The Book of the Sultan's Seal

A SWALLOW EDITIONS BOOK
Founder and Series Editor: Rafik Schami

The Book of the Sultan's Seal

Strange Incidents from History in the City of Mars

By Youssef Rakha
Translated from the Arabic by Paul Starkey

Interlink Books

An imprint of Interlink Publishing Group, Inc.
Northampton, Massachusetts

First published in 2015 by

INTERLINK BOOKS
An imprint of
Interlink Publishing Group, Inc.
46 Crosby Street
Northampton, Massachusetts 01060
www.interlinkbooks.com

 Published as part of the Swallow Editions series.
Founder and Series Editor: Rafik Schami

First Arabic edition, 2011
Grateful acknowledgment is made to the editors of *Banipal*, where excerpts
of this translation appeared.

Library of Congress Cataloging-in-Publication Data
Rakha, Yusuf.
[Kitab al-tughrá. English]
The book of the sultan's seal : strange incidents from history in the city
of Mars / by Youssef Rakha ; translated from the Arabic by Paul Starkey.
-- First edition.
    pages cm
ISBN 978-1-56656-991-0
I. Starkey, Paul. II. Title.
PJ7960.A38K5713 2014
892.7'37--dc23
                          2014033072

Printed and bound in the United States of America

PROLOGUE

Praise be to God

This is *The Book of the Sultan's Seal*, subtitled *Strange Incidents from History in the City of Mars*, a reference to the Conquering Planet, as Mars was called by some Arab astronomers, and from which the name of al-Mu'izz's Cairo (the "Conquering City") is derived, so it is said, as its surrounding wall was by chance built when Mars was in the ascendant. It contains a day-by-day account of the events in the life of the journalist Mustafa Nayif Çorbacı* from March 30 to April 19, 2007, as he himself recorded them in the weeks following this date, addressing his account, in the manner of classical Arabic books, to his friend, the psychiatrist Rashid Jalal Siyouti, who has been living in the British capital since 2001.

The book contains, in addition to the circumstances of Çorbacı's divorce and journey, an account of his transformation into a zombie (to use his own term): a dead man with some of the characteristics of the living, possibly the most important of them being, in his case, the ability to feel loss.

If, in this book, you come across any solecisms, words lacking grammatical inflection, or expressions used in unusual ways, you should know that I have left them as they are because grammatical inflections sound out of place in this kind [of storytelling] and render it unattractive. —al-Jahiz

The Book of the Sultan's Seal does not merely welcome solecisms and bad language but actually celebrates them,

---

*See the translator's afterword (p. 372) for information on the pronunciation and transliteration of "Çorbacı."

imitating speech in all its variety. The author and those who have assisted him have dealt with colloquial language in an open-minded spirit because they like the life that it can impart to the classical tongue. The book also welcomes expressions from foreign languages that have been imported into Arabic, instead of rejecting them or being disturbed by their presence, and for this reason colloquial and foreign expressions have not been distinguished from other words in the typography.

Çorbacı has incorporated various direct quotations into his text (which is written in a disorganized and fluctuating manner), and has added drawings by himself, as well as one photograph, dated 1916, whose place of origin turned out to be the Dolmabahçe Palace in the Beşiktaş district of Istanbul. The text comprises one story divided into nine sections, and involves nine journeys and nine incidents. Each section contains a journey made by Mustafa within the city limits, whose districts and quarters he has renamed, as will be described in detail in the second section.

Each one of the nine journeys is linked to a specific incident in the narrative, each of which Mustafa in time begins to see as a study or treatise in one particular discipline.

From Maadi to Dokki (on marriage)	Separation	March 30
From Dokki to Isaaf (sociology)	First dream and its fulfillment	March 31– April 7
Desert Road journey (psychology)	Finding the ring	April 7–8
From Isaaf to the other world (paranormal)	Meeting the sultan	April 9
Tour of libraries and the internet (on history)	Discovering the Ottoman State	April 10–12
North Giza journey (on friendship)	Divorce and completing the picture	April 13–14
Tour of Islamic Cairo (on love)	Meeting the beloved	April 15
The Muqattam / Cairo Airport journey (erotica)	Finding a clue / Departure	April 16–19
(Later) Cairo Airport	Journey to Beirut	After April 19

Since we like variety, the book is related in Parts 1, 2, 4, 5, and 7 in the words of Mustafa, while Parts 3, 6, and 8 are related by an unknown storyteller whose position is specified by a plural, as here, and who sometimes refers to "our planet" as if it were a viewpoint as all-seeing as destiny. (The ninth part is a miscellany made up of the storyteller's words and texts from Mustafa's notebooks.) In addition to the glossary which we have provided to clarify some allusions contained in the book, there is one observation to be made concerning its title:

The tughra (the *gh*, incidentally, is not pronounced in the original Turkish word) or *tuğra* as it is written in modern Turkish, and pronounced *turra* in the spoken Egyptian dialect, denotes a particular calligraphic shape, well known as the seal which the Ottoman sultan used to record his name on laws and decrees, and stamped on coins. As an official signature, it was placed at the top of a parchment or document and never at the bottom, even if the document was written in Greek.

As is well known, the Ottomans were extremely proficient in Arabic calligraphy, and the tughra was their ultimate achievement in terms of a visual summation of the name of the "shadow of God on earth," as the sultan was called.

And so...

The best way to start, after blessings on the Prophet, is with a quotation from Shams al-Din al-Dhahabi (as quoted from Ibn Iyas), who relates the secret of how the city built by Jawhar al-Siqilli northeast of Misr al-Qadima (or Old Cairo) in AD 969 was named in preparation for the arrival of the Fatimid Imam al-Mu'izz li-Din Allah from the seat of the Isma'ili caliphate in Qairawan:

> When General Jawhar wanted to build the Cairo city wall, he planned the foundations of the city, gathered together the astrologers, and ordered them to select an auspicious time for laying the foundations of the city. On each side of the city's foundations he erected columns of wood, with a rope between each one, and brass bells attached to the ropes. Then the astrologers stood awaiting the arrival of the best time and the most propitious star to lay the foundations. They agreed upon a signal with the builders, that when they rang these bells and the builders heard the sound, the builders

should lay the stones that they held in their hands. While they were standing there, awaiting the propitious hour, a crow alighted on the ropes and the bells rang. The builders thought that the astrologers had pulled the ropes attached to the bells, so they laid the stones they were holding in their hands to form the wall's foundations. The astrologers shouted to them, "No, no, al-Qahir is in the ascendant" (meaning Mars, which they called al-Qahir). So the city's name was decided.

PART ONE

The Epistle on Matrimony

From Dog Alley to Dream Bridge

Mustafa's Account of his
Separation from His Wife, and Its
Consequences

Friday, March 30

Mustafa Nayif Çorbacı said:

Dear Rashid, your emails are intermittent, if they come at all. And I've grown tired of phone cards. But I have a story I must tell you before it sours. How shall I get it across? I've got a lot to tell you, not just the story. You'll find my news really strange. It may even depress you. I laugh when I imagine you whimpering with distress. You were with me the evening I bought a coffee before going to see the girl, remember? It doesn't matter whether you bother to read these words, really. You don't like reading Arabic (assuming that this is Arabic in the first place). I worry that the few people who read, don't read in Arabic. I don't blame them. Even those people who know no other language except Arabic waste all their energy on rotten translations, translations of translations. English rules. Look how our uncles, the Turks, found peace after they adopted the Latin alphabet!

Nonetheless, the fact is that I'm no longer dazzled by that rotten island you live on—England, indeed—forget that shit, man! I'm just writing this, and imagining someone reading it, someone with a really strong and genuine connection with me, a connection transparent enough to transcend every detail of life and reality. Someone I'm connected with outside time, I mean. Because from the day I left my wife till now, I've actually died and been resurrected, or, more likely, at least become a completely different person. I tell you, I want to write to someone whose connection with me transcends my personal identity.

You, alas, are the only one.

As I write these words, I'm thinking of *you*, Rashid. I'll send it to you in installments, whenever you like. Or I might leave it in one big installment, so that you can come back and read it again at your leisure. I say come back, as if you'll be coming back to stay, not just for a vacation. As if coming back wasn't just a gentle melody, like a lullaby before going to sleep. Egypt, England, other places. Bound to travel.

You know that I still remember your wish, for us to leave everything and go to Peru or Guatemala.

I've got a proposal for you. Instead of going to South America, let's cross the Western Desert on foot. We'll sleep in a tent and have a camel for company. One day we'll wake up in Timbuktu.

And there be matters veiled, the veil whereof | Through a recovering sobriety | Was wholly raised for me, yet they remained | Concealed from all besides me. —'Umar ibn al-Farid

I'm now in my seat on the airplane, the engines turning faster and faster as we take off, the asphalt burning under our wheels. And the dawn is orange juice as I write to you:

"The world has collapsed around me and I don't know what to do. Family, children. I've been struggling for three months. Hope is an elastic thing. If you keep clinging to it, you don't get anywhere. I cast it aside and carried on. There was a lot of talk in the office. Gestures from my divorced female colleagues. More than one colleague is getting married and I am bad luck. Change and stability. Happy as a criminal who's gotten away with it, and sad as a house. Ever since my father died, perhaps, I've gotten used to misfortune. The memory wrings my heart, and regret returns. But hope is elastic and I have to go on. I'm not clinging to anything now."

Today is April 19, a hot Thursday. Exactly twenty-one days since I left the marital home in Maadi—the period in which the nine events of my story happened one after the other. I didn't leave Greater Cairo during this period. I feel as though in three weeks I've crossed the whole globe, once from east to west and once from north to south. And as I crossed it, this way and that, I was also treading through five centuries, to and fro. Do you understand me, Rashid? But you can't understand me until you read on.

The metal body that I'm inside has climbed and is suspended in the sky, with everything in it. The plane's nose lifts a bit, but we don't feel it. We just feel—or rather, I feel—that I have completed the first stage of a journey that is far longer than you can imagine. Through the oval window, Cairo gets smaller and fades into the distance. Its features shrink into lines, circles, and lengths stretching into nothingness. It looks like a map, becoming more and more detached, quickly changing into a symbol or a talisman. This sprawling city of twenty million souls, just a horizontal talisman whose meaning is impossible to understand.

Now it's disappearing, and clouds come to take its place, together with the air pressure in one's ears, throbbing temples, and a suppressed sense of shaking. Speed. And you know that, if it weren't for these twenty-one days of madness, you wouldn't have been able to see your city in the shape of a talisman, or feel your sudden distance from it as a sort of closeness.

Meaning: you have to imagine me writing to you a few moments from now, when the fasten seatbelts sign is switched off and I can open the tray table that is stowed in front of me in accordance with instructions and put my notebook on it. Write to you, or mark up the memos piled up between the brown covers of the notebook you gave me three years ago, and circle the drawings. You can imagine me writing to you either here or in the café at the Rafic Hariri International Airport, as they have started to call it.

On the balcony of the Bay View Hotel in Ain el Mreisseh, or behind the window of Lina's Café on Hamra Street toward the Pigeons' Rock at Raouché. The important thing is that you imagine me writing, making fair copies, and clarifying the many things that happened to me during those twenty-one days in the form of a letter, as every book is called in Arabic: *kitab*. When the scene settles in your head, you will continue in your imagination.

Nothing but clouds surrounded by blue.

I have kept in this book to the bounds set by you, limiting myself to things that I have either seen with my own eyes, or I am convinced are true as deriving from trustworthy reporters. —Ibn Hazm al-Andalusi

As you read, you'll notice that there are some sentences or short passages printed in italics. Most of these are stray fragments, like the paragraph I have transcribed above. These are notes I jotted down while on the move. Now I look for them in notebooks or try to remember where they are to be found. The words around them are like a sponge casing. Apart from that, I have nothing except the amazing tale I'm telling you. And I'm telling you the truth when I say that I can still distinguish all of that tale's features. When I focus on a single feature I feel that I have gone mad. But I have learned that I shouldn't always take what happened to me too seriously. In the end, the story tries to pull things together. And whether those things are more or less complicated or comprehensible doesn't really make any difference.

Someone once said to me, about some observations in the notebooks: "This is poetry."

I was rather happy. But what difference does it make whether it's poetry or not?

What makes a difference is that writing things as a book-length letter is better than email or telephone. Perhaps even better than meeting face to face. Writing like this gives things a more palatable tone, just as notes in a jotter can become poetry whether you mean them to or not. They're put in a flowing context and this creates a soothing tone, like a bedtime lullaby.

Interlude

Yesterday I dreamed that I was beside you in the jeep you used to drive in 2000 and 2001 before you settled on your wretched island. Until you left. We were driving along a terrifying mountain road that was just like the Taba Road. Up and down with sharp bends impossible to predict. The surface was dotted with rocks and potholes. Potholes big as whole towns and rocks like the Urals. You had to avoid them as you drove. We were high as kites on Red Sea bango, totally unafraid of having an accident, and laughing. Suddenly we fell into the crater of a volcano. At the bottom was something like a cloud, which absorbed the shock. We were outside the vehicle, crawling on this thing. After the shock, we screamed with laughter. We dipped down and rose up again in the fresh whiteness, and whenever our eyes met, we were paralyzed with laughter, unable to move, waving our hands about and screaming. When I looked up, there were naked women sitting on the edge of the chasm, spreading their legs and squeezing their breasts, winking and gesturing toward us. I kept looking for you to point them out to you, but you crawled away quickly and disappeared. Then I noticed that the hole was much larger than I had thought. I crawled in an unknown direction, terrified that I might have lost you forever.

Mustafa went on:

I said goodbye to my wife one pleasant evening at the end of March 2007, a day before the Prophet's Birthday. I waited a long time for her to collect her things from our apartment on the Maadi Corniche. Then we both went down, each of us carrying their own things in silence. Before she opened her car door, I put my hand on her hair and kissed her on the mouth. I used to do that every time we parted, whether it was hours or days before we would meet again. I noticed that she didn't part her lips to return the kiss as I expected. I didn't wait to see the expression on her face. I felt that it would affect me more than I could bear that evening. I simply hurried toward my own car. I was so impatient that I didn't even look at the street I'd lived on for more than a year, since we had married.

I had no thought except to leave Maadi.

You know how crowded and fast the Corniche is. But our own street was small and quiet. So tucked away that cars basically don't drive there. Just two steps from the Corniche, on the right, opposite the gas station at Maadi's no. 2 entrance, you know, but it's as if you've entered a different world. You can always park, there's a moon in the sky, and the branches of trees. One deserted building, then the house with our apartment in it. In the apartment there's a staircase leading to the bedroom, a large kitchen, and a television that we only used to watch art films on video or DVDs. I even accepted the expensive furniture, as I was told I ought to. In accordance with my mother-in-law's instructions, we had a dining room and sitting room, but no study. I moved cautiously between the vases and flowerpots. It was forbidden to put anything on the wood.

When it was hot, I would make ice tea with lemon. The espresso was always Lavazza. And when I made pasta with thyme I would use a lot of onions and sliced tomatoes but no sauce. In front of us was Hind Rustam's villa, inhabited only by her miserable dogs, which howled at the end of the night, and behind us a garden that attracted mosquitoes, a smell of vegetation, and green light in the late morning. The frogs croaked. Our street was crossed by another dark street, a little more crowded, which I would watch from the balcony, smoking with only my porcelain ashtray and the cold of the winter for company. In our street, the potholes were filled with mud after it rained, and the roses on the sidewalk were never pruned. Even now, I can almost hear the garden hose and the landlady's daughter calling her dog: "Sandyyyyyyyyy!"

Shaaban the caretaker's family lived in the closed-up garage. They were from Kom Ombo. As I walked past him, I would use the Upper Egyptian expression for "how are you doing?" and he would reply in the same dialect, without surprise. One day we discovered his son had been tied to a pillar with a steel chain because he'd lost his bicycle. And one day his daughter was crying because they'd confiscated her mobile after a young stranger had found out her number. His daughter made no progress in English despite the lessons my wife gave her. Friday mornings she would come to us and I would have to get dressed. And all night the stairwell would be filled with bango smoke. Shaaban never sleeps.

In the sitting-room window there were faint, distant lights. No noise, not even a heartache. Nothing in the world called for tears (or so I thought, until very recently). Imagine, nothing of all this crossed my mind as I turned off beside the gas station to join the Corniche toward the ring road before even opening the car window.

It never crossed my mind that my wife had not parted her lips as I kissed her.

An account of the collapse of the marriage

When I turned thirty, the world was made complete by an actually cool woman my own age. My wife, whom you know, right enough! Between two cultures, like me. She'd been brought up in Eng—excuse me, yes, in England, and I studied there. Fatherless, like me, with just one sister who lived abroad and came for visits. I immediately felt that she was liberated, a suitable partner, and I was happy when I discovered that she was ready for pregnancy and life. She was soon at home in the apartment we rented, happy to be my wife, and we were happy with each other.

Our disputes continued to annoy me, however, especially when they were directed toward my drawing, my solitary nature, and even the sex we had. Disputes for no obvious reason. When I spoke to her, she wouldn't even reply. Torture by silence. As if she were saying to me: "We don't face difficulties. We just store them up." Then, the silence. An eternal silence, and tears. I was always supposed to have wronged her, but it was always unclear how. I'd ask her and try to cajole her to return to normal. I'd try as hard as I could, not understanding. I didn't realize how everything had started to exasperate me, and I put up with it all in silence. Silence, because if I had spoken, we would have come to blows. But everything started to exasperate me. Even my nightly rituals disturbed her, despite the fact that she'd known about them before our marriage. She huffed and puffed at my insults. The fact that we were living in a pigsty didn't seem to concern her. She would constantly enumerate for me any housework she had done and not admit to my own contributions. The cleaning woman from her mother's would come—or not—once a week. "Should we get a live-in maid?" Then she'd get angry. I couldn't even complain to her about problems in the office without her getting angry and saying: "Stop complaining!" But I loved her. Every road has its walker.

After I turned thirty I took comfort in the perfection of the world. And in the fact that she was a cool woman who lived between two cultures. But when you have someone imposed on you whom you no longer want to be with, loneliness can be a terrible thing. I kept reciting old women's proverbs to myself: "patience is a virtue," "lying is a failure," and "may God guide you to each other, my son!" But everything that had encouraged me to marry her was like a trick photograph. Her mother's presence, for example, made her freedom a sham. Comfort meant chinois carpets, especially when she got pregnant, after eleven months or a bit more. During one argument I too had thought that pregnancy would liberate her, but after she became pregnant it was actually worse.

Nothing in the sight of her face gave me pleasure anymore.

To this very day, as soon as I remember, I bite my lip and wish I could disappear from the world. No, I don't want to disappear. I want to go back to December 2005 so as not to marry my wife. After she became pregnant, the exasperation became intolerable, I had had enough of being suffocated. No family, no children. I took refuge in Japanese stories—Ōe, Yoshimoto, Murakami, and so on—while hope played with me like a yoyo until I didn't know what to do. I felt as if even breathing was a lie, and the arguments in the office got worse. I was suffocating. Without any pleasure, how could I throw myself on her and kiss her? Not a single road led to Maadi, I was suffocating and confused.

Sometimes I stood on the Corniche, seeking a friend's help in my mind. Who could I explain this to? I wanted things to be as they were before the engagement, before the dowry, before we bought furniture with the blessings of her sister who had come from England especially for the purpose, and added her father's acquisitions to the house—may God curse him! Before her mother said to me "you must become a family man!" How many times did it happen that I failed to control my emotions and she frowned and shouted and looked me up and down? She fussed over her body and put off the accusations. Days of peace then booooom! She'd reveal that she'd completely changed her mind. The law that obliged you to do housework was the same one that stopped you from traveling. She was even annoyed about my not fasting during Ramadan because her mother wanted me to fast. How many hours had I spent miserable when I was supposed to be happy? "Only God and jacking off can help you now," I would say to myself. And I'd enjoy emptying my bowels far more than I should.

The abandon of our first couplings seemed to have occurred with a different woman. Her passion, her curiosity, her rebellion against the usual assumptions. Where had everything gone, when not a year had gone by? Was it marriage that had made it go? A day will come, I said to myself, when the safety catch will break, and she will be astonished, although if she'd paid attention she could have prevented it. Our conversations were silence, or quarreling.

I had begun to think of my days off as a burden. At home, I would wash the dishes vigorously and smile.

Perhaps I was anticipating the sequence of events. After she awoke from a nightmare—I no longer knew when to take her in my arms—I kissed her and pressed on her shoulder and tried to whisper in her ear. She was my daughter and she would tell me what she had seen. But the moment when the barriers were dissolved could no longer be repeated. At the height of my affection she started up and said, in the English whose rhythms I had grown to hate: "You're rubbish at calming a frightened person." I looked for the humor in her eyes, to no avail. Any brief rage on my part made her leave the place without returning or thinking about consequences. It was up to me to mend all the fabric ripped between us. Any bit of behavior that she didn't understand or didn't like. I started to think, and ask myself, why are you taking this silently? How long will you remain silent and take it? I no longer had the nerve to rise above her insults, truth to tell. It was like living with a warning siren that might go off at any moment, and you didn't know what might set it off. Her mother told me: "Woman was made from a crooked rib; if you try to straighten it, it will break!" Is that so? And my mother, to whom I had recently started complaining, reminded me of her pregnancy, of my father's legacy (may God have mercy on him), and of the sacred duties of men.

An account of the Copt Michel Fustuq's prophecy

But none of this was on my mind as I tried to avoid two minibuses like a natural disaster on the Maadi Corniche opposite the Alpha Market, the biggest supermarket you've ever had, Cairo, until recently. The driver was chatting with his colleague in the middle of the road as cars sped around them. Normal enough. Finally, I emerged onto the Ring Road like a donkey that knows its way. When I pulled onto the Great River Road, I recalled the evening I'd been with my Coptic friend Michel Samir Fustuq at the Uruba Café in Zamalek, and he'd said things to me that since that day I've considered to be a prophecy of my separation from my wife.

Maybe, I said to myself, Fustuq's words had reminded me of a book. Something I'd read without concentrating, like most things I read. It had left a sharp, raw sensation. Something like a story of a gang, or a secret organization. Yes, an organization, which had become so strong and with so many branches that it dominated the entire planet. Or perhaps it was a clip from a foreign film—it's dawn, and the man approaching the car intends to kill—preceded or followed by tears. Nothing was clear except the feeling that contrary to the expectation that you would take fright or run away in the face of danger, you were actually happy that it had come. Happy that the danger was a source of pleasure. Of course, you were afraid, but you were happy, as if you had just proposed to a distant lover or, from the furthest place you could imagine, you had unknowingly brought this lover with you. Yes, that was really more like it. A whole lifetime of carrying this danger without knowing it. Then boom! On the heels of an expression that you no longer recall, or a twist in the sequence of events—suddenly, just like that—it jumps out at you, and you have no choice but to welcome it despite everything. Something so frightening it's been hidden from you all this time—I mean, could you really have been so out of your mind?

My conversation with Fustuq was a normal conversation about travel: I love traveling, but out of jealousy and stinginess my wife had forbidden me to travel. I'd spent a year nobly putting up with her laziness and bad manners and saying to myself that now more than ever was the time. Dealing with the consequences of my choice. Believing that people lived by their choices. But what I didn't tell you, Rashid, was that Fustuq had known my wife well before I met her. They had some shared family history. Before he got rich in the 1970s, his father had worked for her mother's father in his little shop in the Birkat al-Fil area. We were all amazed and laughed when we discovered this story. Did Boy named after Pistachios have a more significant role, then? Perhaps my exaggerated reaction to what he said to me in the Uruba Café that evening—the sense of danger (the danger being a prophecy that the world would collapse around me), and the pleasure of that sense—perhaps it was all connected with the fact that some things in life linked this human being and my wife: not just their family history, but also the fact that they had both been brought up abroad and that their brains were therefore alternately subject to two contradictory states of mind: on the one hand, freedom and rebellion Anglo-American style, and on the other, adherence to the filthiest traditions of our toiling classes and tyrannical-head-of-the-family patriarchy, with nothing to disgrace a man except his pocket.

Of course, I didn't realize any of this until everything went wrong.

In Fustuq's case, I didn't understand it completely until after the principal event in my story, when I discovered that he had left the girl who loved him—although she too was a Christian—and married an obnoxious virgin from his parents' church, but that's another story. The first time I went out with my wife—before she became my wife, I mean—I'd met her in the Uruba Café as well. We were with Fustuq and our effeminate African colleague Aldo Mantenzika, or (as we call him at the newspaper) Mazika. There were others with us, and I waited until they had all left to say my two words to her.

Chapter

Farewell, Friday evening: On the Ring Road, the traffic stopped for a minute. This often happens on the flyovers for no reason, as you know. I think it's just a coincidence, when a certain number of cars leave their lanes in a certain direction all at once and as everyone is speeding up. And as always happens, everyone started honking. Usually, this makes me furious, but at this precise moment, I envisaged the noise pollution as an orchestra from whose instruments nothing emerged but farts of every sort, from highest to lowest—from sad and long to short and joyful. I felt a remarkable happiness as I heard an extempore symphony reflecting my life in this enormous city of twenty million people. As if my life up to now had been a bad Arab film, and this farting movement was the music accompanying the final scene.

Abu al-Rushd, I believe it was at that moment that I lost the city (even though I didn't realize it immediately). It would be my job, after leaving Maadi to stay with my mother in Dokki, to reclaim it, which I would only manage in the third week.

For just a moment, I tell you—despite tense nerves, suspended hopes, and my thoughts about how Fustuq's words related to my wife—I passed through an interlude of total clarity. Sometimes clarity is like being stoned: delight in danger equals the end of a marriage. It was only later that I was surprised that the music accompanying this moment should be cars farting during a short-lived traffic crisis on the Cairo Ring Road.

It simply occurred to me that what had spurred me on to marry my wife was three characteristics which I also falsely discerned in Fustuq (on the basis of the fact that the two of them combined the silt of the homeland with the air of developed countries). She was secular by inclination; marriage in her view was a personal decision that continued to be subject to revision; and her values were not the values of her family.

It seems no one can go beyond their family in personal matters. Even me? Perhaps the difference with me is just a symptom of madness. But even I did not go beyond my family in the matter of marriage, except insofar as I regarded it as no more than a license from society to live together. Living together in a context that was acceptable to my mother, to her mother, and to the people we lived among.

I had never ever imagined that marriage to this person in particular would so quickly turn into the conventional scenario in all its details, or that life would immediately turn into empty family obligations, into regulated tedium, and into rules that had no purpose except to preserve a way of life that I loathe. And I thought that she shared this loathing—the one difference being that I did not have the traditional attributes that a wretched husband needs to compensate for his misery: a woman to take care of the house and of her husband, who knows how to deal with him and other people, or at the very least acknowledges that she is supposed to look after herself.

I tell you, it never occurred to me that the values I would be dealing with from the very first day were the values of her family alone—things that I would run a mile from even if accepting them meant sleeping every night with Su'ad Husni— nor that, in the film that she began acting out from the first day, I was really only playing a stereotyped role in a scenario written five hundred years ago, with whose details she had no intention of interfering. In no time at all, Abu al-Siyout, she became a bad-tempered wife who measured everything, even feelings, in terms of money. A man in her eyes meant a feeling of bitterness, or faking love for advantage. I mean, if I had been intending to start a family like this, why would I have chosen a cool woman who lived between two cultures?

Perhaps this will seem exaggerated, but you knew her before we were married, and you can imagine how shocked I was when I found her—the cultured revolutionary, defender of the rights of the individual and of women, the funky rebel that you knew—trying to control the little money that my father had left me, arguing with me because I'd finished the bottle of juice, for example, or ostracizing me for three whole days because I had drunk a coffee with a girl that I might have seemed to have once desired.

I felt that I didn't know her, and that I didn't want to know her, let alone marry her. I carried on making a fool of myself month after month pretending to know her, or pretending that her mother (the worst influence of all on her, as became clear in the end) was basically right, or that pregnancy and children were good for everyone.

Nothing was any use.

Recapitulation

I'm not telling you the story of my marriage. My wife will remain nameless, even though you know her name. What I'm telling you has nothing to do with this tragedy, which, as it turned out, has lost its tragic element. Somehow or other, during the months of the marriage, I was dealing with the facts of the situation, making the decision (even though I did not acknowledge it directly to myself) that this life could not go on. She could be excused for hating me, of course she could. But I am not an institution, not an orphanage or a mental asylum, able to cope with this hate. Perhaps I was deceiving her, of course I was deceiving her, because I was deceiving myself instead of saying to her, "You're the crappiest thing that's ever happened to me, and I'm sorry I didn't say anything before, huh?"

She might ask me: "Do you think that one year is enough to get to know someone?"

And I would answer her in my head: "No, one needs a whole lifetime of misery. A mental asylum or a conviction for murder. Cursed be the father of anyone looking at your face!"

There is nothing easier than making the other party bear responsibility. Maybe it's me who hurts other people. When I thought about my previous relationships, I discovered that it had always been me who had walked away, at an unexpected moment, in a cruel way, with no regard for the feelings of the other party or for the effect on them of my sudden disappearance. I am actually more selfish (and perhaps a little more intelligent) than those I form relationships with: a man infatuated with himself, and with a propensity for anxiety that drives me to behave in a way that makes people angry— perhaps it is impossible for anyone who is with me to be happy.

Do you remember, Rashid, when you confronted me with my true nature as you saw it, and told me that I had a preference for seclusion and a hidden contempt for other people, particularly for their social affairs? That the root of this contempt is an intellectual love of self? That I tend to go for everything I can take from the world, on condition that I don't get tired or sacrifice a thing? You also said that the sole authority I acknowledge is my personal satisfaction, even though I don't always know how to achieve it, which lands me in scenes and situations that I have to run away from, no matter what may happen afterward. I've run out of patience so many times. I always want to be just as I am the whole time, regardless of the context, and because I'm not prepared to make concessions or adapt, I always have to suffer the consequences.

You also spoke to me that day about my more trivial failings: my failure to maintain a sufficient number of friends, my failure to accept others' faults, my constant fear of wasting my time and emotions on something or someone that does not deserve them… and my frightening propensity for detachment.

You know that I don't make any excuse for this. I don't deny it. Only my experience with my wife was completely different. With her I felt for the first time that I had a convincing justification for leaving. Which is what makes me recall your words now.

But as I'm telling you, the biggest problem wasn't my frustration with my wife, or at my having emerged as the villain in a Hasan al-Imam melodrama that I hadn't imagined I would ever actually see, let alone act in. The problem, and the secret of my regarding Michel Fustuq's words as a prophecy, and my feeling that the collapse of my marriage was the collapse of the whole world, was that my experience actually made me doubt all the values by which I lived: individual choice and personal freedom, secularism and rationality in managing one's affairs, respect for the social environment—the attempt to reconcile things by turning cohabitation into marriage, for example—imagining that people can live with each other, physically and mentally, on a non-commercial basis, or express themselves with a degree of detachment from tendencies to hatred or profiteering. A belief that this detachment is what makes people people, or that the mingling of cultures yields knowledge and conscience rather than mad despair.

Call me mad, call my mother mad, she called me mad, liar, scoundrel, murderer, without asking herself what role she might herself have played in all these deficiencies: for example, her family hand-me-downs, which she wanted me to swallow like a drain. In my mind I had only been trying to live with a person like myself who was an Arab and a Muslim but also civilized and contemporary and with a conscience. And now it seemed to me that the picture she presented of herself was just a boastful pretense. Like the female conquests of my Sunni friend Amgad Salah 'Abd al-Galil in Canada, as will be related later, or (and this is really more to be expected) like the streetwise way that Michel Fustuq speaks: she's not a woman, and not cool, and we're not an inch removed from the disasters of this culture and this age.

This son of a madwoman—when everything went wrong, when he found his life reflecting the worst things in the East (treating a woman as if she were a chattel, and observing the outward forms of religion while not working in their spirit; thinking about good works as though they were an account in the bank of the afterlife, for example), and by the same token, the worst things about the West (namely, personal isolation and the inability to achieve a mutual understanding or solve problems in a relationship)—this son of a madwoman imagined that his marriage was a model of the most a Muslim Arab could do to live a modern life, and that his failure was an indicator of the bounds of the possible.

My heart is sick of this world, and will only be cured by journeying to another. Or else, no one in this world should be an Arab Muslim.

What do you think? What if you imagine this world as a building, the pillars of whose foundations move as soon as you take up residence in one of its apartments? The building itself has not fallen, only the pillars have shifted. Perhaps you remember the effect of LSD—way to go—when everything becomes jumbled, so you hear colors and see music, and space turns into time? How about looking at the world as a building under the influence of LSD? A building whose walls and ceilings, staircases, doors and corridors all move while you are in an apartment, and the apartment itself is shifting. You don't know how to go in or out, or stand or sit, or sleep or go to the bathroom. But the building itself is in place?

My heart is sick of this world, as it would be of living in this building.

Recollection of the rest of the journey to Dokki

The point is: As I was passing by the Ahmad Shawqi Museum— on the extension of the Great River Road along the Nile—I became certain: pleasure in danger means the end of a marriage. Memories of a film or a book. I did a rewind of my session with Fustuq while the traffic was at a standstill at the Giza Zoo. The conversation took place on a Friday afternoon. 26 July Street, where the Uruba Café is situated, was amazingly quiet, while Fustuq told me that it was useless to think about traveling freely anymore as I did before I was married. "Just 'cause you married someone classy, you think you still can. Believe me, dude, when you marry, you work on changing yourself."

Fustuq is not a bus like my Sunni friend Amgad Salah. But he is sturdily built with a large square face, and he has a weighty presence that you can't ignore. There aren't that many people you worry about meeting because they monopolize everything with their chatter and are hurt by any sign of boredom or indications of imminent departure. Fustuq is one of them.

The street was quiet as his theatrical voice rang out. His speech went on and on, with no let-up unless you interrupted him yourself. "Okay, Pistachio Boy!" But no sooner had I interrupted him than I recalled that he was one of those people. Either you let him go on talking nonstop, or he'll sulk and make you feel guilty. So I shut up. Time and time and time again, I shut up. Why should I spare this man's feelings?

Now, as I drove from Maadi to Dokki, he appeared in memory like a small barrel on the plastic seat. In an exaggerated sort of street talk, which was intended to remind you that he came from the Egyptian working class despite having lived most of his life as a guest of Uncle Sam (although in fact it merely reminded you that he was reminding you), he kept repeating, "Don't you have any sense of honor? I wish you'd become a man in your house, Mr. Shurba, and didn't go home every night to be slapped on the back of your head like that!"

That day I didn't stand up for my manly dignity. There was no need. The feeling had just assaulted me.

In the weeks following my conversation with Fustuq, for the first time since I had known her I started to help construct the silence between one quarrel and the next. The muddiness in her face made it more pleasant to sit at one's desk than to see her, more pleasant even to wash the dishes, or drive around aimlessly—anything except accommodating myself to a family steeped in distress, or becoming, in this family, a man her mother could approve of—boom! I knew I had begun a process that would take up much more of my time than I wanted.

Like everything, I would have to go through it alone, wouldn't I?

Three months would pass as if I were ill. A genuine illness, the kind that forces you to stay in bed and take medicine. Three months punctuated by temporary separations, aimless driving expeditions, and abortive attempts at discussion.

She stretched her back with the frivolity of a capricious dancer in a B-movie. "I'm pregnant, and that's that!" I stopped asking for her sympathy. Later, when she cried and tried to make up to me, I wouldn't feel anything, just guilt and other people's talk. At night, I would wander around the apartment like an out-of-luck gravedigger. Another attempt at communication? Hysteria followed by sleep. "I'm pregnant, and that's that!" Until we reached the point of leaving, both of us carrying our things in silence. Before she opened her car door, I kissed her on the mouth but she didn't part her lips to exchange the kiss as I'd expected every time we parted.

Chapter

Eventually, I turned off at the Nahdat Misr statue and entered Dokki. The family home.

Before I could breathe a sigh of relief, something like a cockroach jumped up in my throat. I thought I was going to cry. I sighed.

Only then did I realize that I had already left my wife, that I'd quit my apartment in Maadi and wouldn't be going back. And that I would have to make a decision about divorce.

Now the confusion would begin, not just about the events that had caused me to go back to my mother, but about what would follow in the days to come. By the same logic—as is apparent in the notebook—my face that evening seemed to be under the influence of the cockroach in my throat: my eyes holding back tears that I thought would come but never did.

The world has collapsed around me and I don't know what to do. That's what I said to myself. Family and children. Three months of struggle. Hope is an elastic thing. If you keep clinging to it, you won't get anywhere. I said goodbye to it and carried on.

In the office, as I was to discover, I was to be pursued by talk. My divorced female colleagues would make gestures that confused me. I didn't know whether everyone would hate me as my wife did. I started to pay attention to my appearance, more so even than my colleague who was getting married, though it was me who was bad luck. Change and stability. What will she do? I said to myself as I chose a shirt to match my trousers. As I shaved my chin carefully I wondered why I had said goodbye to hope. I constantly thought of traveling, of committing suicide to escape from prying eyes. I didn't dare feel desire. I wanted to be a new person, or to flee. Family and children. Happy as an escaped prisoner and sad as a house.

Perhaps since my father's death I had grown used to disasters. Memory squeezed my heart and sorrow came back to me, but hope is elastic, and I had to go on. Now I was not attached to anything.

So, with no pride or malice, I again made my way toward my mother. "Run to your mama," she would say when I left her and stormed out. Woman was made from a crooked rib. But then again, where could I go? From Maadi to Dokki, my birthplace, to which I always rolled back. Every time I beat it from Dokki, I returned with my tail between my legs. Now I was looking for a climate for my disasters. Nothing but a constant sense of wandering. Three times I passed by the apartment last month, while I was intermittently staying with my mother, and every time I looked up, I felt nothing. On my way back, I stepped on the gas, and when the suffocating feeling had passed, I stepped on it harder. A deep breath. The end of winter was much clearer than this spring.

Everything has been the same since my father died, no consolation in anything.

Perhaps because I'd cried enough during the struggle, from now on I'd notice an exaggerated desire to laugh. In the office, where I kept going—people don't stop going to the office just because their marriages have collapsed—I stayed close to those of my colleagues in stable relationships, like a person who'd had an arm amputated seeking out other people's arms. Our peace of mind shouldn't be tied to women's moods. I craved the company of men: their goodwill and equilibrium. I was consoled by the fact that I wasn't here by chance. If I'd stayed, nothing would have changed and it would have been too much to bear. Impossible for personal relationships to be tests of endurance.

I immediately gave in to my instinct to hide. I didn't want to see my wife or hear her voice. It was hard enough to separate. We remained in communication until she noticed my hesitation. Just a few days, in practice… I didn't want to talk. My colleague Yildiz Zakariyya scolded me: "You said that you loved her." (Yildiz was the same age as me and my wife, and like us had only one elder sister, who was ten years her senior.) But as soon as despair began to blister, I'd throw a bag on my shoulder and move far, far away.

Is it possible for love to be a test of endurance?

A poem on Mustafa Çorbacı's wife
You are an intruder and a blend of races, like a tropical flower lost in our ancestors' myths. I am your exhausted guide. Whenever I pointed the way, you held on to the labyrinth more tightly. We were both lost in myth. How could you play the lead in films produced by children who arrived like an invading army from Anatolia, or creatures from space? I really believed you, and thought that you would refuse to play the victim even though it was a starring role. I said, the days fashion us to hurry our steps. Every story was a jumble of affections, and I didn't understand the point of them until I was impaled. What theatrical text were you clinging to? You are strange and wonderful, like a kiwi fruit that has gone bad before the criminals can peel it. Why did I think you a bird singing two tunes? I found you a single discordant melody that I learned to savor in the evenings. Who tore up the map that we had drawn together? From today on I will not lead! I squatted on the ground crying but you refused my apology. You never missed an opportunity to make me a punching bag to compensate for all your postponed battles, or a drainpipe for the waste that your suspicions had left in your belly. My vengeance grew like a plant you were watering. When your loss becomes certain, I will destroy you as if you were an ancient television that no longer does anything but crackle. You were my bride, the birthplace of my joy. I really believed you. I thought that you would never dissolve in the water of reality. I said I would eat her a mouthful a day. But I hardly tasted you before I was poisoned. My sweet child, to whom I handed over everything… biggest mistake in my history.

PART TWO

The Epistle on the
Subject and Predicate

From Dream Bridge to World's Gate

Mustafa's Description of His Life
after Separating from His Wife

From Saturday, March 31
to Saturday, April 7

Mustafa Nayif Çorbacı said:

That's how the story that I wanted to tell you began, Abu al-Siyout, when I left the marital home the day before the Prophet's birthday. And if you want to hear the rest of it—well, you're in luck.

I said goodbye to my wife on Friday evening.

On Thursday, Yildiz had accused me of withholding information in order to elicit sympathy that I did not deserve. Yildiz Zakariyya—colleague, friend, willowy thing like fire. I thought about her a lot that day. The fact is, her family is a strange and exceptional one that shouldn't have produced so conventional a person. (It occurs to me now that most of the people working at my economics paper are strange and exceptional; then again, if you think about them enough, everyone can seem like that.)

A chapter on Yildiz Zakariyya and her sister Claudine Yusuf

Anyway, Yildiz's father is Dr. Murad Yusuf Zakariyya, a philologist who specializes in medieval French and enjoys a worldwide reputation in academic circles. I met him two or three times in Muqattam. He always spoke in an amusing and measured way, as if you were talking to Muhammad Mandur or Tawfiq al-Hakim in his prime, I imagine. An old-school liberal.

He was from the same village as Taha Hussein, and I think he knew him personally as a student at Cairo University in the fifties, but despite his humble Upper Egyptian origins he married a rich woman from an upper-class family who claimed Turkish roots. Kariman Hanim, Yildiz's mother, had resolved on this name for her second daughter, after Dr. Murad had insisted for their first daughter on a European name, Claudine, whose Old French and Latin origins he particularly appreciated. Anyway, Dr. Murad was only just married when Louis Awad personally gave him a grant to complete his PhD in France, after which he moved with his wife to Holland, then Germany.

As a result, Claudine, Yildiz's elder sister, never actually lived in Egypt until she was seventeen. (I discovered this as I gradually grew closer to Yildiz over time, despite the fact that while Yildiz and I were having our affair she was hesitant to speak about her sister.) It was certainly true that Claudine integrated better into the city than Yildiz, who kept to her own circles and class. She made more friends than Yildiz outside the house, she mingled into street life and identified with the working class (so I recalled now). And perhaps that is why she eventually emigrated again.

What was it that made Claudine emigrate?

On the Thursday, when Yildiz accused me of withholding the details of my relationship with my wife, this was the question that impressed itself on me with an insistence that I wouldn't understand until later—to be precise, when I found out that Claudine's French husband had liked living in Egypt and had been ready to live here with her after they met.

From Yildiz I had picked up an incomplete and obscure idea about something having happened to Claudine and her husband before they were married. Something horrid and cruel that had compounded all the feelings of loathing and exile she'd known in Cairo since she'd come here. I remember Claudine herself speaking somewhat superciliously about the poor health care and undisciplined traffic when someone asked her why she was leaving. I wasn't convinced by these explanations at the time.

I figured that she had suffered some social problem or negative experience with the police, but even after I'd had the opportunity to ask her myself, Abu al-Siyout, Claudine would avoid speaking about what had made her leave. Loathing and exile. From my plane seat I guessed that the reason she left had something to do with the fact that her husband was a foreigner, or that when she had lived with him before marriage, she'd been toying with her father's reputation. But even today I don't know what the reason might be.

Yildiz herself (a graduate of the American University, the same age as me) was seven when she came to settle in Egypt. Perhaps it was this that made her feel it essential to consolidate her knowledge of languages, which Claudine had absorbed naturally, as well as her acquaintance with the intellectual climate in which Claudine had lived while older, and which Yildiz had only briefly glimpsed.

Anyway, when Dr. Murad came back in the eighties with the intention of settling, he bought a piece of land in the middle of the Muqattam Hills with his savings from more than fifteen years of teaching. The two-story house he built and furnished there was built with financial help from the bequest of Kariman Hanim. Like intellectuals before the July Revolution he preferred the old-school, bookish lifestyle, with everything done on time to the strains of classical music and in full dress. He was convinced (and his wife did not contradict him, even if her motives were simply to appear European) that both his daughters ought to have an independent life after the age of twenty-one, and this allowed Yildiz to mix freely with people on the pretext of making contacts.

That Thursday, I thought Yildiz and her sister were truly strange and exceptional, quite apart from the fact that, although they were both Egyptian, one of them had a Turkish and the other a French name. Out of a liberal father and a mother from the petty aristocracy (Kariman Hanim was supposed to be a painter, but the only paintings I saw were dreadful), for an émigrée to be conceived, not to speak of a colleague and friend, a willowy thing like fire.

Recapitulation

To recap, on Thursday Yildiz accused me. On Saturday, the *moulid*, as the Prophet's birthday is called, passed without any celebration in our home. No sweets, no prayers. I remember I spent an hour or more, while my mother read the Qur'an on the sofa, thinking of buying one of those sugar dolls you buy for little girls in the *moulid* to set in front of me, spit in its face, stick a knife into it, pour spirit on it, and set it alight.

I also reckoned that Yildiz had been spreading her message for quite some time. In fact, when I went back to the office on Sunday (for the first time in a year, I drove from Dokki to Isaaf Square, certain that I would return to Dokki at the end of the day, then drive back from Dokki to Isaaf at the start of the next), I noticed an implicit accusation in the way the other unmarried women spoke to me, which upset me without making it any easier to defend myself. How could I explain?

To this day, Abu al-Rushd, a sense of wounded pride takes hold of me whenever I remember. I avoid Yildiz. Her empty confidence and her dependence on clichés. I recoil from her, and immediately I remember her elder sister, the university professor Claudine Yusuf who lives in France, and I tell myself that it would be impossible for Claudine to behave like this. This Yildiz, it's as if she were the head of the National Society for Praiseworthy Morals. She's conscientious and virtuous and she knows everything. But the fact is, she stumbles around like the rest of us. More than us, even, she stumbles. But she'll still take you by the arm, sit you down, and lecture you. Spread her stories without any regard to your wishes. And if you confront her with the facts, she'll collapse.

You know that her motives are not what she says they are. It all comes across as confidence and culture, doing good and pulling ears, but what about the hatred, the cowardice, the self-deception? Specifically, the self-deception. My wounded pride takes hold of me, and her failures turn from a reason for affection into a hateful force. By what right does she judge my motives? When depressed, for example, she feels that she is a chewed-up morsel. Well, I'm thinking, she really is a chewed-up morsel and ought to feel like that. And I wish all the women in the world were not like Yildiz.

On Sunday I've only just set up my equipment on my desk when she asks me again: "Did you say anything to your wife about what happened between us?"

I don't know if I want it to happen again. I won't describe the dirty details, so my scrawl in this notebook will not be revenge. I'd just like it if every woman wasn't as thin and complicated as Yildiz. Even her lust is piety and charity, or rather a settling of accounts. Ready to wager anything for the illusion that she's right, when she isn't. Able to castrate one person and kill another without it occurring to her that she is doing any damage or harm. She is a saint, a victim, and all her actions are peace. Balls, I'm thinking. Even more balls that she's not aware of anything. Listen to her, then observe her actions, and you'll discover: complete separation between her brain and real life. In any possible situation she'll be praying. What a bitch! Religion and drama! And my wife too. It never occurred to me before we were married that she could hold all these dramas inside her. I'm tired of credos and identity issues.

The following day, Monday, Yildiz won't be in the office. And when I ask after her—acting as though we were still friends—they tell me she's taken three weeks' leave because work has exhausted her. I'm relieved. That long a holiday without saying anything to me, though we met only the day before? At least I won't have to see her during the critical period. And despite my curiosity, I'm not going to ask her if she's spending her holiday in Egypt or abroad, though I understand from my colleagues that she's hard up and depressed, so I suppose it'll be in Egypt. In spite of this I know she won't contact me, so—nothing to worry about.

I find it strange how relieved I am at the thought that I won't see her.

An account of the beginning of Mustafa's realization of his historical duty

That Sunday, Abu al-Arshad, the first day after I returned to Dokki, I had a strange feeling as I emerged from the garage. A feeling that I would observe repeating itself on subsequent occasions, and which I would reinterpret more than once.

I mean the opposite of the feeling of danger that equals the end of a marriage, as if something broader and more distant were happening at the same time. Something that only repeats itself once or twice every thousand years.

As I said, the world had collapsed around me. And I was apparently standing on the ruins, gazing out like a defeated general taking a last look at his city, now occupied by invading armies. I stood with a face etched with invisible tears, the same face that I drew on the night I slept in Dokki with half my things in the car and the unborn child a vagrant in my wife's belly, while she pulled at her hair, which I had learned never to touch, after, more than once I'd started to smooth it and she'd shouted at me (do you believe she would actually start a fight with me if I accidentally caught it while we were sleeping?)—and then the household effects coming down the stairs of the building behind us and those squares that had been filled (love, family, a place to live) now empty circles in the dust.

As if my standing there or the general's last glance were a sign of the death of the city itself, the death of Cairo, and perhaps its resurrection in some new form that I wasn't yet conscious of. But when I cried for my father during the night for no reason, it was as if I was crying for Cairo.

Do you remember when we used to sit for ages in Ramiz Dardir's room in Nasr City? How we used to say that some people lived in an endless supermarket? How we'd laugh with genuine mirth when we realized that they really did think shopping was a sufficient goal in life? Well, at this stage, I wasn't thinking of the New World Order or the "way of life" that the Americans were promoting, nor of privatization or the events of 9/11, nor of credit cards or the Wahhabi influence on religious life, but just that the city I was looking at seemed genuinely strange to me.

I seemed to have entered a supermarket whose customers were all Sunnis with beards and women in hijab of the latest fashion. I linked the collapse of the world around me—a sudden suspicion of the existence of a secret organization intent on ruining my life—with a bad dream that I was in a new world with no cigarettes and no Arabic. It was just a moment, as I headed for the Dokki Flyover after leaving the garage, and I saw a Hummer almost make mincemeat of the Fiat 128 in front of it, but I remember.

I had to stop for a small boy running across the road with a bag on his shoulder that read "Spiderman."

Chapter on the daily route there and back

The strange thing is that I started to enjoy the daily trip despite the madding crowds and the temperature that rose daily. This never happened in the Maadi days. Was the pleasure of driving from Dokki to Isaaf and back also part of the program of self-improvement I'd half consciously drawn up for myself to contain my destructive impulses? A possibility. Still, as soon as I saw the office, the anger returned.

Who *are* these people?

For a moment, as I sat in the office on Monday, the world whose collapse I was witnessing would appear to me as a sort of circle, beginning at the gas station and ending with a group of people stumbling over each other, with a car wheel in the middle, turning round and round counterclockwise, like the sun moving around the earth.

Suddenly I'd take out my notebook, in the middle of a long conversation with the obese Aldo Mantenzika, our scandalmongering colleague who was with us—Fustuq and myself—when I first met my wife. He speaks in a strange, effeminate way, and works long hours at the paper. Did you know he is the son of the famous African sculptor Eduardo Mazika? Really Mantenzika, but if you've heard of him you'll know he's better known as Mazika. His story's really strange too. The sculptor fled to Portugal from the war in Mozambique in the mid-1970s, but only became famous in Egypt on the strength of his relationship with the celebrated pioneer of Egyptian painting Hamid Nada, who was his bosom friend, so much so that when Hamid Nada died, he died a few days afterward. To this day, I have no idea why he came to Egypt rather than any other country, or what really drove him away from Portugal. What I do know is that he enrolled his eldest son in the faculty of economics and political science in Cairo University as soon as it was opened. Aldo did well there in statistics, despite the fact that his Arabic was weak, and he ended up working at this newspaper.

So I'm having a long conversation with Aldo about nothing at all, like most of our conversations, when suddenly before my eyes the world becomes a circle. And as soon as I see this, I get out my notebook and make a small drawing, like an amulet to preserve my Cairo, which I will try to reclaim. A talisman or a charm. I'm in a hurry, so I deliberately keep the design simple.

I told myself it was like a visual summary of my world, the daily journey that I would undertake from now to eternity, there and back.

I started from the garage almost at the exit to the Dokki Flyover—beside the gas station, with Dokki Square behind you on the right—though you have to go to the end of Dokki Street to make a U-turn. At the entrance to the Orman Gardens an enormous poster can be seen announcing the Spring Flower Festival. I lingered there longer than necessary to conjure up the scene: dust hanging in the air, a yellow sky, news of war in the region, then the Economic Reform Program. What is it that reminds me of the Economic Reform Program whenever I see the poster for the Spring Flower Festival?

From the Orman Garden to the start of the October Bridge is a straight line. The microbuses battle each other, and there are schoolchildren by the dozen in the rear seats of the taxis. The ads for Concrete clothes along the central walkway feature prepubescent boys and girls in suggestive positions. After that, there is nothing but people waiting for transport at the start of the bridge. Why is everyone in Cairo so grim-faced?

I don't know how to describe Dokki because it's much more familiar than anywhere else. But I can tell you about the wall carvings in the flyover wall, or the smell emitting from the hollow of the turn-off where the dropouts urinate. About the color of the asphalt in the orange light after rain and the glint of the drain covers in the middle of the street. Or the three generations of simpleminded Copts who live in the garage where I start my journey every day. About the bad reputation of the furnished apartments around the Negm Theater. Or the time when, so my civil engineer father told me, there was no district called Mohandiseen.

Dokki then consisted of a number of streets that cut through the fields stretching north of the university and west of the Nile. We lived on the edge of what remained of a village called Dayir al-Nahiya. When he described the working-class pockets that remained there despite the dark concrete and the consumerism around the square and the survey department, my father would replace "Baladi" Dokki, the common term, with Old Dokki. So the low wall that ends at our building is the junction of two worlds: one of them that of suburban destinies, where you find all the clamor of consumption and fast food, and where the human body is constantly deprived of its right to share the available space with cars. The second world is like the villages of the Delta, with its neighborliness and poverty and rural ties. When I passed the garage as I entered that second world, it seemed completely different from the place where I started out every morning.

From Orman to the start of the bridge, Abu al-Siyout, is a straight line. The October Bridge is a separate world, with pedestrians always in the strangest places. That is to say nothing of the lovers embracing on the Nile (all the girls in hijab, even when they are in positions that are debauched by the hijab's standards); the noisy celebrations when they get married (in the same locations where they've been embracing, but at the end of the evening when things are quieter; in a few months they will stop embracing once and for all); people getting off buses to go to work, and people wandering around like stray dogs. The structure breathes on, regardless. With its continual growth since I returned from England, it is a living being that falls ill and gets better, then grows old. When its surface quakes under the heavy cargo traffic, it is as if someone you know is sighing. That's because when you take the October Bridge each day, and occasionally to go to Heliopolis or Nasr City, you start to take notice of it. You could never exchange it for the Kasr al-Nil Bridge, for example, even when traffic is at a standstill, and when traffic is smooth you marvel at its genius.

An account of the fiqi Wahid al-Din
On Sunday, as I was saying, Yildiz interrogated me.

And on Monday, as already noted, I sketched my route from Dokki to Isaaf as I sat with Aldo. I remember that he laughed and said: "Don't try, Safsaf!" That's what he calls me, as if his demeanor wasn't kittenish enough. He would soften the "s" in Safsaf, as he did with all the Arabic consonants. "Don't try, you don't know how to draw!" I also recall that I thought his voice strange. I looked at him as if I were seeing him for the first time.

Now, if you heard Aldo's voice from a distance, particularly when he was laughing, you could easily think him one of those sex-symbol actresses in an Arab film, or else (and this is perhaps more accurate) a girl of fifteen. There is something feminine in the way he articulates his words, that much is certain: something effeminate or "camp," as the English used to say. But neither this, nor the high pitch of his voice, nor even his hopeless games with the Arabic emphatics, could explain the feeling, whenever Aldo came to mind, that you were dealing with a eunuch who was entirely comfortable with his situation.

The voice of this slanderous chatterbox was also marked by a tone or inflection, a sort of stickiness difficult to imagine unless you'd witnessed the sight of the dark brown, coffee-colored, flabby flesh on the folds of every exposed millimeter of his body, even his eyelids. Hanging over the edges of his chair, however wide the seat (and this one was wide), his behind could only be described as a *booty* that disappeared immediately when he stood up, covered over by the piles of flesh that hung down from his belly, the whole figure an enormous egg that turned into a funnel of coffee beans kneaded with oil. Whenever you approached him, his height would scare you because he is so square shaped you think he must be short. A giant funnel, whose height is the same as his width, and every exposed centimeter of his body gleaming, not a hair of any kind on it. Just enormous teeth like ice cubes appearing from the opening at the top, and a faint redness in two narrow eyes. And with every word that he utters in the voice of a fifteen-year-old girl, every millimeter of the funnel shakes in the same rhythm.

Never mind.

I sat talking to the funnel man until Wahid arrived (I say Wahid despite the fact that he insists on our calling him by his full name, Wahid al-Din) sometime after 11 PM. That cheered us both up, because Wahid would be sure to make us laugh. Especially with Aldo there, because he's always relaxed with Aldo—I knew I would fall over myself laughing.

The weirdest person in the office, hands down. I've only ever seen him arrive late in the evening, and it takes extreme effort to get him to say anything. But when he speaks, he does so at a frightening speed, panting and whistling like hell. A sentence is seldom without a Qur'anic verse or a hadith, and generally begins and ends with a vague expression of wonder, along the lines of "heh!" If you're there when he speaks you leave with every centimeter of your face wet. He always behaves as if he were spying on other people, but he acts so hesitant and fearful that instead of suspicion he attracts sympathy. Ustaz Wahid could have been a species of rodent, he's so small and unpleasant. But it has never been hard to sympathize with him.

Still, on Monday night my interest in him went both wider and deeper than sympathy or humor. For the first time, I looked at him carefully and wondered why he was the way he was.

How come he's like that? I repeated.

I mean, he walks with knees bent as if he were crawling or getting ready to jump. His back's always bent too, and he has a striped skullcap on his head. His sprouting beard threatens to turn green. On his feet he has phosphorescent green bathroom slippers over his socks (I swear, I'm telling the truth), and he wears the same summer suit year round, with a donkey jacket over it in winter. If you speak to him, he'll reply, and he'll sometimes ask about Aldo, as if he were coughing, while walking away, but apart from that he'll never start a conversation. Every ten minutes he'll dash to the bathroom to wash. I don't recall who told me that he had a compulsive disorder. The least of my problems.

What's truly remarkable is that he gets his salary without doing anything. He has a respectable position but he doesn't draw any allowance (all of us basically live on allowances), never attends a single meeting, and never proposes a single article, even for the sake of appearances. There must be hundreds like him in this Kafkaesque organization. Ustaz Wahid, however, is distinguished by the hours of his arrival, his appearance, and his total withdrawal from other people. The person who told me about his hypochondria also told me that when he first started working with us, he was first-rate and energetic, despite his strange habits and his tendency to speak in classical Arabic. Then he had a serious illness and kept going back to doctors and was away from work and in the hospital for weeks. When he came back, he was like this, a horror show.

I also heard from the security people that after he came back they caught him watching porn on the internet. I don't know if they saw him playing with himself while he sat there.

On the few occasions I've bumped into him outside the paper, he was walking about looking frightened with the same old skullcap and the same flitting eyes.

No one at the paper knew anything about Ustaz Wahid al-Din, I tell you, except that he was originally from Aswan and that he had no family whatsoever, and no one bothered to ask more. As for me, when I heard his way of pronouncing Arabic and his obsequious way of greeting people, I was convinced that he was an Azhar graduate, as people said.

But his conversation with Aldo about fatwas (Aldo was the only one Ustaz Wahid was comfortable with in the office) was what confirmed for me that he was definitely a *faqih*, or *fiqi* as it is commonly pronounced. Only later was I disturbed by the fact that he did nothing at the paper, came in later and later, and dressed so strangely.

Chapter

That night, Aldo sat him down between us, and started by asking him his opinion of our female colleagues from a sexual point of view. Ustaz Wahid blushed and stuttered (did he take off his glasses at that moment? Was he wearing glasses?), his excitement visible for all to see. "A man has the right, Mr. Mantenzika, heh!—Allah, may He be exalted and glorified, says two, three, heh! Or even four!"

For his part, Aldo carried on in that effeminate way of his, describing his female colleagues in detail: "I mean, up top she's a bit better than the others, or what do you think, honestly, honestly, Wahid al-Din? The important thing is, I know you must have your eye on another woman, because you always like to think about what is down below."

"Heh! Allaaaaah preserve us, 'Amm Aldo! But copulation is allowed by the grace of God, and there is no cop-cop-ulation (pardon the expression!) without what is down below."

When Aldo raised his left eyebrow in his arch way and said to him, "True, Wahid al-Din, but why haven't you married yet?" he stood up again and started to deliver a speech as if it were one long cough.

"Heh!" he said, "Mr. Mantenzika, marriage is all a matter of fate" (he pronounced the "g" in marriage the classical way, and sounded the "q" in *qisma*). "But still, my good man, Aldo Man-n-n-tenzika, the strangest story is that of your friend Wah-h-hid al-Din. I mean, I am honored to be your friend, heh!" He continued with a hysterical laugh. "When I arrived from Aswan, I was engaged, but the g-g-girl (pardon the expression!) turned out not to be a girl at all; I mean (God almighty forgive me!), she'd fallen into evil ways and engaged in debauchery. But God saved me, as I never actually married her." He looked down at the ground and his face turned red again, as he spoke more slowly (this was the first time I'd heard Wahid al-Din speak like this; it was like the tail end of a cough): "As you say, Mr. Mantenzika, it was a problem! I was young and your friend was happy to be engaged." His manner indicated that however much we pressed him, he wouldn't tell us how he found out that his fiancée had lost her virginity. With genuine regret, I just then remembered Amgad Salah. "Then suddenly to find out that your f–f-f-fiancée… heh!"

I would've laughed till I died, but that night as the conversation went on I don't know what happened to me. I just smiled to myself while Aldo emitted high-pitched guffaws, like those of a seductive actress in a seedy film, which echoed all around the building. And I wondered why Wahid al-Din no longer made me laugh.

I had sketched my route once before the fiqi arrived, but when I went back to bed I would sketch it again.

Sometime after one o'clock in the morning, while watching the film *Soldiers in the Camp* starring Muhammad Heneidi, I would wonder if Wahid realized that Aldo was not laughing with him so much as laughing at him, why he relaxed with Aldo as with no one else, what his illness had been when he was away for such a long time, what had happened to him while he was gone, and whether there was any hope of improving his appearance. I went to sleep after the film ended and woke up terrified in the middle of the night. When I fell asleep again, the events of the dream that had terrified me resumed.

Rashid, I was to think about this dream a lot in the days to come, perhaps because since leaving Maadi I'd only dreamed of surface things, the most trivial things. I'd watch Ahmad Hilmi in the film *Zaki Chan*, for example, and dream of the street thugs in his neighborhood forcing him to strip. Or I'd install a new version of Photoshop and spend my dreams reinventing its filters. This was of course with the exception of the repeated dream of the ditch, and a dream or two about my father.

I don't know why my father is on my mind these days.

But apart from my father there was nothing, nothing, except triviality and the insane escalation of puzzlement. That night, when I gave myself up to sleep to the voice of Salah 'Abdullah singing "Hosta costa, high as a kite!", what could I be expected to dream of other than the yarns of a B-movie?

Muhammad Heneidi, a Central Security conscript, saying to the child who is spraying him with water: "Tut tut, little boy, tut tut!" Muhammad Heneidi, a small Ancient Egyptian running away from the fat Sa'idi who is trying to kill him…

A recollection of what happened before going to sleep the night of the first dream

Monday night, after returning late from the office, as well as rediscovering our strange colleague Wahid al-Din (or the zombie, as Amgad called him), a second thing happened in the story I'm telling you. I sat up on the bed and looked again at the circle I'd drawn while talking with Aldo, our prissy colleague.

There was half an hour or more left before the start of *Soldiers in the Camp*. So I turned off the television and got ready to write some observations in my notebook. I'd forgotten all about the circle I'd drawn but as soon as I opened the notebook it jumped out at me. And once again, I entered this confused state in which I thought the circle was turning like a moth around a lamp, time after time after time at the same moderate speed in a counterclockwise direction, its rotation never stopping. My ears registered an absolute silence. My mother was asleep, everything was quiet, the whole world seemed to have stopped moving, time itself had stopped. The earth was stable in the ether, and nothing was breathing except for the moth. Then I started to imagine that I personally was this moth, that the world had stopped and I was turning.

God!

My head was covered in dust, the same magic dust. But before drowsiness could overwhelm and suffocate me, I leaped up, turned on the television, and started to make Turkish coffee. As I came back from the kitchen, I thought this was the thing to say: Don't give in to drowsiness, and just build your world again, the important thing is to build.

In this connection, it occurred to me that the circle I'd drawn in the office didn't show the movement of the road as I felt it on my journey every day. I decided that instead of writing notes I would track my route in pencil on a new page. I didn't dare switch the television off again as I put the coffee down on the table and lit a cigarette. Then I sat up again in bed with the notebook in my hand.

The first sip brought me back to life, Rashid—when I held it in my mouth with a drag from the cigarette, to be precise. I shut my eyes and concentrated. Once again I became a moth leaving the garage and heading for Isaaf Square.

My hand moved over the paper of its own volition, tracing the route with a natural, incomprehensible precision. More than once I almost opened my eyes (another sip of coffee), then didn't. My hand just went on drawing the route. When I'd finished, the film was about to begin and the coffee was still warm. The cigarette was all burned up.

I lit another and took a long drag on it, which I again held in with a breath.

Then I looked at the circle of my daily journey after correction:

From Dokki
to Isaaf

What was this?

As the film began, I thought about what the world would mean if it was reduced to a route. And with a despairing laugh, I said to myself, "Bloody hell! You're confused enough without the world meaning anything! You don't understand why Gulf women have to cover their faces, for example, or why Lebanese editors, our journalistic rivals, insist on putting the word *min* in front of every *dūn* when they want to say 'without,' or why the English are so practical and insensitive that it's impossible to discuss emotions with them except when they're blind drunk, or that it's a matter of pure chance whether anyone can ever form or pursue a relationship. You don't understand why there are borders between countries, what makes some people richer or crueler, nor where to find what everyone says is the most important thing, or why that thing doesn't interfere if it could."

"All you do understand"—I thought, then the film began— "is that there is a fixed route that you have to follow every day (though of course there are other places in the world that could become routes for you or others to follow). I mean, in short, you don't understand anything about anything."

The film's music was getting louder as I took my last sip of coffee.

The first dream

I dreamed that I'd gotten out of bed and gone out into the street, but it was morning and I was in a different city. Was this really a city? Everywhere I looked, there was sparkling water and green speckled with flowers, no asphalt or cars. I looked in vain for Dokki Square. The towers and bridges of Cairo had disappeared. The neon signs, the kiosk windows, the sidewalks, the entrance walls. No constant mechanical noise in my ears. No advertisements or lampposts. All the buildings were stone, wood, or mud brick. Some of them were enormous, reminding one of the Greeks or Romans, but their height was never greater than their width, and they were all beautiful and ruined. I was in the middle of a sandy square, with a road leading down, as if I were on a hill.

The place was completely empty, but from the west I heard the sound of screaming and was drawn toward the stifled noise—drums, pipes, horses' hooves, then a roar and punching—all as if I were hearing them over a radio wrapped in a wet rag. Then the sun appeared, a disk rising from the middle of the water behind an enormous cypress tree. I must have left the hill for the shore: I was standing opposite a line of sandstone that waves were breaking against, with my face to the sun. In front of me were three aged priests, wearing crosses suspended from their necks that they held up in front of their thick beards, and running as fast as they could toward the water. The wind lifted their black habits so that they looked like the sails of pirate ships as they stumbled over the rocks, avoiding the cultivated land. Nothing could stop them. Only a fervent prayer which I thought must be in Greek, mingled with their panting and their unbroken steps over the earth, until they rose and flew off with their legs in a split, each like a ninja in an action film.

They fell into the water without a sound.

Chapter: the rest of the dream

I dreamed I stood up again, knowing that this was a dream, and controlling my terror so that it would not wake me, following the same logic of joy in danger. The feeling that had come over me after Fustuq's prophecy. This time I didn't look for Dokki Square and I didn't find the place strange. On my right were the stones of a building—I didn't know how I had come here from the shore—an enormous building whose dome was as big as a whole village. From the carvings on its pillars I surmised that it was a Greek cathedral.

I was now in the middle of the hubbub, part of a human hill that stretched as far as the eye could see. The people were all in historical clothes, as if in a film like *Oh, Islam!* "Where art thou, oh Jihad?" But it was more convincing. There was gunpowder, food, and drink, and the clothes weren't all clean and brightly colored. The women's faces were covered. From my viewpoint I immediately realized that I was in the middle of a crowd lined up on either side of the entrance to a church as venerable as the center of the universe.

I didn't want to look behind me in case I saw men's insides being devoured by cats and foxes. I reminded myself that I was dreaming so as to able to bear the scene. Torn-off limbs with dogs circling around them. Piles of furniture, rubbish, valuables, and jewelry guarded by soldiers. A turbaned child setting alight an icon twice his size. He pours fuel over it then brings the flame to its surface.

The scene was unlike *Oh Islam!* and more like the documentaries about the Lebanese civil war. Women wailing, men running, and dust thrown up in the air. Nonetheless, there was a general feeling of joy. In the May heat—I don't know what convinced me that it was May—you could smell the stench of blood, burnt hair, and grilled meat. You could hear the sound of artillery as if the earth was exploding, followed by the chatter of voices, no Arabic among them. Yet among the uproar, you could distinguish the expression *Allahu akbar!* in accents that sounded European. And then, in an ecstatic tone, *La ilaha illa Allah.*

In dreams blood has a nauseous smell.

When I raised my hand to my head, I was shocked to find that I too was wearing a turban. It was only then that I became aware of the clothes on my body: thick green cotton tied with a linen belt with a silk coat over it. I was making my way through the jammed bodies to the start of the row, then to the right in the direction of the gate. I seemed to be being carried along by something. There were soldiers, most of them in blue cloaks and a fez like a funnel on the head. Behind their backs a piece of white cloth dropped down like a veil from a gold-faced cube. Most had an eight-pointed star, chiseled from two overlapping squares, in the middle of the cube. Why didn't these men have beards like everyone else? Even I had a thick hennaed goatee.

The noise and the commotion grew until we heard the sloshing behind us get louder. At this point, armed horsemen appeared, like some sort of entourage. Everyone stepped back to make way for their procession. The decorations on their saddles dazzled the eye but it was the white horses that shone. Their white matched the large turbans wrapped around the red pointed skullcaps on the riders' heads. A whistle, and drums. Not one turban like it in all this human heap. I could hardly believe that the eye of the procession was that green young man. Who told me that his name was al-Fatih and that he was not yet twenty-four?

With his Roman nose, his red beard, and his honey-colored eyes, he was really more like a teenager. Could he really be the sultan? But the sheikhs were kissing the hem of his caftan and touching his saddle as the horse moved forward toward the gate. I could hardly believe it: a light prick like the handle of his sword on my head and almost before I was aware of it I was bending over his hand to kiss it. It was as if I had gained the highest honor in the world. Even the sheikhs could not get nearer than the hem of his cloak. Pride, almost flying, as I followed him among the crowds, for he had chosen me rather than anyone. Who could I be? He dismounted and I bent down spontaneously as he continued to keep his back to me.

Just a young man of twenty-four. I lifted my hand to offer him some earth and he scattered it over his turban. The sound of explosions returned. God is most great! Then I heard him whispering, in the same European accent, "Praise to the Lord of the worlds."

He was stepping over the threshold of the cathedral. Suddenly swords glinted in the air and crowds poured like frightened rats around either side of him, running as fast as possible and colliding with one another. There were no turbans on their heads and their wives' faces were unveiled. I lifted my head a little and sighed.

My thoughts wandered away from the heap we were stepping over, sacks placed one on top of the other to hide the floor, sacks filled with something soft and compact like raw cotton. For some unknown reason I didn't look down at them. Being inside the building was like being in a castle in heaven. Despite the Virgin carrying her child and St. George slaying the dragon, I was filled with a feeling of belonging to Islam that I've seldom had while awake.

The sultan bowed in prayer and I bowed behind him. I pressed my head against the ground that was heavy with water, earth, and blood.

It was only then that I had the strength to look behind me and realized that the heap we'd walked across was the corpses of those who took refuge in the cathedral when the sultan's soldiers arrived. A sudden nausea, and I almost woke, but something told me that I had to stay to perform the Friday prayer, so I plunged back into sleep. Once again I raised my head and sighed: Among the icons and the crosses, in the heart of this amazing Byzantine church, which seemed like the center of the universe, with al-Fatih bending before me at less than twenty-four years of age, came the voice of the imam leading the prayer.

Recapitulation

When I described the route from Orman to the October Bridge, I forgot to tell you about the trunks of the green trees that for no apparent reason rise up like poles between the lampposts—higher poles—and the ads. People make their way between the cars like soldiers in a retreating army. A feeling of uselessness comes over you at the Shooting Club crossroads. Once you're on the bridge, the billboards become larger and further apart. Between the Gezira stables and the mini Twin Towers (as since September 2001 I have called the two buildings standing adjacent to one another near the Radio and TV building), a dry river above the level of the asphalt leads to residential areas.

I had often observed the billboards carefully to pass the time: the Kaaba smaller than the bed in a sumptuous bedroom overlooking the sacred area in Mecca; the trinity of butter, oil, and washing powder; the mobile that promises to change its owner into Superman. At the foot of the Isaaf turnoff, on the left, are the remains of a stone and wood building, a factory or station. Opposite this, among the cheap comedy stars and clip artists, 'Amr Khalid, the TV preacher, advertises his show, *On the Heels of the Beloved*, with the same dumb smile always on the verge of hysteria, his eye on the numbers of the hotline to paradise.

Even when the bridge traffic was moving, most of the time you could hardly pass 'Amr Khalid before the congestion began. From above, the mass of cars dotted with pedestrians looked like the Day of Resurrection. I was reminded of the dead rising from their tombs and the popular expression used to mean "at the end of one's rope!": "One's dead loved ones coming out [of their graves]". I felt that the whole of this world was at the end of its rope, everyone's dead dancing around them, and I was content.

I wasn't the only one left standing while everything collapsed, not knowing what to do.

Knowledge is of two kinds, one to be acquired and one to be discarded; and the sea is of two kinds, one to be traveled and one to be feared. —al-Hallaj

On Tuesday, Abu al-Arshad, it would occur to me that Isaaf Square was always the starting point—not always, of course, but certainly since I'd started work as a journalist less than two months after completing my studies in Bristol, around ten years ago. To be precise, from the day I took a taxi from Dokki to one of the ugliest buildings in Greater Cairo, went up in the elevator, found myself in the economic press office of a major newspaper corporation, and learned that I would be writing, then editing, non-economic materials for this publication. From Isaaf Square I learned to go, in order:

—To Zamalek, where my Japanese girlfriend whom I'd met in Bristol had a house, followed by the Uruba Café;

—Across Downtown (the Garden Flower Café, Estoril Bar, Hurriyya Café, and the Swiss Air Café on Adli Street, La Chesa, then the Mashrabiyya and Townhouse Galleries, and the AUC etc., etc.) to Ghawriyya, where I sat consuming the bango that I was addicted to for a full year in the Hawsh Qadam Quarter, the stately houses with their folklore shows and the cafés of al-Hussein on the opposite side of al-Azhar Street;

—Over the flyover, or along Salah Salem Street, to the airport and Nasr City, where my friend the film director had a room on a bare roof in the Tenth Quarter, then Yildiz's family's house, where I used to visit her in the apartment next to her family's on the middle of the Muqattam Hills, or else Qattamiya;

—To Maadi, the home of a retired journalist whose sister (who used to live with him) I was attached to for a year; then my wife's company in the marital apartment;

—To 6 October City (other journalists' houses), and the Carrefour supermarket on the Desert Road—across the Ezbekiyya Gardens, where Amgad Salah lives—

and sometimes, via the same road, to Wadi Natrun or Alexandria;

—To Old Cairo, Souq al-Imam, and Birqash in the early morning.

Also, and particularly after I had started to drive regularly, to a great number of houses and offices in Mohandiseen, Agouza, Ard al-Liwa', Garden City, Heliopolis, 'Abbasiyya, 'Ain Shams, Giza, the Pyramids area, and Imbaba…

Then what?

Isaaf Square was like an opened door, Abu al-Siyout, behind which I could see everything, without taking part in it all:

I saw drugs in all their varieties, with corresponding variations in the classes and temperaments of those who take them and their effects on them and their lives. I saw men who prefer to sleep with men or children, and women like them, then a whole world centered on Downtown that seemed to be all aged foreigners and young down-and-outs who would sleep with them in exchange for various things, the most obvious (and the rarest) being money.

I saw all sorts of women seeking love. The woman who wants you to be a morose failure so that she can pluck you from the talons of despair. The woman who believes she can deceive you. The woman who wants to use you to make a man, or a father, or another woman angry. The woman who feels great and wonderful just because you're there. And finally, the woman who wants you to be a toilet for the feces of her family history.

I saw people who dissect the news bulletin every evening, believing in ideology the way that Amgad Salah now believes in Salafi Islam, and therefore call themselves intellectuals. I saw foreigners who rent apartments to turn them into homes or galleries and hold parties in which they exchange expressions of distress at what is happening to the country; provincial poets who sit in the cafés for a disturbingly long time; writers who pursue journalists; and women writers who form relationships with critics, like the film extras who are always ready to have sex with directors.

I saw murders and torture in the police stations, nervous breakdowns followed or not followed by stints in mental asylums, demonstrations and fights in the streets, actors shooting up in bar restrooms, prostitutes in hijab, and children throwing petrol bombs at each other.

All this and more I saw when the Isaaf Square gate opened. It now seems a long way from my feeling of the collapse of the world and the crazy things that will happen to me in the course of rebuilding it. Only later will it be linked to anger, or a feeling that unknown forces are pursuing me. This despite the fact that the image of the dead coming out of their graves would come in its clearest form as I descended beside the 'Amr Khalid billboard to the middle of the square.

The search for the Mitwalli Gate and the national movement

On Tuesday, on my way to work, I would think it just a whim that I should believe Isaaf to be the starting point for my entry into the wide world. As I made the craziest of U-turns, starting from the Red Crescent Hospital and passing one of the largest Salafi mosques to the whirlpool of the Turguman area intersection, I would laugh at the new name I had unthinkingly invented for it: World's Gate.

Where had I got an expression like this from? Wasn't it a bit of an exaggeration?

I remembered the neighborhood of Bab al-Nasr, Victory's Gate, with Zizu the sausage seller, and Bab al-Futuh next to it (which one was directly opposite Zizu's?). Then there was the dark alley of the tentmakers leading to Bab Zuweila. It was the Fatimid gates of Cairo, then, that gave me the inspiration for this name. There was no doubt that Bab Zuweila was the easiest to remember, too. I would laugh when I recalled, with mock grief, the episode of Tuman Bey, the last Mamluk ruler, who was hanged and strung up there.

For the first time in years, I would recall the sight of our prep-school history teacher relating the incident to us as if Tuman Bey were his father and the Ottoman Sultan Selim his mother's husband. What was his name, oh God…

Ustaz Mitwalli? Yes, I think his name was Ustaz Mitwalli.

With his woolen waistcoat, his trousers rolled up to his chest, and his bald patch that looked like an ostrich egg nested in brushwood, he was the quaintest man in the whole school.

Ustaz Mitwalli could get a laugh without lifting a finger. Not to mention the hilarious things he'd do in class, such as suddenly squatting down halfway through reading a sentence or springing up again like a jack-in-the-box to emphasize a certain idea or chain of thought. He took no notice of our mocking laughter. And he was obsessed with various things he classified under the name of the "national movement."

I didn't understand at the time what exactly this national movement was. For Ustaz Mitwalli, Tuman Bey was one of its martyrs and heroes. In this context, I thought that the common name for Bab Zuweila, Mitwalli's Gate, must be a result of this idea of its most famous martyr (which is what most people take the word to mean), for Tuman Bey was regarded as having a spiritual hold over the area. But in time I would discover that this was nonsense: the gate had been called Mitwalli's gate because the *mutawalli*, or commander, of the soldiers in the Ottoman period had resided there. There was also a theory that it referred to a Sufi sheikh called al-Qutb al-Mutawalli who lived in seclusion nearby. In any event, nothing that Ustaz Mitwalli taught us was at all logical…

Should you ask yourself how I know all this, Rashid, let me tell you that about four months before separating from my wife, I edited a series of travel articles about the Islamic monuments of Cairo for the newspaper. Their authors had taken the contents from books by foreign historians, most of them published by the American University in Cairo. The fact is the topic really intrigued me, so I sought out the books and read up on the subject, and some things stuck in my head.

Now it's true that by the time the Ottomans arrived, the Mamluks had been in Egypt for some time and had mixed better with the peasants. That is where the term *awlad al-nas,* or "children of the people," comes from, referring to those Mamluks who had been in Egypt for generations, becoming historians and rulers.

But Tuman Bey and his uncle Qansuh al-Ghawri were Circassians who came from the Northern Caucasus, while the Ottomans were Turkmen from Rumelia in Northern Greece and Western Anatolia. So what makes the former nationalist heroes and the latter foreign occupiers?

This is another thing that to this day I can't understand, although, if you'd read Ibn Iyas's book, you would know that only two of the Mamluk rulers of Egypt were "Rumi" ("Rumi" cheese being named after them), and that this word "Rumi" simply means Turkish, as is proved by the fact that in Alexandria "Rumi" cheese is called Turkish cheese—referring to the Turkmen tribes who were descendants of the Seljuks and nominally supported the 'Abbasid caliphate, though in practice they controlled it.

When the Mongols put an end to the dominance of this dynasty in Iran and Iraq, a group of them based themselves in the city of Konya in Byzantine territory (the "East Roman" Empire, as it was known), where Persian and Greek mixed with Turkish in their progeny.

I took some interest in this Rumi question because it explained several things. For example, one of the two Rumis who ruled Egypt was called al-Zahir Khoshqadam. For this reason the name of the district in al-Ghawriyya called Hawsh Qadam is written with a "q" despite the fact that it is pronounced "Hawsh Adam." And Mawlana Jalal al-Din, the author of the *Mathnavi*, despite being from Balkh in Iran and having no connection at all with Rum, is called Rumi because he lived in Konya.

In the year AH 569, Saladin commissioned Baha' al-Din Qaraqosh al-Asafi to construct the Tawashi [i.e. the Eunuchs'] Wall. He wanted to construct a single wall around Cairo, Misr, and the Citadel. —al-Maqrizi

But even before the Seljuks seized power in Baghdad, the Turks had ruled here. There was first Ahmad ibn Tulun, and later the Ikhshid and his son Tughrul, who was marginalized by the eunuch Kafur mentioned by al-Mutanabbi. Even the Ayyubids descended from Saladin worked for another Turk, Nur al-Din Zangi, who was the enemy of the Latin Catholics and frequently raided the Crusader realm they had established in Palestine, known as Outremer.

Even Yusuf ibn Najm al-Din Ayyub himself—the Azerbaijani Kurd who brought down the Fatimid state and reclaimed Jerusalem from these Catholics after the Battle of Hittin, then built the Citadel and started building the unfinished wall that was to join al-Mu'izz's Cairo with the old city of Misr, the Old Cairo adjacent to Roda Island—was a Turk by education and culture, Rashid.

About a hundred years after the fall of the Fatimids—practically the only Arab rulers of Egypt since the rise of the 'Abbasid dynasty, and whose fall coincided with the Seljuk migration into Rumelia—Hulagu would make Baghdad famous by wrapping the Caliph al-Musta'sim in a precious carpet to be trampled by horses. He then continued his advance west over Muslim territory until he was stopped by al-Muzaffar Qutuz at 'Ayn Jalut, although in fact Qutuz didn't actually stop Hulagu but defeated a trivial contingent that Genghis Khan's most famous grandson had left in Nablus when he was forced to return to Iran. And it was after that that the caliphate passed to Cairo, under the protection of the Mamluks...

A history lesson, isn't this? Never mind...

I feel sorry for the Sultan of Egypt, how he turned and disappeared as if he were never once remembered: they hanged him unjustly on Bab Zuweila and made him taste the worst of evils! —Ibn Iyas

As I was saying: the day Ustaz Mitwalli told us about Tuman Bey, he was so moved that when he squatted for the second time, instead of leaping up again as he usually did, he fell on his back in tears. I think that he was reading from Ibn Iyas's book *Bada'i' al-zuhur* even though it was not on our reading list, and in fact Ibn Iyas was not on the syllabus at all (Ibn Iyas was also a Circassian, by the way).

What made the incident stick in my mind was that we never saw Ustaz Mitwalli at all after this class. We heard that the school administration had had enough of his strange behavior, and finally dismissed him as a result of the masquerade in our class. How sorry I was when later I heard of Ustaz Mitwalli's death.

As I was saying, it occurred to me to call Isaaf World's Gate on Sunday, the second day after I'd quit the marital apartment, and perhaps I took a certain pleasure in mulling over my grief for Ustaz Mitwalli. As I was coming back from the office, I had the idea of finding the text of the piece that he'd been reading to us, and I made up my mind about it with a stubbornness that reminded me of my wife sitting on the floor and itemizing piles of pictures, papers, and other small things of obscure sentimental value.

Sometimes I felt this was the only time she was really alive. My wife was the kind of person who keeps everything—and spends more time preserving the thing that symbolizes an event than they spend on the event itself. She would even put tree leaves between the pages of a book, and got really angry if they were crushed by someone reading.

In brief, the "pickle" approach to life: instead of eating something, you spend your time marinating it.

The obstinate need to do something useless—to find a text that reminded me of my preparatory school—and an enthusiasm for chewing over old sorrows: these were among my wife's few distinct attributes. So when I found myself following this logic, I remembered her. It was not exactly nostalgia, but rather an adaptation to the sort of madness that might temporarily compensate me for my loss. As if in this way I could achieve the partnership that had eluded me for a full year while we were under one roof.

Then again, I knew this wasn't my nature, there was no danger that I'd continue to apply the "pickle" theory in my life.

So I went to the balcony off the hall without fear.

Something ghabar, yaghbur, *that is "it remains." And* al-ghābir *means "the remaining." Al-ghābir is also "the past." It is an auto-antonym.* —Lisan al-'Arab

There used to be a cupboard on the balcony where I kept pigeons and rabbits. I still remember the plump pigeon who would fly away and come back to me, as well as the psychologically disturbed rabbit who managed to climb the wall and commit suicide. On that balcony, which looked out over both Dayir al-Nahiya and the street, memories are mixed up with the fights of our depraved neighbors in Old Dokki and with the long waits for my mother to come back from work or from a day trip to Port Said, bringing with her a gas station to fit my cars, each the size of a matchbox.

Even today, whenever I go onto the balcony, a moment passes when I forget that this enclosure is barely large enough for the body of a person rummaging through the piles of books belonging to my father. After the books got to be too many, my mother would have sold them by the kilo, had it not been for the peaceful coexistence agreement that the parents drew up together—"At least we'll have some peace from the noise of the riff-raff below," she said—and the homeless books were gathered there. On Sunday, after sunset... I was moving as if in slow motion.

"What are you after in there now, for God's sake?" my mother's plaintive cry followed me. "Okay, but shut the door behind you to keep the dust out!"

A strange thing, my friend. As if the route from the dining table to the entrance to the balcony behind my father's desk had grown longer, or changed into an outer-space channel connecting two separate planets. My mother at the table was on one planet, and the balcony where the books were stored was on another, and I was flying between them. The nearer I got to the balcony, the softer and stranger my mother's voice became; and the farther I moved from the table, the more I assumed the spirit of a child playing with a dove. My plump dove, the color of cow's cream, with a yearning in its eyes (two shirt buttons) for a country I had never visited. Its beak between my fingers was a sunflower seed I could almost crack. It rests in my hands until I let it go. Then it flaps its wings and looks at me, flying further and further away. Yet it seems to me that every so often it turns to look at me before continuing on its airborne journey...

I came to in the middle of the dust—the *ghubar*—my hands groping for the light switch as I hunched over (I was a little taller than the ceiling), then straightened up to shut the door. Dust mingled with the smell of old paper and a musty sensation like the air that surrounded my father. Something between coffee and Kent cigarettes and a gray-green dressing gown.

The place was in darkness. A single bulb dangled from a hole in the wood. It seemed to have actually burned out. Only a pale glimmer, because the door was ajar, allowed me to find the switch.

Ibn Iyas's account

Finally, I went to fetch a candle and some matches from the drawer in the meat safe and came back. Although I'd shut the door behind me as my mother carried on wailing until I went into the balcony-cupboard again (this time I didn't leave the door ajar), I felt that I had entered another planet. I was no longer a child playing with a dove with cream-colored feathers, but was completely separate from this place and time. My country was a wooden vault holding weighty secrets, which I had to look for among the rows of books, because they (the secrets) were printed on paper. Even the smell of oil from the kitchen did not change the feeling that I was on another planet. I was like an exile on his way home. I remember: as soon as I had closed the door completely, I crawled.

You could stand with your head bowed inside the vault that the hall balcony had turned into. In the darkness, I recalled a strange dream, which has repeated itself in different forms throughout my life.

I had fallen into a wide ditch that was like a complete world. Something like a cloud at the bottom absorbed the shock. This time the cloud was like heaped-up dust and paper. Deep piles of dust which the palm of your hand would sink into, wrappings that looked the color of my father's dressing gown in the light of the candle that I'd placed between my feet, a succession of notched incisions. I was outside the world, crawling on this thing, dipping in and out of the gray-green moistness. Whenever I felt tired I would lie down on my back and stare upward.

It seemed to me that in this ditch, for some unfathomable reason, I had moved from my mother's planet to the planet of my father's books. I traveled to this dream, and without realizing it, candle in hand, I started to crawl. I clasped the books and pushed them away from me, pulling them down and plunging into the few gaps between them. Pyramids, mattresses, and pillows of books, and I was in the water. You can imagine the quivering light when I finally squatted down and lit the candle. Shades of gray and yellow in that vertical tomb, and I was exactly like Ustaz Mitwalli, may God have mercy on him, as my hands turned over the paper creatures that came up to me one after the other, they seemed to be breathing. I don't know how long I spent among the books and the dust. I'd forgotten my wife already. I even forgot my father. I don't know when the book came into my hands, or how I reached the page I was looking for. What made the words stick in my head as though I had memorized them? And where did the book disappear to when I had finished?

"When they came to Bab Zuweila, they took him down from his horse and loosened the ropes holding him. The Ottomans stood around him with swords drawn. When it was clear that he was to be hanged (it was here that Ustaz Mitwalli squatted for the first time), he stood up on his feet at Bab Zuweila and said to the people who were around him: 'Recite the fatiha for me three times.' Then he stretched out his hand (Ustaz Mitwalli was fighting back tears) and recited the fatiha, and the people recited with him. Then he said to the hangman (the unfinished jump) 'Do your job!' When he put the noose on his neck and raised the rope, it broke and he fell onto the threshold of Bab Zuweila (here Ustaz Mitwalli fell but did not stop reading). It is said that the rope broke twice and he fell to the ground, then they strung him up with his head uncovered. When he had been hanged and his soul departed, the people gave a great shout for him, and there was much sadness and regret… (all this mingled with tears)."

Ustaz Mitwalli seemed to be in front of me, wanting to speak, or perhaps I had become Ustaz Mitwalli. Just crouching and leaping up in the light of the candle. Then I was in the hall, with my mother wailing "the dust"—"go clean yourself up, go on!"—and the other planet was a lump of salt that had dissolved. There was nothing left of it except for Ibn Iyas's words, and it was as if I had never been on the balcony. I went back to the dining room where my mother was sitting: the collapse of my marriage, Fustuq's prophecy, the fateful trek from Maadi to Dokki, then the journey that repeated itself every day, from Dokki to Isaaf.

Recapitulation

In El Galaa Street, the aggression of the street sellers, fights between drivers (even those who are colleagues), and the feeling, increasing every day, that we really are a nation of animals and the government is not to blame.

As for the land of Egypt, it is a low-lying, depressed country, the country of the Pharaohs and the dwelling place of tyrants, only distinguished by the Nile. It is more to be slurred than praised. Among its inhabitants you will find cunning, usury, evil, slyness, and deceit... —al-Mas'udi

The important thing was: All through this first week, I would go to the office in a good mood, only to find them piping on about morals. People in Egypt are very moralistic, but their motives are all hypocrisy and vice. Between ambition and lifelessness there is reaction and falsehood. The only exciting thing about Yildiz: if you wink at her, she will get excited. But I'm scribbling to take revenge now (that's what I did the whole of the first week), and I wanted to tell a story, not take revenge. Maybe my colleagues annoyed me because I was forced to be with them in the office. I had no one else, just my empty room in Dokki. It was all the same, Yildiz or Michel Fustuq, the girl engaged to the very young man or Amgad Salah.

My daily task was to rediscover the madness of each one of them. Whenever I spoke to one of them in the day, Abu al-Siyout, I spent the night drilling into his motives. And whenever I noticed a contradiction in one of them, I would curse all of them to myself.

In time, I started to extract general results that made me feel I was more and more on my own. I would feel perplexed, get angry, and stumble around until I was stilled by fear. Once again, I thought about the need to keep to a firm daily plan that would preserve the course of my work, social appearances, and my parents' happiness. No?

An account of the girl engaged to the boy
Let me return to the sequence of events:

On Monday evening, after I had sketched my route twice, and observed without laughing our colleague, the fiqi Wahid al-Din, I awoke terrified of the priests falling into the water. And when I went back to sleep, I saw the rest of the dream. What *is* this?

Now, before looking for Ibn Iyas's book on Tuesday, I had been playing the Lost Ark video game and copyediting an essay about the merits of step-by-step constitutional amendment, when the girl engaged to the boy came in for a smoke.

By the way, this has no direct connection with the story I'm telling you, except that, at the paper, I worked in a plywood cubicle inside one of the big rooms. Its advantage was that it had a window that let in natural light. It's true that the window looked out over the rooftops of the poor quarter of Sidi Abu al-'Ila, which reminds the viewer of the country's sorrows. But even refuse and quicklime and such things have their own beauty by day. And there was a door you could close from the inside to separate yourself from your colleagues and feel free.

It's for this reason that the girl engaged to the boy came to me rather than anyone else whenever she fancied a smoke. She would sit in the corner with the hand holding the cigarette behind the chair. It had to stay a secret from her fiancé, who also worked with us. She didn't really smoke—she just liked to provoke that dolt of hers, stepping just an inch outside the circle of disgrace. Under the influence of our dissolute, dark-skinned colleague, most likely. And without the fool knowing. What bounds did she overstep, anyway? I don't think she suffered a moment of suspicion that the circle her father had erected around her may have stopped her natural development. No anger, no curiosity. An impeccable manual of behavior, but nothing worked. Not a thing.

"I can't do anything that would annoy them!" That's what she said about her family, and blinked: "I mean, why...?"

In short, her father knew what was good for her. And her father would allow her to marry the boy on condition that he guaranteed her rights. All the material details of their life together would be determined by her father. And she agreed one hundred percent, no? The problem is that the boy's apartment isn't up to standard. I mean, in exchange for the hymen, surely there's a better apartment? The skimpily dressed dark girl, as though unaware that she's half-naked, is the closest thing in my life to a woman I desire. Suddenly, she lifts one leg off the other. "Okay, I'm off to pray!"

"So you behave like this but you also pray?"

An investigation into values connected with work and life

I thought a lot about the boy and the girl that day. Presumably, she loved him and presumably, he loved her. Both were over twenty-five and had never known another body. Both were prepared to wait for the apartment before knowing the other's body. That is, he would pay to sleep with her and she would sleep with him and be paid. For a year or more they would wait, and neither of them would feel that anything was amiss. Their love, which was measured out with a ruler, would not be affected, and they wouldn't know any other body until they died. Right? He would revise his English vocabulary and she would smoke behind his back. As the Prophet Muhammad advised early Muslims, if you can't have halal sex, you should get your mind off it by fasting. I steered the Lost Ark over the screen and kept thinking. A production company for boys and girls who lack the simplest conditions of trust in a partner. Whoever is cleverer wins. I left the screen and went over to the window.

Are these human beings?

Despite that, only one thing would remain with me: the relationship between the betrothed girl and the dark-skinned woman.

I could picture the two of them heading off to the prayer room, one behind the other. The prayer room was like another cubicle in the reception room for visitors, hardly big enough for two bodies, and divided off by a curtain rather than a door. As they make their way there, I think that despite the stark differences between them, there are actually many things they share.

The engaged girl's love for her family is the mirror image of the other woman's family upsets. The absence of sexual awareness and the exaggerated exploitation of it are two sides of the same coin. And then the thing they clearly have in common: revulsion at the idea of actual physical contact: men's bodies.

As far as I'm concerned, until now, this is all conventional appearances to emphasize moral innocence. Just as the dark lady complains continuously about sexual harassment, as she calls it, despite the fact that she is physically incapable of going for ten minutes in a row without drawing the attention of a man to her body, so is the pretense of revulsion the sick echo of the values of a society that claims it is conservative when in fact it is just closed. Despite my roaring anger, I had to occupy my mind with something else.

I decided to put the matter to one side temporarily.

"How you doing, girl? Kiss, kiss, cuddle, cuddle!" —the comedian Muhammad Sa'd in the film *Allimbi,* directed by Wa'il Ihsan, 2002

It's possible that I was annoyed by the boy and the girl because for days I'd been watching comic B-movies, and every film contained a love story. The heroine is a virgin, and the hero has to undertake a series of ludicrous exploits in order to take her virginity—impossible without a legal contract. Sometimes he is engaged to her before he embarks on his adventures but some all-embracing disaster prevents him from actually marrying her. Occasionally I laughed out loud, but in any case the films generated noise in the room. This helped me fill up the empty time. It was clear to me that the world that had collapsed could simply be added to all the remains of previous worlds. I no longer preserved the material evidence that I was there, as I had when I was younger—the important thing was to continue with the new without fear.

As soon as the void was filled, my appetite for lust would return. Little by little. Everything impels us to be monks. I had to resurrect desire in my body. Tonight, in fact, I would shower. I would gather my things together to be ready to travel. My lust for other countries. I would roam the world like a fool. And when I found my goal I wouldn't marry her under any circumstances. Nothing would make me get off a tour bus going at 170 kilometers in an unknown direction. After the dawn call to prayer I took comfort in the thought of setting out on comic adventures that would culminate when I took the virginity of a peasant girl I loved. A Sa'idi, a girl from Upper Egypt who'd never been to school. I knew that this would never happen.

There is a Sa'idi girl who'll make me coffee and leave me alone. I like the idea of her being my property, to do with her anything I like.

• • • • •

That night, I don't know why, Abu al-Arshad, I felt heartbreak over my wife. Not in the sense of sorrow about us splitting up. I wasn't heartbroken for our relationship or our life or our love, nor for any part of what might have remained of the lovely thing that there'd been between us before our marriage (not a single part would remain). For, as far as all this was concerned, I breathed a sigh of relief. As usual, when I escaped from a human problem that I'd dragged myself into by mistake, I was happy to have left it behind, and—for the first time since that thing started—confident in my actions.

What I am saying is that I felt heartbroken over *her*. I acknowledged to myself that I had deserted her and that— despite the fact that she deserved to be deserted by every man in the world—she does demand heartbreak: her neuroses, her negativity, and the terrible paralysis that afflicts her in relationships. Her silence. I recalled that she had hardly any friends. As soon as she got to know someone, she quarreled with them, at work and in life. And since she was unable to make up with anyone, she would lose them quickly, usually without hope of retrieving them. Her heart was black as coal. Without being free of the female crap that's traditional in Egypt, she had all the English problems of psychological isolation, excessive reserve, and gloom. Like the English, she was totally incapable of expressing her feelings, which made every expression of her feelings hysterical. It was nice to feel genuine heartbreak over her because it meant I could stop grieving for myself, for the faults that she'd accused me of, and for my inability to go on. I recalled that my wife was just a variation on the shitty confusion and unease that surrounded and tormented me everywhere in Cairo, just one more deformed child of the marriage of cultures.

An event
As I was saying, on Tuesday, the girl engaged to the boy came. On Wednesday, there was something new on the subject of the break up. Not an event in the sense of being unexpected, I mean, but it lessened the anticipation without reducing the

confusion. Less than a week after leaving Maadi, my wife had an abortion. She sent me an email telling me that she didn't want to look into the face of a killer like myself (she actually wrote "killer" in English) and that she and her mother had gone to the apartment to take back her dowry. I asked my own mother to go and collect my own stuff, which she did immediately after the weekend, while I sat nodding off in the office.

I mean—this is what I felt at the time—I would hide in the office while the apartment had its guts ripped out. My head would suffer the same bouts of nausea that afflicted my wife, and a sharp knife, because I'd left her vomiting over and over until our child came out with the sick. I'd feel then that she wasn't doing it on her own. The apartment and our happiness as well. The whole world was vomiting. Even before the abortion, a thick brown liquid would come out, whose smell suggested death. Then I would weep for my father.

More than six years since he died, and I'm crying for him now?

Chapter

But as I was telling you, with the exception of this email and what followed, me sitting in the office while my things were spirited from Maadi to Dokki after me (or so I imagined) on the back of a camel with a litter—with the exception of that, the dream was the only thing to happen the whole week that I passed in my old, deserted room. If I was having a conversation with myself—that's all—I started to talk about World's Gate whenever I headed toward Isaaf Square. As I was telling you, after thirty—as I noticed when I got used to the room again—books started to take the place of B-movies for me. My addiction surprised me, as did my choice of subjects.

I read a long book about an American in China. He had promised himself that he would go there and cross the whole country by train. He didn't have sex for a year. I wanted to do the same. His life was as it should be. Nothing had collapsed. He didn't have to keep working. Take a nonstop train and look at other people, even if I don't speak to them. Then get off in some faraway place and don't think of returning.

I stayed up reading another book about China. If I traveled, I'd take this one with me: a local artist of just thirty (I'd reached that age weeks before my marriage), whose world had collapsed, so he'd made a decision and just taken off, traveling all around China on forged papers. I didn't need forged papers. My situation was between that of the American and the Chinese. The big difference was time. They both had a year or more. I could hardly get three days. Never mind, perhaps something will happen and I'll never come back. That's how I always thought about traveling. Sleep and smoke as I liked, and scrawl in this notebook: even without traveling, these things can make the end easier.

For ten days, in short, I just read and stayed in the office for no reason. Something that happened periodically, staying in the office like that. Usually when I didn't have a woman. And in the absence of a woman, as chance would have it during those days, the office was empty. It had something to do with political questions that I didn't like to interest myself in. In the office, as in the country as a whole, there were insect values, and nothing happening, no production. You would go in at the peak of the weekly working cycle and find no one. Everyone was desperate to finish his business as quickly as possible. I begged the company of losers.

Gradually, I started looking at people with stable relationships in the way that someone who has just managed to drop the sack of shit he was carrying on his head looks at the sacks other people are carrying. They're all oozing shit. I no longer believed in the high-mindedness of my former journeymen. Nonetheless, until the strange events started that drove me in the second week to record this story, from its beginning, I continued (with a curiosity prompted by anger) to rediscover the madness and insanity of my colleagues. Coming and going I would analyze them.

And in the hadith: Cut the moustaches and leave the beards.
—al-Mu'jam al-Wajiz [Short Dictionary]

After investigating the circumstances in which my agitated drunken friend Amgad Salah 'Abd al-Galil joined the ranks of the Sunnis, for example, it became clear that even when the conversion happened (about four months before I left the Maadi Alley apartment), it had nothing to do with political Islam, with jihad, arms, or even a revolutionary tendency. Basically, Amgad didn't have the intellectual capacity for these things. A personal choice, then—I thought it impossible that the conversion could be just a temporary blip or a variation on the theme of reactionism through ignorance. I mean, it's ordinary enough for a man to turn religious, but why should he grow out his beard like those terrorists in the soaps, or be delighted when ignorant people call him "sheikh"?

I thought that something must have affected his brain. That he was one extremity of a wide network, without a doubt conspiring with the people behind the collapse of the world. In whose interest, except for this sort of person, was it for religion and identity to be so conjoined? In essence Amgad hadn't changed so much as a fingernail (let alone a fingertip)— his stupidity, his complexes, his love of laughter and an easy-going life. None of that had changed. The only difference was the beard, the prayer mark on his forehead, and the endless number of newly forbidden things. Not to mention all the rituals. I started to think that this sort of madness and delusion turned people into cogs in a machine that would destroy their humanity. Without knowing it, they were implementing the plans of a network whose aim was the collapse of the world or the end of everyone's rope: all our dead loved ones rising out of their graves.

The infection could spread without a single change to their personalities.

A chapter on the names of the quarters of Cairo

On Thursday, nothing happened. I recalled the dream and went on analyzing it. I had no idea who that young sultan called al-Fatih might be, nor the whereabouts of the Byzantine church that he prayed in, nor in which period. Just as I had on Wednesday, Tuesday, and the other days, I woke early, took a shower, had breakfast, and brushed my teeth. I postponed my first cigarette until I reached the office, where I smoked it with a Turkish coffee and worked for six hours without a break.

"And he taught Adam all the names" —sura of the Cow, 31

All this was on Thursday. You know that ever since leaving Maadi, I'd had in my head a map of Cairo I wanted to draw. I'd taken with me from Maadi a case of books that had stayed in the car for weeks during our temporary separations. After dinner that evening I got out three books which had old maps in them and spread out paper and pens on the dining room table to experiment. I would start, naturally, with the Nile, then try and incorporate the residential areas along its two banks.

Five or six times, I crossed out what I had drawn and tried again. Each time, the drawing became simpler, with thinner lines and larger white spaces. I wanted something supple and abstract, like an abstract picture—an Arabic calligraphy design, for example—so I stripped the Nile of its two islands and restricted the residential areas to Maadi, Dokki, and Isaaf. I paid no attention to streets or flyovers. Five or six lines for each area and I finished the picture as I wanted. I just had to give the places new names.

Without any effort, I had already named the whole of the downtown area Bab al-Dunya ("World's Gate"). Now I sat thinking: if Isaaf was the point of departure, then Dokki, with the Dokki Bridge and the Dry Nile Dock—yes, I found myself calling the 6 October Bridge the "Dry Nile," its ramps becoming harbors—must be the bed that inspired my dreams. Let's make Dokki (and with it Mohandiseen, Agouza, and the University) a bridge, yes, "Dream Bridge."

I spent more than an hour racking my brains for appropriate names for the remaining quarters. Maadi was a small street like an alley with Hind Rostam's dogs, the landlady's daughter's bitch (Sandyyyyy!), and the dog adopted by Shaaban the caretaker's daughter, as well as a large number of stray dogs that came and went all day long. Let me call it… "Dog Alley."

As there was a secret reason that I went with my Sunni friend Amgad Salah 'Abd al-Galil to the Desert Road Carrefour supermarket rather than anywhere else we could have gone—a secret that even I didn't know—the word "secret" had to be included in the name of this place. Bab Zuweila reminded me of Khan al-Khalili. A khan is a covered market, with intersecting streets lined with shops on either side. A mall like the Carrefour, that is. Quite natural, then, for the Carrefour to be… the "Khan of Secrets."

I wrote the names in their places, and drew lines between them, to show the journeys I'd made within Greater Cairo since the Prophet's birthday in the year AH 1428. From Dog Alley to Dream Bridge to World's Gate (and back again), and in anticipation of what would be, as you know, sooner or later, from World's Gate to the Khan of Secrets.

To The Khan of Secrets

World's Gate

Dream Bridge

Dog Alley

Only then did it occur to me that there were important places that did not appear on the map. I chose four that seemed to be fundamental in my life. The place I went to observe my favorite animals; the place where I left and came back into town; and the place where I'd discovered love Japanese-style on the banks of the river (that is, in an apartment close to the Nile), where Fustuq's prophecy also came to me.

On a fresh piece of paper I drew a camel, an airplane, and a tree. I copied the emblem of the Gezira Club from an old ticket I had, and the Carrefour logo from a plastic bag, then wrote under each picture the new name of the place.

The Giza countryside beyond Feisal Street and the Pyramids, with the village of Birqash and the camel market: Sand Port;

The airport, and the surrounding areas of 'Ain Shams, Heliopolis, and Nasr City: Plane Yard;

Gezira (or Zamalek, to be precise): Japan River;

As for Muqattam, where the house built by Yildiz's father (the world-renowned philologist Dr. Murad Zakariyya) stood in a quiet, wooded spot on the middle hill—as well as the family apartment, and an empty furnished apartment which he sometimes rented out; he had made a separate apartment for each of his daughters, Yildiz and Claudine, so that they could live independently—I found myself naming it: Tree Hill.

Like this:

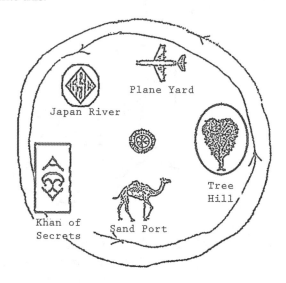

I knew that this was just a start and that I would draw the map again, but I was pleased with what I'd done stage by stage. When I'd finished I trimmed the two sheets and pasted them into my notebook. I had nothing else to do and I felt that I'd achieved something. From now on, with this map under my nose, I would seek inspiration from the circle of the first journey (after correction) to construct a geographical representation of each journey I undertook. I would draw it with my eyes half-closed, opening them by turns to check my progress against the drawing and make sure the distances were right. In this way, I could construct a pool of preliminary drawings before the final implementation. I didn't shower. At midnight I masturbated and went to sleep. My dreams were trivial, as always.

Friday morning, the fact that I had the day off took me by surprise.

•   •   •   •   •   •   •

It was my first weekend since moving to Dream Bridge—the room was still empty—and I didn't know what to do with myself, so as usual I drove to World's Gate. I noticed, as I reviewed all the places I could go, that the new names no longer surprised me or made me laugh. With the afternoon call to prayer the Dry Nile Dock was like the end of the world. 'Amr Khalid's smile was as it always is on the right. I parked in my usual place in El Galaa Street and returned on foot through the Tawfiqiyya Market. I turned off beside the Américain coffee shop, past the Odeon Cinema to Champollion Street, and returned from Ramses past the High Court building that looks like a Roman temple. After stopping for a while in front of the newspapers, I climbed up to the roof of a building I didn't know. From the Press Syndicate came the sound of shouting. Another demonstration? Then I remembered. There was a referendum on something they were calling "constitutional amendments." Next week? From here I couldn't see anything except the Rivoli Cinema. Behind the High Court some buildings swallowed up sun as if they were made of dust. In Champollion Street there was a lighted, empty café. A woman sobbing on a low wall. Death and destruction.

An account of the fulfillment of the dream

For a moment, while I was on the roof, I imagined that I had returned to the amazing city of my dream, with its water, greenery, and white horses. I knew that I was in Cairo and that there could be no confusion about this. There were billboards, kiosks, and sidewalks; no wood, no flowers, and no end to the cars. Even the sunlight was yellower, its fluctuations more powerful. Every few meters, though, a blond youth like a copy of al-Fatih would appear to me as I walked along, and each time he would assume a different form: a shoeshine boy squatting in front of the Café Américain; an apartment building's doorman in a well-known street; a taxi driver parked by a metro station. And every time I would be on the point of going up to him and asking, "Are you the sultan?" then at the last moment think better of it.

I realized that I was under the influence of the dream and was sleep-deprived and hallucinating. The debris I had left behind me in Dog Alley had left me sad and confused. Even though al-Fatih's appearance had been a mere hallucination, I nonetheless had a feeling deep inside me that I was still living the dream. Despite the fact that it had only occurred once.

To travel through the streets of Cairo was to reproduce the extraordinary state of the dream city at the moment I had been there. As if an entire age were ending and another beginning, as I'd felt when I went back to Dream Bridge from Dog Alley.

My stopping place, or the general's last glance, was a symbol of the death of Cairo—or its transformation into something else, with no place for anyone but shoppers, men with beards, and women who, after the latest fashion, covered their heads. All this, despite the fact that the significance of the idea was far clearer in the dream. And I was the only witness. This is how I would explain the shock on my face that evening.

What was going on was much bigger than constitutional amendments. The chanting of slogans reinforced the suggestion that the world as I knew it was coming to an end. So too did the heavy boots of Central Security on the asphalt. I could only just hear them, in fact, but they still rang in my ears. The afternoon sun crept slowly toward the west.

When I spotted three priests moving toward Isaaf (viewed from a distance and high up, they looked tiny, but they were certainly priests), I recalled my feelings the evening I was with Fustuq at the 'Uruba Café, and immediately I was certain that since that day I had been on a journey. It was true that I didn't know where it would lead me, didn't even know which stations I would stop at to rest. Days would come when fear would triumph over delight in danger, but it comforted me that the end of the world had not been entirely in vain.

I mean, I'd said goodbye to my wife in order to embark on an essential mission the day of the Prophet's birthday. As is proved by the fact that the rebuilding of the world I was undertaking was somehow linked with the movement I'd aspired to since my soul had turned its back on marriage.

I had to travel.

Chapter on going to the Khan of Secrets

To put it more simply, that first weekend after I left Dog Alley, I realized for the first time since Monday evening that the dream—unlike my trivial dreams and even my dreams of my father—had a meaning that would be fulfilled. I had never ever in my life believed that dreams had significance, even though I rejoiced in the story of the Prophet Joseph and his ability to interpret them. Now everything was changing. Naturally, I didn't know exactly what that meaning was. Like a nail of ice in my breast, anxiety made me retrace my steps down from the roof of that unknown building, thinking the whole time. I almost felt grateful to Fustuq for giving me permission.

Love should never be a test of endurance.

There was no escape, then, from subjecting the society around me to close examination, I thought, or continuing to analyze my colleagues. Everything had a meaning, everything was connected with everything else. So it made sense to work on rebuilding my world. Despite my anger I would rebuild it through movement. Through movement I would come to know my direction. Would I meet my son or daughter at a future stop? Then I recalled that my wife had had an abortion and that when I had stopped playing the role of husband, my chance at fatherhood had disappeared. I wandered until I found myself in a side alley. Seven children kicking a naked old man who was making a high-pitched sound like a cat mewing.

She plucked desire from my heart, she stripped love of desire, she got rid of our joy at the first corner like a wretched cat that the owners of a house are fed up with. She made even the Maadi apartment into a sad place. Then she continued to burden me with the cares of her own dejection rather than mine; she wouldn't let me sleep.

After a second wander along Marouf Street, I retraced my steps toward the car in El Galaa Street.

Once again I drove around aimlessly, heading north toward Plane Yard. Ten minutes, then I turned and went back again. I would have liked to have someone with me, but I was averse to all the possibilities: the army of spinsters and divorcées, Michel Fustuq, the gang of artists and writers. Apart from that, there was a friend or two, perhaps three journalists from other papers. Who else? I wouldn't look at the list of contacts in my mobile. As I had just come to important conclusions on the subject of himself, I would speak to Amgad Salah.

Among settled people there is much depravity, evil, nonsense and trickery to secure a livelihood right or wrong, so the soul is preoccupied thinking about that, and in devising a means to that end.
—Ibn Khaldun

A short journey, in principle, to the Desert Road. When we went out, I would usually drive him there, we would wander around the Khan of Secrets for a bit, then choose a café and take a seat. Coffee and cake. A long way, as he liked to say, from civilization. A journey different from the sickening daily commute. After I turned thirty Amgad Salah proved to me that I was actually better attuned to non-intellectuals. OK, what induced me to marry an intellectual? Fuck intellect, fuck the mother of marriage. To feel the possibility of human interaction without philosophical questions. *Sakan*, with its two meanings, comfort and housing. One needed a hot meal at home, even if only once a week. A meal you don't just prepare for yourself. Boredom, the killer of love and mercy. I wanted innocent companionship and pure debauchery.

Just to build, it didn't matter how. With Amgad Salah you could build as you sat there.

For years I had been persuading myself that I enjoyed his company. In his presence, my brain went to sleep. We chatted without actually saying anything as though we were two forty-something government archivists. I liked the resonance of his laugh. His ignorance, his loneliness, and the fact that he was a resister. Gradually, it became clear to me that what really drew us together was anxiety and our propensity to suspect others. Without thinking about it, I sensed we could be in each other's company. Ever since the project of his marriage was accomplished, his mood had been happy. He had let himself go a bit, talking of food and halal sex.

But for the hundredth time, at the Dry Nile Dock, I found myself wondering what the Khan of Secrets was for, what the Khan that was right at the beginning of the Desert Road was for.

You know, don't you, Rashid, that the West Bank of the Nile, where the Pharaoh's tombs are situated, is always more relaxing? There you have a hint of a journey, as if you were traveling to Alexandria. The joy of setting out with no frustrating hardships. Then all your purchases in one place. You drive a long way and emerge carrying all sorts of things. And you know that you'll go there again. Coffee out of town, with no tension. Near the desert, and the atmosphere is free of anything that would stir up memories. As if you were on the surface of the moon. The company of a thin-haired Sunni there. Among the corridors of goods, with people shoving each other like animals, it is possible to be in harmony with the class you belong to. If you hadn't been hit by an existential crisis, at least, you would feel from a very long way off that it was possible to be in harmony.

In the Khan of Secrets, after leaving Dog Alley, and the sultan's dream that had been fulfilled, the third move in the story took place, the last big step before plunging into the deep.

Now, as I reflected, it occurred to me that if Amgad and I hadn't agreed to meet, the whole story would have disappeared into thin air, and I would never have gone through any of this madness. For a few moments I was convinced that this would have been better for me—I mean, that life without the story would have been better for me. But then I started to feel that it was inevitable, with or without Amgad Salah.

I had to go to the Khan of Secrets after the fulfillment of the dream.

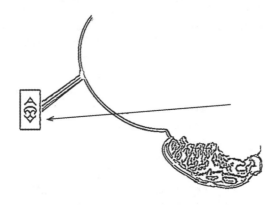

PART THREE

The Book of the Demons

The Khan of Secrets

Chapters Recorded by the
Storyteller on His Journey to the
Khan of Secrets and the Biography
of Amgad Salah

Saturday and Sunday, April 7 and 8

Praise be to God

On the second Saturday evening, Mustafa implemented his agreement with Amgad Salah 'Abd al-Galil. He had spent the day reading and sleeping. How many times had he played with himself? Anyway, before night fell, he headed for the Ezbekiyya Gardens and gave Amgad a ring on his mobile to come down to him. A trip out with Amgad Salah always altered Mustafa's view of himself. Amgad was a retired police officer who had joined the paper at an advanced age after leaving the service, then going to Canada for two years to study business. He was an athletic man, anyway, large and competitive, and his behavior exemplified the values of the middle class and relations incompatible with the West. He was, as Mustafa liked to say, culturally illiterate. And now, after converting to Sunnism, that equation had become more complicated.

Mustafa liked the idea of having a Sunni friend. What struck him every time was how shallow and stupid Amgad's faith was. Totally devoid of spirituality. Amgad said, for example, that he'd gotten a mark on his forehead as soon as he started praying regularly. There was no way to make him acknowledge that this had been deliberate, which would be obvious to any donkey because the mark went from side to side. He had marks on his nose, and between his eyebrows, as well as on his forehead, which made it look like a map of a desert island in the Pacific. His chin was like the sail of a ship wandering through the ocean waves. He shaved his head and moustache, which exaggerated the lecherous look of his lips.

"Hello, Salah Pasha!"

Mustafa had started to imitate the archivist's ethereal voice. That's how the two friends spoke. This way of speaking was Mustafa's reaction to Amgad's size and (after he'd turned Sunni) his gloominess. He was always aware that Amgad filled the car. It was true that Amgad answered him in the same tone, true that the roughness of his voice didn't weigh down his movement and nothing about him was threatening, but Mustafa continued to be taken with the appearance of his friend and say that when someone was that large he had a certain presence.

"Hello, sir!"

But Amgad wasn't paying attention to Mustafa so much as to the headlines on the billboards. Was it because, in his days of paranoia, they contained encoded messages to him?

"I found something to hang on to, that's all," he would reply if Mustafa asked him what had made him convert, and would gesticulate wildly: "It's not a joke, Darsh!"

The way to the Khan of Secrets started from the point where his daily journey ended, behind World's Gate. To the right, over the 15 May Bridge, through Bulaq Abu al-'Ila, as the night drew in. "As if you were a traveler, wishing you had a map. Where the roads begin to quarrel, you lose your way in the curves." On his own daily journey, so Mustafa recalled, were all the questions that come to your mind at a port of call. Three days or a bit more: what forced him to stay for the rest of the week? "Before you lines stretch out and intersect, then lead to no one." Mustafa was fine, so long as there was movement in his life. If he stopped at a stopping place he would feel unwell. Better not to stop.

Here he is, on the 15 May Bridge, negotiating the right of way. The lights of the Bulaq secondhand clothes market during an attempt to start a conversation about anything other than religion with Amgad Salah. He wouldn't let him. Mustafa was battered by different impulses as the cold got worse. The crowd was everywhere. He looked at the shelves of worn clothes and the wet doorsteps. The women were like ducks in gallabiyas.

Now another quarrel began about the Prophet Muhammad's advice for men in the presence of the female form: to avert their eyes.

"But how can you not look, Amgad?"

"You have to stop looking, sir!"

After Lebanon Square, where the 26 July Corridor starts, leading to the Khan of Secrets in a northerly direction from Dream Bridge, Mustafa felt that he was really on his way. By night, the 26 July Corridor was like a closed tin can, and he a light wandering along its uneven base, with its variously shaped speed bumps. He was going wherever the road went. Life was a series of rectangles. Why then did he imagine the scene in the drawing like the page of a book? A page full up to the edge, divided lengthwise by the long rectangle of the road.

This strip was produced by the car's headlights, he told himself. The writing represented the darkness of the night, broken up by the street lamps. The whiteness on the page? Perhaps the humps.

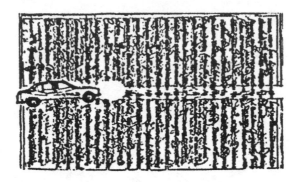

Inside this book/can, Amgad Salah was the sole remaining link with the world. Mustafa grew tense at the shrinking possibilities for conversation. One after the other, he enumerated the names of his colleagues, in the hope that they might open up a conversation, but Amgad grimaced and turned his face away, uttering religious imprecations. "Leave it, leave it," he kept repeating, as Mustafa dodged a speeding Hummer. "I mean, do we have to spend our whole lives in that place?" There was terror in his eyes as Mustafa braked. "Watch out, Ustaz Çorbacı!"—a hole in the side of a hump—"No, sir, it won't do to talk about that place!"

Mustafa looked across his chin at the side of the road and started with fright. It was hard for anyone to talk to Amgad because he was disturbed, and his confidence had fallen so far that he had no fixed opinions. Most of the time he had nothing to say. Just looks, and nothing else, which ruined every possibility for conversation. Seriousness turned into laughter according to your reaction to the conversation, and this made you fear that laughter would turn serious. "What's wrong with that place, Salah Pasha?"

Disgust on his face. "Oh, for God's sake!"

Where the street lights were less bright, the sky had some color. There was no sign of stars, but sometimes something between violet and orange was visible on the ceiling of the sky. Amgad Salah started to ask about Mustafa's wife, and his separation. Mustafa replied curtly. He kept trying, and he thought of imitating a TV peasant as he used to do with his friend Rashid in days gone by. He gave his friend Amgad a stupid look and repeated: "Is it true, boy, that you still want to get engaged?"

Amgad (taking up the same accent and mannerism): "Eheeeh!"

Then he let go of the steering wheel to pull that fundamentalist mountain by the arm, which made apparent the tension on said mountain. Amgad pushed him away violently then laughed. From archivists to TV peasants, words slipped out, like the theatrical jokes he'd given up. Together with songs and music, porn and zombie films, vampires and death metal. Even television, pick-up lines, and insults that involved the word "religion." Amgad had given them all up. He no longer smoked or drank. Instead of hashish and cocaine he used musk, sticks of incense, and Sheikh Shaarawi tapes.

He must have heard of the historical link between learning and religion, as well. Because he started talking about books and reading—articulating the word carefully like a turbaned sheikh or Arabic-language expert, one letter at a time, though his trusted sources were all still rubbish. "Onward, Prince!" As the car turned off at the Cairo–Alexandria Desert Road exit he was complaining about the names Mustafa had listed for him and their wicked intentions and ugly deeds. They claimed to have culture but they were nothing!

"And where were they, Ustaz Çorbacı, when I was being butt-fucked?"

Amgad coughed as Mustafa ruminated on the steps that his wife was putting off till later. After their relationship had come to an end, he had imagined the worst possible scenarios. Anger like urine retention. How do you feel about alimony and deferred payments? He went back to the peasant wisdoms soaking the dust of his forefathers. There's payment to support one's wife, and payment in return for divorce, right? You can still legally drag a woman to the marital home against her will, right, and if she doesn't obey she becomes a recalcitrant wife and is deprived of all payments due to her... There are fifty thousand ways to make a woman miserable... and the saliva stuck in his throat.

"Happy on the Corridor, Salah Pasha?"

"You, sir, are most obliging."

Anger was always fear in disguise. You could control guilt with logic. But anger was a sort of inhibition. If only he could pull off Amgad's beard! Everything Yildiz had said to him. It leaves no doubt that they always punish you for no longer desiring them, instead of thanking you for risking matrimony. Three months and nothing, not a word... The sluts! Mustafa growled like a rabid dog. Yildiz was the spinsters' *qibla*.

Once again Amgad coughed, as the laughter turned into words. Once again he sounded like he was disclosing secret intelligence no one but him knew about: sincere affection at the mosque; how He spared us the decay of non-Sunni living; the houris in Paradise.

The more carefully Mustafa looked at his prayer mark, the less he could believe that it was there.

Amgad Salah's madness

That evening on the Corridor, Mustafa's mind continued to wander until he recalled the last time they had been out together before the separation. When the conversation about psychological problems dried up, Amgad began to tell him about the Organization. All the colleagues whose names he'd just been listing, they weren't necessarily agents, but they were conspirators. Amgad had recounted situations that sounded to Mustafa like textbook symptoms of paranoia, but when Mustafa recalled the symptoms now as he was driving, they immediately reminded him of what had happened to him at the office, what had happened with his wife, and how he had been feeling about the whole world for a long time.

For example, everyone knew how scared Amgad was of his colleague the fiqi Ustaz Wahid al-Din. He'd avoided him like the plague since his return from Canada. He called him the zombie—"Is the zombie here?" he would ask as soon as he entered the office. Well, without any warning, Ustaz Wahid al-

Din would materialize in front of Amgad in the elevator of his apartment building, or at the door of his usual café in the Sea of Japan, where no one could reasonably expect him. He would be smiling and looking straight at Amgad, and as was his habit at work he would leave without saying anything.

When Amgad told his colleagues about this the next day, they showed no surprise. As if they were the ones who'd sent Ustaz Wahid al-Din to him—orders they were carrying out as members of the Organization?

It was impossible to deny that Ustaz Wahid al-Din had also appeared to Mustafa in unexpected places once or twice, and each time had taken him by surprise. But in the absence of any feeling that the world was punishing him, this didn't matter to Mustafa and he didn't even wonder about it. This in addition to the fact that he had never felt the slightest fear of the fiqi; thus far, he had only aroused his curiosity.

Another example. Amgad told Aldo Mazika, their fat, effeminate colleague, that he was going out with an Italian girl (he wouldn't tell him her name or where she lived). He was certain that Aldo had never met her in his life. Then, when the girl canceled at the last moment, he went to the disco on his own and found her there with Aldo.

So, when the psychiatrist told Amgad that he harbored insane suspicions and tapped his shoulder, muttering "psychotic episode," Amgad decided that the doctor was a conspirator as well and stopped the sessions. That night he threw his pills into the trash—which Aldo had encouraged him to do, telling him that psychiatrists were mad and he should never listen to them. And even today Amgad didn't doubt that the Organization existed and was active. He had simply decided to give his mind a break. It was impossible to recognize its members—even Mustafa could be a member, of course—"So far, I make it you've have five telephone calls," he told Mustafa—and if he dug in and resisted, what would he gain except for a mind ache?

The Organization could not be defeated except through remembrance of God.

I know that there are some people who have been seduced by demons. —al-Jahiz

Some time ago, about five years previously (in the weeks preceding his admission to a mental hospital, slightly less than a year after returning from Canada, to be precise), the retired policeman had got drunk for the first time in Mustafa's presence, and complained to his friend Çorbacı about a creature that was tormenting him, which he called the zombie.

"Son of a bitch," he said. "He disappeared when I went to Ontario and all that." He gave an obscene snort that was coarser and deeper than his normal voice. "But now he's appearing to me again in my sleep, sir."

Mustafa knew the popular meaning of the word "zombie": someone who was drugged or doltish, like those moving corpses they make films about. But as he'd never in his life had any interest in this sort of film, he had no clear conception of the creature. The word was linked in his head with the word vampire, but while he knew what a blood-sucking human bat was, he wasn't quite sure about the distinguishing features of a zombie.

Nor would he have bothered to watch Romero's films if it hadn't been for an extraordinary conversation one evening, during which he'd sensed for the first time since he had known him that Amgad Salah was actually crazy, years before any mention of the Organization.

The pair of them had been at the bar in the Jazz Club in the no man's land that lies between the end of Dream Bridge in 'Urabi Street in Mohandiseen and the Sea of Japan to the West. Unusually, Amgad was sitting and staring into a bottle of vodka, which he was drinking straight out of. He usually brought his own bottles into the bar or kept them there for when he showed up. Sometimes, when he felt down, he would drink straight from the bottle. Mustafa was holding a plastic water bottle, with a lit cigarette hanging from his nostril. No one knew how it had got there or why he didn't remove it.

"You know, when you take Ecstasy, things can happen" (so he had written in one of his notebooks). "I mean, if you take enough of it, you don't feel any pain or anxiety or anything." About an hour previously he had swallowed three Euro-brand tablets, and if he'd drunk anything, he could have died of hyperthermia and dehydration. But now, as he listened to

Amgad's complaints, a chemical happiness swept over him like a crashing wave, making him sympathetic to everyone and everything. "The shape of things changes, the light becomes brighter, and you feel as if you've entered a locked place. I don't know how to describe it but the main thing is that you're happy, as it were, *despite* yourself and this happiness makes you really in tune with other people."

He listened with great emotion as Amgad told him: "Before Ontario"—about three years before the present time, as Mustafa calculated it, then realized that what Amgad was telling him about coincided with the illness that had turned Wahid al-Din into the strangest person in the office—"a zombie would appear, but it would only appear when I was asleep and there was only the one. Now there are six or seven of them and they come to me when I'm awake." He stared again in silence. "At any fucking moment!"

The Ecstasy surged through Mustafa's body like a rope of hot metal twisting his insides side to side and up and down. Sometimes just side to side. It turned his brain into a sky. God in heaven! A sky that rained down a happiness he wasn't sure would last. A rope of hot metal like a cable. It exhausts but does not burn you. He had learned not to resist.

When Amgad sat up straight that evening so that he was in the light, darkness all around him, he looked like the icon of an unknown saint that had somehow come alive. But he stayed as he was, as if he were about to cry—though every time, after saying something like "No, chief, I'm really in a shit situation, Mr. Çorbacı!," he would either stare into the moist bottle or snort in an even more uncouth voice. Then he'd quickly take another slug and go back to staring again.

A gushing happiness and a longing. Mustafa remembered, even though the memory didn't stop the metal rope in his body or decrease the conversation's effects on him, that for two weeks after today he would feel a hole in his brain in the spot where it had rained happiness.

For this reason, when he watched Romero's films they would affect him twenty times more than normal, and he would suffer the state of confusion, ennui, and slight depression that he had recently discovered was one of the side effects of the drug. Hashish produces a state of equilibrium. He remembered that he had a joint of mango bango and half a bottle of tequila at home, as if he'd prepared for the anxiety he would feel once the effect of the tablets wore off.

Just a slight crunching in his nostrils drew his attention to the fact that the cigarette was alight and that the fire had started to reach him. He took the cigarette out and got up to put his arm around the mountain of muscle who was sitting next to him, with an overwhelming affection.

One, two... he squeezed hard.

Chapter

The first time they admitted Amgad to the sanatorium after he'd come back from Canada (so Mustafa recalled when he saw the prayer mark as they went along the 26 July Corridor, on the way to the Khan of Secrets, the first Saturday after he'd left Dog Alley), it was fast on the heels of a completely weird incident on the October Bridge.

In brief: When a policeman stopped Amgad in a perfectly routine check and asked him for his license (this was during the weekend) Amgad simply slapped the policeman twice on the face without even getting out of the car. He slapped him, and when the man retaliated by opening the door and started to pull him out by his shirt collar, the first thing he knew was that he had been thrown on his back, with Amgad's iron knee like an artillery shell on his chest, pinning him to the asphalt, and the muzzle of a revolver, which had appeared from God knows where, in his mouth.

Until he turned religious, Amgad used to carry a Belgian FN-49, which he had licensed, for no obvious reason, at the time he left the service. The policeman imagined that Amgad must be secret police or intelligence, and started to shake and apologize, hardly able to breathe with this black monstrosity on his chest. If the superior officer at the police checkpoint hadn't turned out by chance to be an acquaintance of Amgad's from their police academy days, it really would have been a nightmare.

The officer quickly let his classmate go, but the next day he spoke to Amgad's brother and told him what had happened.

Later that week Mustafa was standing smoking with Amgad in the newspaper's outside corridor when Amgad's mobile rang. As soon as he looked at the screen, he started to hiss "fuck, fuck, fuck!" and turned around, his hissing getting louder, without explaining a thing to Mustafa. This might have been in the winter of 2002.

Mustafa remembered the sight of his Sunni friend jumping—with an elegance that didn't tally with his size— from the corporation railings down to a lower floor before running back up and shouting: "That zombie, the son of a whore, can bite my ass, Darsh!" And he threw him the old black Ericsson mobile, the model that people used to call "the works" because it was heavy and metallic like the old dial-up phone sets.

Mustafa recalled that when he put the receiver to his ear he recognized Amgad's brother's voice at once. "Hello, yes, good evening, sir! We're sorry, sir, but could you hang on to him for us until we can get to you...?" Of course, it was impossible. Amgad disappeared within minutes, with Aldo winking at him from where he stood at a distance with the young Coptic lad who was called Michel Fustuq and who spoke English just like an American.

It was very embarrassing.

So embarrassing that the chief editor himself came out. The chief editor who looked like King Kong in a full suit stood and lectured the young men gathered outside: "Colleagues, at the end of the day this is a place of work. Our colleague may be suffering some nervous stress for some reason, but this doesn't mean that we can all leave our work and spend the day chatting in the corridor." Mustafa remembered that he'd laughed from the bottom of his heart at the cold giant's words (Mustafa had possibly never met a colder person in his life than the chief editor of his economics newspaper): that Amgad was affected by nervous stress or that watching him voyeuristically was a waste of work time.

That day, leaving Amgad's mobile with the security guard at the corporation entrance, Mustafa went straight from work to the house of a friend, where he sat till morning smoking hashish and wondering what would become of Amgad.

The fact is he never found out, even after Amgad had left the sanatorium and got his phone back somehow or other. The first time he saw him again, after about three months, Amgad was squatting in the lounge of his apartment—the same apartment he'd pass by tonight as they went to the Khan of Secrets—with a large cooking pot full of water under his arm. Before he was allowed to say anything, Mustafa had to squat in front of Amgad and put his hands in the water.

Either that, or the retired policeman would block his ears with his fists, shut his eyes, and croon: "Dum, dum, ding, I can't hear a thing!"

From then on, Mustafa learned that he shouldn't raise the subject of the zombie whatever happened, nor under any circumstances mention their colleague, the fiqi Wahid al-Din.

"Dum, dum, ding, I am out of here!"

Because as soon as Mustafa remembered Wahid al-Din and asked about the zombie, with his hands in the water in the pot, Amgad closed his eyes. For a very long time, he continued to say nothing, then grasped Mustafa's hand under the water and leaned over him to whisper like madmen in films:

"You know, Darsh, the zombie can take anyone's place and come to me. You remember when I threw you the telephone in the office: it wasn't my brother Mahmoud on the line." He tightened his grip on Mustafa's hand. "It was the zombie!"

He said nothing more until Mustafa tried to get some further explanation, at which point he blew up and started to talk hysterically about the future: the terrible things that would happen when the brain bite infection spread. When a zombie bit you, you'd become a zombie as well, and would try to bite other people. Stupid people that didn't understand. And the danger, the danger of an epidemic that threatened everyone.

The whole world was on the point of collapse. That was what Amgad told Mustafa that night. Then he took his hands out of the pot and turned around with a sudden violent energy. After a moment, he stood up and went into his room, locking the door behind him without saying a word.

Chapter

Now, on the 26 July Corridor, Mustafa recalled how Amgad had put that state behind him and had kept coming to work, though he'd started to refuse to go out to bars. Perhaps this was the true beginning of his conversion to Salafi Islam.

In the two following years, nothing in his conversation indicated any awareness of danger, or that the world was threatened with a plague, until when he began to indicate, on appropriate or inappropriate occasions, the need to embrace religion. Only when it became difficult to talk about psychological problems, and he was on the point of becoming a Sunni, did he mention an Organization.

It was true. Since the session when Amgad had made up his mind about the existence of a secret Organization—Mustafa now recalled that this was the same week he'd sat with Michel Fustuq in the 'Uruba Café, the night of the exaggerated wise-guy performance and the obscure prophecy, and about four months before his separation from his wife ("How I wish you'd be a man in your house!")—Mustafa had not stopped thinking about the story. It never occurred to him that the Organization might be connected with what was happening to him at home. He neither scorned the subject nor shut the door on it. Not even in a daydream did he head-butt Amgad Salah and spit on the ground in disdain.

It was as though a lightbulb were hovering over his head (like Gyro Gearloose in the black-and-white Arabic version of Mickey comics) when an ingenious idea occurred to him. There really was an Organization, one whose existence was grafted onto their place of work. Its basic purpose was to dissolve the employees' minds, so that they wouldn't discover what was being done to them. If there were those who wanted to destroy the nation, for example, what better way to do so than to turn the people into cogs in the Islamization machine; otherwise, they would have to destroy their minds some other way. Of course, Mustafa realized that thinking this way would be turning the tables on Amgad Salah. Amgad believed that converting to Salafism had saved him from the Organization, while the fact was, as his friend Çorbacı saw it, that by converting, he was simply obeying orders.

For this reason, Mustafa realized early on that it was impossible to confront Amgad with the truth.

The matter was very delicate. Any slip on his part would confirm Amgad's suspicion that he was a secret agent. He decided to try to ascertain his friend's feelings by chattering about other subjects over the course of a series of trips to the Khan of Secrets. But the circumstances of his escalating quarrels with his wife and his growing wish for a divorce had kept him from Amgad until that day.

Only now that they were on the road did he begin to recall everything that the impassioned Sunni had told him about himself.

Amgad's return from Canada

It had all happened after Amgad returned, as suddenly as he had left. As Mustafa understood it, the story began when they'd threatened to kill him. He didn't know how Amgad had ended up going to Canada in the first place. Every time he told a different story. He'd been living there on the pretext of studying, and suddenly there was a revolver between his legs.

"Its muzzle was exactly at the base of the penis," so Amgad told Mustafa, "right where it joins the testicles."

Amgad had told Mustafa this during a previous trip to the Khan of Secrets. At the time he had a beard and the first signs of a prayer mark on his forehead, but he still smoked hashish. For the first time, he had spoken in that strange and totally incomprehensible way about secret agents and international conspiracies.

What did they want?

"How should I know, sir? Was I going to wait to find out? I packed my things and left."

Now, in the middle of the book/can that he would draw later, Mustafa started to suspect that Amgad might be right. He was still convinced that his Sunni friend couldn't prove anything he said, but this tale of an Organization was not implausible.

Most probably, he said to himself, that business with the revolver was some sort of trivial fraud operation: drugs or prostitution. Some goons who'd had the idea of holding up a rich foreigner whose only interests, other than food, were sex and junk. But the fact that what had happened to him was a scam on the surface didn't mean it couldn't have a frightening interior.

That night Amgad was relatively calm and went on giving thanks to God that he'd packed his things and left.

Cocaine compounds paranoia, Mustafa told him.

"What cocaine, Darsh?" He was serious, certainly, the grief and fear in his eyes proved it. "You know, there are a lot of Israelis in North America..."

Once again, he told him about the king's life he'd lived there. Then the same smile appeared on his face that had drawn Mustafa to him the first time they'd met; as if he were a child caught stealing sweets who was expecting punishment when he saw his captors were laughing. Every day a new woman. Sometimes, three in the same breath.

"White?"

"All colors, sir."

He would buy cocaine and share it around. Bottles of Absolut Vodka in every direction. Of course, with time it became clear that all the women were bought and paid for. Amgad's talk was a mixture of boasting, bravado, and flattery, but his pride in himself was really sweet.

Mustafa recalled that he'd once come back from the Khan of Secrets almost whimpering. Amgad had told him things that made him think his Sunni friend had never known a woman any other way. He actually cried when it occurred to him that Amgad's experience confirmed the saying that a woman was chattel; if she slept with you she'd be damaged goods, and you'd be crazy to think of marrying her.

During this period, Mustafa realized that Amgad was ten years older than him—he didn't look it, my friend, a wild bull!—and that he'd been disappointed in the only relationship that he'd had before he went abroad.

"No, of course I didn't love her or anything," he'd said of this relationship. "She was a bit like your aunt, Umm Ihsan!" But gradually his voice became gentler: while he was respecting her virginity, others were having it off with her.

"Did she confess?" asked Mustafa.

Amgad lifted his head as the Greeks and Syrians do to mean no. "They were the ones who told me!"

A woman's body is to be loved, but her tongue, mind, spirit, and everything that indicates her humanity is to be hated. —Wajdi al-Ahdal

Mustafa recollected all the women in the office that Amgad had tried with, and the ambiguous formula that had brought them together in the first place: Amgad was keen to make friends with someone who'd scored there. Yes, your brother Mustafa Çorbacı, the hero, had scored with women in the office. Amgad was jealous of him without hating him, but was he trying to get something out of it? Anyway, they could smoke hashish together. Amgad used to target the pretty, upper-class girls in the office, which convinced Mustafa that he was more than averagely stupid. These girls were further than the clouds were from his culture and his type. They couldn't be expected to mistake him for prince charming, or indeed any prince at all.

Nonetheless, Mustafa never said to him, not even once, that the reason for his failure was obvious. To fulfill your desire you had to pay for it in the usual currency: self-control, coded expressions, lies that could be believed, a convincing balance between confidence and passion. Or else you had to pay cash. It was never in your interest to get drunk (as Amgad Salah used to) and charge, whether by making passes at the women or by coming to blows with the men.

Mustafa never said anything, perhaps because he figured that when Amgad lived in Ontario he had discovered all there was to be said. Certainly, something had changed in his relationship with the world after he'd spent that year there. Only in his relationship with the world, Mustafa thought, not in his madness. After he'd come back his rhythm was faster and he was more inclined to find slowness and confusion strange. Disorganization. But (and more importantly) he had clearer ideas about women. He started to say, for example: "Why do people think it's so easy to judge women?" or "A girl may wear next to nothing but still be respectable!"

Despite the adventures that he boasted about, he seemed to have discovered there alternative possibilities for relationships.

Situations and settings in which the woman was not chattel. But at the same time he realized that these possibilities were closed to a person like him. So he decided to act as though there were no distinction between his own experience and these possibilities. According to the Salafi viewpoint there actually was no distinction: neither the attraction of the male nor the desire of the female had any influence on the legal status of things. As a Sunni, Amgad could get himself a reasonably pretty girl twenty years younger than himself, and this would also be better than scoring in the office. That was how he reconciled himself to his failure where others had succeeded, by describing them both (his failure and their success) as mortal sins.

Did anyone think, Amgad Pasha, that marriage Wahhabi-style would solve your crisis?

Mustafa had a vague memory of a conversation he'd heard a bit of, without taking part, before the start of Amgad's conversion. Amgad Salah had been sitting on the revolving chair in the big room in the office looking at the others out of the corner of his eye and shouting: "I swear there's nothing but halal and haram in the world!"

Çorbacı almost cried for the third time when he realized that Amgad Salah's breakdown hadn't started until his father died, exactly as had happened with most of his friends. A man's father dies and he is at the end of his rope. His personal mood (even if he hated his father) merges with the general mood in Cairo, and he deals with this either by resistance or submission. And how could Amgad Salah resist, except through paranoia?

In the case of Amgad in particular, the story was quite clear, because his father had been a senior official in the Ministry of the Interior. When he died, his youngest son lost all the influence that he'd relied on. No one was prepared to assume responsibility for Amgad's needs either inside or outside the service. Even his fellow officers couldn't believe they were finally rid of him, because he'd been a huge embarrassment in ministry circles. He felt that without a father he'd become like a public toilet where everyone could relieve themselves then leave.

This was why, so he told Mustafa, he resigned.

The grieving who do not confront their grief. Their lives become conditional on possibilities that are in no way likely until all possibilities become hot air. Just a beard and a mark on the forehead and an infinite number of forbidden things, in addition to all the rituals. Until the day came when Mustafa would look at the mark on his retired policeman friend's forehead and not believe it was there.

Chapter

Mustafa had a cousin who worked as a doctor and he explained to him how to procure dead skin. He assured him that the operation could be completed within two weeks. "It's very simple," he said. First of all, you injure yourself, making a broad but superficial wound in a place near the bone—the forehead, for example? The forehead or the knee was just as good—but it was better to pierce than to cut. To make a fresh, flattened wound. The most important thing is not to let it heal. Once you've injured yourself, you just repeat the injury.

"You just carry on scratching and don't stop!"

After enough of this, the living cells will stop growing. From the flesh of the skin, darker, rougher tissues will emerge, and take the shape of a raised circle, like a sand dune shifting in the desert.

Chapter

On the Saturday evening, the first weekend since Mustafa had stopped at Dream Bridge, as he drove his Sunni friend to the Khan of Secrets, he became disturbed that the latter seemed determined to raise the subject of his separation. Amgad kept telling him that he felt that he—Mustafa—was egging him on to speak about himself, then not talking. He shouted in jest: "This is cheating, you're a cheat!" And Mustafa didn't know how to hide his anger.

They went back and forth about it through the entrance to the Dandy Mall. All the time Mustafa was doing his utmost to explain the problem in a way that Amgad could understand. He tried posing as reasons for the breakdown of the marriage anger, misery, conflicting temperaments. All this, only to discover that in the view of his retired policeman friend, he was simply repressing his wife. The problem, that is, lay in Mustafa's patriarchal authority.

"Oriental blood," he told him. "You just don't want to admit it."

"Admit what, Amgad?"

"And what's more, she was always kind of a hippie girl."

"She what?"

"She was always kind of a hippie girl," he repeated. "That must be why you suffocated her."

Mustafa started the TV peasant conversation again, to keep from getting worked up.

For more than a month, I've been avoiding the friends who liked her, he said to himself: artists, poets, generally older than me. They could only see the glittering surface and the rising sun. I couldn't say to them: today there is nothing to keep me from leaving without separating. Was I avoiding them, losing their friendship, only to end up with a donkey who thinks the problem was my patriarchal authority?

The light was shining in the towering arena of the supermarket, but the neon was like a whirlpool in the sea: nausea. Mustafa concentrated on their distance from the city. This was really why he'd come. After the world had collapsed, where could he go, except for the Khan of Secrets? "In the dictionary traveling means traversing distances. It doesn't matter if they're short or long, vertical or horizontal, on the surface or in the depths. To have experienced a journey you only need to have traversed a distance." He pulled Amgad by the arm across the entrance corridor. The groceries were piled high, as were the clothes. As usual, they headed for the electronics. Mustafa stopped without realizing it. He could just see Amgad eying the cookers, drifting toward the microwaves and toasters on his own. He no longer moved in tandem with Mustafa as he used to, when Mustafa thought he must have been afraid of being on his own. *My dubious journey, which always promises new stations and always costs me more tickets.* Mustafa had only to straighten his head so as not to see Amgad. A face like his wife's flying past in the distance. Change and stability. A hot meal and a fuck. From where he was standing he looked at the cameras: silver, black, and metallic colors. Gardens of silicon, beneath which pixels flow. He stepped closer and stared. Lenses of different apertures, a photographer's bliss!

The big camera his wife had bought for him wasn't practical. If he was really going to move he'd need one of these. One the size of a packet of cigarettes.

To put in his pocket and fly.

• • • • • • •

"Where have you been, Mr. Çorbacı?" The pillar of bloated rubber was coming up to him.

"What?" he asked impatiently.

"Did you see that mixer, sir?"

Delight on the pillar's face. He paid no attention to anything except kitchen gadgets.

Once again Mustafa left him and made for the DVDs. He needed a B-movie collection to fill the space in his room. The book selection proved limited and disappointing, as did the stationery. Amgad Salah was carrying two copies of a work by Sayyid Qutb, claiming that it was the "finest nectar." With some difficulty they found a place in line. Shaving supplies and cans of juice. As they were packing their purchases into bags, Mustafa noticed that the light was gentler outside the supermarket—the space belonged less to the Egyptian middle class than these rows of goods. With no people pushing and shoving like beasts, there was no reason for nausea, he thought.

From our own planet, outside the enormous square occupied by Carrefour, we can see Dandy Mall as a broad, twisting lane: keep walking and you'll return to where you began. But were the white walls really that dusty?

In Mustafa's memory everything is gray. But the sensation of travel comes back to him as his eye cuts through the fancy kiosks in the middle of the lane and settles on the rows of shop fronts on either side. You're walking on tiles, almost skating, relieved for a moment to be separated from everything. The asphalt and the red bricks, the flies and the trees, the air, the exhaust fumes, and the sight of the sky. You adapt your walk too to a ceramic rhythm and feel that you're in a submerged airport where planes seldom land. Another reason to come to the Khan of Secrets? "Don't you miss flying, Sheikh Amgad?" Here was the sheikh jumping up and down with all his weight as he listed the merits of the mini-microwave that he'd made up his mind to buy.

In front of everyone?

And we forget his sorrows and his beard.

Mustafa jumped up and down with Amgad and was happy for no reason. Perhaps his happiness came from the fact that this place really was like an airport, in that you might be anywhere on earth. Then there was a light-skinned child so small that the microwave Amgad had decided to buy could hold all of him, no exaggeration. He was sticking his tongue out at Mustafa. His family seemed to have left him to do as he liked, and Mustafa couldn't see anyone with him, either in line or in the supermarket.

Now he was playing blind man's buff with Mustafa and laughing: sweet enough to eat!

Chapter

Two steps forward for Mustafa to pretend to attack the child, and Amgad had suddenly disappeared. He must be somewhere between the Syrian sweet shop and the Costa window. But Mustafa had hardly spread his arms out when he stood pinned to the ground. Ustaz Wahid al-Din, their zombie colleague, yes, flesh and blood, was pushing a large, empty shopping cart, the most striking aspect of which was that he was a long way from the shopping area. Outside the shopping area, you don't see shopping carts unless they are full of plastic bags on their way to the parking lot. Wahid al-Din was dragging his feet in his usual furtive way, walking with no obvious aim.

But as soon as he was opposite the young boy, he stopped and turned around. Suddenly, his movements became confident.

For the first time in his life Mustafa saw Wahid al-Din's back straighten and his face expand without embarrassment. He didn't doubt that Wahid al-Din was looking directly at him. His eyes were fixed on Mustafa's eyes without expression, and Mustafa was uncertain whether to say hello or to pretend to ignore him and look for Amgad. He also noticed that

Wahid al-Din was wearing round old-fashioned glasses. For a moment, and this was the really surprising thing, he was certain he was looking at someone else who only resembled his colleague. Someone a little older, with a light beard instead of stubble. The agitated way he was moving had a certain gravity, so that rather than creeping along, he seemed to be exploring.

But it was suspicious, Mustafa thought, that this person was deliberately trying to give the impression of being Wahid al-Din. Why should this unknown stranger be deceiving me today? The unsteadiness at the two points where his lips met was more like sarcasm than anticipation. Who could Wahid al-Din's double in Dandy Mall be? Leaving aside his excellent posture, his steady stance, and the cheerfulness of his wrinkled face, the man's eyes were on him. And he was overwhelmed by a powerful sense that their meeting wasn't an accident. He was convinced that nothing in this world was an accident, in fact, but sometimes the feeling was so powerful that it hit you in the face. Like now.

When he asked himself whether he'd ever seen Wahid al-Din in glasses, he started thinking instead about what the appearance of his double here might mean, and about the possibility that it might have some connection with the Organization or the dream, or the prophecy—three things that were undoubtedly connected, though he had not the faintest idea of the secret that linked them. Suddenly, he came to, to find fingers like rubber burrowing into his shoulder, and discovered that without his noticing, the phantom with the out-of-place shopping trolley and the small boy in tow had disappeared. When Mustafa turned around, he blinked, because Amgad, who had just as suddenly reappeared, was holding something to his eye. He mustn't draw his attention to the presence of Wahid al-Din.

When he opened his eyes—he would continue to remember this moment—something that was a color between black and gray was moving away from his face, acquiring a faint sheen, and his Sunni friend's rugged voice was saying, "Have a look at this ring!"

Amgad jumped again when Mustafa tried to make out the engraving, which was large and blurred because it was still so close. Despite this (as would be explained by a visitor from another world, which Mustafa seemed to foresee), he could immediately make out its four constituent parts, and he let his mind wander over everything they suggested to him, still in a state of surprise from having seen Wahid al-Din.

Bagpipes
A boat
A water skin
A gazelle horn scabbard for a dagger.

For a moment, Mustafa thought that he might be looking at a map of the whole world in one engraving. This idea was reinforced by his realization that this was a decorative drawing of hard-to-read Arabic calligraphy (for some time, he had been taken with the idea that letters might depict a map). In the north there were three columns next to one another like a very thick flagpole. The curves emanating from them to the east came together in a tapered line like a sword. To the west was an egg with its yolk, sitting on the trunk of a fishing boat in the south. The pole was joined to the trunk, and the sword emerged from the egg. Everything was connected by endless circles and arcs.

Later, after he had discovered everything and various preposterous things had happened to him, Mustafa would photograph the engraving on this ring with his large camera and reproduce it. It was shaped roughly like this:

Without thinking, he'd stretched out his hand to take from Amgad whatever it was Amgad was holding to his eye. At that moment the latter, his Herculean figure looming, noticed the scared look on his friend Çorbacı's face and asked him, in a slightly shaken voice: "What's the matter, sir, why are you shaking and that?"

"And what's up with you, Bashbushti?" replied Mustafa, trying to smile.

Only then did he realize that the engraving was very familiar. He must have seen it dozens of times, in names, trademarks, religious expressions, and even on a small coin bearing the words "Arab Republic of Egypt." But this was the first time he had made out all these allusions in it. From a distance, when he looked at it out of the corner of his eye, he noticed that it looked like a bird with an enormous comb and a hooked beak. For some unknown reason, without asking himself what it meant, he recalled the Qur'anic verse: "And every man—We have fastened to him his bird of omen upon his neck!"

But he quickly pulled himself together and resumed his conversation with Amgad.

"What is it that's written on this ring?"

"In the name of God, the merciful, the compassionate..." But as soon as Amgad said this, Mustafa began to have doubts. "Could it be something else?" Then he laughed shyly. "Look, I liked the look of it, that's all!"

"In the name of God, the merciful, the compassionate! What's that, Amgad?" sighed Mustafa with disgust. "You're making that up!"

They were quiet as they looked at the engraving. Most of the examples that Mustafa had seen really had had the expression "In the name of God, the merciful, the compassionate" on them, and sometimes "Muhammad, may God bless him and grant him peace." He didn't know why he had instinctively challenged Amgad's interpretation of the writing on the ring. But even odder was the fact that the ring actually bore another, completely different phrase, of which he could only make out the word "Ibn" ("Son of"), surrounded by circles of intersecting words.

"To be honest, I don't know what it says!" said Amgad as they stared at it. "But now I'm sure it's not 'In the name of God, the merciful, the compassionate.' Come on, why don't we go back to the shop to see what else they've got!"

The other one nodded enthusiastically. "Did you buy it?"

"I could take it back, chief. I came to fetch you for your opinion and that. I mean, I know that you love musk and the sweet customs of the Prophet…"

"Is the ring a custom as well?"

"But of course!"

Getting the ring

The way to the silver window was longer than Mustafa had thought (there were intersecting paths with no logic to them in the Khan of Secrets), along a passage that branched off from the one leading to the restrooms. We say "window," because the shop as Mustafa recalled it was like a box of glass containing three silver shelves. It was surrounded by a square meter in which the salesman could walk about. Just a plastic chair, plus a calculator and a Visa card machine on top of the box. No door and no windows. Mustafa looked up at the high ceiling. Everything was gray. There is a colorless detachedness to airports. The really strange thing was that again without thinking about it he really did feel that he was in an airport. The walls were streamlined and sad. For another moment (though it seemed a very long time), as his gaze hovered between the ceiling and the walls, Mustafa remembered again what airports had meant in his life. The time when his father was working in Libya, his university years in southwest England on the coast of the "Manche" (or "Channel," as the English call it), then the search for his aunt the year she went on pilgrimage and didn't come back.

Between one place and another, there is always a dead time locked in buildings with colorless walls and high ceilings. He recalled that Plane Yard, like the Khan of Secrets in his current situation, promised an arrival that always remained at the stage of being fulfilled. Absolute time, or an eternal place. And there you seemed to be content to stay out of line.

In that absolute time, your compensation was the sense that you were moving away from the foundation pillars and blocks upon which your world was built—that is, the sense that you no longer had a world. Nothing mattered as you followed your Sunni friend to that window. Amgad said, "Hey, sir!" and

Mustafa looked in no particular direction. Amgad was asking the cheerful young silver seller whether the inscription said "Muhammad, may God bless him and grant him peace," while Mustafa stood two or three paces away, staring at the ceiling to shake the dust from his head. Very slowly he returned from his vision of Plane Yard to the conversation between them:

"This is basically Turkish script, sir!"

"Turkish, ah!"

"But naturally that doesn't stop you..."

"What do you mean, Turkish?"

"Turkish, sir, Turkish script. I mean, this writing is basically from Turkey or something. Of course, sir, that doesn't stop you from finding pieces with religious words written on them, 'In the name of whatever,' or 'Say, he is God, one,' things like that. But Turkish here, sir, isn't understood, because it's not Arabic at all, sir!"

"You mean, this isn't 'Muhammad, may God bless him and grant him peace'?"

"You could really call it Turkish calligraphy. Unfortunately, sir, this is the only piece I've got left. This shop is your home, sir, you can change it for something you like at any time. No offense, sir, I showed you a Throne Verse, something more than excellent, to be frank, but no offense, sir, you insisted on this one."

"Okay, what else could I exchange it for?"

"Turkish, sir, Turkish calligraphy."

Suddenly, something with four legs seemed to dart between Mustafa's shins. He sprang back in fright.

"What's up, Mr. Çorbacı?"

"How should I know?"

Amgad smiled at the shopkeeper with the same self-confidence that had made going about with him change Mustafa's view of himself, before Amgad had become a Sunni. When he was dealing with shopkeepers and waiters, or even garage and parking attendants, he would take on the spirit of a kind and generous feudal gentleman. But why was the shopkeeper now suddenly grimacing and turning his face away from him?

His tone changed as he spoke to someone Mustafa couldn't see.

"Come here, boy!" he shouted.

Until he realized he was talking to the little thing that had made him jump. A glance to the left and he recognized his little white-skinned friend walking toward the shopkeeper with his head bowed. He was no taller than a couple of hand spans. As soon as the shopkeeper started talking to Amgad again, the child took advantage, and stuck out his tongue at Mustafa. Mustafa stepped forward, looked at the cheerful young boy and asked: "Your son?" This made the shopkeeper ignore Amgad a second time, and gesture with a mixture of pride and embarrassment.

Amgad was still hesitant as he examined the rings that the shopkeeper had brought out on a piece of dark-blue velvet. He turned them over in his coarse hands like someone tapping a watermelon to learn from the noise it made whether it was sweet.

"What do you think, Darsh? Should we take this one?"

Suddenly the whole of the Dandy Mall was flooded with Salah Abdullah's song from the film *Soldiers in a Camp*: "Hosta Kosta, high as a kite..."

"This Throne Verse is beautiful, Amgad," said Mustafa. "I'll take the Turkish one for myself."

"Sure?"

"Yes. I'll settle up with you. Just let me try it for size!"

As soon as he put the ring on his finger—as if it had been custom-made for him—he was shaken by a new terror he could not explain. Just for a moment, during which Michel Fustuq's talk about him leaving the marital home and then the church dream went through his head. He was thinking about how the fair-skinned young boy had turned out to be the shopkeeper's son, which would explain why he was wandering around the place on his own. If I'd looked for him when he vanished, he wondered, would I have reached the window on my own? As it turned out, he'd come to the Khan of Secrets in order to obtain a ring, with an inscription that was at once familiar and obscure—perhaps the inscription had some connection with the events of the dream? Then there was the appearance of Wahid al-Din's double and the fact that his wife had been a bit of a hippie from the beginning. Without any question or answer, Mustafa knew that Amgad had this evening handed him his place in a battle from which he—Amgad—had withdrawn. He didn't know how, he just knew.

One last time he sneaked up on the child and tickled him, before leaving.

If anyone dismisses them or criticizes them, they call him an unbeliever. Each of the heads of the group becomes a sheikh in his own right... judging, ordering and forbidding... —al-Jabarti

It would've been better for them to walk around a little after putting their purchases in the cart, but Amgad immediately headed to the cake display window. Mustafa followed him slowly to the circle of light. The waiter there was more polite than was necessary. Once again, motion takes place as if in a dream, the yellow light frightening Mustafa when he sees it on Amgad Salah's face. The atmosphere is calmer than it should be, that's all, he said to himself. But he was apprehensive as they sat down. And indeed, hardly a minute had passed before the conversation turned to Amgad's persecution in the office, which is what he'd been dreading. An Arab soap opera whose episodes would never end. He recalled Amgad saying that they shouldn't talk to him like that, their colleagues. A sheikh with a beard and a prayer mark on his forehead—he said this without laughter or irony—should be treated with respect.

So far, he recalled, he hadn't succeeded in raising another subject. Even his separation was madmen's talk.

"Ustaz Amgad Pasha Salah!"

"Yes!"

"A beard without a mustache is a joke"—he couldn't believe that he'd succumbed to the explosion—"It doesn't look nice, not at all. And then, my friend, what's all this got to do with religion? The Prophet of God had a ponytail. I mean, if you mean to follow his example!" Then he shouted: "Piety isn't a mark on the forehead!" After which he hurried on, still shouting about the Day of Reckoning and the Resurrection.

He didn't come to himself until Ramses Square. Was he thinking about Yildiz all the way? It was better to avoid quarreling with Amgad Salah because he either immediately retreated or he hit you. He knew that Mustafa wasn't afraid of his blows. Still, the silence was absurd. Yet at least the subject was closed. He was no longer obliged to explain the basic meaning of the word Islam, nor his separation. At their next meeting Amgad would look for an opportunity for revenge. But for now, Mustafa was dropping him off outside his house as he did every time.

Amgad leaned through the car window to bid him farewell, looking around him like a hunted man. "Al-salam 'alaykum," he said.

And you, he was saying quietly to himself, are a laughingstock and a coward.

•   •   •   •   •

Still, what had happened to Amgad in the sanatorium? What had he seen during the periods he'd spent drugged? Mustafa knew they'd given him electric shocks once, before he'd joined the newspaper. He also knew, though, that Amgad didn't like to recall that incident, although the operation in itself hadn't hurt him physically. He always said that sanatoria were quiet places and a good opportunity for rest and recuperation. And so they were, insofar as Mustafa understood them, most of the time.

But how had the experience, and its subsequent repetition, affected him?

In moments of clarity it seemed to Mustafa that the sanatorium itself had given Amgad the chance first to formulate these tales—the zombie, the Organization, the regal life he had lived in Canada—then to put together a life that would remove him from them, and finally, by embracing the Salafi lifestyle, make it possible to do away with them altogether.

It was as though he'd been writing stories during this time in the sanatorium, stories he would quickly burn when he came out... until he found one flimsy story for himself that would actually spare him all life's details.

The characters that he played in turns with Mustafa—the archivist, or the peasant on TV—had he found models for them behind those doors?

Mustafa thought that if it hadn't been for the sanatorium, Amgad wouldn't have any stories.

Chapter

As he left Amgad at the Ezbekiyya Gardens and stepped on the gas, Mustafa was struck for the first time by a strange fact: he'd been working as a journalist for a decade now—how many decades in the life of a smoker?—but in the last seven years he hadn't budged from in front of the screen. How could this happen? It amused him that as a consequence, everyone he knew, he had met at the paper, though they had very different reasons for being there: Yildiz, and the dark girl; Michel Fustuq; Amgad Salah... even his own wife, who had been working for a foreign insurance company and had called on them to arrange for an ad. It amused and scared him that this was true.

As if, on the pretext of writing articles, he had spent the whole time arranging the moment when he would wait for his wife to collect her things from their apartment in Dog Alley, after which they would each emerge carrying their things in silence. Without being conscious of what he was doing, of course.

Seven years in a plywood cubicle without getting to know anyone outside the company. That evening, as he returned to Dream Bridge, he wondered among other things about the basis and point of his job. How had the office turned into a world that needed no one outside it? Gradually, as the journalism he was looking for became synonymous with movement and travel (instead of correcting endless empty words on a screen), and as movement itself transformed from mental relaxation to a means of uncovering the truth—the basis and point of the job—Mustafa sensed that Amgad Salah was bearing him a message (was this why he had started going around with him in the first place?).

There really had to be an Organization. Otherwise, what was it that was making him dream about things that he saw during the day on the streets, or pay attention to rings and children and familiar faces in public places? What magic had turned Isaaf into World's Gate, and Carrefour into the Khan of Secrets? What had made him so far incapable of desire? Other than taking a deep breath and gradually discovering how to control his life, what could arouse his desire to embrace his wife?

"I'll never ever leave you!" A scene or two of what he had put up with in her company, and his tears would dry up. "I'll never ever leave you!"

In a dream, before he left Dog Alley, he put his hand over his eye and coughed as he leaned forward. Into his hand there fell a pearl dripping with blood, then the appearance of things changed. He was giving his wife the pearl but she jumped up and said (with her usual hysterical English rhythm), "One eye! Of course, you won't give more than one eye. Do you think we can see properly without the second one?" Most of the time he maintained an exaggerated self-discipline. No one knew how distracted he really was.

He wished he could stand on his head or take off his clothes and run down the street. How could he forget that after being there, he was now here? Once or twice the light faded in his eye for no apparent reason. He would be sitting in the light of the window in his cage at midday, minding his own business, and suddenly the light would fade. Everything had stayed the same since his father died. There was no comfort in anything. Why was all this happening? And why did the map of Cairo that he was imagining seem more and more like an engraving, a work of Arabic calligraphy? An engraving that might resemble the ring that was still on his finger?

The really frightening thing was that all the people around him, all the people working in this office, were disturbed, but paid no attention to the causes of their disturbance.

No one was aware of anything except for Amgad, and Amgad just got on his nerves.

Chapter

Once upon a time there was a wretched, mad Sunni who behaved like the extremists from Saudi or Afghanistan. As he sat with his friends he would repeat the disgraceful words of the sheikhs, whether or not appropriate, like a parrot. One or two months went by during which time this Sunni was convinced that what made him function in life was something called "inner electricity," which relied on a special connection; he believed that his movement and his life depended on the plug being in its socket to close the circuit, and that he had to carry the plug with him everywhere. He started explaining everything that happened to him as being due to the plug having come out of its socket—whether it was his nervous breakdowns, the surges of anger that came over him, paranoia, anxiety, repression, or abandonment. He felt that everything depended on the closing of the circuit, and he suspected this might be because the members of a secret Organization were trying to control his life. He resolved to reconnect it because it was the sole key to the inner electricity of any wretched, mad Sunni. One day a voice came to him in a dream and he went and bought a small sack made of cloth, which he stuffed full to the last centimeter with an enormous mass of those colored mini-pamphlets in which they print verses, prayers, and sometimes complete suras of the Qur'an. He buried a plug without a wire among the pamphlets, together with an electric socket, then sat with a bowl full of water in front of him, recited the sura of Ya Sin with his hands under the water, then dried them on the bag, and finally slipped them into the bag and put the plug in the socket. Meanwhile, he was extolling God with the traditional Islamic formulae, adding: "With God's blessing, we are closing the internal electricity circuit which will put peace in our heart!" Whenever something disturbed him after that, he would reach for the sack, and after reciting "In the name of God, praise be to God," put his hand into the pamphlets to check that the plug was in the socket to ensure that the circuit of inner electricity was closed, then smile and say "Amen!"

That evening, Mustafa recalled a day when he was supposed to go to the Khan of Secrets with Amgad. After Amgad had gotten into the car beside him he found he was coughing harder than usual, then as soon as they got onto the 26 July Corridor, he started to cry. All his muscles were twitching, almost begging Mustafa to turn round and go back. When he asked him why ("But why, Salah Pasha?"), the voice of the retired policeman trembled as he replied: "They took away my plug, Mr. Çorbacı, they took away my plug!"

"Didn't you bring the plug with you?"

"No, I left it at home!" He started to whimper again. "I can't get a hold of myself at all when the plug's been taken away and that."

Mustafa would also recall how the story ended, when Amgad discovered the plug had been loose for seven days, although he had been in a good mood. It happened that another bearded individual in the mosque had told him that electricity was originally an innovation, and therefore continued to be disapproved of on religious grounds, even though it was legitimate to use it so long as the intention behind it was not invalid. When he found that his heart was at ease and the plug was loose, he became convinced that the circuit and the idea of inner electricity were both errors, and that if he didn't free himself from them, he would go to hell. Mustafa recalled the day he'd come to the office with a plastic bag full of small pamphlets, which he'd distributed to his colleagues. When he asked him why, Amgad had replied: "Praise be to God, Our Lord gave me guidance, Mr. Çorbacı! I threw away the circuit and burned the sack here in the yard behind the garage, but then I thought that instead of leaving these eloquent Qur'anic verses in a corner, our colleagues might make use of them, sir!"

Chapter

The Chinese artist whose book Mustafa had read said that those who do not know themselves are incapable of forming relationships. Relationships only serve to distract them from an inner emptiness, which exposes them to collapse at the first obstacle. It was obvious that Mustafa was completely ignorant of himself. So where did this conviction come from, that it was his knowledge of himself that had made the world collapse? His knowledge of his propensity for continuous misery. That this was the end of his rope. Or at least the limit of what he wanted. It was knowledge, so he felt, that precipitated breakdown. Knowledge meant that you had standards for judging your partner, and that your partnership would fail when you measured by them. If he had been empty inside, he would not have been forced to judge. Now, when he thought about his dark-skinned colleague—the nearest thing in his life to a woman he wanted—it amazed him that he had not given in to his passion for her since they first had contact, years before he met his wife. He knew this about himself: that whenever he crossed the path of this dark-skinned girl, he would stumble over something that would make him retrace his steps. She could behave like a spoiled child, with the same malice and stupidity, and her morals were the opposite of her actions (the "dissipated youth" theory). He didn't believe ninety percent of what she said. He hated the social contradictions she embodied, the fragility of the truth in her head, and the fact that she gossiped without thinking about what she was saying.

Despite this, he had never met anyone in his life whose weakness had melted him to this extent: his crazy need for compassion. The dark girl conducted herself without any moral catalogue, and yet her prettiness remained. By contrast, what had made him leap over the obstacles in the way of his wife was that her roots in a different society excused her contradictions, or that half of what she said convinced him. But she was no less stupid or manipulative. Even the way she rose above society was no more than the actions of a rebellious adolescent, as removed as could be from any real rejection of the status quo. Her roots in another society hadn't helped except to disrupt the balance: he didn't know from one moment to the next whether he was in Birkat al-Fil or in the Mayfair district in London. Crossing the path of his wife, had that in itself been pure ignorance?

When would he enfold the dark girl and taste her flesh, with all the ignorance that he lacked, and all his desire for passionate love during sex? When embrace her soft neck and smooth her hair? At night he dreamed of her silky body. A cuckoo in her lungs. All the tenderness that he had given to his wife—wasn't she more worthy of it?

Amgad Salah's marriage

On the evening of the second Sunday, while the apartment was spewing its guts and Mustafa was sitting half asleep in the office, Amgad Salah told him that he had gotten engaged. As if he were saying that he'd eaten kufta for lunch. The previous day in the Khan of Secrets he'd been talking about claiming his legal rights before his wedding night; now he believed that waiting would increase his manliness.

The sister of his who had found the bride was divorced, so Mustafa understood. Divorced and in niqab. The bride was also like a curtain. Young and uncouth, but he was happy. He related a hadith to Mustafa about the reasons for a woman to marry: wealth, beauty, and knowledge of the faith. He confessed she lacked both money and beauty. Knowledge of the faith was enough for Amgad Salah, regardless.

"Are you ready?"

He wiped the yogurt from his beard.

This comes through the heart, not the convulsions of the tongue. This comes from seclusion, not the wedding night. —'Abd al-Qadir al-Jilani

That evening, Mustafa noticed for the first time that he had not been thinking as much about his wife. It occurred to him that the things we count as precious are much cheaper than we realize. To have a wife, for example, or a job. For live cells to continue growing on your skin. Amgad Salah insisted that tattooing was haram. You'd never suspect that he'd get a tattoo on his forehead big enough to block out the eye of the sun. It meant nothing so long as he was addressed as sheikh.

"That's what my marriage was like!" Mustafa thought. "To go to bed and smoke as I like, and to scribble in this notebook. Anything but that. To hell with family and children so long as I can travel!"

He reflected that everyone had his own madness. To find something to cling to, or else put a camera in his pocket and fly.

Chapter

As we said, he was aware that he was no longer thinking about his wife. He recalled, instead, the matter of the zombie. The zombie, like the blood-sucking vampire, is a dead person who has some of the attributes of the living. But he isn't intelligent or seductive like a vampire. He can't use sex to kill. He doesn't have the distinction of surviving endlessly through time. The zombie doesn't usually assume multiple guises or sleep in a coffin, and he isn't affected by sunlight like a vampire. He doesn't have two fangs to plant in the side of your neck. He just rises from the grave, driven by some unknown force. A stinking, decomposing corpse wandering a short distance for a short period of time. A dumb, primitive intelligence, rather than extraordinary powers. Just a corpse—a *jifa*, as Mustafa liked to describe him, borrowing al-Jabarti's word—a corpse that feeds on human flesh, especially the living brain. The zombie, in short, is a dead man who eats your brain, biting into your head to make you become like him.

Except for the moments when he recalled Amgad Salah's madness on the 26 July Corridor on that Saturday evening, the subject of the zombie hadn't crossed Mustafa's mind since the time Amgad had first spoken of an Organization. Now, though, he started to wonder what lay behind Amgad's having called the fiqi Wahid al-Din a zombie (was Wahid al-Din the zombie he'd complained about in the Jazz Club, someone who could assume the guise of anyone else?) and then failing to complain about a zombie who appeared to him from then on. Mustafa remembered a feeling of terror churning his stomach when he had watched Romero's films, but what preoccupied him now was the metaphorical meaning of eating the brain. A dead man taking over your mind so completely he drove you mad. Was this what had happened to Amgad?

At some stage, Mustafa would read about the origin of the word zombie, far removed from the culture of Hollywood, and would realize that "zombie," according to the voodoo beliefs current on the island of Haiti, meant a dead person restored to life by a voodoo sorcerer, with no voice or will; he would be employed by the sorcerer as a servant or soldier, or else the sorcerer would utilize his spirit in various ways (Mustafa would read about similar phenomena in Oman, where the magic, as in Haiti, originated in Africa). In voodoo, the sorcerer is called a *bokor*, and this *bokor* has the power to neutralize a man's life—a man whose family thought him dead, whether or not the *bokor* killed him. Usually they will have buried him years ago when he appears among them again, as if he were the same person, but without speaking or recognizing anyone or anything. Just a human vessel for someone else's impulses, moving without living, bearing through life not his cross but his grave.

At some point in this tale, as we are aware from our planet, Mustafa would personally feel that he had turned into a zombie. But contrary to the two definitions—the Hollywood definition and the voodoo definition—he would feel that in his case a zombie was a person whose consciousness combines history and desire into a state more like death than life. He would feel, despite the contradiction this implied, that when he died he had become more alive than ever, and that his death was like a miraculous rebirth.

And that his personal bereavement—his grief—was the same as his joy in the beloved.

Chapter

The Chinese artist talked about the path. Three years had gone by as he walked. Walked through the desert and over the ice, near the mountain peaks. Thirst and humidity. He'd be arrested and fall ill or be lost. His things would disappear and he'd be exposed to death. Hunger and the wilderness. But he kept walking. That's how he felt his life would go on. Yesterday was behind him, and tomorrow morning would arrive in rooms that would temporarily accommodate him. Only the road stretching before him meant that he would go on. Mustafa had a notebook with him. So long as he had the urge to scribble, he would be all right.

Better to go on without Amgad Salah.

Chapter

You are like tea sweetened with basil near the end of the path to the top of Mount Sinai. What is it that pulled from your cheeks a black creature like a tortoise? Who exposed your face to the witch who gives birth to anger, the bright surface of your brow marked with the brown seeds of death? Tell me, what keeps your feet between two narrow lines, as if you were trying to avoid the barbed wire on the borders of a rogue state, or crossing a yellow minefield with an antique compass? You look like someone who knows his way, but you know nothing! Where do all these circles of respect come from, when the pious phrases so stutter on the tip of your tongue that they sound like a cough? Where has this cough come from, when you are in the face of eternal happiness? I cried for you twice, when the acacias were plucked from your throat and when you assaulted the world in Pakistani dress. You are like a mocking laugh, so by what right do you exaggerate your violet diligence? By what covenant that rejects friends have you proclaimed your devotion to God? Would that I had not indulged in your company or delighted in your chestnut-colored disappearance amid the whiteness. Now the caravans of laughter have departed for the graves and your grimace has destroyed the spirits of the world's desires. Now, unwillingly, forever. The girl we loved together has gone to a place whence none returns, and you let her go willingly. Does red doubt ever overcome you about the value of jumping on nails? When will you dance? Will rose roots spring to life in your belly? When the rags settled on your shoulders, I cried for you for eternity. But as long as there remains a laugh or a glass of tea, I will see you as a drop of wine clinging to a pink window in a tumbledown building. I still hold fast the reins of my ignorance, and you are a growth of the devil.

PART FOUR
The Epistle of the Sultan

From World's Gate to the Heart of the Tale

Being Mustafa's Description
of His Meeting with the
Muslims' Imam

Sunday, April 8
and Monday, April 9

Mustafa Naif Çorbacı said:

My dear Rashid, on the third night of the second week, the night of Sunday, April 9 (you will recognize the significance of this date in a bit), our Master the Sultan expressed himself. Only two days had passed since the return of my things from Dog Alley. I was still reading about the Chinese artist and contemplating the collapse of the world. Suddenly, despite everything, there turned out to be a reason to stay at the office after all.

Now, you must pay attention. I'm not mad, and the things I'm telling you all happened just as I'm telling them. I didn't have a nervous breakdown as a result of the separation, despite my previous and inevitable subsequent breakdowns. You know that my breakdowns don't involve hallucinations, and the mental clarity that I have enjoyed since I moved to my mother's house is not just an illusion.

You know, there was strange comfort in the return of the books and clothes. My desk, my chair, my stapler, and the printer. All of us back in my old room, just like before I married. We found strange comfort in settling down with each other there.

And the serene lucidity arrived as soon as we'd settled down. It was a genuine serenity, as is proved by the fact that in the space of a week, all the people I work with were saying "What's happened to you?", with smiles on their lips as big as the crescent moon in its first quarter. Even before ten days had passed, they had started to comment on my excellent timekeeping, as well as a noticeable improvement in my output. Add to this that at home I was reading quickly and with greater concentration, absorbing more. My retention is attested to by the notebooks in which I recorded transcriptions of my readings. Even my mother, when she saw me sleeping at night as I seldom had before, getting up early to go to work—when she saw how my appetite had improved, how tidy my room was, and how the rituals of cleanliness and self-respect that I periodically abandon had reasserted themselves of their own accord—said: "God preserve you for your youth, my dear!" And she sighed with a smile of the same size on her lips, despite her depression about my family situation.

I'm not telling you this to boast to you. It's important for you to realize that the period I'm talking about (a period that could be defined as the first Monday to the second Monday)—apart from disgust with colleagues, degeneration, and analysis—was all lucidity and stability. So it wouldn't follow logically that what happened should have happened solely in my head. In short, what happened was that the Muslims' Imam came to inform me of my historical task. His coming was a harbinger of the journey for which I'd been longing ever since the start of my problems with my wife. A mystical, inner journey, as much as a journey on earth or in heaven.

But until it was time for the journey... I wasn't to know that the separation itself, with all that had preceded it—Michel Fustuq's prophecy, Amgad Salah's conversion from a lost hobo into an unarmed terrorist, all the way back to my decision to marry my wife—had been nothing but a preparation for this, the journey.

I'm also telling you this so that you'll know there was a deeper reason for my lucid serenity. In the days that preceded the return of my things from Dog Alley, while I was in my empty room, I reached the conclusion that my marriage had been a Greek tragedy, which begins and ends within twenty-four hours. Blink and it's over. "A midsummer night's dream of buying a quarter-kilo of dark-roasted coffee at three in the morning." Perhaps you still remember, Rashid: buying the coffee on the way to her house was the beginning of the relationship. That discovery astounded me. Time after time I asked myself whether I'd gone mad in the last act.

In addition to insisting on leaving my wife when she was pregnant, and my job being in the balance after I'd quarreled with my colleagues and insulted the editor-in-chief in the corridor (I had to submit a written apology in January), I felt that the whole world was against me. Was it conceivable that everything could be wrong and I alone be right?

But the more I focused on the streets and the people in them, the clearer it became that the office was just a mini-model of something all-embracing and all-powerful. Something like the resurrection of the dead from their graves on the Day of Judgment.

He also said:

As I argued with my female colleagues over an issue of the glossy magazine named *Hijab Fashion*, Abu al-Arshad, seeking theological backing for the sexual revolution in the fact that the author of *The Perfumed Garden* was a judge and a religious scholar—which prompts me to make clear that *The Perfumed Garden* was just one of many Arabic equivalents of the *Kama Sutra* of the Indians, inhabitants of Sind and other countries that ride the elephant—I felt I was facing this thing alone. And even when I left the office, I found that the streets misunderstood me just as much—as if I were noticing scowling faces and farting children for the first time. It angered me that in every sphere of interest, a small mafia managed to turn a straight line into an exponential number of circles and bends. However straightforward your interest—to park your car, walk along the sidewalk, go up in the elevator, eat a plate of koshari, or buy a kilo of milk—there are people who will complicate your life.

As I slap greetings onto colleagues ("God bless you, Mr. Khalil; all best wishes for your pilgrimage, sir!"; "God's light on the newspaper, Mrs. Fakhriyya!"), I remember, for example, that now you only ever see women in sacks or with their hair covered. Some of them are exactly like whores, except that their hair is covered. Even the street girls who distribute boxes of tissues and bags of air freshener have put scarves over their heads. Things like this occur to me and I shudder with anger. And Yildiz's opinion that I broke my wife's heart seems to me closely connected with all this. What makes me doubt myself is that no one takes the same view of them as I. As if there were a tyrannosaurus rex on the street that I have to kill all by myself.

On reflection, during my move from Dog Alley to Dream Bridge, as I stayed in my cubicle and made that trip to the Khan of Secrets, I realized that if I had a free moment it was very possible that I would do something disastrous. My anger guaranteed it.

Order and cleanliness simply corrected what returning to my mother's had distorted. So order, cleanliness, and unwarranted comfort led to lucid serenity. I mean, gradually, during the first ten days after leaving the ruined marital nest in Dog Alley—despite the dream, and the ring, and moving the furniture on a camel with a howdah—I'd accustomed myself to being a normal human by my mother's standards and the standards of my colleagues, and this helped me cut down on thoughts that made me angry and concentrate on my work. What helped me even more (and this is important) was being in the right kind of mental state to confront the strange things that were coming my way, as if I knew... I'm telling you all these details so that you'll believe what happened to me in the middle of the following week, Rashid. If you don't believe me, I won't press you. But it happened. And if you hear me to the end, I think, you will believe me.

And, as I was telling you, what happened was that he expressed himself. The sultan.

An account of the appearance of the Muslims' Imam
You remember our colleague Ustaz Wahid al-Din, who appeared several times to Amgad Salah and eventually to me as well, in the Khan of Secrets? He was a weird character, as you know. So did I stay late in the office to amuse myself by watching him?

In the past, Abu al-Siyout, when I stayed to watch him—always in the absence of any woman—I would feel a curious pleasure come over me, immediately followed by a pang of conscience. Ustaz Wahid al-Din was like a human embodiment of the collapse of civil society in the third millennium. Was it right to turn him into a laughing stock?

I feel sorry for civil society, and it makes me sad to see people and cars bumbling in unwarranted panic twenty-four/seven. Even after midnight, after leaving him in front of the computer screen and going out (is he looking for porn? will he find it? and if he's in luck, will he sit there and play with himself?) I would discover that the traffic was still like bumper cars at the fair: round and round in too small a space until they bumped into each other—booom!—then, after pausing to quarrel, went round and round again.

Wahid al-Din was now exactly as he had been in those days, with his skullcap, summer outfit, and failing steps. He seldom appeared before ten in the evening, after the neon-lit rooms had emptied and the cleaning staff had scurried out from their corners, like piglets in a garbage heap at night. I knew that the security guard would come to check on me sooner or later to ask me when I would be leaving, so he'd know when he could lock the door. I knew he had to sit there all night and liked to exchange greetings with me.

But I was in no hurry as I sat working at the computer in my cubicle.

"Muslims," they tell you, "Christians and Jews; don't they know all are descended from the same line?" —Badi' Khayri

The night the caliph spoke to me I wasn't, in fact, working. I was playing the Lost Ark race and thinking about Fustuq. I'd met him by chance that morning in the office and he'd spoken to me briefly about an emotional crisis he was having with the girl he loved, Lilianne. She wasn't a Muslim, but an atheist from a Protestant family, and her father would never agree to their marriage. "Because, I mean, she's not from the same church—but believe me, that's not the problem," he said. He was silent for a moment, as he put his hand on my shoulder. "Tell me frankly, Mustafa, would you marry someone you'd already slept with?"

Wow, so that was it, that was the nub!

When he saw me open-mouthed, Fustuq quickly changed the subject, and started talking about work. And when I came to the story of Aldo, he said: "Because you don't pay attention to anyone, Shurba! Look, I've severed my relationship with him, believe me!" But I paid no attention to the details of their quarrel, for I was still shocked by his question, "Would you marry someone you'd already slept with?" What disturbed me even more was the fact that he'd started, for no good reason, by talking about sectarian crises.

Here you have someone whose father is a wealthy plumber, I thought (I don't know if I told you that my wife's grandfather on her mother's side had been a master plumber in Birkat al-Fil). A westernized young man whose father owns one of the most famous bathroom supply shops in the country, whose life was a byword for apartments and travel, books, and languages, most of his years spent between Boston and the British School in the Sea of Japan…

Why does he never miss a chance to describe the Copts as victims, hint that he is one of them—"Oh dear, Pistachio Boy!"—meaning that he too is oppressed? Why does he have to criticize any manifestation of backwardness among Muslims? Their conservative morality, their materialism, the father's absolute authority over his children, their ostentatious displays of faith... if he himself lives in exactly the same way, to the extent that he refuses to marry the girl he loves simply because she has given her body to him. The only difference is that he isn't a Muslim.

"Because you're a Muslim, you just aren't aware of it": suddenly, I recalled all our conversations of this sort. I would tell him about my experience with the Sunnis, for example, and his face would turn pale and he would say nothing, probably thinking, "Let alone what they'd do to a Christian." Several times, he'd frowned and said, "I'm scared."

Just when you thought he'd understood how serious the matter was, he'd start talking again from a viewpoint as narrow as the eye of a needle. Like a reel, he'd repeat that American fable about the descendants of the Pharaohs holding out under humiliation by barbarians from Nejd and Hijaz. They stop them from building their houses of worship, remove them from government posts, and even force them to change religions in special "conversion houses"—really, now? These barbarians do even more than that, actually: "You just don't know about it, believe me!"

In his American edition, Fustuq is my idea of hip-hop: black, or Hispanic. You can see him in sagging trousers, with a boom-box on his shoulder the size of a duffel bag, swaying slowly on the corner. And that must be why, when he talks about the tragedy of the Copts, he makes them sound like the blacks. But he often does this in his street Arab edition, with the hesitation of a man fearful that he may be trod on by a bearded bus, which makes it twice as funny. The persecuted minority and the slaves' revolt. You remind him of the old colonial edict "Divide and conquer" and he replies: Look around you, man. Not that I deny the existence of sectarian crises. After he's agreed with you about the need for secular citizenship, however, he'll then come back talking about a priest who can drive out devils, or write pious verses about the Virgin Mary.

In the middle of talking about liberalism, freedom of religion, and the need for a secular regime, you'll find that he's started praising the bravery of Deacon Zakariyya Butrus, who's lived abroad forever—only to discover, in time, that this Deacon Zakariyya Butrus was in fact expelled from the Coptic Church, and that all he ever does is appear on TV, slander the Qur'an, insult the Prophet Muhammad, and attack the religion of terrorism, as he calls Islam. It's not that Fustuq is defending secularism, then. It's just that Christianity should be the sole religion.

All this madness and the world's en rose, I was thinking that evening (I'd lost the Lost Ark race for the third time because the cleaner was determined to scrub my desk at the critical moment), exactly like my wife's lunacy: a confounded confusion of allegiances.

And I concluded that Fustuq's liberalism was nothing but cunning, usury, evil, slyness, and deceit. Even Fascism was kinder than a lie codified for the advantage of... what percentage of mankind? To claim that you're suppressed in order to express racist sentiments. It's no better than "God said" (as if God spoke to them alone, sons of a whore!), and that evening with every moment that passed I lost more sympathy for Fustuq.

Note

Neoliberalism angers me more than anything else. In practical terms, neoliberalism means that life is a supermarket. It's what you buy from the supermarket that defines your identity. And the more your choices increase—a thousand types of orange juice, for example, or seventy different sizes of aspirin packet—the more the world flourishes and the possibilities for fulfillment multiply. Would you like your milk 1% or 1.5% fat, or fat-free? Which brand of dark Irish cheddar do you prefer?

So you break your head in a daily job that kills any rebellious instinct in you until you yourself turn into a commodity. Your time, your concentration, your enthusiasm. A job whose only purpose is to increase the supermarket's size.

Recapitulation

By the time the security guard blocked the door and said "Good evening, Darsh!" I'd remembered how depressed I'd become after my conversation with Fustuq in the corridor that day. And as I responded to him I was on the point of gathering up my things and leaving when I heard footsteps in the corridor outside.

The security guard turned (I am always struck by the body-building of the corporation's security men, especially their puffed-up chests and their attention to their moustaches, as though the moustaches were warhorses and they the cavalry) and I could see the corridor clearly again. In that time I noticed a striped skullcap instead of the usual spotted one. That's how I was certain that Wahid al-Din had arrived.

"Hello, sir!" I said to the security man. I left my things in their place to stand up to shake his hand. I knew that it was a feeble excuse for indulging in an old touch of humor, but I had persuaded myself that I needed to make sure Wahid al-Din really had changed his skullcap.

I'm telling you the truth, Rashid, when I say I was also afraid. After the Khan of Secrets I no longer trusted Wahid al-Din, especially now that I'd noticed I no longer laughed at him as I used to in the past. But my desire to laugh again overcame the memory of that Monday. I was almost daring myself to greet him and ask where he bought his skullcaps.

What happened was that I had to urinate. The security man went away shaking his head in the direction of Wahid al-Din and winking at me. When I came back from the restroom, the mad fiqi was sitting cross-legged behind my desk in the cubicle. I was stunned and shouted at him, "You here, Wahid?"

But instead of blushing and stammering or saying to me "Wahid al-Din, please!", as he usually did when someone shouted at him, he smiled with a frightening calm and motioned with his head for me to sit down.

(I could almost hear "Sit down," pronounced with a foreign accent.)

I pretended to be sarcastic as I slumped down on the chair opposite. "Present and correct, sir!" I said.

It was as if I were persuading myself that there was nothing new, that the fiqi had suffered a short moment of insanity, that was all. Although I was still afraid and knew that something was up, I took a cigarette out of the packet and composed myself as I looked him in the eye. As if I were challenging him, or were afraid that he might be someone else. Someone else? Exactly. This was certainly the reason for my fear. Finally, I lit my cigarette as he put his hand in his waistcoat pocket to take out… glasses, the same glasses as I'd seen him wearing that evening in the Khan of Secrets. Can you believe it?

I was still playing it cool: "What's your news, Ustaz Wahid al-Din?"

An incident

The transformation began with the first breath, as he held the glasses in his hand to put them to his eyes. Fuck, fuck, fuck! The strangest thing I've seen in my life, no exaggeration: this transformation from our colleague Wahid al-Din, the faqih, to the person I'd seen pushing the shopping cart in the Khan of Secrets.

Sometimes in the course of a thriller, a character's appearance will change, whether through a liquid mask or by a fast and frightening cosmetic operation. I seem to recall a scene much like what was now happening with my colleague, at least in terms of speed. The secret-service agent is sitting in front of the mirror with something like dough in his hand. On his hair there are paints and powders, and sharp and shining metal contraptions lie about, in keeping with the general suspense. Then in a single movement said agent straightens up and slaps the dough on his face, quick as a flash. You watch in the mirror as he becomes someone else. Just like that. In just one moment, the moment he put his spectacles to his eyes, his beard seemed to become a little heavier, and the touch of green was gone from it. The only difference was that his features hadn't really changed. Just a slight relaxation in some of the tiniest face muscles, and a tautness in others. A marginal rise in the level of the shoulder. A change in the look of the eye.

But (and this is the frightening part) it really was another person. I had no doubt at all that I was sitting in front of someone different from my colleague, although I knew that he was so like him that anyone who hadn't seen the transformation for himself wouldn't be able to notice the difference. What frightens me now is the realization that I was the only person to have had the experience.

A blow ahbarat *his skin, that is "left a mark" on it, and his skin* hubira *if signs of the wounds remain after it has healed...* —*Lisan al-'Arab, under* hibr, *"ink"*

If the security man had come back and seen us sitting together in the cubicle, he wouldn't have believed that the person with me was someone other than the fiqi Wahid al-Din. That night, as I recorded what this person said to me— the person who, it would clearly emerge, was the Imam of all Muslims—my face looked like a deep wound in the paper of a notebook, scared and shouting.

Of course, I still didn't acknowledge what was happening, despite the fact that I knew in my heart—I knew that our colleague the faqih Wahid al-Din had turned into another person who would turn out to be the last of the Ottoman sultans—I just stopped pretending to ignore him and remained silent. The person sitting in front of me had so far also been silent. We were like this for a period considerably longer than necessary, he looking straight at me and I staring at the floor. Until I realized that I was shaking, so I coughed.

From then on, this moment (I have no idea how long it lasted) was transformed in my head into one of those dreamlike states that have visited me ever since I left Dog Alley, like the journey between my mother's planet and that of my father's books in Dream Bridge, or the vision I had of Plane Yard before acquiring the ring in the Khan of Secrets.

I mean: I coughed, and was ready, when the shaking had gone, to confront the truth that I could only acknowledge completely in a dreamlike state. What was new, as I raised my eyes slowly from the floor, was the sudden certainty that, since the moment he had put on his glasses, the actions of this person sitting in front of me had been entirely premeditated.

He knew everything that was happening to me and wanted to leave me like this until I weakened and became putty in his hands. It wasn't clear what he would do to me once I was putty. What did he want from me on this dark night?

"All this has come from Wahid al-Din, the son of the dog's religion!" I was thinking.

I was forced to remind myself of the muddle I was in. This wasn't Wahid al-Din, but his miraculous double who'd made me stop in the Khan of Secrets, the night I bought the ring, when my friendship with Amgad Salah finished in an unexpected way. The remarkable thing, in retrospect, is that as much as I was afraid, I felt—instead of the anger that might be expected to accompany the feeling that you are the victim of a conspiracy, or that someone is making a fool of you and sapping your nerves (however unknown, exciting, and unusual this person may be)—instead of all this, I actually felt a bubbling pleasure like that I recalled feeling on the day I finally left Dog Alley. A pleasurable danger meant the start of a journey, the journey, the exemplar of the mystical departure that I had never believed in until I came back here from Dog Alley via Dream Bridge. Fuck, fuck, fuck! Even so, this second idea seemed to encourage me.

My fear was increasing, and with it my pleasure, but I was ready for the confrontation.

Come on, then!

I stretched my back and looked the double in his eye as I took a deep breath. Perhaps he had prepared himself for me. The ghost of a smile seemed to play on his lips as I looked into his eye, which was cupped like a date behind his glasses:

a confident smile with something paternal about it. Paternal? God knows, there was a compassion and a concern like those that in dreams I look for in my father's eyes. Impossible that this should have any connection with the faqih Wahid. I didn't understand why I was compelled to repeat that to myself.

The cigarette was completely finished. I took a quick breath after I'd stubbed it out between my feet, without taking my gaze from him even for a nano-second. The fear that gives joy reached a new peak when I observed that in the minute that had passed, a second change had come over his face, a change that suited the paternal state, as well as (by the same logic) that of the secret-service agent in the film.

He had aged, as if he'd become twenty years older in a single minute, with all the characteristics of an old man. Once again, I tell you, the change happened in a hidden way, extremely fast and frightening, and it could be reversed, as I would discover with alarm, with the same facility: when the old man became middle-aged again, the muscles of his face would revert to their normal combination of relaxation and contraction. Then the shoulders would drop marginally to their original level, just as if nothing had happened, and hey presto! The tremor returned as I looked for an ashtray while, at the same moment, extinguishing my cigarette on the ground.

Chapter containing the rest of the incident

Like someone under hypnosis or possessed by a devil (no, no, someone bitten by a zombie!) I found myself turning toward the window. Between religious mutterings—"Praise be to the Lord of the worlds," I said, without realizing that I was imitating the young sultan of the previous Monday's dream, "There is no God but You, praise be to You, I have been among the evildoers," I continued—I raised both my arms in a single dramatic movement without turning my face from the window, then pointed to the double with both hands and screamed: "No, no! You are not Wahid al-Din, you are no way Wahid al-Din at all!"

When he remained silent—as I turned around it seemed to me that the smile on his face had become broader, and the care and compassion in his eyes had intensified—I understood that my moment of weakness had arrived and that I was a piece of dough. I would find out, finally, what the devil who had possessed me would do with me.

"Yes," he said, and this time his voice came out loud and clear, "we are Mehmet Vahdettin Khan. Sit down, Mustafa Efendi Çorbacı!" Khan? For a moment I thought of asking him whether he was from Pakistan or something. But his manner made me keep silent and listen to his words. "We are highly appreciative of your gullibility and amazement at our appearance," he continued. "By the felicities of the Lord of Truth we will provide you with all explanations. First, tell us, Mustafa Efendi, what is the source of your annoyance with this puppet who is not of our religion?"

Although I was used to the eloquence our colleague the faqih exhibited in Aldo's company, I immediately observed that this was eloquence of a different order. But still, how did he know that I was thinking of Fustuq?

Despite my confusion and delight in danger, I observed several details of his speech that would be confirmed in the following hour. There was a clearly articulated "d" before every soft "g," for example. Those letters that are difficult for foreigners—Hā', 'ayn, and qāf (he pronounced his qāfs, unlike ordinary Egyptians)—were articulated softly, and the "w" turned, fully or partially, into a "v" (like a Persian "w"). There was a French-like influence on the letters of prolongation and the vowels.

When he said *Wahid al-Din*, especially when he was absorbed in what he was saying, it sounded like *Vahdettin*.

The main thing was that I sat down as he told me to without understanding a thing, with more than one sarcastic comment on the tip of my tongue that I did not articulate. I had hardly digested what he was saying when I noticed that he also had a tendency to leave out the definite article on numerous occasions, and a tendency to substitute a "z" for a "*dād*" in some words, and in others to substitute a "d" for an emphatic "t." All of a sudden I recalled the faulty European pronunciation that I'd heard in the dream. The religious mumblings resounded round my head, the climax of the danger safely passed.

I don't know how to describe to you the state I was now in.

Something like contentment, but mixed with a fiery curiosity. Whenever I was about to ask a question, though, the response came of its own accord. That night I recorded five things said to me by the Padishah (as I learned to call the last of the Muslim sultans, that is, the last reigning caliph), but until I drew my face on my return home I didn't notice how deeply the incident had gripped me while it was taking place, and how shaken I'd been at the appearance of our Master the Sultan… in particular, when I realized that he'd started to talk about Fustuq. I was stunned that he knew what I was thinking without my telling him.

At first I was nervous. I didn't know in what sort of Arabic I should reply, though I did have the idea (the last joke of the night) that I should recite from the Qur'an and follow it with "heh"!

What actually happened was that I nodded my head and felt a smile of satisfaction divide my face in two. I clenched my fingers in the shape of a rose that had yet to open, and drew them downward beneath the Padishah's face. As though I had shed a tear? What I do remember is that I lit another cigarette then started talking. I spoke so warmly and openheartedly that I was surprised at myself and thought: do you need a ghost to open your heart? Before I knew that he was the Padishah I had told the Padishah everything.

—That I was drunk, lost like a hemp plant amidst a field of corn;

—That after I decided to divorce my wife, I no longer knew why I'd married her;

—That I'd suddenly noticed that my contact with other people had been restricted to the economics newspaper I worked for;

—That I'd been having strange dreams (I didn't relate the vision to him, just said "strange dreams"), and analyzing my colleagues, who are the same as my friends, in particular Amgad Salah, and the puppet whose history has already been given ("How did you know that I was thinking of him at that moment?");

—That I feel, in short, that my life no longer has any meaning and that nothing motivates me except hatred of others;

—And that I'm tired and confused, Master (what made me call him "Master"?).

The Padishah sighed, paternal compassion welling from his eyes, exactly like my father when he would caress me in a dream. So I didn't believe it when he stood up, moved toward me, and patted my head tenderly—his dignity was apparent in his walk, even in the narrow area of the cubicle—and after he'd turned his back on me and looked out the window, he quickly turned his shoulder as though to avoid a blow, and said:

"Our son, Mustafa Efendi Çorbacı." It was as though the prick of the sword handle that had preceded my greeting the young sultan in the dream was returning with the movement of his shoulder. From where I was, I drew his hand toward me and bent to kiss it as I sat there. He was exactly like the young sultan. He didn't pull his hand back, resist, say "I seek refuge with God!" or even turn around completely. He just looked at me and continued to caress me without moving. When he turned away from me toward the window, he left his hand on my head for a moment, "For the scene of our subjects' circumstances to be so degraded arouses our great sorrow." (He pronounced the emphatic "h" in *huzn* like an ordinary "h." Every "u" vowel seemed to be preceded by a "y" and pronounced without lengthening.) "And when the images of decadence were revealed to the eye of your intelligence in the place of this diwan" (here he gave a mocking laugh, as his right hand traced a circle around the corners of the cubicle, as he pointed through the window with the tip of his beard to the roofs of Bulaq Abu al-'Ila), "We have seen fit by the fortunes of His all-knowing, all-powerful grace, to entrust to you the initiation of our intent for the land of Egypt and to plant the might of eternal beliefs in the manner of our illustrious ancestors."

"What was that you said, Usta?"

An account of the five things that the caliph said

I nodded. For some unknown reason, Abu al-Siyout, a sense of peace had descended on me, despite how much I had been shaking. All my confusion came out in the "What was that you said, Usta?" that I said to myself (despite the fact that this irreverent form of address, "Usta," used for blue-collar workers and such, would actually turn out to be a perfectly respectable title in Ottoman Turkish); as soon as I'd said it, I felt more relaxed than ever. As though, once I'd established the identity of the Padishah (how had this word taken root in my brain?), I relaxed and was no longer afraid of the ghost that had his sights on me. Apparently, I was still hypnotized. I didn't realize that the smile on my face was still getting wider as I nodded again and again at what was being said to me.

By nightfall, I wouldn't have retained the complete text of what he said, so as quickly as I could (having established the identity of the fiqi's double), I recorded his meaning in his own words. Even now, as I tell you who he is, I am shaking.

The fiqi's double, so it was clear to me, was none other than the Commander of the Faithful and the Guardian of the Holy Places—Hazreti Sultan Mehmet Vahdettin, to be precise—Owner of Blessings, Refuge of the World, the shadow of God on earth—the thirty-sixth and last sultan of the Sublime Ottoman State and the twenty-fifth caliph of the House of Osman (the last to rule Muslims on earth), who was born in 1861, the same year that his father, Sultan Abdülmecid I, the son of Mahmud II, died of consumption, and who himself died in exile in Italy in mid May 1926.

That's what I was to discover during the research I embarked on in the succeeding days, with the aim of plugging the historical gaps in my knowledge of what was happening to me: the Commander of the Faithful resurrected in the guise of his namesake, with the crooked back and a green, sprouting beard.

As I was saying, I recorded these five things, in a quick and condensed form, as if they were the record of the proceedings of an editorial meeting. I put them under the heading "*Khatt Humayun*," as I had been taught to describe the sayings of the "Osmanli" Sultan, as he pronounced it—not saying "Osmani" as we do. To each of them I attached a miniature drawing by way of illustration, so that they would stay clear before me however many twists of fate or time might elapse. Now, as the airplane takes off, the miniatures seem clearer in my head than any words, as if the notebook were empty of everything except for these symbols, the symbols of the facts on which my tale is constructed.

When I recall them, I cannot believe that they really mean what they do.

First:

The dream you had last Monday night was an integrated inner representation of the conquest of Constantinople on the twentieth of Jumada al-Awwal AH 857 by our great ancestor, His Highness Mehmet II, known as Mehmet the Conqueror (may God have mercy on him). This was the good news that the Honorable Prophet prophesied in his hadith: "Let Constantinople be conquered, for its emir is the best of emirs, and that army is the best of armies!" The blessings and peace of God be upon him who spoke the truth! The soldiers that you saw in their blue uniforms with long head coverings and flowing white cloths were the janissaries, and the awe-inspiring horsemen were the sultan's sipahis.

The gravest incident on the night that Constantinople was captured, as you saw, was the taking of the cathedral of Hagia Sophia and its transformation into the mosque of Ayasofya, when Mehmet the Conqueror prostrated himself before the one God there on the first Friday following his entry into the city. This was followed by the move of the state capital from Edirne to the "Red Apple," the pearl of Devlet-i Ebed Müddet or the Eternally Lasting State, of the whole world, and perhaps even of the whole of Creation.

By this means, the word of God conquered the West before the East, and the "Apple" became our property, Mustafa Efendi, and that of all Muslims. When Mehmet the Conqueror singled you out for a handshake, that was a sign of our coming. For you, together with six others from different provinces of the Sublime State, you have been charged by us with reviving the nation and religion of Islam.

Second:

Our Rumi calendar was abolished in 1917, but this year would be 1430, not 2007. In either event today's date, April 9, corresponds to the twenty-first of Rabi' al-Awwal of the year 1428 after the noble *hijra*, which is the 505th anniversary of the execution of Tuman Bey, the last of the Mamluk Sultans, who were the patrons of the 'Abbasids in Egypt, on the twenty-first of Rabi' al-Awwal in the year 923.

I believe you also dreamed of that, even though you were awake in your mother's house at the time, and read the account of the event by the Circassian outsider, Muhammad ibn Ahmad al-Hanafi, in that book of his which is famous in Egypt:

And with the death of 'Ali [ibn Abi Talib] was completed the period of the caliphate that the Prophet (may God bless him and grant him peace) had specified: "The caliphate after me shall be thirty years, then it shall be a vicious kingdom." —al-Jabarti

In this connection, I should note that today is also the anniversary of the date on which our family really assumed the caliphate, because on the day he left Cairo to return to Constantinople, Ghazi Yavuz Selim I took with him Muhammad al-Mutawakkil 'ala Allah, the last of the 'Abbasid dynasty who had lived under the protection of the Mamluk Sultans in Egypt, since the fall of Baghdad at the hands of Hulagu Khan in AH 656 (the title Ghazi is linked with the names of emirs and sultans who led armies in person, while Yavuz includes among its meanings determination and sullenness), knowing that Ghazi Osman Bey was born in the same year that Baghdad fell. Aren't you struck by the fact that Baghdad fell for a second time exactly five years before we appeared to you?

As for the conditions for holding this position, they are four: knowledge, justice, competence, and soundness of body and mind... there is a difference of opinion regarding a fifth condition, namely Qurayshi lineage. —Ibn Khaldun

In Constantinople, shortly before his sudden death, Yavuz Selim received from al-Mutawakkil 'ala Allah the reins of the caliphate and (from the Sharif of the Hijaz, on his behalf) the noble relics of the Prophet: banner, sword, and cloak; he became Khādim al-Haramayn al-Sharīfayn (or the Servant of Mecca and Medina), accepting the keys to the Kaaba and the Prophet's sanctuary, and from that day the Sultan of the Osmanlis became King of the Two Lands, Ruler of the Two Seas, Breaker of the Two Armies, and Servant of the Two Sanctuaries. Or so they taught us, Mustafa Efendi. The result was that he became Commander of the Faithful and the Caliph of the Prophet of God (peace be upon him and his family and companions), not only in name as the 'Abbasids had been in Egypt, but in fact as well as name. For the first time since the star of the 'Abbasids had risen in the House of Islam, temporal power was united with spiritual power.

The incorporation of the province into the state at the hands of Selim (may God forgive him) made the rule of his son, Kanunî Suleiman the Lawgiver—the tenth Ottoman sultan whose reputation is well known in Europe (ten being a blessed number, Mustafa Efendi)—a fulfillment of God's words "To God belong East and West" (God's words are true). And perhaps it was God's wisdom that made Selim harsh and bloodthirsty, as he is known to have been, since if he hadn't killed his father, brothers, and sons, the way would not have opened before the most fitting candidate for the sultanate and caliphate, Suleiman the Lawgiver, the Poet Muhibbi, as he used to sign the verses that he sent to his wife, Hürrem.

It was Suleiman the Lawgiver who retook Hungary and Baghdad, spread good, extended justice and fairness throughout the State, and presided over its most glorious age.

We also decided to tell you about ourselves today to bless the memory of the five hundred and fifth anniversary. The number produced by this date in the science of hidden numbers is ten, which in turn equals a simple "one," the highest degree of blessedness. Do you not know how lucky you are, Mustafa Efendi Çorbacı?

Third:

The engraving on the ring on your finger is nothing but our own tughra (the "tuğra," or "tughra," is the Osmanli Sultan's seal that you will find on every imperial decree, as well as on walls, ceilings, and printed material in all sorts of places). The text reads: "Muhammad Wahid al-Din Khan ibn 'Abd al-Majid al-Muzaffar Da'iman (ever-victorious)." The tughra is a talisman that looks beautiful, but hides its meaning from everyone, except for those with penetrating insight, as the curves and directions of the lines are changed to suit the composition.

Let us explain to you how it is composed with pen on paper, for we ourselves have learned something of the art of calligraphy in *ta'liq* style from the calligraphers of the Dolmabahçe Palace. My father, Abdülmecid Khan, was a skilled calligrapher who gained his diploma from Mehmet Tahir Efendi, may God forgive them both. (Here, I am attaching to my notebook the piece of paper on which he made all this clear to me):

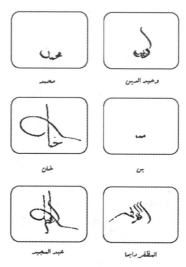

And now that you have ascertained that you are walking on the earth with my name on your finger, here is my photograph, in case you still have any doubt in your heart.

(I immediately recognized the old Ilford paper and the black-and-white tinting technique. After he had given it to me, I felt I had a treasure in my hand, not just because it was a picture of my Master, but also because it was a piece of photographic history. I put it carefully between two sheets without using any adhesive material.)

Fourth:

Eight years ago, we offered the noble commission that we have now resolved to entrust to you, to your colleague, the crazy policeman Amgad Efendi 'Abd al-Galil. When he failed to endorse it, we abandoned him for you. Among the reasons for our optimism was your name, which you inherited from ancestors you no longer know. You bear the name Çorbacı, that is the man that carries the pot of soup to the soldiers under his command. The Çorbacı was equivalent to a Bimbashi, or lieutenant colonel, in the rankings of the janissary officers, who are known to you—as a result of the way the word is written in Turkish, "Yekcheri" (that's how he wrote it for me)—as *Inkishariyya*. Similarly, the word Bimbashi itself, Mustafa Efendi, you pronounce it "Bikbashi," don't you?

The janissaries were the first regular army in the history of the whole of Europe, would you believe it? They were the sons of Balkan and Caucasian Christians, who, after converting to Islam, were loyal to the sultan alone. As they were not free men but slaves of the sultan—they were later called kapıkulu or "servants of the Porte"—they were not permitted at first to let their beards grow. And they were blessed by Hajji Bektash Wali (may God be pleased with him) and took from him the symbol of the Bektashi order with the eight stars, which they engraved on their rectangular helmets. They started to be known in their ranks by the tasks they attended to in addition to assuming the responsibilities of battle. So there was a *wakilkharaj* and an *odabashi* (referring to the "land tax" called *kharaj* and the "room" or *oda*, as I believe you call it here in Egypt, even though it is not so called in standard Arabic). Çorbacı itself equals the overseer of a thousand in the Mamluk rank system, because he was responsible for a battalion of a thousand soldiers.

The janissaries were both the good and the bad fortune of the State, Mustafa Efendi, until they were discontinued by my grandfather, Mahmud Khan II (may God have mercy on him), just before the period of the Tanzimat reforms that my father initiated. Corruption had become rife among them, and chaos swept through their ranks. The Egyptian forces under the command of the Albanian Muhammad 'Ali and his son Ibrahim would have defeated the armies of the State, had it not been for the intervention of Britain and Austria. You should know, Mustafa Efendi, that Muhammad 'Ali, who appeared to have seceded, actually planted unshakeable Ottoman values in the soil of your country; and that the origin of his good fortune was also the janissaries, as he entered the service of the Çorbacı of the town of Voula, which lies within the present borders of the Hellenic Republic, after the death of his uncle Tusun, who had raised him on his being orphaned. The fact that you bear this name, even though you and a large number of previous generations have forgotten the fact, is an indication that you are a genuine Osmanli.

The divine breath that gave me freedom of movement refused to allow me to divulge my paths between the heavenly dimensions, where I sing His praises while awaiting the great gathering, and the earth and its water holes. You will see me or my double in the form of a student of the religious sciences, your poor colleague Wahid al-Din Marzuq al-Qurani. (Believe it or not, this was the first time I had heard the name of Ustaz Wahid al-Din in full.) But you must know that I shall not return to you after tonight, despite the fact that when I offered the noble commission to Amgad Efendi, I met with him a number of times over a period of three months.

For there are difficult and ever-changing conditions for traveling to the lower places. But by speaking to you tonight I shall have fulfilled my objective.

I tell you: Amgad Efendi did not deliberately lie, but he only told the truth in one of the things he said to you. There really is a tightly knit conspiracy, which he called the "Organization"—a conspiracy that is wider and deeper than the boundaries of your understanding (you, the inhabitants of the lower places, that is), though the people of the divine dimensions like myself, by virtue of their powers and the will of the All-Merciful One, can appreciate it. It is like a turning circle, my son, which has no beginning and no end. Suffice it to say that, should it be fulfilled, the task we have come to entrust to you, however easy or trivial it may seem, will disrupt that circle, which will then have a beginning, allowing the slave of God who seeks the truth the ability to confront it. I will leave it to you to work on explaining the conspiracy within the limits of your understanding and to link it with your life and your constant desire to travel—this is a part of your mission I suspect you actually started before my visit—and will give you (apart from clarifying that the conspiracy is not confined to this paper or the journalists working on it), no more than two pieces of information.

The first of these is that the Christian puppet Michel Samar Fustuq, your wife (he gave her name in full at this point, adding the word "Hanim" after the first of the three parts), and of course Amgad Efendi 'Abd al-Galil, are all fundamental parts of its fabric.

The second is that in your life, and in the crisis that you complain of, there lies a perfect symbol of aspects of the conspiracy itself. As if these things were a microcosm of the theater of history, as if your behavior and choices were a means to influence historical events.

I am telling you, without any illustration or support, that Amgad Efendi's submission to the primitive ideas of the Najdi heretic Muhammad ibn 'Abd al-Wahhab is no different in its essence from the profligacy of the Osmanli apostate Mustafa

Kemal, whom some of the sultan's people regarded as a father
after they had again become barbarians in the Turkmen legions,
and agreed to use Latin letters and European headgear in place
of the alphabet of revelation, the fez of Oriental modernity,
and the turban of our ancestors. You have no doubt heard the
expression "Atatürk," Mustafa Efendi. Doesn't it prick your
heart that this ignorant Fascist should be a father, "Ata"? But
there is no difference—and this is the second piece of information
that concerns you—between what you have started to call the
Salafiyya (God forbid that the real Salaf or Predecessors should
be linked with such apostasy, stupidity, and bloodshed) and the
secularism of that despicable liar Mustafa Kemal.

Fifth (the commission):

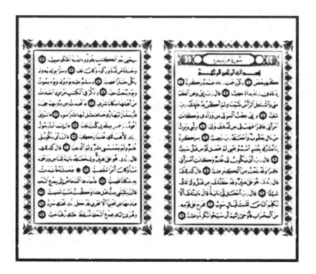

In that "thing" that they split off from the rest of the State
and called, arbitrarily, a republic, they still describe me as a
traitor. I, who was ready to renounce everything in exchange
for salvation and the fulfillment of my father's dream of a
cohesive union of people and communities within the domain
of the sultan.

I am confident that in the next three days you will read
about, and fully acquaint yourself with, the details of the

collapse and fall, and learn the real facts of the part that I and my treacherous friend Mustafa Kemal played in them. So I will not burden either myself or you by describing the development of events from the outbreak of the Great War, through my taking up the sword in the mausoleum of Abu Ayyub al-Ansari (may God be pleased with him) three months after the first battle (like my father Abdülmecid but unlike my brother Abdülhamid II, I girded myself only with the sword of the Commander of the Faithful, 'Umar, and did not carry the sword of Ghazi Osman, which would have been an indication of the desire to fight), until I left the country on board a British ship (the Bosphorus was closed, Mustafa Efendi, so there was no way to leave the country except on a British ship), which happened on the eve of the secession of the new "Father of the Turkmen" in Ankara in Asia Minor, Constantinople having already been occupied by the allies on November 17, 1922.

I will not recite the facts to you; leave it to the historians to tell you the extent of my misery and piety. Suffice it to say that when death came to me four years or a little less later in San Remo, I could not afford the funeral service so I remained unburied until my son-in-law, 'Umar Faruq Efendi, the husband of Sabiha Sultan, came (may God bless their place of rest), bringing with him money and a winding sheet. 'Umar was the son of my cousin, Abdülmecid ibn Abdülaziz I (may God have mercy on him). Mustafa Kemal left my cousin as nominal caliph for two years after my departure, having also made me powerless as caliph in October.

I assumed power from my late brother Mehmed Reshad, who was a Mevlevi dervish, distracted from matters of war and conflict by his devotions. He was the last of the Ottoman sultans to compose Persian poetry, Mustafa Efendi—which put me, the frugal old man, in a difficult position from which it was impossible to escape.

This was less than three months before the shameful defeat of the Axis Powers. However, as soon as the Allies occupied our country, I started to bless the resistance, for I utterly rejected the Treaty of Sèvres which the Unionists and the Young Turks had signed in defiance of my wishes. These people had revolted against my brother Abdülmecid, deposed him in 1909, and committed the most awful atrocities on the non-Muslim peoples of the empire. When I sent Mustafa Kemal to Anatolia on the pretext of dissolving the remnants of our armies there and disarming them as the treaty required, I gave him a secret undertaking to join ranks and revive hope and preparedness...

Which was what he and his republican successors held against me.

His descendants and sons of the "Father" today call me the Traitor Sultan, just as Ghazi Abdülhamid, the unifier of the Muslims and reviver of the hope of continuity in the State, was called the "Red Sultan," in reference to his alleged bloodthirstiness, though he never signed more than two decrees of execution in the thirty-three years of his reign.

I am not hurt by their lies so much as by the single act of treachery that I actually did commit, and which it later appeared was the hidden reason for what befell my people. When I left, leaving even the sultan's servant in the palace, I had in my possession, amongst the little that I took to the island of Malta where the ship carried me, an envelope of Italian leather in which were seven small pieces of calfskin parchment bearing the complete sura of Mary in the most perfect Arabic Qur'anic calligraphy.

The choice of the sura of Mary rather than any other seemed to be a way of indicating the generosity of the State throughout its history and its openness to Jews and Christians and even secularists. It reminded us that Suleiman the Lawgiver, the tenth Ottoman Sultan (ten equaling one plus nothing, Mustafa Efendi, again: the good tidings of the Unique One), was not only Sultan of Egypt and Shah of Iraq, but was also Caesar of Byzantium. The State, like the message sent down to mankind as a whole, was a focal point for a variety of peoples, just as Constantinople was, while the civilization of the imperialist West was for the Europeans alone, and for the Christians to the exclusion of the Jews.

That empty republic that Mustafa Kemal detached like a tail severed from a puppy in the dog factory founded by Europeans—what do you think of it? The republic hated itself from the very first moment, for it tried to make a clean break—against the wishes of the people—with its alphabetic and ideological heritage, and the spirit of its glorious identity. It was said that the enlightening Qur'an was revealed in Mecca but recited in Cairo and inscribed in Istanbul. The contents of this envelope were a definitive indication of the ability of the calligraphers of our State.

The opening parchment was written in *ta'liq* and *nasta'liq* script, and each of the remaining sheets in one of the six styles invented by Yaqut, the calligrapher of the caliph al-Musta'sim—the last of the 'Abbasid caliphs to be in charge of the Islamic state that would be crushed by the horses of Hulagu Khan: *thuluth, naskh,* and *muhaqqaq,* followed by *rayhani, ruq'a,* and *tawqi'.*

Its Sultan, Ikhtiyar al-Din Orhan Bey, the son of the Sultan 'Uthman Jawq... was the greatest king of the Turkmens, with the most wealth and territory. —Ibn Battuta

When you read the history of the Sublime State, you will know that each Osmanli sultan since Ghazi Orhan Bey had to learn a manual trade as part of his upbringing. My father's skill, as I have mentioned, was calligraphy. I was only a few months old on the eve of his death, but he left this envelope to me alone (rather than any of my brothers), telling me that it was the most brilliant thing he had accomplished in this field.

It was a rainy day and the sky was overcast. The English policemen took us in two cars to the Red Cross, after concealing their badges so that it couldn't be said they were raiding the supplies of the wounded and injured. But during the journey to Malta—less than one day, Mustafa Efendi—I had lost the envelope. How? I don't know.

This is the sole piece of treachery I have actually committed, and your task is to correct its long-term results.

(At this point, he stretched out his hand in a greeting of peace, and pressed my hand firmly, as he continued:)

"We, Vahdettin Khan, entrust you, Mustafa Çorbacı, with the task of finding one of the seven lost parchments of the sura of Mary. It will be for six other representatives of the provinces of the State to find the six others, not necessarily within the confines of their own region, for the parchments have been dispersed throughout the world without order or logic since we lost them on the way to Malta, and it was not ordained for us to have the office of caliph in the Hijaz. You must know, Mustafa Efendi, that finding the lost sura of Mary and reassembling its scattered leaves is the first step toward frustrating the universal conspiracy that is being carried out against the Muslims."

(The caliph let go of my hand again and seemed to relax.) "I don't know where I lost the sura of Mary, nor where the parchment might be after all these years. But I will tell you some riddles that may help you reach the start of the road.

"I swear to you that I do not know the solution to these riddles except literally, but the True One (may he be exalted and glorified) revealed them to me in a dream. Do you know the dreams of the dead, Mustafa Efendi? The dead also dream, and sometimes their dreams convey secrets to them. Here are the riddles: the first clue that will lead you to your goal you will find through a woman: a woman you know in the Biblical sense, Mustafa Efendi" (he laughed in a clearly paternal way). "God keep both us and you from sin. This woman was named after the palace to which my brother Ghazi Abdülhamid Khan retired, isolating himself before they deposed him. It is a Turkish word meaning, in Arabic, *najma*, or 'star.'

"Did you hear everything I said to you, Mustafa Efendi? Is it fixed in your head?"

(And before I could reply): "I hope so!"

•   •   •   •   •

Before the caliph sat up straight for the last time, and the change that had come over him at first was reversed, so that he again became our colleague, the fiqi Wahid al-Din, he spent an hour telling me about his father, his uncle, and his brothers (the suspicious death of Abdülaziz, the isolation of Murad V in the Çırağan Sarayı Palace after 'Abd al-Hamid had assumed power from him, and how Abdülhamid never stopped smoking), about his own love for Oriental and Western music, the compositions he had written for the piano, his life, and his cousin, Abdülmecid ibn Abdülaziz. He also told me the story of his friendship with Mustafa Kemal, how Atatürk had promoted Turkish nationalism (despite being born in Greece), destroying the efforts of Abdülmecid to put an end to sedition and ethnic strife for the sake of a state in which Turk was not superior to Arab except through deed or civilization, and his personal anguish in the face of all this.

Before I wrote an account of all he told me that night, I transcribed what of his speech I could still recall.

Chapter, being the partial text of the caliph's words

"We have directed to your trust the endeavor of finding the lost parchment, on the basis of the tested loyalty that you possess, and your knowledge of conditions of our responsibilities in the land of Egypt. We have great faith in the glad tidings attached to your name as being a bearer of the reasons for a glorious victory at the hands of the soldiers of Egypt, the strongest on earth. Our most extensive hopes are placed in Him..."

"Efendi is your title, our dear son Mustafa, but you are now more like the Grand Vizier—our minister and companion, Your Excellency Mustafa Pasha Çorbacı, isn't that sweeter to the ears that will be pleased by its tones than your present title...?"

"The blessing of social advancement and civilized regimes is endowed through the virtue of intellectual striving in the eternal, permitted orders. The first cause thereof is the pursuit of knowledge and advice, forging a harmony between the ranks of the umma and those under its protection outside the true community of believers, and pursuing the most important advancements and the greatest toils without fear or distraction..."

"If we examine carefully the weakness of Islamic power since the destruction of the Eternal State and the disappearance of blessed events, the reasons therefor can be summed up in the umma's lack of culture and its severance from the branches of knowledge belonging to non-Muslims. We have already mentioned to you, Mustafa Efendi, the saying of the True One, 'To God belong East and West' (God's words are true). If anyone should head in one direction and ignore the other, he removes the bases for our success and weakens the foundations of our Islamic nation's power, and his reward shall be an evil path..."

"The marriage of East and West is like your anticipated divorce, Mustafa. There is no alternative to implementing it, even though it be nothing but the most hateful historical event permitted."

"When the Muslims refrained from adopting harmony among the types and varieties of knowledge and the many forms of its intersection across differences, the Sublime Empire collapsed, and decadence overtook the umma. Your discovery, together with the other delegates, of the sura of Mary, will be the first stage of an escape from the cage of retreats and will spread new reasons for the body of the umma to fortify itself."

"With the destruction of the Eternal State, the scattering of the groups of the umma along short-lived paths of authority, the loss of connections with true identity, and the absence of any hardy kernel to be adopted at the center, we have seen a delay in measures of improvement throughout the human field as a whole, and the real and total deception of the systems on which the efforts of mankind depend. For this reason the dead will emerge from their graves in the guise of ghosts from whom their successors will have nothing to fear…"

"As we are full of insight springing from the blessings of the Creator of the world, and confessing from our self that yearns for him the sin we have committed in losing the parchments of the blessed sura of Mary, we have hastened to appear, by virtue of the paths opened before us by His blessing, to the one to whom we have seen fit to entrust this solemn undertaking, and all our confidence is in buttressing his efforts…"

"In these circumstances, we desire above all for our objective to be fulfilled in the revival of the umma and thereby the reordering of mankind as a whole. For the death of our State is the end of civilization, Mustafa Efendi…"

An account of what followed the appearance and disappearance

The phrase "the death of our State is the end of civilization" was the last thing the caliph said to me, Rashid. Afterward, all at once, he took off his glasses, put his face into his hands, and sat weeping, so hard that it reminded me of Ustaz Mitwalli, my history teacher (though unlike Mitwalli's, the caliph's tears were almost silent). When he lifted his head to wipe away the tears he looked like someone who had woken from a long sleep and did not recognize where he was. "Heh!" he exclaimed, "what made me s-s-sit here? You, sir?"

"Absolutely not!"

"And where's Ustaz Alllllllldo, eh?"

By the time my face was drenched, I knew that the operation to put on (or remove) the mask was complete. In front of the mirror the secret-service agent had spread the dough over his face and become someone else. By relaxing some tiny muscles and contracting others, with a marginal drop in the level of the shoulder, and a change in the look of the eyes... there was a different person in front of me! The change had happened in exactly the same quick, terrifying, hidden, underhand way. No time at all had passed before I was sure that the caliph had reverted to being the eccentric fiqi looking for Aldo Mazika. I was so worked up and impatient that I don't even recall how I ended up in my room with my notebook in front of me, scribbling with such speed and concentration that my hand hurt, but I still went on.

I recorded the text of the Padishah's speech so far as my memory would allow, then turned to documenting the things he had told me in his own words, devising miniature drawings that would remind me of each piece of information individually, however much the circumstances differed. The cathedral that became a mosque with the conquest of Constantinople; the number 505 in today's dating; a man wearing a fez with the name of the Sultan on the ring's engraving; the eight-pointed star connected with the janissaries who gave me my name; then two pages of the Qur'an, with the commission to find the missing sura. I left Wahid al-Din in the office, blushing and stammering.

To travel is to seek a day's happiness in city maps. —Ali Badr

Even after I'd finished recording the caliph's words, I didn't sleep a wink until the time came to go out.

Just after dawn I photographed the surface of the seal with a large camera (as already noted). I printed the picture from the computer and transferred the enlarged engraving into the notebook. I was struck by its strong resemblance to the line of my journey as I had felt it obscurely on the night of the first Monday when the dream came to me. When I put them next to each other...

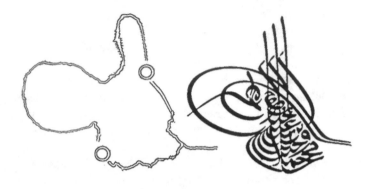

I couldn't believe that when I'd tried vaguely to work out my route inside Cairo, I was, without knowing it, drawing a tughra. At that point I realized that there was a hidden meaning to the vague drawings that I made whenever I went somewhere. I needed to discover this meaning, however much effort it might take.

The important thing now was to fulfill the commission. First I must discover the Turkish word that meant "star," and how it could lead me to the beginning of the road.

PART FIVE

The Epistle on Plans and Antiquities

From World's Gate to the Heart of the Tale

Mustafa's Record of His Historical Research and the Things that Interrupted It

From Tuesday, April 10
to Thursday, April 12

Mustafa Nayif Çorbacı said:

Immediately after the meeting with the caliph, Rashid, I spent three days reeling violently, only saved by researching the history of the Devlet-i Ebed Müddet, from the second Tuesday to the end of the week. Three days in which, when I wasn't reading, I would transcribe and summarize in the notebook, as though I were discovering everything for the first time. Dream Bridge, World's Gate, the computer, the elevator, shoes, the shape of the flame that emerges from the lighter, the feel of the steering wheel, the smell of the skylight, Aldo Mazika's raucous laugh, the girl engaged to the boy, and the end of my relationship with Amgad Salah.

I was still dealing with the shock of discovering that our fiqi colleague Wahid al-Din was himself the last caliph to assume the sultanate directly from the line of Sultan Selim. He assumed the office in order to rule, not as an honorary position as in the days of the Mamluks or like his cousin Abdülmecid Efendi at the time of Mustafa Kemal. Or else he was his double, who somehow or other impersonated him. When I recall what he said to me about Islam and the Muslims ("The death of our State is the end of civilization, Mustafa Efendi"), I feel my head throbbing, and the place deserted by lust filled with another driving force. If lust is the usual expression of the instinct for survival, a different expression of the same instinct had taken its place in my body: fulfilling the order of the sultan.

At first, I experienced the situation in sudden flashes, of which I recorded three (as will become clear in Part Six). From the start, however, they left inside my brain a deeper darkness, and were followed by longer and more violent periods of forgetfulness. Wednesday morning, also, I hadn't slept a wink when I discovered that the flashes had disappeared and I seemed to have reached a pinnacle of bewilderment.

A feeling I'd never had in my life, even during the breakdown you witnessed with Ramiz and me during those days. You remember Ramiz al-Dardir, Rashid? You remember the day we got news he'd been found dead, lying on his back with a needle in his arm in his aunt's bathroom? In those days I was terrified of everything. But this bewilderment was completely different from any sensation I'd known before.

Imagine you just woke up one morning and looked around and didn't recognize anything. Not the furniture, not the room, not the sun creeping through the window. Even your body, which woke up just a moment ago, seems not to be yours, as though someone else has taken your place on the bed and left you to be a sort of hidden spectator. When you go out into the street, the sensation is repeated. You really do seem to be seeing everything for the first time.

You didn't exactly lose your memory. In some buried place, you know that this is your bed and this is your mother; and that the flyover you pull onto as you turn in front of the garden is one of the landmarks of the quarter you grew up in— the quarter whose name was Dokki until you started to call it (and the area surrounding it) Dream Bridge. You know, that is, enough to let you cope without anyone noticing anything odd, provided you don't start in on the details. But your direct experience of all this is that you don't know anything about it, nothing at all.

Now your loss of the city was complete.

All day you applied yourself to your ordinary duties, haunted by a feeling that you were not yourself. As if you were acting your own part or—and this is worse—as if a stranger had perfected your part so well that you no longer knew which of you was driving the car past the Red Crescent Hospital, editing an article about Hamas's disputes with Fatah, or surreptitiously giving the girl engaged to the boy a second cigarette… You were doing all this as another person, or else someone else was doing it for you. In a brief interlude in your bewilderment, you realized that the reconstruction had begun in earnest.

To build something anew from the beginning, you first have to clean up the site of destruction. But I felt I didn't know what sort of cleaning was needed before the foundations were laid.

An account of buying the camera
The first thing I did before work on the second Tuesday was to return to the Khan of Secrets and spend all the money I had on me on a remarkable camera the size of a packet of cigarettes. The thing that obsessed me, now that I was carrying it with

me in the car—after anticipating the purchase, choosing it, and paying for it—was the word *athar*.

On the 26 July Corridor, I recalled that this word, when pronounced with a "t" instead of a "th," acquires a mystic dimension. *Atar* is a material thing connected with a person for whom a deed is being performed: something in the past that changes the future.

On Lebanon Square I thought that when I'd started to take photographs—I used to develop my black-and-white film between my bedroom cupboard and the bathroom, then print them near the bathtub on a secondhand Beseler enlarger with no timer and no red lamp—what I was most concerned about was that the picture should be a true *athar* of the camel that I'd photographed (for many years, I photographed nothing but camels), that is, a material record of the light that came from the animal at the moment the picture was taken.

I learned to sympathize with the primitive tribes that reject photography on the basis that the camera steals something from their soul. When you photograph someone, you really do "take something from his *atar*," because the light that comes from his face is itself the chemical (or, in digital photography, the electronic) transformation that creates the picture.

Since the *athar* is basically something that the creator / artist leaves behind on earth (note that *khallaf*, the Arabic for "leave behind," is connected with *khalīfa*, or "caliph")—a person, a book, a building, an idol, part of a place or event—there must be a connection between the mystical and the historical *athar*.

When you read books, know your state [the better to know] what speaks to you in them, for your states are the home of speech and your ego its bearer. —Ibn 'Arabi

Yes sir, for three days after buying the camera, until the third Friday after my departure, I occupied myself constantly with research into Ottoman history and the history of Cairo.

I'd spend hardly an hour inside my usual cubicle in the office, reading or surfing the internet, then run like a madman from book cover to file to a stray piece of paper to stick in my notebook. Like that, the whole time, night and day, here, there, and everywhere.

I neglected my appearance and my editorial duties, which disturbed my mother and my colleagues, but I was hardly aware of the howls or the backbiting. My father had completely disappeared from my mind. I never took the ring off my finger. I hardly slept. Without effort I would disappear into a palace or monastery, and scenes would appear in my mind's eye as though they were real. I would write and sketch, to conjure up the most important events over a period of seven centuries, Rashid, and research whatever would be of use to me. I went to the National Library, the university library, the newspaper library, the British Council library in Aguza, and the Spanish and Russian libraries in Dokki. Then a friend of mine smuggled me in to the AUC Library in Tahrir Square (he had a membership because he was an old graduate).

Whenever possible I photocopied pages, or else transcribed what I could. At home, I would surf the internet and dip into the balcony without embarrassment. No dust and no disguise. Just sultans' titles and Persian phrases. "What on earth for?" I would say to myself later. In my whole life, I had never read at such amazing speed—a year and a half's reading in three days, no exaggeration—but at the time I was so absorbed and happy that it never occurred to me there was anything odd about it.

The following Monday, when the urge subsided, I discovered I'd been driven by some extraordinary force, with the aim of hastening my readiness for the task. I thought I noticed the face of our Master the Sultan giving me a paternal smile as the fiqi Wahid passed in front of the room where my cubicle was situated. What I noticed as I read was that whenever I embarked on a subject or uncovered an event, I felt that I'd fulfilled a mission within the city. More than once, I discovered that I'd mixed things up between different periods, just as I'd felt toward the tughra on the ring when I'd first seen it. These things were related in one way or another to Cairo. With the same pleasure I'd experienced on the drive from Dream Bridge to World's Gate, the pleasure in the awareness of the journey that I discovered for the first time after separating from my wife, I rediscovered all that could be known about the Sublime State in Arabic and English.

The sensation was as powerful as it was surprising.

Although I didn't think about it directly—as I had the first Sunday when I drove from my mother's house to work after leaving Dog Alley—the pleasure didn't subside for one moment for a whole three days. It was clear that it didn't come from driving, walking, or trekking between the legions of books distributed between two areas that I'd renamed immediately after the departure (I mean, Dream Bridge/West of Nile and World's End/Downtown).

The pleasure of travel came from research and reading. Reading was also the best way to escape from the state of awe and weakness that had come over me after the Commander of the Faithful had manifested himself. I said to myself that I was fulfilling his wishes regardless, but the truth was that I was also employing a stratagem to overcome my bewilderment. So long as I occupied myself with something connected with the mission, I would be all right.

I stuffed full my head, which seemed to have become wider and longer and to have absorbed far more than its capacity.

A detailed account of the State on the internet

It was on the internet in particular that my objectives were achieved. I found a site in English and Turkish with the 35 tughras from that of the first Orhan to Vahdettin (Osman did not have a tughra) and spent an hour (which seemed like a week) studying their development from primitive exercises in calligraphy through various more creative stages until they settled into their accustomed shape after Sultan Mahmud.

I copied Orhan, Suleiman, and Abdülhamid onto the first page of a brand-new notebook in black ink.

As I struggled for accuracy, I noticed (much easier to produce a tughra if you are a calligrapher, by the way, and not, as I am, an amateur photographer and draftsman) that despite their differences all the tughras had two things in common: the three vertical strokes that descend from the top; and the two arcs, which may or may not form complete circles, one inside the other on the left.

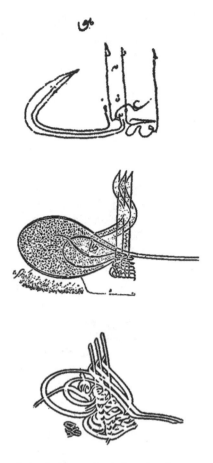

Another website informed me that the three vertical strokes symbolized the three continents that the Sublime Empire aspired to, together with their rivers: Asia/the Tigris, Africa/ the Nile, Europe/the Danube; that the wide arc represented the Mediterranean, which the Ottomans turned into a sort of Islamic pond in the middle of the world; and that the narrow one (their smaller Balkan pond) was the Black Sea.

All at once, I recalled the map I was drawing of Cairo.

For a long time, I'd known it was developing, and I'd had the idea that my Cairo also had to have three continents and seas. As well as Tree Hill, I recalled, there were Plane Yard and Sand Port (both in raised areas like mountains), and as well as the Sea of Japan, Dog Alley, and the Port of Bulaq situated in the middle of World's Gate, at the shrine of Sidi Abu al-'Ila, where Sheikh Mustafa Isma'il used to recite the Qur'an back in the days when my parents got married.

More than once I returned to the scene I'd seen in my dream, Abu al-Siyout, and was horrified to realize how precise that dream had been in relation to the description in the history books of the first Friday prayer after the conquest of Constantinople.

I was attracted in particular by the person of Mehmet the Conqueror—how he built a shrine over the tomb of that Companion of the Prophet Muhammad (who had been martyred in the siege of Constantinople at the time of Yazid ibn Mu'awiya in the year AH 674), for no other reason than to prove that it was he, Mehmet II, who was referred to in the Prophetic hadith that the Padishah related to me (at least, he claimed that this place really was the grave of Khalid ibn Zayd al-Khazraji, better known as Abu Ayyub al-Ansari); how he preserved the relics of Byzantium even while turning churches into mosques, and stamping an Islamic tattoo onto the body of the city; how, being also from the north of Greece, he assumed the spirit of Alexander of Macedon, and listened, in alternation with the Qur'an, to readings from the biography of Alexander composed by Arrian of Nicomedia. He imitated his arrogance and language, to the extent of commissioning a Greek writer to compose a biography of himself on the same type of paper on which Arrian's book had been printed. Even the pictures of Alexander engraved on medals and coins—Mehmet wanted similar ones for himself. Casting aside the religious prohibition on representing humans, he listened to the advice of the Italian intellectuals living in the country he ruled over, to the effect that a realistic drawing of his image could guarantee him immortality. The young sultan had it in mind that Islam, when it first began, had targeted the two neighboring civilizations: Persia and Greece. One of them, and through it his own lineage, had embraced the religion of Islam. And despite the fact that the second one remained in error, he felt that he was the legitimate heir to both.

An account of hiding the news of the Sultan

From the very first moment, Rashid, I wanted to tell someone, anyone, of my fear and my fervor. It is perhaps for this reason that I spent those hours recording the caliph's words in my notebook. Immediately I felt the need to buy a small camera, and thought about the word *athar*. So far, I had nothing at all to indicate that what had happened to me was real.

Nothing remained of my meeting with the Padishah except the picture he'd given me and the piece of paper with his handwriting on it. Try to imagine anyone's face if I told them where I got these things.

I mean, if I'd told someone and persisted in my explanation, that person would've been extremely disturbed, thinking me sick in the head like Amgad Salah, giving me medicine or committing me to a sanatorium, as had happened more than once with my Sunni friend. (From the very first moment, I'd known that it would be necessary to speak to Amgad Salah, but before I could consider the best way to confront him with the subject I needed to escape from the state of bewilderment I was in.)

You're a doctor and you know: anything that goes against the ordinary, without irrefutable proof, should be treated as though it's madness. Most likely I understood all this without admitting it to myself. When I recalled, at an advanced stage in my research, that our Master Vahdettin hadn't asked me to keep our meeting to myself, or to keep my commission secret, I was surprised that I had not, even for a moment, considered revealing it. Apart from Amgad Salah, indeed, I wouldn't tell anyone. Only after I go to Beirut and meet new people will I think of confessing to *you* in the form of a book.

And now, even if you decide that your friend Çorbacı has gone soft in the head and become like the mental patients you treat in London, I am certain that this confession of mine will please you in the end. At least, you'll like the idea of writing a book in the manner of a classical history book, composed in a language like that of those books, but in the idiom of people living today.

As I say, I'm sure you'll like it, or at least appreciate the usefulness of a tale that left my mother confused and frightened for my future—because I suddenly left the paper I'd been going to for the past ten years without even completing my leave paperwork—and that made me suddenly leave the woman I'd fallen in love with. (The love story is in parts seven and eight.) You're right to wonder about the value of all this effort, and the money spent on it, since I myself don't know how finding the sura of Mary will lead to a solution of the Muslims' problems. But I swear to you, Rashid, that this question really no longer bothers me. As I say, once you believe in something, the issue is settled. It's not important whether there exists a rational explanation for the things you commit yourself to, or which demand your belief.

Looking for the parchment of the sura of Mary is exactly like that: you do it, as you told me once, because you have to, isn't that right? And the necessity is connected with the fact that you believe.

Then again, Abu al-Arshad, it's useful as well as pleasurable to read books and to see God's many countries. There are many sides to the question—beginning with the worn-out cliché that it is less important to arrive than to travel. At some stage in this research, I observed that—in relation to the first step in fulfilling the commission—the story would no doubt bring some advantage. I mean, did I have anything more useful to do after the world had collapsed around me? After the drawing, the photography, the copy-editing, my colleagues at the paper, friendship, love, and roaming out of my base through the many quarters of Cairo, I finally thought I'd found, under my foot, a meaning for my life. My life's meaning lies in what I despise and ridicule, would you believe it?

Finding the sura of Mary will make no difference to anything now, and forget the historical results that the sultan spoke of.

An account of the difference between modernity and the Khawaja's complex

The fact is that I was not in harmony with the history of the State during the First World War and its aftermath, but I had to be sure. There were many conflicting views about Abdülhamid in particular—as the architect of the previous three decades—

relevant to this part of the study. Power mad, an emperor of destruction, and a vain obstacle in the way of democracy, certainly.

But he was also a sincere broker in the contract of Islamic unity. I haven't issued any judgment, either positive or negative. It just struck me that Theodor Herzl—the giant among the Zionists, no less—offered him a sum sufficient to cover the debts of the state in exchange for Palestine, and he refused. He also offered shelter to Jamal al-Din al-Afghani and other Muslim names that I'd heard in the context of the struggle against imperialism.

The son of a bitch was a genius of international diplomacy. More than once he was able to sow the seeds of discord between Britain, France, and Russia, and cooperate with appropriate caution with the German Kaiser Wilhelm II. In this way he was able to extract the state from its crises, despite its economic weakness. I also came to the conclusion that Abdülhamid, when he stood aside from the industrial revolution, nationalist thought, the liberation of women, and the other things they call "progress"—they all came from you, from the West, these things, why can't anyone believe that the Muslims were doing battle against themselves when they embraced them?—when he stood aside from them, as I said, he was merely avoiding the follies of Enver Pasha and others who fought on the side of the Germans and massacred the Armenians after Abdülhamid had been deposed in the name of the constitution.

European bias deprived the Sublime State of many of its possessions... on the argument that religious extremism was one of the bases of Islam... as if, when the Muslim state protected the Jews, it was protecting Muslims; or as if its Christian subjects (except those that truly did stir dissent) were done injustice —Muhammad Farid

In the same context I observed that it was Mustafa Kemal who banished the Christians from the borders of the Republic that he established with the Allies in the Treaty of Lausanne in 1922, after the military heroism on which he based his leadership in the Dardanelles area. He then brought in the Muslims of Rumelia like himself, who had been born inside the borders of the present Hellenic state. If you think about it, that means that it was this secular republican who was responsible for the end of ethnic and religious diversity, because the Turks of the so-called homeland had nothing to unite them except Islam—neither ethnicity, idea, geography, or even an alphabet—and this part of the discussion about the link between secularism and progress made me laugh.

It was Mustafa Kemal who suppressed the Kurds and reneged on the treaties he had made with them: he wouldn't have won a single victory without them, by the way. It was he who despised the Arabs and paved the way for Turkey's despicable position on its fundamental responsibilities for this part of the world, all in exchange for a hollow little republic. It was he who restricted modernism to imitating Europe and rejecting the past as if it were nothing but shameful filth. But even he, when he embraced nationalism, could find nothing to build it on except for the community of Islam, isn't that so?

Applying the words of the sultan

When I looked carefully, Rashid, I found that the Padishah Vahdettin was right in the general picture he had drawn for me. But I said to myself, you have to look at the details. Sources confirm that Abdülmecid ibn Mahmud actually used to practice calligraphy from his youth onward, and that he launched the Tanzimat movement to continue the modernization started by his father. But the most important thing is that Abdülhamid saw in the Empire a defense against the plague of nationalisms that was spreading throughout the world. For this reason, he drew his personal guard from all races and made them wear their own national dress. The Empire, he said, was its peoples' refuge from the weakness of division and clannishness (he was extremely far-sighted in perceiving the worthlessness of the nationalist idea, which would divide the Muslims and turn the Arabs into servants of the Western powers, despite their weaknesses, then leave simple or sadistic soldiers—if not highwaymen—to turn their homelands into theaters of corruption and espionage). Quite natural, so I thought, for people seeking a homeland to turn once again to Islam, but why should Islam be just a beard, a mark on the forehead, and an endless number of forbidden things? Not to mention all the rituals.

Was this, I wondered, what Islam had been like in Ottoman times?

We lost faith in our countries, so they turned into prisons, and no one knows how to arrange his escape from them. —Burhan Ghalyun

For the third time, Rashid, I recalled Mutawalli and the nationalist movement. I remembered the words of Ibn Iyas that I had read, and the conclusion he came to that Tuman Bey, unlike his uncle Qansuh, was good to his people and careful with their money. Tuman only ruled for three months and seventeen days, I recalled. After that, he heroically resisted Ibn 'Uthman (as Ibn Iyas called Sultan Selim) until he was defeated at Rabdaniyya, where the 'Abbasiyya Quarter stands today. Then he died, through the mercy of God. I found myself feeling empathy, not with Tuman Bey's patriotism—he was defending a ruling dynasty against others more powerful, and I will cut off my arm if he'd ever heard of a concept called nationalism— but with the nobility that the words of a historian from the same family had bestowed on him.

Those who ruled Egypt after the death of al-'Adid (the last Fatimid caliph)... were called kings and sultans. They can be divided into three groups: the first group were the Ayyubid kings, who were Kurds. The second group were the Bahris and their descendants, who were Turkish Mamluks belonging to the Ayyubids. The third group were Bahri Mamluks, who were Circassians. —al-Maqrizi

I recalled that patriotism (contrary to what everyone says) represents nobility, regardless of the angle of allegiance. I even sought an excuse for Khayyir Bey, the Mamluk governor of Aleppo, who was the Mamluk traitor siding with Sultan Selim. Perhaps he too was a patriot in some sense or other. People say that Abdel Nasser was the first Egyptian to rule Egypt, and they draw a parallel between Abdel Nasser's coup (past several other figures) and the downfall of Tuman Bey related by Ibn Iyas. But they forget that Ibn Iyas himself, as well as Tuman Bey, whose downfall he relates, was by their own logic not even Egyptian.

Since the arrival of 'Amr ibn al-'As in AD 642, I figured, it was impossible to speak of any Egyptian identity as opposed to other, "newcomer," identities (otherwise we would all be traitors and imperialist bastards and nationalism would be a separatist Coptic movement). The Ottomans themselves never made this mistake. They never said "we were the first people to live in this place" and they never made any distinction between locals and "newcomers." For them, identity meant merely that power should remain in the family: the power of destiny that had enabled them to conquer Constantinople, then (in contrast, once again, to the racism of European imperialism) to utilize the different races and religious communities to attract civilization from every quarter of the earth.

The Egyptian they refer to when they talk about Abdel Nasser (in general, Abdel Nasser was no less ruthless or dictatorial, though probably less successful and more stupid, than the least successful Mamluk sultan), this Egyptian who had to wait centuries before achieving power, was nothing but a peasant: one of those ignorant upstarts we look down on and make fun of their lowly origins, perhaps because our own origins lie among them, though we don't want to be like them. Before the modernization of the education system none of them played any part in history, except for fiqis like Wahid al-Din al-Qurani. I mean, are these really the only Egyptians?

I imagined that it would be impossible for the fellahin, with their loose morals, their subservient way of thinking, and their reluctance to take risks or to travel, to create a vibrant society, let alone a multicultural one. My brain recalled how indifferent, servile, and deceitful they are whenever they are in power, as well as shortsighted in the pursuit of advantage and wealth. These are the filthiest people to have ruled a country. I mean, the fact that they had become Muslims early on, or were prevented from mixing with Muslim newcomers later, why should that make them any more Egyptian than other people living in the country? True, after the Ottoman conquest, Cairo was no longer the first city of Islam. Cairo had been the seat of the caliphate. After Saladin had restored the black emblem of the 'Abbasids to the mosques, al-Zahir Baybars summoned the 'Abbasid caliph personally to live, with curbed powers, under his protection. The Ottoman conquest turned Cairo into a provincial capital, the best things in which were Istanbul-bound, but it remained the second city and retained most of its income, in practical terms, among the representatives and emirs of the State. So the Ottoman conquest added Turkish greed to Mamluk tyranny, and the Mamluks' Turkish-influenced Arabic became mixed with Osmanli Turkish, which had itself already been steeped (via Persian) in Arabic. More of the same, really. And yet today the Ottoman conquest of Egypt gives me an alternative to all those broken homelands to which I might conceivably belong and a means to understand what has made my life so difficult. It gives me something cleaner than Ustaz Mitwalli's shirt and more exalted than the Jama'a Islamiyya, more valuable than the wretched island on whose territory you live, Rashid. It gives me something far more plausible than the American minority complex and the Civil Rights Movement, more spacious than the cubicle I work in as a journalist, and more genuine, far more genuine, than the mark on the forehead of Amgad Salah.

The problem of identity

Suddenly, Abu al-Siyout, I found myself thinking: does the problem lie in religious adherence? Is it religious adherence that makes you unable to see a woman without a knotted rag over her hair, get into an elevator without hearing someone giving glory to God, or cross the corridor without tripping over a group of people praying or an ordinary employee assailing you with the call to prayer?

Everyone talks about religion. Everyone articulates their problems through religion. Everyone plays the fiqi and lays down the commandments. Not a good word for anything, beyond the things that have been agreed on ever since al-Ghazali closed the door to independent thinking, may God forgive him. Nothing except for devotions and prohibitions. Especially prohibitions...

As though Islam had for a millennium and a half produced nothing except makeup to suit your hijab, or a vapid young man in a full suit smiling inanely on a satellite TV channel, his eye in the middle of his bald head, as he shrills: "The hijab, viewers, is an order from God, so why shouldn't we all adopt it?" All the fine things that Islam has given us—poetry, architecture, calligraphy, miniatures, Qur'an recitation, the *dhikr*, Sufism, philosophy and science, the Family of the Prophet, God's saints, stories, love, wedding customs, social duty, fine morality—people ignore them all completely. If anyone mentions them, he only does so to criticize or prohibit them. And if there were a Sublime State today, mightn't these things have come back?

A review of the idea of nationalism

As I was nearing the end of my research, I became convinced that Vahdettin had actually been a friend of Mustafa Kemal, and that he was more protective than Kemal of the Empire's territory and peoples. I knew that he had apologized for the massacre of the Armenians, for which he had not been responsible, for example, whereas Kemal, to the day that he died, continued to deny the existence of any massacres. In 1920, he objected to the Treaty of Sèvres, which would curb the Empire's authority and divide what remained of its territory into zones under European control, despite the fact that he had no means of preventing it.

Vahdettin supported the resistance from the first moment. He only fled on board a British vessel, as more than one Turkish historian vouchsafes, to prevent his country from embarking on a civil war it could not endure under occupation.

They all rode and went to Muhammad 'Ali and said to him: "We do not want this Pasha to rule over us." "And who do you want, then?" he asked. "We do not want anyone except yourself to be our guardian," they told him. At first he refused, but then accepted. They brought him a red fur with a caftan on it, and Sayyid 'Umar and Sheikh al-Sharqawi came to him and dressed him in it. —al-Jabarti

From my reading, and my memory, a picture of Egypt with its manifold interconnections began to crystallize in my mind. I understood what the Padishah had meant when he said that Muhammad 'Ali had planted Ottoman values in us. The great Arab state that Muhammad 'Ali strove to found—and it was the Ottomans, helped by Britain and France, who caused the enterprise to fail—was nothing but a new Sublime Empire. It almost proved to me that the enmity between the Arabs and the Turks was itself nothing but another European invention.

Our Master's point of view was that names make no difference and the important thing is the value: Ottoman value lay in the diversity of regions and objectives under a central authority believing in absolute power.

In time, the sultan-caliph who had appeared to me seemed like one of those tragic, fatherly personalities who as soon as they are dragged into history for a moment are ejected from it by their good intentions, their serenity, and a sort of frustrated hope. So they leave the celebration just as they entered it, without a chickpea to their name, and most likely without a halfpenny either. He reminded me in particular, as I recalled his tears, of Mohamed Naguib. But he reminded me even more of my father. Although names like Ben Bella and Allende also came into my head, I recalled the sight of my father behind his ebony desk with its flaking sides, wondering at what was becoming of his country, tears in his eyes.

Testing the new camera

The second Thursday morning, I hadn't slept. I spent some time staring at the crescent moon which hung large and bright in the sky after dawn had broken. I wanted to use the new camera I'd bought in any way possible but I couldn't find anything to photograph. Five centuries of history were at work in my head, with overlapping maps that I wouldn't draw of the route of my movements within Cairo: the world that had collapsed, and the areas that were being reconstructed. My passion for the camera hit me with no preliminaries.

In the end I took it out and sat fiddling with it. I charged the battery and read the instruction manual. I kept my eye on it as I moved between my room and the hallway, looking at papers in the natural light that was coming in, still weakly, from the window. Then, when it was ready, I turned off the instant screen, and, with my right eye closed, put my left eye to the miniature viewfinder situated behind the lens. I wanted to see the world as the camera saw it, not look at the live picture on the screen. I sat looking through the viewfinder from various angles, pointing the lens here and there until I settled on a particular spot among the piles of books deep inside the wall. There were two books leaning on one another in the shape of a thick triangle, with a third, smaller book on top of them. I looked at the three books for a long time through the viewfinder, thinking about the vault, thinking that it was a vault, and that it was at the same time a cupboard that had been the balcony of my childhood.

The strange thing, my friend, was that as soon as I took the camera away from my face, I was seized by a violent tremor which I explained to myself as due to lack of sleep and too much coffee and cigarettes. Taking a deep breath, I put out my cigarette and put the camera on the television.

The art of history is one of those arts in which... the learned and the ignorant are equal. since on the surface it is no more than conveying information about time and nations. —Ibn Khaldun

I seemed to need historical information as an awning over my head so that I could see without being blinded by the sun. This was the first time anything like this had happened to me, by the way. I was lying on the sofa in the hallway of the family home recovering from the tremor, while at the window the morning of Thursday, April 12, 2007, was just dawning. I saw the whole of my life before me, not as I had imagined it in the preceding days as an itinerary or a talisman or a map, not in the form of a door or a bridge or a khan or a hill or a courtyard or a road. I saw my life differently, and I knew that this was in preparation for the second dream before I knew when that would be.

You know that moment when you remember a film clip, a single, very quick shot from a scene that you may have otherwise forgotten? In my case, for example, Fustuq's prophecy brought back a shot in which nothing was visible except a man approaching a car at dawn and you knew that he intended to kill. Its effect was in part due to the proximity of other shots, about which I can remember only that they had crying in them.

The second Thursday morning, as I told you, I saw my life in front of me as if I were recalling one of those shots, with one difference, namely that I was the hero (which is what makes me say that it was the first time this had happened to me).

Despite being the hero (actor and character at the same time, that is), I didn't feel I knew any more about what I was

seeing than I knew about any faint memory of this sort—
though I had no doubt that what I was seeing was indeed my
complete life, with no omissions. As if the whole universe were
a single film in which we acted and watched alternately, but of
which we understood no more than a moment.

In the shot, I was stepping over a high threshold to walk
through a door, one hundred percent certain that with this
step I was finally and irrevocably leaving behind someone or
something quite fundamental. As if I had only now, when I was
sure of escaping, poisoned my mother and father, for example,
or given away my country's military secrets to the enemy.
And now, after this total ruin, I was crossing the threshold
to confront the world anew from the beginning. A single
step, after which a new life would begin for this treacherous
murderer, a life in which I would understand nothing, while
beyond this new life, like destruction or ashes or the remains
of a crime, lay everything I had known in the world before I
took that step.

Like the danger that gives pleasure, the idea pleased me
so much that I gave in to the tremor (which had come back
more forcefully) and said to myself that perhaps every life in
this world was just one shot of a film. Perhaps every life was
like a scattered memory that arrives or doesn't according to
circumstances, and until it comes you can never see it clearly.
But as soon as you see it and come to know its true nature, it
becomes like a member of the living dead: a zombie wandering
the pavilions of the present in the certainty that his historical
life has ended and that he (and his body) are buried in a grave.

The marvel of the digital photograph

"*Hosta costa*"—I suddenly remembered the words, as the song
started going around in my head—"*Hosta costa, high as a kite!*"

I mean, I ask you, what except for a super-universal
struggle contrary to the laws of nature could make me, after a
situation like this when I was tired and exhausted, pull myself
together and, with the energy of a boxing champion who's been
in the ring for only a minute, retrieve the camera from on top of
the television, and squat down in front of the balcony with my
left eye to the viewfinder to photograph the spot I had settled

on as I'd tried out the camera without shooting—the spot where two books were leaning against each other in the shape of a thick triangle, with a third, smaller book on top of them—adjust the frame until the scene was as I had seen it when I'd been trying out the camera, then press the shutter for the first time in the history of my possession of this camera, and then, after I'd taken the picture, find nothing of what I'd seen in front of me as I was taking it has appeared on the screen, not a trace of the vault or the three books, just a magnificent doorway in the morning light? I continued to look in disbelief before taking the camera with me to the computer and comparing the doorway on the screen with different pictures on the internet until I realized that it was the original Sublime Porte, that is, the gate of the Diwan in the Topkapı Palace built by Mehmet the Conqueror, and that just as I'd drawn the tughra without recognizing its shape on the evening I'd heard the *Hosta Kosta* song, I had now photographed this venerable antiquity that appeared in front of me in the browser window that I was adjusting for focus, as an exact image of the picture on the camera screen, without recognizing its shape and without its being there, simply by concentrating on a particular point in the middle of the vault. This was after seeing my entire life as a passing shot from a door whose features were also unclear. But when I connected the camera to the computer and downloaded the picture, I could see on the computer screen only the frame that I'd photographed of three books deep in the wall. The picture of the Sublime Porte had been erased from the camera's memory. I sat stunned, banging my hands together. *Hosta costa, al-banknota, taralam, taralam, mali al-jakotta, taralam, taralam…*

    Let's dance, people, let's dance

The text of al-Jabarti's account

All this, I'm telling you, before eventually going back to the hallway vault, without feeling that I was traveling among the planets, without recalling my plump dove or the suicidal rabbit or imagining that my mother was in one world and the books in another, but merely passing through an imaginary door that would bring me directly, by way of the Topkapı Palace, to the awakening of the community of Islam.

It was night, and I was reeling from lack of sleep, with a candle in my hand. Paper and dust.

I seemed to know that what had happened once, before I sat down with the sultan, would happen again. I deliberately started on a dream that I'd had almost since childhood, and was not surprised when, with the same dreamlike feeling, I fell into a ditch, the bottom of which was made of colored felt, the kind they use to make fezzes. Everything was bright red, and the world was in the distance without my having traveled. With the same incomprehensible facility, I continued to rummage through books by the light of the candle, without getting out of the ditch, and without losing sight of the felt, knowing that what I wanted would make itself known to me, despite the fact that the books had been thrown down in no particular order.

Exactly as had happened to me with *Bada'i' al-zuhur*, the relevant part of the book *'Aja'ib al-athar* seemed to come to me of its own accord. Did the books know that I was on the track of this page in particular? Perhaps they, all of them, were blessings from the sultan. Deliberately, without anything metaphysical happening except that right away I found a page I might have spent a week looking for, I imagined that the sultan would materialize from the paper and dust, just as I had met him in the clothes of our fiqi colleague Wahid al-Din, and would recite to me. I could hear al-Jabarti's words articulated with that same Turkish fluency, and despite the fact that this time there was no ambiguity about myself, nor was my identity confused (God forbid!) with the Sublime Self, I went along with the voice resounding in my head with a pleasure that surpassed the pleasure both of the inner journey and of reading.

The conclusion I came to, Rashid, was that the Egyptians, just as they were angered by Tuman Bey, came once again to love the Sublime Empire. Like me and like Sheikh Mar'i al-Qudsi, the author of *Qala'id al-'uqyan fi fada'il Al 'Uthman* (Sheikh Mar'i lived more than 150 years before al-Jabarti), there were people who felt an allegiance to the sultan.

"On that day it was announced that the French would depart, leave the forts, and surrender the strongholds at noon on the following day. When Thursday came, and the noon hour passed without anything happening, there were various stories. Some people said that they would depart on the Friday, while others said that they had postponed until Monday. Then people started to hear the clamor and talk of Ottoman troops, and the clump of their boots, and when they looked, they found that the French had all left at night, abandoning the great citadel, as well as the other forts and strongholds and barricades, and gone to Giza, al-Rawda, and Kasr al-'Ayni. Not a shadow of them could be seen in the city, Bulaq, Old Cairo, or Ezbekiyya. As usual, people rejoiced to see the newcomers, of whom they held a good opinion, and went out to meet and greet them, heaping blessings on their arrival. The women ululated with their tongues from the arches and in the markets. There was much noise and shouting; young people and children gathered as they always do, and voices were raised in a shout of 'God grant victory to the Sultan!'"

So just as there was a Mutawalli, there was a Selim (this happened in 1801, during the reign of Sultan Selim II, the father of Mahmud; wasn't it a happy chance that the Sultan at that time should have the same name as Yavuz, the first imam?). Without making any deliberate choice, I pulled out a different volume of *'Aja'ib al-athar*; this was the Dar al-Sha'b edition, and each part was like an exercise book, held together with staples. I dusted it off as I left the balcony and put it between two notebooks on my desk, with the words "as usual, people rejoiced to see the newcomers, of whom they held a good opinion" ringing in my ears.

The homeland is treason. Every homeland is treason. The idea of the homeland is treason. —from the novel *Shay Aswad* ("Black Tea") by 'Ali al-Maqri

For the first time in my life I felt that I—even I—had nationalist tendencies. Most likely, my nationalism, like that of Khayyir Bey, was of a misshapen sort. But like Khayyir Bey also, I had found an outlet for it. Today, having discovered, like everyone else from Mauritania to Pakistan, that the Islamic state, whatever and wherever it might be, was the nearest thing to a homeland I could hope for, and having formed the view that allegiance to a religion, regardless of belief, was actually the obvious choice, I realized that my personal misfortunes, precisely as the Sultan had said, were the historical result of all the imaginary homelands in my life.

From the start of the United Arab Republic to émigré societies in Western cities, I thought: complete independence or sudden death, the proclamation of the Suez Canal as an Egyptian limited company. We said we'd build it and we built the High Dam. Lifestyles and loads of money. It astonished me that neither the struggle for self-determination nor adaptation to Western civilization had solved the problem. They say that if you were an Ottoman subject, you were the property of the sultan and the Porte, and that under the Ottoman state system there were no rights of citizenship or human rights. OK! I asked myself which was better: Egyptian-style citizenship (as Ahmad 'Urabi famously put it, "God created us free and didn't create us to be an inheritance and a piece of property") or the slave of the sultan?

I put aside sarcasm and stupidity and spent a full hour thinking about the subject with mathematical seriousness, as if it were an algebraic equation, and came to the conclusion that personally I would prefer to be the sultan's slave.

An account of the honorable name Çorbacı

During all this, Abu al-Arshad, I spent a long time thinking about the janissaries, or Yenicheri as our Master called them, and tried to imagine my great-grandfather as a military commander, an important figure, reclining on a high chair and distributing soup from a pot the size of a barrel to a thousand soldiers, each with a moustache, under his command. But I could only see a sepia print of my oldest uncle, may God have mercy on him, who had turned into a licorice seller going round the cafés with his decorated pitcher.

I figured that my great-grandfather was either the slave of a genuine Çorbacı whose name he took, or a yogurt seller from Jabarti's time that people got confused about. I could excuse the Padishah for his mistaken conception of my ancestry, telling myself that he didn't know how common this name was among us—impossible that every Çorbacı should be descended from such a high rank—but then I recalled that the janissaries who had come with Selim III when Egypt was conquered had married and settled down, and their circumstances had changed to the extent that their Turkish colleagues at the time of al-Jabarti found it difficult to understand their speech, and the Egyptian janissaries at any rate rejected their Turkish counterparts, fearing for their positions. I pictured them as my police and army officer relatives.

Their social and material circumstances were also much more difficult than one might have expected from the plunder and deception they were permitted to undertake, and their ranks meant nothing but a measure of age because there were so many of them.

Maybe, my friend, I said to myself. Maybe my great-grandfather, the janissary, was in difficult circumstances. Why not? For the hundredth time it occurred to me how strange it was that the kapıkulu, or servants of the Porte, of Christian origin should turn into fanatical Muslims generation after generation, passing on the little power that remained to them. Like the civil servants of today, their loyalty was to their families, and they didn't care three halfpence for war or the sultan.

Suddenly, I tell you, I felt that my name was a story. Mustafa (blessings be upon the Prophet) means chosen. I was chosen as well by the Muslims' Imam, but I am also named after Atatürk, my adversary. Isn't it extraordinary that I should bear the name of my adversary? As for Çorbacı, the commander of a thousand men, who distributed the pot of soup, so I carried on thinking, I knew that my father came from a village called al-Wastaniyya in the district of Shubra Khit on the Rosetta branch of the Nile in the governorate of al-Buhayra, though we buried him in the family tombs in Shubra Khit itself.

My great-uncle told me that his grandfather, or grandfather's grandfather ("old Çorbacı," as he called him without explaining further) had been present at the battle there between Murad Bey, the Mamluk feudal commander, and the French expeditionary forces under the command of Napoleon Bonaparte on July 13, 1798.

My uncle, may God have mercy on him, was a liar and a thief, and no one believes him about anything, but why shouldn't "old Çorbacı" have been a janissary supporting Murad Bey? I was pleased by the possibility that "old Çorbacı" might be different from the licorice or yogurt seller I had imagined him to be all my life, the mere possibility pleased me. But what made me feel really proud was that, regardless of any of that, I bore the ideal name for fulfilling the mission that I'd been charged with.

An account of the end of the state of being overwhelmed and beaten down

On the third Friday night, I finally slept... a long, deep sleep with no dreams. During the last hour before I slept, I'd had a friendly clash with my mother that made me laugh more than anything. "Won't you eat or sleep, son?" she screamed. "Suit your disgusting self!" I was squatting at the end of the hall, half on the balcony and half in the hall. Without turning around, I smiled and shook my head gently, knowing that that would anger her even more.

"Bless the Prophet!" I said.

Then and only then, when those three words had left my mouth, did I feel that I had finished my research.

I had the idea of traveling to the countries of mankind. — *The Thousand and One Nights*

This feeling filled me with a sort of pride, I recall, as if I'd finished a doctorate in three days. "One of the Sultan's miracles," I said to myself. Immediately I had a positive intuition that I would be traveling. Afterward, when I was in bed and my mother was huffing and puffing in the room between the piles of papers and the notebooks, I heard her rabbiting on: "You're not an animal grazing in a pen, you're a human being!" I thought of correcting her and saying "These pens are for sleeping, nonna" (when I tease my mother, I call her "nonna," as you address a baby), "animals graze in fields, may God's name protect you!" I just laughed to myself until the light went out and the door was shut. Then I noticed that for the first time since December 2005 I was happy.

As I went to sleep, I said to myself that this was the first time since leaving Dog Alley that I felt my situation was not a punishment. Not a punishment, I mean, so much as a historical condition. The beginnings of an idea started to play inside my head, an idea that at this stage I thought naïve and superficial (although it would be confirmed in more than one guise during the coming week).

The organization Amgad Salah feared, without knowing that he had fallen victim to it, the organization that was the universal conspiracy the sultan spoke of, was simply history itself, history in person, and the madness caused by the appearance of a zombie eating someone's brain was nothing less than an attempt to change the course of history. Perhaps the zombie was an angel guarding the path of a new radiance of which I was, I felt, the center. However utopian or impossible that may seem, however much you feel that you are an ant facing a robot the size of the sphinx who is programmed to crush ants—so I thought, before I went to sleep—or that the task with which you have been charged is a fantasy, nothing will stop you from completing the journey on which you have started. A day or place will certainly come when it will be recalled that you took part in the revival or knew what ought to happen on the ground. Without meaning to I had started to sing God's praises.

History cannot be defeated except through remembrance of God.

A summary of the research

I was worn out with the collapse of civil society and the disturbance of values essential to work and life. Ever since I had left my wife and my life had changed, I'd had nothing to do except to analyze my colleagues. What was there to have prevented the caliph from coming to show me the way out? Perhaps patriotism would require no more than a faithful execution of his words.

Of course, I knew that the matter wasn't that simple. I knew it would be difficult for anyone to believe that the way out lay in finding a Qur'anic parchment. And however much I myself believed it, I would never have an answer to the question of how. How would finding the sura of Mary written by Sultan Abdülmecid, then lost by his most useless of sons between morning and evening, how could this lead to an improvement in the Muslims' condition? But I also knew that faith knows neither logic nor calculation. Either you believe or you don't, that's all there is to it. In order to have a Lord, or a homeland, you have to put your trust in something, however fanciful or arbitrary it might seem.

I found myself standing on the bed, staring at the copy of *Bada'i' al-zuhur* open on the floor in front of me, and shouting:

"This Tuman Bey is of no importance, by the way, Ustaz Mitwalli, I'll show you how the nationalist movement works! The nationalist movement is called the sura of Mary, Ustaz Mitwalli!"

What inspired Mitwalli to poetry

This notebook is unique—(that is what I felt, the moment I saw on Youtube some clips of scenes cut from the accession ceremony of our Master Vahdettin on July 4, 1918: horsemen, clerics, and a gilded throne in a large square; puffed-up fezzes, and no end of steeds and standards), despite the fact that it is full of mementoes, clippings and stamps, pictures, tickets and receipts, most of them from the first twenty-one days; this is in addition to the drawings that reminded me of my commission—unique and sad. During a moment of turbulence I catch a glimpse of it in the pocket of the seat in front of me, and I feel sorry for it. There is nothing in the world more miserable than a notebook that someone carries with him to try to rebuild his world.

Nothing, perhaps, except for a sultan-caliph being forced to leave the country in secret on board a British vessel. Or a religious community no longer defined by anything except a beard and a mark on the forehead of a human body which—for no obvious reason—is blowing itself up...

I recalled that there were other notebooks like it—at least seven. Seven Osmanli notebooks bursting with hundreds of memories and fears, in the pockets of airplane seats, in which seven researchers are looking for the lost sura of Mary. Victims of madness and travel. They cannot imagine life without notebooks to rip pages from and load them with glue as punishment, exactly as I do.

You, Rashid, have to imagine me writing to you with shaking hand, opening the notebook beside the plastic cup on the plane's tray table. Imagine me between the balcony overlooking the Ain el Mreisseh Corniche and the Rawda Café beside the military baths on the Beirut Corniche, as I record new information or rummage around in the information that I recorded secretly.

Nothing except the commission and to go on.

The poetry that Mustafa wrote on the sultan

You are the ghosts of the youth that fled like puppies from a purple blaze on the banks of the Bosphorus, shouting your exhausted conscience. In the overcast daybreak, the cities console you with a glimmer of the last of the dervishes, where the heaped-up domes poke their needles in the pillow of the sky and the *fuqaha'* eat their turbans like unleavened bread. Did you hold on to the covering on your head in the face of the English mists, was it in the glow from your medals that you bet on the dawn of an age overflowing with different climates? On the shreds of your decrees are shapes like ovens, and on your grandfather's head is a brown tombstone, no longer a sign of civilization. Now, the cloak that you—or your brother—kissed is closed, as you mutter, in Persian *"Masnavi, ma'navi, mawlavi, is the Qur'an in the Pahlavi tongue,"* then leap over the steppes like two wings flapping continuously over the continents' shores, while your hands rummage like mice in sacks of possessions for rice fit for pavilions or candles to be translated into Italian gold. You are a dead father, or a hermit smoothing the hair of his absent sons, and behind the rubbery glass of your spectacles are tears lifeless as ashes. Who will sharpen the swords of your dreams to come, or send your gifts across the ages? Who except me believes that you are you, believes that a stuttering monster is your double, or keeps close to your companions through the airports searching for an icon with no face? Your family has a drum like an orgasm, your name is a stew of pearls in a dish like a sea amid the table of the worlds. But I see you as an old man in a decommissioned ship, staring at your receding country.

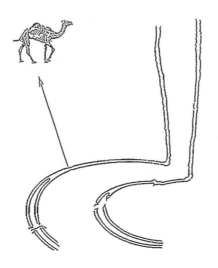

PART SIX

The Book of Friends' Secrets

Sand Port

The Narrator's Description of
What Followed His Meeting with
the Caliph: Stories to Turn Heads

Friday, April 13
and Saturday, April 14

Praise be to God

Here is the text of the three illuminations that Mustafa recorded immediately after the appearance of the Sultan. We thought it preferable to postpone this until the beginning of the current part, so that it may throw light on the many succeeding events and how the sultan's appearance led up to them.

1. Without a woman, you feel that there is a hole in your belly crying out its need to be plugged. You know that the plug must be the right size, but you don't know the size. You only know that the possibility of finding it is almost nonexistent. Days and months pass in which you're happy for the hole to stay as it is, without a plug. You keep yourself busy drawing and taking photos, or writing articles for an economics newspaper, or with friends-colleagues whom you can no longer persuade yourself you understand or share any fellow feeling. All the time, the hole still in your belly, you tell yourself that the world is better this way and that you don't need a woman, but the hole keeps throbbing inside you, and you try to ignore it. Until a day comes when you when you meet a woman you are happy to sleep with, whom you think will fill this hole, and you're convinced (or convince yourself, knowing that you are not convinced) that she'll serve as a good plug. So you get closer to her, then marry her. The rest I have told you. You have to find a woman to complete your life.

2. To be born a Muslim in this age means that you are perforce a different person. Your historical formation is not a logical result of the situation you're in. I mean, take these silly examples: you've resolved to deal with time in a generous spirit; it is in your nature to grant priority to interpersonal responsibilities and feelings over the demands of work; you explain visible phenomena by reference to the supernatural as well as physical laws; and everything runs, for you, from right to left. This is the complete opposite of the contemporary expectation that time is like an impaling spike, gain is more important than affection, and everything, even emotions and ideas, has a material explanation, in Latin script. So it is quite natural, in a moment of clarity, that you should wake up one day and fail to recognize anything around you, and be surprised even at your own body. There are now only two

choices for a way out: either to blend in with the age to such a degree that you forget you were born a Muslim; or to be a Muslim, narrow-minded, extremist, mediocre, in line with the conditions of the age. There has to be a third choice.

3. When you speak of nationalism in the absence of a nation you believe in, you're either a liar or a fool. A homeland is a place you're comfortable with and happy to take part in forming—just as you feel comfortable building a house or a life with a woman you love—and insofar as it allows you to express and fulfill yourself, you will feel it is your homeland. It doesn't matter where, or even in which language, in the end. However many stirring words you regurgitate about the land and the mortal remains of your ancestors, it's no use if the homeland is a bogeyman, however familiar its features. A place where every day people are at the end of their rope, or where, when you try to live with a free woman—caught, like you, between two cultures—they call you "family man" and find that the world equals silence and tears. How could this be your homeland? What remains, after the characteristics of the homeland have disappeared, is an intimacy that it is impossible to replace and your need to belong to something— the religion into which you were born, for example, would be enough, if you could find a convincing form for it—anything. You have to find a true meaning for identity.

The story of the divorce, and solving the riddles, Friday (daytime)

Friday morning seemed to have come late. Mustafa woke up refreshed and calm, unusual for after such a long sleep. Like a leisurely day in the middle of a long holiday—for several weeks you've had nothing to do—a single thought gripping his mind, namely that he must get divorced. Had this too come from the Padishah? Who knows… From the time the Commander of the Faithful appeared to him and explained why the sky folded down over the earth, Mustafa had no longer been certain of the source of his feelings and decisions.

In the past, he'd thought a lot about the matter of free will and predestination. If everything is preordained, where do reward and punishment come from? And although he believed in fate to some extent, he had always resolved that a human being had a choice in what he did and even what was done to him, so the idea that everything was preordained perturbed him...

All this had to happen for him to be able to reconcile the two ideas and understand that they were not incompatible. There is a path marked out for you: you can either follow it or depart from it, and reward or punishment comes in accordance with that choice. His own path had been marked out for him by the Muslims' Imam, from today at least, but it was up to him whether to follow it or to remain as he was. It was also up to him to choose to stay with his wife and pay no attention to Fustuq's prophecy, then deny to himself that the sultan had appeared. But he chose his fate. The son of a madwoman...

The first thing he did when he woke that day was to go into his mother's room without knocking and yell into her ear: "Is there a registrar working today?"

She was asleep. The moment he saw her, before she jolted awake, he noticed the increasing signs of age on her neck and face. He still didn't know that he would leave Cairo, but he had an intuition (and this was new in his life) that it would happen sooner rather than later. Only at this moment did he feel a deep sorrow, because his mother had become old and lonely and it was impossible for him to stay beside her. For the first time since leaving Dog Alley, he recalled his elder sister who lived in Australia (the last time he'd spoken to her she'd said: "What's so strange about wanting a divorce, since when have you done anything properly?") and his brother, whose death in infancy they'd told him about. It weighed heavily on him that he hadn't been able to give his mother a grandchild or set her mind at rest on the subject of his marriage.

Still, the idea in his head was a stronger one and, as always happened in his life (in relation to his mother, at least), Mustafa preferred himself to the other person and yelled again in her face: "Is there a registrar working today?"

"Whhhho, Mustafa?" she stammered (and before he knew it, he was kissing her on the cheek). "Wwwwhere's the rrregistrar?"

Mustafa didn't know how the scene changed from his mother in her bed to the front of a tumbledown apartment building behind St. Theresa's Church near his mother's family home in Khulusi Street in the neighborhood of Shubra...

By nagging and joking, plus the tea that he'd made her—the first time he'd made her tea in years—Mustafa was able to persuade her to speak to his aunt Hafiza about a registrar. This was after the Friday prayers. It occurred to him that for some time his mother had stopped getting angry that he no longer attended prayers, though she continued to burn incense in the hall and would shut the window on the stupid sermon coming into the kitchen from a very loud loudspeaker. This was the first Friday he could remember on which prayers had passed from start to finish while she slept. So far, there was no indication that she'd noticed. He watched her as she savored the tea in bed. For one moment, something arrogant, almost French, came back to her in the way she set the edge of the glass on her lip, something he seemed to have seen in the days of his childhood or in another place or planet. As he sat in front of her, cracking his knuckles on his knee, he found it astonishing that his mother, despite coming straight out of the Shubra Intersection, had once been a babe who lived it up. Was it credible that the new working-class neighborhood of Shubra could ever have produced such beautiful, classy women? It pained him that he'd paid no attention, not once, to her need for love and affection since his father died. For exactly half a second he thought of telling her about the sultan. But before he could open his mouth, something in his brain kicked in, and he stood up and left on the pretext of letting her talk with her sister. "Sorry I have to make you do this, mama!"

His mother was already hesitant and sad. Her depression about the end of her son's marriage was made worse by her unease about letting him do as he planned, and her wish that he should reconsider before he took the final step. "You're always in such a hurry," she said to him. "I mean, what would happen if you waited until we could consult your relatives, or even until they could come with us and be witnesses, rather than bringing witnesses in from the street?" In reply, in a tone serious enough to persuade her, Mustafa repeated the things that his wife had castigated him for, then made a joke, reminding her that his wife had within a week gotten an abortion and called him a "killer." "I, a 'killer'? I, mother?" he asked, using the English word, as he watched the effect his words had on her from one moment to the next. He was dying for her to come with him to the registrar, but why? He could ask one of his colleagues, take the address of a registrar, and go—taking with him two witnesses from the street, easily enough—but the presence of his mother would give the proceedings a legitimacy that he needed. Was this why her words were affecting him now? His resolution was stronger, at any rate. And when he found out the address of the registrar that his aunt Hafiza recommended, his reaction was completely the opposite of his mother's: instead of hesitating and thinking the errand too difficult, he became more enthusiastic.

Shubra

Mustafa hadn't intended to put the Shubra district on his list of sketches. It wasn't close enough to the world he'd been reconstructing for himself—his world since he'd started work on the paper—and whose collapse after his separation from his wife horrified him.

Nonetheless, for a period that seemed much longer than it was, as his mother reluctantly got herself ready to go out, he stood at the window of his room opposite the hall balcony, preparing himself to play with his fat pigeon and revisit the intersection area in the light of the information he'd acquired during his recent research.

For example, he'd always secretly wondered why the Bulaq Canal Street had been given that name when no one could find the trace of any canal there. Only during his research did he find out that they had built a canal for Muhammad 'Ali from Bulaq—the most important port in Cairo through the ages, opposite the Sea of Japan, which in those days had been called Bulaq Island—to bring water to the new quarter that the Pasha had constructed on the boundaries of the Qalyubiyya Governorate, erecting there a palace that he built twice...

From our planet we say: Until the scene changed from his mother's bed to this apartment building near St. Theresa's

Church, via both World's Gate, where the newspaper building was, and the Qolali tunnel that reminded him of his childhood, Mustafa was still by his mother's bed, waking her up to come with him to the religious registrar—the only kind allowed in Egypt—where he would divorce his wife. He was preoccupied with his mother's family's unusual history and memories of his childhood linked to that history.

At this point there came into the world 'Aziza Hanim Farahat (Engineer Nayif, Mustafa's father, had given his wife the high-fangled title of Hanim on the basis that he himself was a simple peasant and dazzled by the lights of her family's civil standing, although they were not in fact Pashas, or indeed, anything of the sort). The fact was that her father had been a cloth merchant exactly like Engineer Nayif's father, but he died early, together with her mother, in a car accident; she was seven years old when they disappeared from her life. From that time, she had been brought up by her only sister until she graduated from university and went to work for a travel company in Alexandria. There she had met a failed revolutionary called Nayif Çorbacı, and they'd come back together to get married on the edge of Dayir al-Nahiya.

Her brothers were older, and had better luck in life. They'd all moved in time to better-class areas. Only his aunt Hafiza, who had brought up his mother, had stayed home. All the appearances of splendor that Mustafa's father had made fun of had disappeared both from Tante Hafiza and from Shubra. She married and had children, her husband died, and her children married, and still she sipped tea from a china cup and put one leg over the other on the balcony she called a veranda. Her hair remained uncovered when everyone else started covering theirs with hijab. People laughed at her French vocabulary and supposed she must be a Christian, now that nothing remained of the world that had turned his mother into Sitt Hanim. From this point of view, perhaps, Khulusi Street was linked in Mustafa's head with the empty arrogance of the dispossessed aristocracy, which would stamp the interlude of divorce in the coming months with that same feeling, of someone too poor to clothe themselves who nevertheless stands on ceremony.

Suddenly he was standing between his mother and his aunt, in front of him three swarthy young men in Upper Egyptian gallabiyas whom he'd never seen before in his life. He'd had to hire two witnesses before appearing before the registrar to fulfill the conditions for a divorce *in absentia*, and this was the task he was now engaged in: he first had to ensure that the witnesses weren't Christian and that they had proof of identity. It also seemed necessary for there to be two women gossiping on either side of him. Legends and fairy tales. For a very long time he looked back and forth between his mother and his aunt while they conferred as though debating a judgment they would be delivering on the Sa'idis, as Upper Egyptians are known. When he could find nothing to do, he sighed and said: "How's it going?"—to which, one of the three men smiled shyly (or suspiciously) and replied, "Count your blessings!"

Today, the episode of the divorce comes back to Mustafa like a dream. All those details, no logic to them, and mixed up with memories of his youth. Those sharp shifts of angle and viewpoint. The loudness of a voice and the variation in its tone. His inability to calculate the time at any moment of his memory, and then the interaction of relatives and strangers in ways without any precedent in his life. As if some giant intelligence, tired of the woes of the world, had lain down to sleep after a long period of wakefulness, and Mustafa's only purpose in existing on this earth was to represent the vision of this intelligence.

From the day he'd written a piece on the institution of the Azhar, Mustafa had had it in his head that a registrar, even if he no longer wore the jubba and kaftan of the Azharite faqih, would be a conservative, well-dressed person, with a formal manner. You wouldn't see his wife, for example, even if you visited him at home. And if you did see her, she would never be young and pretty and dressed in revealing clothes. Mustafa, as his aunt Hafiza had told him, would appear before the registrar in his office, where the man earned his bread. So where did all these bottle caps come from?

The plump temptress with the red hair and something like a skimpy nightdress over her flesh, walking back and forth with the tea tray in front of the two Upper Egyptians Mustafa had eventually chosen—they were standing opposite each other in front of the door, backs straight as though on military parade, and eyes almost popping out, despite the great seriousness on their faces—was she really the registrar's wife? Why did Mustafa imagine, then, that she was pushing her nipple into his mouth as she poured him tea? And had she really winked at him as she moved to serve the next person in turn?

He didn't care. He just looked in the opposite direction, where a thin girl in a purple top and jeans was squatting with headphones in her ears, nodding silently.

Perhaps the scene has changed in Mustafa's mind. What he finds strange now is that it didn't astonish him at the time. Neither him, nor the two women swallowed up by the large sofa where they'd sat down as soon as they'd come in, their depressing mumbling growing softer and softer until they almost disappeared from the place—as if those bottle caps were perfectly routine for a registrar's. But when he recalls the registrar's office, which was clearly also his home, Mustafa can see only the high ceiling (behind the two Sa'idis was the apartment door, the kind with two wings he was familiar with from his aunt Hafiza's and which was linked in his mind with the church bells next door), and three tables of varying sizes, all covered to the last centimeter with serrated circular metal bottle caps.

Up to the very moment he left, his mother and aunt hard on his heels, followed by the two witnesses, no one would comment on the bottle caps or explain why they were there. Mustafa was almost certain that he'd seen the Stella beer logo on some of them—at a religious registrar's? He also thought he'd heard the sound of church bells (impossible at this time). But what comes back to him most clearly is the sight of the lame dwarf wearing red track-suit trousers and a pajama top draped over his shoulders. He was almost rolling as he walked quickly toward the largest table, to retrieve a long government logbook from beneath the bottle caps, which his hairy hand removed from the book as though he were shaking it clean, a mock sadness on his face as he sat and placed the book in his lap, saying: "Good things lie in what God has chosen." To which the girl with the red hair replied (a hoarseness in her voice suggested some agitation, though the tone was completely motherly): "It's all fate, your reverence! God willing, He'll compensate him with someone better. All he has to do now is swear the legal oath when you ask him." Mustafa felt that the whole business of the divorce was an interlude in a farce. But instead of being disgusted, he felt that it was his right to watch and enjoy it, even though he was the principal actor.

But in the midst of all this, what reminded him that he'd married and was now divorcing according to the Hanafi rite, even though the Çorbacı family was Shafiʻi, and that this was because the Hanafi rite was the official rite of the Ottomans and of Muhammad 'Ali after them?

Solving the sultan's riddles

For three days, the caliph's riddles had been tormenting Mustafa. Who could this woman be, whom he knew in the Biblical sense and who could put his foot on the beginning of the road? The moment they'd finished, as he was leaving the ground-floor apartment, his mother and aunt Hafiza on his tail and the two Saʻidis behind them, the answer flashed into his head: the wooded hill that Sultan Abdülmecid had turned into a palace, decorating its walls with stars—another Tree Hill in Beşiktaş, Istanbul—because it had a name that in Turkish meant "star": Yıldız.

Although he didn't know what to do with this solution, he seemed to feel a fatherly hand patting his shoulder, and he relaxed. He didn't want to speak to Yildiz—colleague, friend, and a willowy thing like fire—after she'd reprimanded him and issued her invitation and her insulting words had wounded his pride. He was relieved when he found out she was on leave the first day he went to work after leaving Dog Alley because it meant he wouldn't see her for three weeks. Should he seek her out now, with his heart so full of loathing for her? He didn't come to a definite conclusion, though he knew that since the solution to the riddle lay in her name, she would inevitably again become a presence in his life. However, as we can see from our planet, there was a fatherly hand on his shoulder to comfort him.

He said to himself: I can forget about it for the rest of the day—I deserve to celebrate, for God's sake—and tomorrow is another day.

Of course, no time at all had passed. It was only two weeks since he had left his wife. But the sultan's appearance alone was enough for him not to give a shit. People tell you the most important thing is to go slowly and take your time, thought Mustafa. But time, in practical terms, is just a sensation. Five days since the sultan's appearance and he felt that he'd gained three lifetimes' worth of time. In the space of two weeks, he'd gone back to Dream Bridge; the world that had been completed by his marriage had turned into a wreck; and he'd received news of the abortion of his unborn child and over twenty accusations. That's not to mention the dream, the map, the ring, the research, and the appearance of the sultan, followed by the task he had entrusted to him. Even the weather had changed since he'd left Dog Alley—the dust became painful when the wind blew, and afterward the air was clearer and the wind remained, but some days the temperature kept rising and falling until finally it rained and the weather settled between the two extremes—the weather, too, eventually came to a decision. At night, when he went out in a shirt without a T-shirt underneath he felt a gentle sting as the air hit his face. The shade by day could also be like that, but even the sun was bearable.

•   •   •   •   •

Now, in Beirut, where he landed only three weeks after his exodus, Mustafa recalls that his wife had sulked at him, and nothing in the whole world could change that. Sulked at him or just sulked. She'd been sulky before she was pregnant and even more sulky because of his reaction to the pregnancy. Her father had mistreated her mother, her father had left her with nothing for three years when she was dependent on him, her father had threatened to spray firewater in her face then died. His wife would sulk with or without him. The world itself made her sulk and there was no more to be said about it... When he decided they should separate, she sulked more and more. And now that he'd divorced her, she'd sulk more and more and more, despite all she'd said and done previously. The earth turned and she sulked, he thought. Her reality is to sulk, just as his reality, maybe, is to be fed up. And this, he thought, is all that it amounts to when two people meet in this world; this cannot be changed. That rational story they tell us, the happy story about two like-minded people meeting, falling in love, living together with affection and compassion, and begetting children, who are also happy...

This story that motivates us and helps us accept our wretchedness, that we use as evidence that we are in the good camp not the bad camp, evidence that we have values we can hold up like armor in the face of the mad and the evil—when is this story ever true?

In Beirut, Mustafa came to the conclusion that any meeting of two people was nothing more than a clash between sulkiness and ennui, or between any two things that can clash under one roof, whose shelter is the only thing shared by these two like-minded people who meet, fall in love, live together with affection and compassion, and beget children who are also happy. He came to the conclusion that the meeting of two people in this world is no more than what they can salvage from such a clash.

[Cairo's] throngs surge as the waves of the sea, and can scarce be contained in her for all her size and capacity. —Ibn Battuta

At noon, the streets empty and his mother sitting beside him in the car, they made their way back to Dream Bridge— this was the second time on the third Friday since he walked out that he'd driven over from World's Gate—Mustafa felt that Cairo had changed her clothes and was now a babe with a familiar shape. Only his mother's comments threatened to make him feel yet again that he didn't know anything. How could he change his mind after going through all that fear and grief, with all the guilt and the readjustment of engines that went with it? Then again, if we regard Fustuq's prophecy as being the first sign of disintegration, we'll realize that four complete months had gone by since the collapse of the world, each day equivalent to a month or a year or a complete chapter in the tragedy of the collapse of the Sublime State. For four months, that is, Mustafa had been suffering because unknown powers were punishing him. And even if we subtract from that total his days of reason and stability, it is impossible to calculate the pain and effort in a single day, considering that until he'd finished his research the previous evening there'd been not a moment's respite from the feeling of being punished.

What son of a bitch would dare say to him "You decided to get divorced too quickly"?

An unreliable story

When you feel a knock on your forehead, then you know your brain is a locked door. What if a hand were to reach out and open it? Sure, there is someone outside wanting to come in. (Someone very ordinary, whose name is also Mustafa Çorbacı.) But now, suppose we were to imagine a hand reaching out and opening the door, would that mean that the world, relationships, and all of life would actually change?

Until the door opened, once, and everything did change.

Mustafa thought this had happened to him before. Once or twice the door had actually opened and he'd been able to peer inside his own brain. It happened when he was studying in England, perhaps, or during the period when he moved away from Dream Bridge and spent all his time in the Sea of Japan. But because the incident was never completed, no change had resulted.

There'd been an attempt, that is, to open the door into his brain, possibly followed by a second attempt, but neither had succeeded in doing more than pushing the door ajar. And when he peered in through the half-open door, he found nothing. Or perhaps he found people or things like people, whose ghosts continued to haunt him in a half-hearted, intermittent way. Then the tapping on his forehead returned and for the first time he noticed that he was sitting with his elbows on the table, his arm bent over his head, beating his head with his fist. One beat, followed by another, then another, until he discovered there was no one outside as he had supposed.

It is he who is shut up inside, afraid to go out.

Then you ask yourself what might encourage you to complete the mission. But you're hardly done asking when the dream comes, the story begins, and the contents of your brain are spilled all over the table. You know you have left and there's no hope of going back inside.

Every story begins with a dream. The Friday of prayer in Ayasofya was followed by the Friday of tourism downtown (the Ottomans, by the way, used the word we use for "tourism" to mean simply "travel"), when the young sultan appeared to Mustafa and he saw the three priests running as he'd seen them in the dream. He wouldn't find the beginning of his path until his pending divorce was complete—on the basis of the tested loyalty that you possess, Mustafa Efendi, and your knowledge of…

The story of Mustafa's conversation with Amgad, Friday evening

Better to sleep on it, he said, but then he remembered Amgad. Ever since the caliph had appeared to him, he'd wanted to talk to his Sunni friend. He didn't know whether he would have to tell him what had happened. He only knew that Amgad was closely connected to these things and that he might help. Those moments when he suspected he'd gone mad, he'd compare the caliph's appearance with what had happened to Amgad throughout his life: interlude after interlude after interlude of psychosis.

So now, coming back from Shubra, instead of driving to the garage, he dropped his mother off at home and turned the car around to go straight to Amgad's, with no clear plan. "Just a little errand, nonna!" he told her.

Something kept changing in his sense of the world that was moving alongside him out the window. The streets were still empty, which allowed him to recall some of the things he'd discovered in his research about the areas he was driving through. Tahrir Square, for example, the place that defines Cairo—Mustafa had heard that its name had actually once been Isma'iliyya Square—was much less old than he'd thought. None of this had existed before Khedive Isma'il decided to found a modern, French-style city between Bulaq and Fatimid Cairo, Mustafa recalled, when he needed something to make him look good to the European dignitaries attending the opening of the Suez Canal in 1869. Tahrir didn't exist before this. Neither Tahrir, nor Suleiman Pasha Square, Opera Square, Ramses Street, the lions of the Kasr al-Nil Bridge, nor Isaaf Square. Not even the Dry Nile, whose construction had commenced, as Mustafa also discovered during his research, with a new carnival of architectural situations and settings in 1969, exactly a hundred years after the opening of the canal. Never mind that Dream Bridge itself belongs with the next carnival, Mustafa thought.

The whole of World's Gate, from beginning to end, was effectively a fashionable something that they'd put down in an empty area where the city of Qahirah had gradually encroached on the city of Misr before the Ottoman invasion. Of course, you know they were two separate cities and had nothing at all to do with one another until Saladin commissioned the eunuch Qaraqosh to build a wall to connect them. (At this point, Mustafa recalled the common expression "Qaraqosh's rule." He knew that Qaraqosh was cited as a prime example of repression and recklessness because he forced the Copts, who formed the majority of the population of the district, to work as laborers in the construction of the wall, and didn't bother with the impoverished Muslims: the term was originally a Christian one, then...). World's Gate was therefore roughly as old as Mustafa's grandfather, whom he had never seen, the father (God have mercy on him!) of Engineer Nayif al-Hajj Sayyid Ahmad Çorbacı, the biggest cloth merchant in the town of Shubra Khit in his time and, so it was said, in the whole of the governorate of al-Buhayra.

Ezbekiyya

As Mustafa approached Amgad's apartment building on this third Friday, shapes moving up and down out the car window, he noticed that he was looking at the city not as a completely unknown place, nor as a place with which he was gradually renewing his acquaintance, but in a third way—as though Cairo were a geometric arrangement of infinite complexity, constructed of a multitude of surfaces interacting with one another, each surface made up of a million interlocking architectural shapes, each of which told a historical or geographical story independent of the rest. Although this new vision weakened the effect of the sigh that Mustafa had let out when he uttered the divorce oath, repeating the familiar phrase after the lame dwarf while the red-haired girl winked at him for a third time—although he no longer saw Cairo as an attractive girl, exactly—there was a certain pleasure in looking out at the Ezbekiyya Gardens without feeling the interplay of his ideas come to an end at the sidewalk by the wall where his father had bought used books until the government closed the place down and moved the booksellers to kiosks inside the garden wall. Already before Mustafa was born, the garden had shrunk, its design irrevocably ruined. It had become as dingy and lackluster as the lions on the Kasr al-Nil Bridge and everything else in the Khedive's city—antiques piled up and neglected amid the household junk.

As he slowed down and looked at the tall palms and casuarina trees, he recalled that the Ezbekiyya Gardens had originally been named after an Atabeg, as he had learned to call an army general in the Mamluk period.

Ezbek ibn Tatakh al-Atabeg (may God have mercy on him) was the strongest right arm of Sultan Qaitbay, famous for building the fort at Alexandria. It was Ezbek who, between the seventies and eighties of the fifteenth century, dug the lake, built the fort and handled the installations, until, as Qaitbay wanted, he was able to turn the empty area east of Bulaq and west of Mu'izz's Cairo (as the Fatimid city is called after its founder) into a residential suburb in the chicest fashion, until the sultan died and the looting began in the reign of Qansuh al-Ghawri, increasing greatly after the Ottoman conquest. Three centuries of intermittent destruction, until the Ezbekiyya regained its glory in the days of al-Jabarti, so much so that when Bonaparte came, he found it as it had been in its original splendor three centuries previously. As Mustafa took his mobile out of his pocket to call Amgad, having parked by the dilapidated French arches with the working-class shops behind them, he recalled with some alarm that just seventy years after the French invasion, the neighborhood's splendor had disappeared for a second time, its lake filled up and vanished without trace.

• • • • •

As we were saying, from our planet: Mustafa dropped his mother at home, with no clear plan, except to go to Amgad's. When he pressed the key with a green receiver on it—he hadn't lifted the phone directly to his ear—the idea of pleasure in danger came back to him with a startling clarity, as if he were sitting once again with Michel Fustuq in the 'Uruba Café, with the theatrical tone of his Coptic friend's voice ringing in his ears: "Going home every night to be slapped on the back of the head like that… " In the minute and a half which passed between the moment he pressed the key and the moment Amgad Salah's voice reached him, Mustafa felt as though he'd never heard this expression before, as if he really were a well-balanced Cairene, married for several months, with nothing to threaten his employment as a journalist at an economics paper with offices in El Galaa Street, and who had never separated from his wife at all.

The city that was the world hadn't lost its familiarity only to regain it in another form after his research and his divorce.

Sultan Vahdettin hadn't taken on the form of his Azhari colleague Wahid al-Din to charge him with finding one of the seven parchments containing the sura of Mary in the handwriting of his father, Sultan Abdülmecid.

The personal history of Amgad Salah, Mustafa's fickle friend who'd become a Sunni, had no connection with the feeling that still came over Mustafa, that the whole world was against him and punishing him, or that the world was about to collapse, as his Sunni friend had alleged after suffering a psychotic episode.

As soon as he heard Amgad answer the phone with "al-salam 'alaykum" instead of the usual "'allo!", the mere feeling that he hadn't actually heard Fustuq's expression before made Mustafa blurt out (completely seriously and with a sort of gushing expectation that he hadn't bargained on):

"How are you, Amgad? Look, I was wanting you because I caught sight of the zombie you were telling me about some time ago, remember?"

As soon as he'd said it, he was conscious of a long silence on Amgad's part. He immediately realized the seriousness of what he'd done, and expected something bad, which made him absolutely delighted when he heard his friend reply— letting out a new sigh—"OK, where are you? Standing down below, Mr. Çorbacı, are you?" A hint of laughter, which had been simmering, as always, from the start of their conversation, now brimmed over. "OK, come up! Or will you wait for me to come down to you to get a breath or two of fresh air? You know the wedding's getting close, God willing, and, to be honest, I'm fed up with sitting at home like this!"

"Cool!" he said, and wished he hadn't been so cheerful, because at this moment it was as if Amgad's sigh had given him the green light to tell Amgad everything with impetuous abandon, everything that had happened from beginning to end, and to ask him about the link between our Master Wahid al-Din, the zombie, and the Organization. "Cool!"

Driven once again by a power he didn't understand, Mustafa forgot, or pretended to forget, that his Sunni friend was psychologically disturbed and constantly on the verge of a breakdown, and told him everything one step at a time— from the beginning of the dream about the conquest of Constantinople, when he cooperated with the young Sultan Mehmet II in turning the cathedral of Hagia Sophia into the mosque of Ayasofya by holding the Friday prayer inside it, to getting the ring with the tughra engraved on it (through Amgad himself) in the Khan of Secrets, and the transformation of their fiqi colleague into His Highness the deceased Sultan Vahdettin ibn Abdülmecid for precisely two hours in the newspaper office, during which time he had told Mustafa of the existence of an ancient cosmic struggle between the Islamic umma and those supernatural forces that Amgad and Mustafa after him called the Organization (Mustafa didn't mention to Amgad this time either that his hunch after talking with the Sultan had proved correct, in that the Sunnis had proved to be exactly like Atatürk, opposing the umma in this struggle), until the caliph charged him with finding one of the parchments of the sura of Mary in the handwriting of his father, Abdülmecid ibn Mahmud.

Amgad seemed to hesitate when Mustafa, to avoid going to the Khan of Secrets, insisted that he had to return to his mother before too long, then headed, without asking, toward the Sea of Japan. For some unknown reason, he wanted to hold their conversation at the 'Uruba Café, the place where Michel Fustuq's prophecy had first reached him. He recalled that it was also on a Friday that Fustuq had spoken the words that brought his marriage to an end, at the same time of day, during a time of the year when the weather was similar. He expected to find 26 July Street quiet in the same disturbing way, as his voice rang out with the news of the conspiracy and the sultan. And though his voice didn't ring in the end (perhaps it rang loud enough in Amgad's ear), and despite all the ideas that came to him on the way, his determination to tell the story never wavered.

What happened was that Amgad found himself sitting on the sidewalk with a higher than usual small table between his legs. The table had on it the elbow of his divorced friend, while the friend himself was bending the shisha tube over his head, blowing molasses-soaked tobacco directly into his beard and chattering into his ear. Even today, Mustafa doesn't know how he could have failed to notice the effect of his words on Amgad Salah.

"When Amgad looked at me, during that time," he wrote at the end of a notebook he'd filled during the three weeks in which the story was brought to a conclusion—a fine Italian notebook with a calf-hide cover, brown like the sura parchment, which his friend Rashid Jalal al-Siyouti had given to him some time ago, and which he had kept for a fateful occasion—"I imagine that he must have seen on my face that same pleasure in danger. Perhaps it appeared as a dumb smile accompanied by an unexplained widening of the eyes, as I said to him, for example: 'You're right about this Organization,' or asked: 'What I want to know, Amgad, is this: was the zombie that appeared to you actually Sultan Vahdettin?' I imagine that in the middle of all this he could see the face of the beast he'd been fleeing for ten years now reincarnated as his closest friend. For half an hour, I, Mustafa Çorbacı, Amgad Salah's only ally and confidant in a world ruled by conspiracies, became a member of the Organization originally founded to persecute him, just one other face of the zombie who wanted to eat his brain and then propagate among mankind a plague that would end the world as we know it. All the demons that had touched Amgad and that he was unable to avoid except by joining the opposite side in the struggle—perhaps for half an hour in the 'Uruba Café one mild day in April, I became them all."

The Sunni may have appeared composed as Mustafa sounded off to him, or perhaps his anger was just an ordinary annoyance with the smoke. What was certain—and this is something Mustafa will never forget—is that Amgad never said anything. Didn't reply to his questions, and didn't comment on his statements. Before Mustafa could finish talking, he suddenly stood up, knocking the table, then straightening it with a violent movement of the hand, and stepped quickly in the direction of the road. Mustafa would remember his straight back, his taut arm muscles, the sight of the table shaking between them, and the glazed expression on his face. He remembered Amgad saying, without even trying to make his excuse convincing, "I have to go at once, Mr. Çorbacı. I'd forgotten, I've got an important appointment with my mother-in-law." Already he had walked into the street and flagged down a taxi that was hovering on the opposite side of the road, under the flyover.

Mustafa shouted: "Hey, wait, I'll give you a lift, at least!"

And his Sunni friend's impatience and quavering voice reminded him of when he'd leaped over the corporation's banisters and threw his mobile at him about eight years before.

"What do you mean, give me a lift? You've smothered the mother of the beard with your mother of a shisha—how will I go to the mosque with a beard like this?"

From behind the vehicles parked under the flyover the taxi drew away, with Amgad inside it. Mustafa stood staring, the shisha tube still in his hand.

They asked 'Amr ibn 'Ubayda: "Can a demon throw a man to the ground?" He replied: "If it were impossible, God would not have made a proverb of it." —al-Jahiz

Mustafa didn't see Amgad after that encounter. On his final day in the office, he'd just hear that, after entering the asylum again, the recently betrothed Sunni had been forced to postpone his Islamic wedding celebration, to which he wouldn't have invited anyone from the corporation anyway. Mustafa thought he'd lost him when he confronted him with the futility of the Salafi school the day they'd gone to the Khan of Secrets, the first weekend after he'd left, but in fact he hadn't lost him until sometime later.

Now the picture was gradually becoming clearer before his eyes, without, however, filling all the gaps, disparities, and cracks that prevented its completion: that what had turned the fiqi Wahid al-Din into a horror film when he returned from his time off from the paper because of illness, maybe the cause of the illness itself, was the role that he was fated to play, without his knowing it, by assuming the spirit of the sultan—if not in all the lands of the Empire, then at least in Egypt. The fiqi certainly didn't know that this was happening to him, so would he know when it happened? And was the process so emotionally and psychologically taxing as to turn him into a clown? Amgad had gone to Canada to escape from the spirit of the same sultan when he appeared to him and demanded that he find one of the parchments of the sura of Mary. He was influenced by Romero's films and called the intermediary a zombie before he had anything to do with the idea of the Organization.

Perhaps his choice of term was inspired by his conversation with our Master, without acknowledging to himself that this zombie had originally come to win him over in the war against what the term "Organization" itself signified: the conspiracy unfolding against the Muslims. Until things became very confusing for him, and he began to think that the zombie and the Organization were fighting on the same front against him personally, instead of confronting the fact that they were rivals in the existential struggle between Islamic civilization and history that had been raging since the collapse of the Sublime State. The murky confrontations that Amgad had encountered, nurtured by his paranoia over lawbreakers in Ontario, or the occurrence of the biggest "Islamic" terrorist attack on New York while he was there, Mustafa Çorbacı's marriage to a girl who'd always been a bit of a "hippy," and Aldo's high-pitched, effeminate cackles… everything that happened to Amgad was driving him toward submission to the thing that would spare him having to decide.

Were the mystical forces of history that the sultan had mentioned to Mustafa, without specifying what they were—powers dressed up as Atatürk, as European colonialism and national independence movements, then as neoliberalism and religious fundamentalism ("the tail end of the same turd," as Mustafa called fundamentalism in his notebook, alluding to the fact that Salafism was the logical extension of nationalism)—were they all the time striving to win over the person on whom the Sultan's choice had fallen?

Everything is fate, he said to himself. And although he realized that he'd hurt Amgad by talking to him like that, he also knew that if he hadn't told him anything, the picture wouldn't have appeared before his own eyes with such amazing clarity that it didn't require completion: something that just glows, like the appearance of the ring as soon as Amgad Salah had pushed it under Mustafa's eye in the Khan of Secrets. Though the existence of that thing didn't mean it was understood or resolved. Something like an apartment building whose foundation pillars dissolve as soon as you move in to one of the apartments.

That was how the matter had been when he related it to his Sunni friend. Did the picture need to be any clearer?

Mustafa continued to repeat this question to himself as he wandered around the Sea of Japan, recollecting and reviewing things without anxiety or torment. He had noticed the rear end of a small funeral, and the dead man carried on a bier looked—as they had said about his father's bier in Shubra Khit—as if he were flying, propelled by a force of his own.

Without anticipating disaster of any kind, he knew that the story of his life would finish before the end of the week.

Sea of Japan

At first, he walked along 26 July Street. The street is broken up by the 15 May Bridge, which already looked like a tributary of the Dry Nile before any construction to connect them started: swollen vertebrae, thought Mustafa, from the island's spinal column.

For half an hour, as he walked, he was preoccupied by the flyovers and the possibility that they might have some symbolic significance for Cairo. He'd always felt that the Dry Nile, in El Galaa Street in particular, blocked water and light from the world beneath it. In Cairo many main roads are cut lengthwise by flyovers—the first being Dream Bridge Street, where his family home was situated—but El Galaa Street, despite being one of the widest of these streets, was where he felt most that the flyover reduced light and constricted space.

Because this was the biggest flyover in the city?

Maybe, but Mustafa had a suspicion that this feeling wasn't based in actual reality. The effect of the flyover on the view and the traffic was only apparent at World's Gate because everything seemed clearer at World's Gate—because the first time Mustafa had seen things, he'd seen them there.

Now, as he crossed 26 July Street on foot for the fourth or fifth time, with the shadow of the bridge blotting out the little light remaining in the sky, Mustafa imagined that the flyovers, which had become—after the carnival of architectural situations and settings that had arrived a century after the Khedive's city—the city's most important distinguishing feature, had a function other than to try to outwit the shortage of space and the traffic above the water or to shorten distances.

The flyover takes you from one world to another, true, but it also creates a mist like a magnetic field over the area where it stands, transporting it too from one world to another. It leaves it more crowded and more contemptible, almost transforming it from a district in the Khedive's city to a village that has forgotten its own name. Peasant women in black dresses walking on the asphalt in the middle of the road beside the idle freight trucks, like tractors that have lost their way to the fields; parking attendants shouting at the siren on a broken-down crane; or a rubbish-cart donkey, spooked from being surrounded by motorcycles. Between cross roads and street ramps the air is thick with clouds and pedestrians like stray buffaloes; if a car hit them, they would low. You'd only see this under the flyover or in the imagination. So could the flyovers—or the whole carnival of situations and settings—actually be part of the grand conspiracy?

A feeling of being at the end of one's rope was again taking shape in Mustafa's head, not just in light of Amgad's reaction to what he'd said but also from this urban vision and its associations. The picture had become clearer after Amgad's reaction, and now Mustafa started asking himself what had made Fustuq, Mazika, and his wife parts of the story.

When he found no immediate answer, he decided to take a long walk there and back from the Umm Kulthum apartment building, where the Star of the East's villa once stood on the Nile, to the ceramics museum in the direction of the Gezira Club. He wouldn't think about anything, but simply look at God's people spread out among familiar things, things whose existence in their place under normal circumstances would comfort him. For the second time, he passed the apartment he'd rented for his Japanese girlfriend in one of the narrow lanes between Shajarat al-Durr Street and Mansur Muhammad Street, walking more slowly at the beginning of his excursion. He noticed the enormous differences in dress and manner between people, and it frightened him to think how much one life could differ from another within a single square meter of dug-up sidewalk surrounded by pale black-and-white squares.

When he returned to 26 July Street, he felt that the presence of these things no longer comforted him and that the world had changed for the third time in a single day. He squatted out of breath on the sidewalk in front of the Akhnatun arts complex: the building of the Aisha Fahmi Palace (he'd discovered this by chance during his research), built by 'Ali Pasha Fahmi, the Nazir al-Jihadiyya or Minister of War, who took over the post in place of Ahmad 'Urabi after the failure of the 1882 uprising. When he grew tired of looking at the building and contemplating the world's ups-and-downs—the same feeling of neglected antiquities piled up, in poor taste, in the middle of modern clutter—he got up and walked to where he'd parked his car in front of the 'Uruba Café, then turned round and drove off.

A second story

Rather than going to swimming pools or parks, Mustafa liked to go to Sand Port, where the Birqash camel market was held. The last time he'd persuaded his wife to accompany him there, he'd asked her jokingly whether camels were a source of healthy milk or a form of Jeep Cherokee. Sometimes they reminded him of birds, ostriches or flamingos, and sometimes they were extraterrestrial creatures, like something between insects and reptiles. Enormous, either way.

For her part, his wife kept to the traditional description of the camel as the Ship of the Desert. Mustafa remembered how her eyes had widened as she spoke to an Upper Egyptian sitting in the market during a visit, and the Sa'idi had told her that camels were now only useful for their meat—"Yes, yes, at the butchers!" She nodded her head slowly with a vague smile on her lips: "Are we eating our ships now?" she asked, as if they were people of the desert—and sure enough that's what they were, if they wanted to be Arabs of any kind, or even Muslims. "Land ships" wasn't the only way of describing them, of course, but Mustafa had often thought about how the Forty Days' Road had been plagued by highwaymen. He had the idea that the demise of the camel as a method of transportation was what had put an end to Arab travel literature: letters sent by travelers. When people stopped riding camels, it meant that the well for this kind of literature had dried up. The journey from the Maghreb to Mecca was no longer worth writing down.

To this day, he often thinks that his love for this creature is perhaps another result of what moves him to scribble in his notebook, or that he scribbles as a form of motion. He loves camels because they are the traveler's ink.

Going to Sand Port, Saturday

Again he was driving. The third Saturday evening since leaving Dog Alley, after talking to Amgad Salah on the day of his divorce, Mustafa Çorbacı was again driving alone. With no clear, or even unclear, direction this time. As if the city were a cinema screen and the car a balcony seat. Traffic would slow him down but he kept driving. Distance and air. Happy with the divorce and with traveling. More happy than ever that he'd been chosen to fulfill the commission.

When the phone rang in his pocket that evening he pulled over to one side—we think he was on Salah Salem Street when he pulled over, in Plane Yard, to which his destiny was rapidly leading him—then got out of the car before answering. He had an overwhelming desire to walk on foot, and the phone was an opportunity at hand, especially since parking was permitted there. What didn't occur to him, with his mind on Amgad Salah, was that the call might be from the Christian puppet he'd been so annoyed to meet the day he was introduced to the Padishah. So he was alarmed by the word "Pistachios" on the screen and hesitated before replying in an official tone: "Hello, Michel, how are…"

"Hey, Uncle Shurba, how are you doing these days?" The Pistachio Kid interrupted him in the same fucked-up manner as always, unaware that he was talking to someone who'd changed 180 degrees since he'd last seen him. "Hey, do you think you're so important you can let the phone ring for an hour? Not to mention that it's been a month" (since the previous Tuesday, in fact), "with no message and no missed call, not even a fragrant letter, you leave your lover like that, like mist on the windshield!" And, before Mustafa could speak, either to defend himself or anything else, "No, you've been standing me up big time, Chief Shurba, and that's rotten of you, believe me. You don't tell me what happened with your wife or ask for my opinion. Is it because I'm a Christian? You've started to sit with Sheikh Amgad all the time, soon you'll have a beard too and will screw us in the head. You wearing a short gallabiya yet? Listen, I'm meeting friends early tomorrow morning at the farm and I want to see you there. Tomorrow early, I'm telling you, Shurba, don't get up at 3 PM then say sorry I missed it! OK? I'll be pissed if you do that! I sent you a big map too so you don't get lost on the way. Not a squeak about not being able to come, hear me? I'll be pissed, I'm telling you! And anyway, it's easy to get there, I mean you won't get lost, believe me! Listen, you…"

"OK, son, Pistachio Kid, but I'm on the street right now." It was only anger that finally allowed him to interrupt Fustuq and stop the conversation. "I'll come, yes, I'll come!"

Then he pressed the key with the red receiver on it before he could hear the reply.

As he got out onto the sidewalk and walked quickly away from the car, as if fleeing his place of imprisonment, for the first time Mustafa felt that the little barrel had failed to evoke any feeling of guilt. If being hung up on had hurt his feelings, he could eat shit. He'd respected his feelings the whole time he'd known him, but why?

By and large, the fact that Mustafa was careful not to hurt Fustuq hadn't made it any easier to deal with him. He had to persuade himself to endure Fustuq's never-ending horse shit, put up with his Sa'idi complexes and his ethnic stupidity—either that or the Pistachio Kid would sulk. As he strolled along Salah Salem Street on the outskirts of Nasr City, it was for the first time blindingly obvious to Mustafa that it made no difference to him whether Fustuq was offended or not. He could be angry, he could go to hell. Serve him right!

Why should it make any difference to Mustafa—a small barrel in two versions, one a black or Hispanic rapper, and the other a falsetto street bum calling for an international neoliberal regime, while profiting from local corruption and setting the worst example for national unity between Muslim and Christians... After all, this was a mere puppet, not even of our faith, wasn't it?

What really preoccupied Mustafa was the party he'd been invited to and the fact that he'd decided to accept the invitation. Ever since he'd made up new names for the quarters of the city, he'd known that his inner and outer journeys, which started with a dream whose content he hadn't immediately comprehended, would certainly take him, if not to Birqash, then somewhere else in Sand Port. (For this reason he would sketch his route to Sand Port rather than Shubra, where he had divorced his wife, because Sand Port had become the more enduring place in his life.) He had correctly prophesied that in this unexpected journey he would discover new proofs of the Padishah's truthfulness.

We did not forget that bodies have narrow destinies. —Sargon Boulos

The trick is in the imagination, he found himself thinking as he walked along the edge of Nasr City, gazing at the concrete and molten asphalt, like an industrial desert in the shades of gray that had taken the place of the yellow wasteland northeast of Cairo. When you can imagine a situation different from the one you're in, then you're moving. In theory, there's nothing to stop you completing a journey of a million light years in a single day and changing from that greasy old man wiping the dirt from his hand on his gallabiya as he hawks a toy fiddle, to the owner of the orange Hummer who parks across the street then walks away, chin up, in a leather jacket. Mustafa recollected the Padishah's words about Muhammad 'Ali— from an orphan with no income under the protection of the military commander of a small Greek town, to a real rival of the sultan—and he too wondered at the vicissitudes of time, how quickly circumstances could change.

The Padishah was of course referring to the fates of cities and peoples and, as the centuries followed each other, the ripping up of maps. What was in Mustafa's mind was something closer and more straightforward: people were always terrified that their lives might change, and always had a judgment ready for any such change, even though reality was full of opportunities and carried no guarantees.

People were so afraid of a worse life, and this cost them the opportunity to see the world from many angles rather than only one. It may be hard to be a sweeper after you've been a journalist, for example, but on a much deeper level, if it happened, it's very likely that you would see the world afresh, completely anew and afresh, and that you would find some compensation in this for everything.

Mustafa thought that Cairo itself was a place ripe for change. If you were to change from one thing to another and then became a third thing, so he said to himself (and the weather was fine enough to give his walk both a joyous energy and a balanced enthusiasm), if you became a third thing, this could only increase your humanity in human terms. There is more than one life in a human lifespan, and the best things happen without your being aware of them.

I was sent from myself as a messenger to myself, and through my miracles my soul was guided to me. —'Umar ibn al-Farid

Mustafa stood for a moment stroking the trunk of a large and most likely dead mulberry tree, feeling a pious gratitude to whoever had allowed him to be born again, seeing with an eye that was not his eye, and hearing with an ear that was also like the sultan's seal, like the ear of the history of Islam. This was the first indication of the return of the craving that had been snatched from his body since his marriage had turned sour. With his hand on the tree trunk in a relatively empty area in the middle of Plane Yard, he sensed in the rough bark something that seemed to respond to his fingers, as if it was tender or alive. And until he suddenly felt the impulse to embrace and kiss it, he paid no attention to the fact that he was standing out in the open, groping a mulberry tree.

He was also conscious of wanting the bark to be a woman's skin. For the first time he recalled, with his whole body, that skin of this kind could exist apart, totally apart, from his wife.

Beside the tree, Mustafa remembered the bier he'd observed flying in the Sea of Japan. He recalled a modern poem he'd read somewhere or other about how when a dead man lies on his back, the world is shortened, and it occurred to him that if there were nothing except for our bodies, we would have no destinies. What proved this was that fateful decisions are all made in a moment, with no consideration for the age of the body that's making them or their effect on its existence: the decision to marry, the decision to divorce, the decision to procreate, the decision to join oneself to another body which will die, or to finally part from it, or to make one's peace with an aged father before it's too late.

Fateful decisions do not take into account the life of a body. Like our destinies, which manifest themselves as pale memories or shadows, they are giant containers in which all our perceptible features sink away.

For a longish period, Mustafa considered the subject of fate: how it was really a mistake to suppose that the end of a human body was the end of its destiny. He said to himself that the Padishah's destiny, for example, was a lot longer, more complex, and more extensive than his body. Mustafa downed a double espresso in the first café he came to and walked slowly back to where he'd parked his car when Fustuq's call came. He got in, shut the door, and fastened his belt, then looked in the mirror as if he'd noticed something on his face.

And only at that moment did he see clearly that he was no longer Mustafa Nayif Çorbacı: he was now the Chosen Çorbacı—like the Prophet Muhammad himself, a *mukhtar*—or a *mustafa*, as his name suggested. He sat up straight in front of the steering wheel and looked again in the mirror above his head, then yawned, stretched, took a packet of cigarettes and a lighter from his pocket, and put them on the dashboard below the mirror. Then he turned the car around.

Rasm *(drawing, mark, or illustration): a trace. It is defined as: the remains of a trace. It is also defined as: a trace without a person. It is also defined as: a trace that remains on the ground.* —Lisan al-'Arab

When he took the car out at six o'clock in the morning on the third Saturday—he'd bathed and slept, after giving his mother some affection, eating her food with gusto, and reassuring her as much as possible that the divorce was a good thing and the future wide open—he recalled that he didn't know how to get from Dream Bridge to the villages to the north of Giza except through the area of the Pyramids.

Even if he *had* known, he thought, as he printed out Fustuq's map from the email and folded the paper emerging from the printer into his pocket before leaving, he'd want to take his usual route via the Pyramids to Kirdasa, without looking at the map until he reached a certain canal there whose name he didn't know. He hadn't touched any food (as his sleeping mother would've noticed had she been awake) and he was pleased to be going to the home of his favorite creature without having eaten. Exactly by the garage, he recalled that when he'd gone to photograph camels in the past, always at this time in the early morning, he had followed the examples of the anonymous funeral portrait painters during the Roman period in Egypt, the creators of the faces of Fayyum and Hawara that continued to be produced until about AD 300 (three hundred years before the arrival of 'Amr ibn al-'As, the Arab general who annexed Egypt in the Prophet Muhammad's lifetime, at Rawda Island). Mustafa had read a lot about them after seeing their work in a large exhibition held in the Mahmoud Khalil Museum at Dream Bridge, the same week he'd joined the newspaper.

These artists drew people on wood using warm wax or dye dissolved in resin; they did so from life, during the person's lifetime, so that at the end—usually many years later—a tablet with the person's likeness could be inserted into the mummy casing at the position of the actual face. The raw materials used demanded a high speed of execution because they dried immediately. Most likely, they had used a lens like a projector to reflect the face of the person being painted onto the wood, to achieve such astonishing verisimilitude with light, shade, and texture. Mustafa was convinced that these drawings were a form of photography, but what interested him even more was that these anonymous artists, in order to be confident in their purity of mind, and out of piety in performing the task with dedication, would refrain from eating from the time they woke until the completion of the required portrait. The artist would then take his fee and go home.

Some months after Mustafa had joined the newspaper, when he started to take photography seriously, he became fascinated by the idea that artistic work should be a devotion in the literal sense. He was absolutely convinced that if he was fasting when he looked at the face of a camel he was photographing he would see something infinitely purer and more beautiful.

From Dream Bridge to Sand Port

Now, as he headed right instead of turning back at the Orman Garden, and continued along the Cairo University wall, passing the Bayn al-Sarayat area and the Bulaq al-Dakrur Bridge, to turn to north again behind the university and head toward al-Malik Faisal Street—King Faisal ibn 'Abd al-'Aziz Al Sa'ud's catastrophic legacy to the city, and one of the destinations he'd imagined himself heading for ever since he realized he was on a journey—he was thinking that even if his fast that day was not for an artistic work, it was certainly for the sake of purity of mind and piety in one of the first steps in his commission. The flow of traffic on the Sudan Street extension, and the blazing light. Behind the nick in the road to the right—were those train tracks? By God, they were!—was a world not of this world called Ard al-Liwa'.

Now, unusually, Mustafa was in a completely good mood. He hummed the Hosta Costa song without feeling any anxiety. Pricking up his ears, he contemplated the extent of the various worlds and how they adjoined each other. At the start of the bridge, for example, he called to mind a boy about ten years old in one of the alleys of that world some time ago, who'd tried to sell him a bundle of straw on the basis that it was a packet of bango, and when he refused to buy it, had produced a penknife. Hatred of mythical proportions was visible in his face. He called to mind a group of wrinkled women smoking a shisha in a circle around a fire, its smoke truly blinding. Behind them were emaciated crops and rooms made from plywood and metal sheeting. How old was this memory, and why was he certain that it was from the same place?

Ard al-Liwa', he thought, was the ideal drawing of the city that had become a village, or else the village that had become a city. He wondered whether the secret of his interest in this duality was the existence of his family home on the edge of Dayir al-Nahiya. Then he concluded, rather, that he felt something similar had happened to Islam and the Muslims. As though the Free Officers, on the planet from which our Master the Sultan had come, had hatched a revolution against the rule of Muhammad 'Ali's family under the shadow of European colonialism (also on that planet) and had built the flyovers above the fine quarters of the Khedive's city there.

As if it was this that had led to the weakening of Islamic power and the disappearance of blessed events, to use the Padishah's language, from our own planet. The history of this Islamic capital since the mid-fifties had been a microcosm of unseen revolution that had led to decline: a blow from above on the top of the head of the Islamic umma.

Mustafa, however, had only just bowed his head when he found himself in the middle of a spluttering of cars, microbuses, bicycles, motorcycles, and pedestrians. This spluttering was associated in his mind with Faisal more than anywhere else. When he'd crossed the short flyover—and as usual forgot to bear left toward the street island diagonally opposite, in order to cross over (he'd have to wait a bit at the lights) via the side road connecting Faisal Street directly with Pyramids Road (grander, wider, older, and more pleasant)—he realized that he could take Faisal Street the whole way, and wasn't too alarmed.

Something attracted Mustafa to Faisal, he confessed to himself for the first time, and this had occasioned more than one argument with his wife when they'd been on visits to al-Maryutiyya or 6 October City, because he always forgot to make that turn, as though he deliberately wanted to get stuck in the filthy trail of traffic and knew it.

Faisal, he said, was the narrowest main road in the whole world.

With the packed housing, the tinpot apartment buildings springing up around it, the appalling manners of the drivers, the rudeness of the coffee sellers and shop owners, and the force of pedestrians hurtling like ants between paralyzed cockroaches, Mustafa knew in the depths of his heart that Faisal was the most perfect example of the collapse of civil society in the whole of Greater Cairo. The place where you could see with your own eyes the failure of all those imagined homelands—from the American "way of life" to a sudden, violent death.

Perhaps for this reason, although he was usually annoyed by traffic jams to the point of exploding, he consciously or unconsciously decided he could put up with them whenever he came to this place.

Today he was in a good mood and not in a hurry about anything. The congestion couldn't annoy him. The route would become clear to him when he sketched at the end of the night—he'd sit upright in bed for a second time in front of a B-movie he liked; then, when he'd finished everything, he'd go to sleep and the second dream would come to him (as will be recounted later), and when he woke up he'd draw his face for the last time.

Faisal Street would be revealed to him like the page of a book, like the sketch he'd drawn of the 26 July Corridor after the expedition to the Khan of Secrets, with the difference that this time, although the page was still full of writing, there were no lines in it, no sections or margins, no boundaries of any kind. A stream of motionless traffic in the distance; that was the shape that Faisal Street took in Mustafa's imagination. Except that, as he made this journey, he again felt he was trapped inside a book. Only, this time, on a page that looked like this:

Just words, complete or incomplete, repeated or not, spread horizontally with the car in the middle, as though the car, with Mustafa inside it, was a piece of steel tossed into a gravel yard in broad daylight.

After he'd bypassed Kirdasa and reached the small canal that he knew there, the first concept of the story he was passing through would take shape in Mustafa's head in the form of a book. The story he was scribbling down in detail in the notebooks and seeing more and more as the purpose of his whole life. A book of travel literature, social history, or autobiography. A book in the old style, in the form of a letter to a friend...

Or else it was a perfectly integrated situation, the closest metaphor for it a book based on three weeks in the life of a man. Every time this man makes a journey by car during these three weeks, he sees himself on one page of this book. And each page is followed by a crudely drawn map of the route he follows, so that they appear before him unadorned, just as he sees them.

On the road, as he passed the pyramids, he would see from behind the walls and palm trees the edge of the pyramid of Khafre, built on land higher than that of his father, Khufu, and son, Menkaure. Then his position changed, and he saw, on the other side of the three pyramids, phosphorescent crops, dark sand, olive-green water, and scenes from which he took away the asphalt and for no particular reason inserted Ottoman sipahis with their narrow turbans and blue vests, gilded scepters in their hands, on red saddles that flowed behind them—alone where they were supposed to have fought the Mamluks, with no Mamluk helmets or swords threatening them with death, he saw sipahis bereft of leggings, embroideries, long-sleeved robes, tunics, and other Mamluk clothing that he'd read about or seen pictures of during his research.

Only fine horses with saddles like the trains of wedding dresses, and horsemen in black and white uniform with turbans—he remembered the dream of Hagia Sophia and felt an incomprehensible pride.

No other male is like the camel when it is excited, for it becomes bad tempered, so that its foam becomes visible... [then] it spews less and eats less. —al-Abshihi

Shortly after passing the canal, Mustafa stood in the fields to look at the map Fustuq had emailed him, have a cigarette, and see if he could see a camel or two. He said to himself that it was still early and he'd most likely speak to Fustuq from here so that he could describe the route to him; either from spite or pettiness, he didn't want Fustuq to think the map had been useful. The air was clear today, with the smell of dung and ravenous mud on his tires, the air cleaner than the air of Faisal, and something like the joy of nature itself. He looked at the clover and the palm trees in the distance and felt the power of lust in his body, and to the sound of a faint twittering and bleating in an unknown direction, desire swayed to and fro in his body.

Had his sexual craving returned at last? Good.

As the faint bleating of a camel now reached his ears, Mustafa imagined he could feel the hand of the Padishah on his shoulder again. The Padishah's hand reminded him that peace of mind was also a blessing, and that with the appearance of the camels he had wanted to see, with the joy of nature, and desire, he was promised an amorous encounter that would restore to him, from where he knew not, his confidence in the value of contact with women. A whole herd now arrived—accompanied only by a small, barefoot child, holding a cane and wearing a blue gallabiya—but Mustafa latched onto a young camel whose age he reckoned at around four years. It was balking, frothing without bleating, and the child was hitting it to no effect. The child started running beside the herd in a scene that Mustafa thought like a postcard of the Giza countryside—complete and utter kitsch—then left the herd and approached the unruly camel, which was half kneeling in a way that left its whole body twisted over the shoulder of the road.

As its nose widened in a series of soundless puffs, it seemed to Mustafa, as he watched the foaming and steaming, that the camel was talking to him. He actually saw the camel lift its head to him, and shake it a bit as Mustafa looked into his face, following the movement of his breathing, which resembled words and sentences. In a language like the unarticulated speech of ghosts in a dream, Mustafa heard the camel say to him: "You and I are one, we have done with this world. But today, when nature is happy with itself, and desire is stirring in our two bodies, there is no place for us in the forefront of civilization and no female will slake our thirst. And what does this lousy driver want from me, anyway?" He took in his words and gestured to the camel, looking him in the eye, as if to reassure him that he understood, then went back to the car in the middle of the mud with his mobile in his hand.

Be patient with me for a moment, then you can go. All that you said about me has reached me... —Ziyad al-Rahbani

"Hey, dude, are you pistachios at everything in the world, even maps?" he asked Fustuq. And without intending to, he extracted from him a confession that the gathering of friends was really an engagement party and that he was going to formally register his betrothal the following day in church.

"Who are you marrying, buddy? The girl who goes to church? Damn your religion, man. But why didn't you say anything yesterday when you phoned?"

Fustuq made the excuse that he hadn't wanted to impose the cost of a present on Mustafa but there was an obvious embarrassment in his voice; it cheered Mustafa as he sat in his car with the map in his hand, smoking. "Good L-l-l-lord!" he said to his Coptic friend.

Till he turned round and drove off, waving to the camel.

As he drove off (an event that would fill his lungs with optimism), he saw a small white bird that seemed to return from the middle of the field and circle around the restive camel before settling on its back. The camel was shaking its tail teasingly and turning its head toward the bird.

•   •   •   •   •

After arriving with relative ease and greeting those guests that he knew, Mustafa would take the Pistachio Kid to one side. They were both in their swimsuits, beer cans and hamburgers in their hands. For ten minutes he quizzed him, one question at a time:

Did you leave your girlfriend?

"Believe me, things just weren't working out! Then, because you've quarreled with the bit you've got, you say to me 'did you leave?'—I mean, I left you, you left me, or you leave me and sit stringing me along? Grow up, man!"

And why are you getting married so quickly?

"Come on, would I say to my father, 'What's up with you?' They were afraid that if I didn't marry I'd go back to *her* again. Believe me, I thought hard, Shurba, and talked to a lot of people, here and in America. Look, I can't put my name on a woman I've slept with. You may not be a believer yourself, but with me, this is something sacred. I mean, it's no use. Because you haven't got any self-respect, I mean, you can't appreciate what I'm saying. Ha ha! Our Lord sent you Sheikh Amgad to give you guidance. Ha ha! I mean, don't make fun of me, what did you gain from marrying out of love, and all that talk, and now you're lying there like a woman stuffed into a meat safe, I mean have you gotten out of the safe or not yet, buddy?"

Okay, but why this silly girl?

"There's no one without faults, Shurba, and this one's much better than the others, believe me. And then, she's not stupid or anything. Just because you don't know her and are seeing her in the middle of the engagement and so on. Believe me, believe me, a good wife shouldn't have to keep her belly in the market any longer. What's more, this girl's religious and well-mannered and her family is very respectable. Why do you want your friend to let good things go and frolic in the mud? Just because you fell into the trash can, you've got a grudge, yes, you look like you really have a grudge!"

Michel, Michel, do you realize that this decision of yours really makes me sad?

"My friend, you'll be making Indian films about me, with plaintive love songs and a baby doll under the wheels of the car—what's wrong with you?"

•　　　•　　　•　　　•　　　•

But Mustafa's understanding of the ins and outs of his Coptic friend's marriage would not be complete until he went to the restroom by chance and heard him talking to a third colleague of theirs (as would become clear later) about him (Mustafa) and his wife, whom Fustuq didn't yet know he'd divorced.

He was talking without knowing Mustafa was listening.

So, by a chance that wasn't a chance, the great discovery of this journey would be made, a discovery that would hurt Mustafa's soul perhaps more than anything else in his tale, in the long term. There was no rational explanation for his presence in that little restroom at precisely the moment when Fustuq was talking to their Australian-Egyptian colleague, another Copt, who worked in the same corporation (but in a different department from the economics paper), and whom Mustafa knew superficially. Fustuq and the Australian-Egyptian were standing against the wooden wall outside the toilet, and Fustuq was talking to the other man (while Mustafa was inside) and letting him in on some new facts. As a result of this coincidence, not only would the ins and outs of the old prophecy become clear to Mustafa, but he would also discover for the first time, with no filters and no streetwise pretensions, the inner thoughts of the Pistachio Kid.

•　　　•　　　•　　　•　　　•

On the farm, he recalls, there was a circular swimming pool surrounded by the most elegant of chaises-longues, almost like marble, with towels like velvet atop them and atop the towels people in swimwear. "What about going inside and relaxing a bit in private," he said to his colleague, the dark-skinned girl from the office. She laughed and straightened up, showing the outline of her pubic region through the bikini that exposed the flesh of her superlative thighs (or so he thought), then sighed in a way that brought his gaze to her bosom, the tone of her voice lending her words the opposite meaning as she replied: "Okay, but won't you ever get some manners? Ooooh!"

After hearing what he'd heard behind the restroom wall, Mustafa rather lost the plot. What he recalls is that his urges got the better of him, with the water, the sun, the Italian sausages, and the Meister Max beer (alcohol content 8%). His body began to respond to the hip-hop playing over enormous speakers—an American DJ, a friend of Fustuq's respected for his professionalism, who was scratching on a turntable—and Mustafa enjoyed flirting with the dark-skinned girl and two others, one a beauty from Belgrade who lived in Sharm El Sheikh, where she taught diving full-time.

From our planet, we surmise that the scandal of Fustuq's indiscretion from behind the wall only happened later, because Mustafa spent the whole day on the farm, and he knows that he left shortly after hearing the gossip.

The funniest thing—or so he told himself at first—was that Fustuq was ill at ease with his relatives and would only greet Mustafa from a distance. Despite this, it was clear that his Coptic friend was either disturbed or angry, seemingly infuriated at his bride, who was sitting alone in a modest party dress inside the house (which had been furnished with exaggerated luxury), talking neither to any of her bridegroom's vagabond friends, nor to the "prostitutes." Mustafa noticed this as he mischievously asked some people he knew about "Charlie" (that was what he'd learned to call cocaine when he was in England, and had taught all his drug-using friends to do the same): "Isn't Charlie coming today?"

At one particular moment, perhaps the second near the end—Mustafa had found no cocaine or opium, as if the Padishah were saying to him "The beer is enough!"—the old plumber would come out in a bright Hawaiian shirt and khaki shorts, looking just like a first-class tourist on a Caribbean island, and make his way through the groups of people, applauding in the direction of the DJ and the turntable: a second barrel, the older Fustuq, cracked and fragile because he was older and less balanced on his base. He was followed by a sullen priest and someone carrying a case; the latter stopped the music to announce "The crowning of the bond of two souls," and the casual gathering changed in the wink of an eye into a formal occasion with buffet, roses, wedding procession music, and countless women wearing evening clothes in the middle of the day.

Could it be that the dark girl had gone home?

People's faces had changed without Mustafa noticing. Even the pool deck saw an amazing number of energetic workmen in red uniforms, fanning out to clean where the swimmers had been a short time ago and to fold up the chaises-longues.

Michel was in a shiny black tuxedo, standing in front of a transparent marble statue of the Virgin Mary set on the buffet, kissing the hand of his father, Fustuq *père*, the only person who hadn't changed his clothes between when he'd first appeared before the sitting guests, and when he had, like a cursed prophet, reinvented the world with a snap of his fingers. Mustafa, despite himself, thought that his father-in-law must have resembled this old plumber, that he was next in line among the rich men of the cesspools. He circulated a little among people who'd suddenly woken to the world, until he came upon the bride, still silent although she was now surrounded by well-wishers, no feeling visible on her greasy face, which was just like a clown's face, with three layers of make-up.

In the midst of these comings-and-goings of family and businessmen, Çorbacı no longer felt anything, except the need to take a piss.

•　　　•　　　•　　　•　　　•

And, as soon as he'd shut behind him the door of the first toilet he chanced upon at the end of the corridor—he'd discover that the small room he'd entered was actually a wooden cube fastened to the house from outside—he heard the voice of his Coptic friend ring out.

What Fustuq was saying to his colleague about Mustafa, in English

"Goodness me, thank God I got tested for every STD, and assured myself of the Divine Mercy. And now, everyone is happy for me except him. So far as his wife is concerned, you could feel bad for him, because he didn't know. But for him not to be happy for my sake! Yes, I mean our colleague Mustafa Çorbacı, who else did you think I was talking about? A delusional person, and also misguided, what can you say about someone so pathetic? Today, just think, he had so much to boast about, he had to give me a lecture on the nature of marriage and who I ought to marry. God, you know what?— he's talking, and I'm a second away from saying to him: 'By the way, Shurba, two weeks before your wedding I was giving it to your fiancée from behind, do you believe that? From behind, man. Then I took it out and put it in her mouth because she likes the taste! Just two weeks before, she was writhing with pleasure while I gave it to her, do you believe it?' That would have been the absolute truth, at least if I'd swapped 'before your wedding' for 'before the beginning of your relationship with your wife.' The horny bitch really loved me. Of course the relationship was a secret, and I was happy when Mustafa fell for her because it meant I'd be free of her. I was sure she wouldn't tell him about our relationship, and what's more, she'd give herself to him claiming to be a virgin. That's natural. You shouldn't be taken in by what he says. If there'd been any doubt about her virginity, he wouldn't have married her. Everyone in Egypt takes that very seriously. If you don't care about it, then what does it mean to be Egyptian? And who knows, perhaps she had a quick hymenoplasty as well, the horny Muslim bitch! He wanted me to marry Lillian to take revenge on me, that pathetic artist, because no doubt he realized at some stage or other that she was soiled goods. He thinks himself civilized and he's a Muslim! Anyway, by their wedding, I'd gotten to know Lillian. Mustafa Çorbacı's wife was no longer of any interest to me. But I continued to regard him as a friend, despite my history with his wife coming between us. I continued to regard him as a friend and to trust him. Until last week—when I was still reeling from the Lillian affair, remember?—I decided to consult him about it. His reaction was extremely strange, as though he wished on me the bad times he'd fallen into before me. It's odd, you know, the way these Muslims behave, everything in their lives is based on uncleanliness..."

Everything I've suffered in the way of wounds and burns, doesn't compare with such chapters. I wasn't expecting it of you especially, and I could hardly believe it when they told me. —Ziyad Rahbani

When Mustafa had left the little toilet, after hearing Fustuq's words to the Australian-Egyptian, his head was full of a Lebanese song about two friends who hate each other, but despite that their friendship continues. He repeated the words as he stood in front of the buffet with the statue of the Virgin on it, his brain working feverishly to absorb and digest what he'd heard.

Recovering from his shock, the first conclusion he came to was that his wife—his ex-wife as she now was—had never told him about her relationship with Fustuq, although she'd told him about several other previous relationships. It had seemed that, like him, she didn't see virginity as a condition for purity and didn't believe in deception when it came to relationships. There were no inhibitions of this sort between them at all. So why hadn't she told him about the only relationship in which he knew the other party? Did she think it would make a difference to him that this party was a Christian? And exactly what, he found himself wondering, could have attracted her to a human being of this sort?

She deserves it, he said. She deserves to have a cowardly pimp stand and talk about her like that.

But from another point of view, as he sought a blessing from the subject of the sura with his finger on the Virgin Mary's marble head, the information seemed enough to confirm the sultan's statement that his ex-wife was a party to the small conspiracy to spoil his life—through which he viewed the larger conspiracy against the Muslim umma, as he had also been instructed. As though a piece of information like this was proof of her evil intentions from the beginning: she was neither cool nor a woman, true enough; she was unable to rise above the instincts of hatred and profit. But what was more important—something that the Chosen Çorbacı didn't know, or was not convinced of—is that his ex-wife had no intentions that went beyond a scenario written five hundred years ago (the traditional marriage scenario had actually been scripted centuries before that: before the Arabs came, before most Egyptians became Muslims)—a hateful scenario which this chauvinist barrel wouldn't spare himself, despite all the trappings of luxury and Europeanization.

As we were saying, he recovered from the shock that his ex-wife hadn't told him. But he remained disgusted with Fustuq as he'd never felt before in his life. And his disgust made him really hate himself. Later, when he remembered this disgust in particular, he would feel that if you'd mixed nausea with fear with depression, and made each of these ingredients as strong as possible, this still wouldn't have been as strong as his loathing for Fustuq.

Now, after kissing his fingers, which had brushed against the Virgin, he wiped his face and rubbed his eyes, then went outside to find his Coptic friend in the same place behind the restroom wall, but with the Serb beauty. Mustafa shook his head haughtily left and right as he walked, as if he were a rich house owner welcoming poorer guests, and noticed something that made him even more conscious of Fustuq's awkwardness over the engagement than his embarrassment at what he'd been saying to the Australian-Egyptian. This was that the Pistachio Kid smiled in a strangely pleasant way at finding him there, rather than prattling on in a loud voice as he usually did when Mustafa appeared before him. "So you've come to me at last for a special occasion, Shurba?" he asked. Mustafa stood close to him in an exaggeratedly pompous way without saying anything. For some five minutes, as he joined in the conversation by shaking his head, he continued to stare hard at Fustuq, as if this was the first time he'd seen his Coptic friend.

He was shaking his head contentedly, but what was going around in his head was that the Organization's work could only be easier with non-Muslims—the Copts and the Balkan Christians, for example—there. The goal of the Organization (so he found himself thinking) was not Western domination of the Muslims—politically and economically, domination was a done deal—but rather to plant fundamentalisms. Fundamentalisms, so he heard himself saying in the tone of a great thinker at a cultural conference, are nothing but the nationalisms that Abdülmecid ibn Mahmud tried to eradicate: fundamentalisms are nationalisms after they've grown big and fat, but before they've dissolved in that neoliberalism that turns the world into a supermarket.

Immediately, the existence of a firm mystical link between his marriage and the conquest of Constantinople became fixed in his head: an example of a duality he'd found himself pursuing ever since the caliph appeared to him. As if there were a connection between the collapse of civil society in Cairo and the digging of the Suez Canal, for example; or between the Crusades and the use of electricity to torture and intimidate people at the Imbaba police station; or (the closest thing to what was going round in his head at that moment) between Fustuq's moral compass and his ex-wife having been brought up in (excuse me!) England.

Everything in his life, if he thought about it this way, would be another example of the marriage of east and west, Mustafa Efendi: the most hateful thing history has allowed.

He didn't utter a single word in the presence of Fustuq, however. In fact, he would never speak to this little barrel again. From when he left Sand Port to when he finally left Cairo and would no longer see him, Mustafa Çorbacı would not direct a single word of any kind to his Coptic friend Michel Fustuq. On the one occasion he bumped into him in the office, on the Tuesday—when Fustuq started to take him to task for what he'd done to the Serb beauty at his engagement party— he would shake his head at him as though he were a rich house owner welcoming some poorer guests, smiling with exaggerated affection, then avoiding him until he left the place.

The story of Mustafa and the Serb girl

When Mustafa decided to go—it was after four in the afternoon—he took the opportunity of Fustuq being busy with his fat cousin (at whom he nodded with the same inexplicable superiority), and took the Serb beauty to one side on the pretext of taking a walk in the mango grove attached to the garden. He carried on asking her about her life between Belgrade and Sharm El Sheikh before enticing her back to his car and suggesting they go for a drive. As they exchanged smiles on the dusty asphalt, Mustafa was giving himself an excellent opportunity to get out of his system the anger he'd suppressed from the moment he'd looked at Fustuq—the intense loathing he'd felt at first had since been turning into a multi-layered anger.

The pretty girl, whose name he'd forgotten as soon as he made her acquaintance at the pool, accepted and got in beside him, to the sound of another Lebanese song on the car stereo, this time hip-hop, suiting the rhythm of the first part of the day. "I speak through silence. There are those who call for my death. My voice is loud in Beirut..." He drove her to the banana trees and the small canals. They kept talking about various things, while he (driven by desire, true, but without any wish to have it fulfilled) had only one thing on his mind.

Ever since he'd learned that she was a Serb, he'd been thinking about the massacres in Kosovo during the Bosnian War in the nineties, during which Serbian nationalists had marshaled all the Christians' historic anger at the region's fall to the Sublime State at the end of the fourteenth century. Now he wanted to find out how easily the Organization could take control of the Balkan Christians of the Byzantine rite, whose priests he'd seen jump into the Bosphorus in his dream.

After ten minutes' drive, during which the Serb girl expressed, in broken English and with drunken emotion, her great love for Fustuq's family ("I don't understand how a whole family can all be such wonderful people!") Mustafa parked in an out-of-the-way place and again suggested a walk along the canal.

The Serb girl yielded to his flirtatious tone as they walked, her head fuddled with the wine. His sweaty palm crept forward until it clasped her hand, which thrashed about in it like a fish and started to mirror her sighs and shudders. Thick locks of blond hair like plaited threads tickled the back of his head. The smell of her skin was somewhere between curdled milk, the silene with which they flavor tea in Sinai, and mud. It now came to his nose more forcefully. But just as he felt he was about to kiss her, and could see the tender expectation on her face—no watchers in sight to worry about—he straightened up to face her, put his hand gently on her shoulder, then took half a pace back to broach the subject.

"I didn't tell you I'm a Muslim," he whispered. "I hope that won't upset you."

"I don't understand. Why should it upset me that you are a Muslim?" Her face froze and her eyes widened a little. He felt the fish go stiff in his palm and gripped it with all the force of his desire, smiling sweetly as she continued: "The fact is, I respect all religions."

"Really?" He took his hand away from her shoulder, and blew her a kiss. The softness returned to her face but with no expectation of an embrace. As he let go of her hand, which immediately started to jump around again, he recalled that this was exactly what he wanted. "As a rule, I'm a secular person, and I'm not bothered about these matters, but aren't there tensions between Muslims and Christians in your part of the world?"

"It's different in my country. I understand that repression and imperialism over several centuries made some people dislike the Albanians and the Muslims, or hate their unjust treatment of the Orthodox Christians, who owned the land centuries before the arrival of any Turk or Albanian. But we coexist with them extremely well, despite the fact that they have always been the aggressors." Mustafa listened and thought: leave aside the fact that more than eighty percent of the civilian casualties had been Bosnian Muslims (where had he gotten this fact from?). "And if you went back to the beginning of history"—yes, baby, that's exactly what I brought you here for—"you would understand that it was the Ottoman butchers who killed their brothers and sons, sucked their blood and gorged themselves on the flesh of the Christian peoples, it was the Ottomans who occupied us, slaughtered us, and deprived us of our church when they came. The people you're talking about us having problems with are the descendants of the Ottomans!" When she found that he was still smiling sweetly—her face was red, the anger in her voice unmistakeable—she pulled his hand toward her and continued: "I love all Egyptians and understand that a man cannot choose his religion, but frankly, I am not comfortable with this religion of yours. Can you deny that it was spread through occupation and slaughter, or that it deprived people of their rights? What religion encourages a man to visit prostitutes, says that a woman has to cover her face, forbids people from enjoying a drink, cuts off the hand of a poor man, or pelts a woman with stones until she dies?" All this, with Mustafa still hanging on to his sweet smile. "I don't understand how all this can be a religion! Can you deny that Islam is against progress and civilization?"

They'd stopped walking and were near the edge of the canal. She had her back to the water and he was in front of her, his palm still in her hand. She pushed it away angrily. Over the water to the right the sun hung like an orange ball of fire.

"I understand you must be a secularist, otherwise we wouldn't have been able to have a conversation with each other, you and me." Oh dear, that bad, is it? "But regardless of all that, you have to understand that things are different in our country, and it's a matter of honor, our love for our homeland, and who we are." The idea had by now jelled in his head and he knew exactly how he was going to vent his anger. "They are usurpers!"

"You're right!" he whispered again, leaning his body against her. "Islam" (by now his voice had begun to get louder as he pulled her other hand, spread his chest, leaned back, and took a deep breath): "Islam really is the enemy of civilization!"

With all the energy he could muster, and before she realized what was happening, he let go of her hands and pushed her over the edge, taking his aim from the orange ball of fire in the sky.

"Islam," he shouted, in Arabic this time, over her screams and splashes, "Islam, you daughter of the dog's religion!" Then he ran to his car, got in, and headed for Faisal without looking back.

A third unreliable story

Whenever Rashid was apart from his Belgian girlfriend—for months they were both in their own countries and he saw her only intermittently—he had such severe pain in his stomach that Mustafa was worried about him, especially when the pain started to be accompanied by depression and tingling in his fingers. But the evening he went to the doctor's, he came back angry, not saying anything—he'd undergone all the possible tests—he and Mustafa both having concluded that the symptoms were psychosomatic. This was years before Rashid specialized in psychiatry.

The first signs of clinical depression, as all the certainties of their upbringing fell apart. That was in the time of Ecstasy, delight in depravity: *The Time of E-s*, as Ramiz al-Dardir, their third friend, who died of a heroin overdose, titled a screenplay he wanted to write before he skedaddled. That pain could occur for no material reason—Mustafa's astonishment made a mark on his being. (For the rest of his life, Rashid, whenever he felt pain, would be uncertain whether its source was physical or not.) The important thing was that the pain increased over time. That is, the closer he became to his Belgian girlfriend, the more his stomach hurt and the longer the pain lasted, until it confined him to the house, so that he let his beard grow. His mother said: "An evil eye has hit you, my son!" And his father called her the dregs of European civilization.

When Rashid eventually went to Europe, he was closer to her, but he had so many preoccupations in his new life that his stomach no longer hurt when he left her. This only confused Mustafa more. When Rashid found something to occupy him, his symptoms disappeared completely. And in fact his relationship with his Belgian girlfriend grew tense over time; he started to find it a burden to meet up with her, and their relationship gradually evaporated. His mother relaxed a bit and his father started to laugh and call her "the sprite." He grew to love other women.

As for Mustafa Çorbacı, he remained convinced that all pain entails separation.

The story of Mustafa's conversation with Aldo on Saturday night

As he drove around aimlessly on that third Saturday night after finishing his walk in the Sea of Japan (after Amgad Salah had left him suddenly, upset about the shisha smoke in his beard), for the first time Mustafa suspected he was the mad one. Before that—until he spoke with Aldo Mazika, who would turn things on their head for him—he had suspected that *he* was the sick, hypnotized victim of the Organization, but it consoled him that even if he'd been mistaken in his explanation of what was happening to him since he'd seen Istanbul in the dream, even if Vahdettin was nothing but a satanic visitation, he, Mustafa, could only be an example held up by God. Of course, in a sense we are all examples held up by God, but for whom, if not for ourselves?

But is it of any benefit if the example is also the person for whom the example is being held up?

That's what he would be wondering less than twenty-four hours after the episode of Amgad's sudden departure, when Aldo Mazika spoke to him on his return from Michel Fustuq's farm near the village of Birqash, which adjoins the boundary of Imbaba in the north of Giza: another way of reaching the Delta, in fact, parallel to Shubra, where he'd divorced his wife the previous day.

Mustafa had been surprised by the absence of Aldo from the engagement party, the true nature of which (as already related) Fustuq had only informed him by chance at the last moment. But there were now sacks and sacks of contempt in his heart for Fustuq. Pure contempt and repulsion, the like of which he had perhaps never felt for anyone in the world.

On his way back over the Malik Faisal Bridge, however, while it was still light—the Meister Max was evaporating from his head, but he was still repeating: "Civilization, children of the dog's religion! Filth, you pimp, you son of a plumber!"— he wouldn't hesitate to take his mobile out of his pocket and answer an unrecognized number while driving. Aldo only called from unrecognized numbers, as if he were really a secret agent or a member of an intelligence organization being pursued by the authorities.

Mustafa would immediately recognize the smarmy voice that tickled letters and spontaneously brought back the sight of dark brown, flabby flesh. The words stretched out sensuously without having the desired effect. "What did you do with Amgad when he went with you to Zamalek, Mustafa, tell me!" So that Mustafa was concerned for his Sunni friend and the words were stuck in his throat, though he knew it: Aldo exaggerated things and enjoyed playing the complete fool, embarrassing and terrifying the world on any excuse. "Where did you get to just now, after the disaster you caused, I bet you're at young Michel's, the traitor!"

But even though he knew all this, it was hard for Mustafa not to feel concern.

"Listen, Safsaf!" the effeminate African would go on with a savored coolness when he noticed Mustafa's breathing becoming difficult, like a girl crooning her words instead of speaking them. "Amgad went totally off his head after you took him to Zamalek!" He gave an exaggeratedly effeminate laugh. "What did you do to him in Zamalek, tell me! The thing is, now it looks as if they want to deal with him in a very bad way. I have to meet you tonight to STOP them!"

"Who are these people we have to stop?"

"No, I can't tell you anything on the phone, Safsaf, but by the way, you are the cause of this disaster. Tell me now, how and where shall I see you tonight?"

"Anywhere, Aldo!" said Mustafa, pretending to be calm, and recalling that Aldo didn't just spend his evenings in the office but also worked there on weekends: "Are you at the office now? Shall I come to you?"

"No, no, don't be stupid! Do you want them to discover us, or what?"

"Who are they, Aldo?" he replied, his patience running out.

"Listen, Safsaf, I'm going to tell you something very important. The best place to talk about the Amgad situation is Khan al-Khalili in al-Hussein—don't ASK why now! Just tell me, can we meet there in exactly, exactly an hour? Okay? Inside, in the Naguib Mahfouz Café where we went last time we went, okay?"

Khan al-Khalili

In a week or less, Mustafa would have forgotten everything that happened during the time that Aldo specified as "exactly, exactly." When, sitting by the sea in Beirut, he recalled the evening of his meeting with the camp African, he wouldn't remember the road congestion across Dream Bridge to World's Gate and from there to al-Mu'izz's Cairo over that little bridge that always felt as if it was about to collapse. He wouldn't recall the woman with the deformed arm who ran up to him after he'd parked behind al-Hussein Hospital, laughed mockingly when he'd given her two pounds, and in an almost threatening tone, said: "A parking spot here costs ten pounds, sir!"

In Beirut, Mustafa wouldn't recall the pungent odor all through the pedestrian tunnel that links the area of al-Ghawriyya, called after the Sultan Qansuh, with the al-Gamaliyya Quarter, named after the Amir Gamal al-Din Yusuf al-Istidar (that is, the official responsible for the houses of the sultan and his retinue), from al-Azhar Street, nor the trucks with bored soldiers and policemen parked along the edge of spaces cleared in front of the mosque. Here, everything started to be covered in shiny ceramics, and enormous sunshades had recently been erected along the façade, reminding him of the green tree trunks and lampposts he'd noticed after his separation: perhaps these sunshades were the biggest phalluses without a function in the whole city. He wouldn't even notice the human masses that hurtled through or between them, as the waiters dragged him by the arm to sit down in a kebab shop or café, or the salesmen in front of the souvenir shops who were testing on the tourists the theory that torture by shouting in several languages would attract customers inside.

He wouldn't distinguish, in his memory, between the noise of the wind against the car window on Faisal Bridge and the noise of the car horns from the traffic jammed on Tharwat Street, nor even the noise of the oriental band that he'd found playing when he reached the Naguib Mahfouz Café, then made his way across to Aldo, who was sitting at a table with three chairs in the corridor linking the two large main rooms, ensconced in a corner away from the crowd. He wouldn't recall how it went through his head that the place was kitsch and ostentatious, to suit an effeminate male buffalo... so much so that their conversation, punctuated by gulps of coffee and tea with baklava and sticky pudding, as well as an overwhelming sense that they were up against a secret operation or a security-service strike, and that their presence in a place with an oriental band and sticky pudding was a cover for arrangements they were making—their conversation would only come back to him as a natural extension of the phone call he'd received on his drive back from Sand Port and Michel Fustuq's farm. As if nothing separated the two conversations.

Magic is a deed in which, through his assistance, one gets closer to the devil. —Lisan al-'Arab

After Aldo Mazika had said "By the way, you're the cause of this disaster," he immediately added: "They won't leave Amgad alone, Safsaf. He was tired out when he spoke to me and we met. He was complaining about you, not Wahid al-Din, imagine! But if you help me, we might save him!"

"Look, Mazika!" (nearly screaming), "Either explain what you're talking about or I'll leave, okay?"

"Okay, but calm down, man, you're in too much of a hurry! God preserve us, the 'ghosts' will discover us, then they'll go and inform on us at home. And then Amgad's people may also have spies, even here, you don't know, he may have a brother in the security service. Not a word! Keep your voice down, Mustafa, and listen to me, please!"

Mustafa had hardly had time to give out a sigh when he was drowned in a quivering coffee paste and could no longer see anything except for some sparkling ice cubes and two red circles that he'd forgotten were eyes. He was blinded by the scent of expensive cologne, while a nearby warmth betrayed fierce sweating in the lower regions, with the discordant tones of the zither in the microphone and the murmur of the customers.

"There are important things you don't know. There are disasters and calamities. I'll tell you what they are now. But keep your voice down a bit and keep calm, please, Safsaf!"

Aldo now leaned further toward Mustafa.

"Look, you've noticed of course that Wahid al-Din is comfortable with me in the office and not with anyone else, and of course you've also noticed that Amgad Salah is not comfortable with Wahid al-Din. But have you ever asked yourself why things are like that? Look, frankly and briefly, this Wahid al-Din, for a very long time" (he whispered more softly to emphasize the suspense) "for a very, very long time, I mean, he's been possessed by a demon, God preserve us!"

He turned his face to mutter or pray before continuing: "Of course, you won't believe what I'm telling you and you might even laugh at me, but with us in Africa these things are quite usual!"

With us in Africa? Mustafa knew that Aldo had been in Portugal aged six to thirteen then come here and not left—all his siblings had left either before or after his father's death, but he'd stayed—and that despite his travels all over the world, he'd never visited Mozambique, where he was born, or anywhere else in sub-Saharan Africa.

"Listen, he's been possessed by a demon for a long time, but I'm the only one in the office he's told about it. The demon that possessed him is called Sultan, and this Sultan" (without turning around this time, he made a quick sign of the cross, while muttering in Portuguese) "when he took possession of Wahid al-Din, he'd make him appear in places without his knowing, and speak with people as well. But what you're completely unaware of, Safsaf, is that when Amgad Salah's brain gave for the first time, it basically gave because Sultan let Wahid al-Din appear and talk to him…"

•   •   •   •   •

It was a conversation that would later remind Mustafa of his meeting with Vahdettin.

Not just because he would record its contents when he got back to Dream Bridge. Not just because it would open up new lines of inquiry for him. That evening, before he wrote in the notebook (with almost the same extraordinary speed, even if the size of the article was infinitely smaller), he would read about the civil war in Mozambique and magic among the Bantu, to which Mazika belonged (Aldo, in addition to Portuguese and Arabic, spoke the language of the Makua tribes, whose origins went back to these tribal groupings). And not just because it contained some incredible and unexpected information. The conversation would remind Mustafa of meeting the sultan because it made him doubt himself. For this reason, he wouldn't calm down completely until he was convinced that Aldo had no knowledge that the sultan had appeared to him, Mustafa, and that there was not the slightest suspicion that he had told Amgad what he had said: when Amgad spoke to Aldo, all he had said was that the zombie had bitten Mustafa.

At this point, Mustafa recalled that the effeminate African would never know he was charged with the commission, and that the tale had become his tale, nor that a few hours earlier he'd woken up to the true role of their Coptic friend, Michel Samir Fustuq; to the connection between this and his atrocious disappointment with regards to his wife, and then between that and their friend Amgad Salah's conversion to Islamism. Nor would he make a connection between these things and the collapse of civil society as embodied by their colleague, His Excellency the Sultan, the fiqi Ustaz Wahid al-Din.

It would certainly become clear to Mustafa that the African was working for the front opposed to the Islamic umma, but it would also be clear that he was doing so unaware that there was a struggle, let alone that one of these people might be party to it. The disturbing thing about all this was that Aldo would of his own accord that evening make some unprecedented confessions, which would clarify for Mustafa some old puzzles, and would with total sincerity explain to him "important" facts about the situation.

●　　　●　　　●　　　●　　　●

"Look," the conical man would continue, still leaning over him, "Wahid al-Din trusts me because it's I who helped him find out the name of the demon who took possession of him, and eventually helped him get rid of it as well. Do you believe me or not? Tell me! Look, I'll tell you the story from the beginning, but promise me that what I say will remain a secret between you and me. Okay?"

Aldo Mazika's story with the fiqi Wahid:
A digression by Mustafa

This is my interpretation of the story I heard tonight from Aldo (so Mustafa would write in the same brown notebook, under the title: *Summary of Conversation with Mantenzika in Khan al-Khalili on the Night of Saturday, April 14th*):

The fiqi Wahid, during his illness at the newspaper that I didn't witness, exhibited a series of strange symptoms, which he complained about to Aldo. At the time, which was several months before I joined the paper, Aldo was the only other person to spend evenings at the paper. His patience with the fiqi's strange habits, plus his constant questioning about his health, made the fiqi's complaints possible. He told him that when he prayed he was often surprised to find on his body an extraordinary kaftan of colored silk he'd never seen before, which quickly disappeared as soon as he noticed it, to be replaced by the cotton flannel gown that he'd been wearing when he started. Or else he would bang his head on something smooth and cold while prostrating himself, then notice on the prayer mat an antique sword, which would also quickly disappear. He had strange dreams in which he would be sitting on something resembling a mastaba covered with expensive decorated material, with people bending in front of it, or riding a decorated horse through green meadows, with a bow in his hand and gazelles as far as the eye could see.

Sometimes the décor of a very ordinary scene out of his everyday life would change into a scene from one of these dreams, suddenly, just like that. He would be in the washroom of his apartment on Malik Faisal Street about to take a shower, when all of a sudden the place would turn into a large Turkish bath, all made of red Belgian marble. Or else, climbing the stairs in the corporation in World's Gate, suddenly he would be in white clothes on a carpeted wooden roof, borne aloft by seven men, a sea breeze full of salt hanging in the air.

And every time, the dream disappeared as soon as he became aware of it.

Later, when the fiqi had gotten used to these things, he began to discover himself in places where he'd never been, as if he were sleepwalking but without actually sleeping. More than once, he found himself with their retired policeman colleague, Amgad Salah, a long way from the office, and every time Amgad seemed to be angry or afraid without the fiqi knowing why. But when he asked Amgad about it, the retired policeman would turn away from him or make ready to hit him.

Still—so the fiqi Wahid informed his sympathetic colleague Aldo Mazika—all this was one thing, but the bouts of seizure he was suffering were something else. Wahid had complained to Aldo of these convulsions before quitting work for an appointment with a senior consultant. At first, the doctor had diagnosed them as an uncommon type of epileptic fit that came in middle age. But the treatment had no effect, and after numerous examinations and a more detailed consideration of the symptoms, he confirmed to him that he didn't have epilepsy and confessed that he didn't know what it could be. At that point, the fiqi decided to go to the hospital and disappeared for many weeks, during which he exploited all his contacts and relatives in our corporation and in al-Azhar to get himself examined by brain specialists and professors of neurology, and to have all the possible tests and X-rays done. To no avail. The last doctor simply told him: "Your condition is psychological." When he had completely lost hope of finding a cure, he sought out Aldo at home to try what Aldo had been advising from the start.

Aldo lives in a privately owned villa in Dog Alley which his father bought in the eighties when he first came to Egypt. It was disturbing to me to visualize all this happening in the area of my marital home, several years before I got married—though fortunately, I had never visited Aldo there while I was married, nor, indeed, have I to this day.

You ought to know, at this juncture, that Aldo is a non-practicing Catholic, although it is also clear that he is influenced by the pre-Christian beliefs of the Makua tribes to which his parents belong, and that his aged mother, Sitt Azuka, who still lives with him, is a witch. This was what amused me most, to be honest: a piece of information that was in itself an "important" secret, because witches in a Makua community never advertise their extraordinary powers, which, even if not used for evil purposes, can expose them to punishment without trial and are not unlikely to lead to their being killed.

Aldo's view from the first moment was that Wahid was possessed. The kaftan and the sword belonged to the evil spirit that had possessed him, and the dreams and visions represented scenes from the spirit's life, while the convulsions—the clearest indication of the presence of a spirit in the body—represented its fickle mood swings. As for his shadowy meetings with Amgad, they were the first step in the plan the spirit wanted to implement through the fiqi: to strike madness into those around him one by one. Aldo was the only person protected, as he was the son of a witch—so he told me—and he could see that the plan had worked with Amgad, as proved by the fact that Amgad actually embraced Salafi Islam. So far as Aldo was concerned, for someone to become a Sunni was far better proof of madness than any psychotic condition. I believe that if I'd told him about my meeting with the sultan, he'd have thought I was on my way to getting a beard and a mark on my forehead.

The important thing is that the fiqi Wahid had had a convulsion once while at work in the evening, and there was only Aldo in the whole office. He heard him cheeping "Sultan, Sultan," found him writhing on the corridor floor, and immediately thought he'd discovered the name of the spirit: naturally, he didn't make any connection between the sword and kaftan and the Ottoman Padishah.

To cut an epic short.

On the night the fiqi went to Aldo, the witch's son sat him down on the floor in an empty room and brought a cooking pot full of water, which he put in front of him. He told him to close his eyes for five minutes then put his hands in the water and not remove them whatever happened. (I've only just realized the secret of the pot of water that Amgad put between us following the first of his nervous breakdowns that I witnessed: Aldo had given him the same advice. But Amgad quickly stopped having anything to do with the conical man, regarding him as a member of the Organization that was targeting our newspaper. And despite never going to Aldo's house or knowing that his mother was a witch, he held on to the idea of the water container when he was afraid of the zombie plague, adding some alterations of his own.) To this day—as proved by the fact that after I spoke with him at the Uruba Café he immediately went to complain to Aldo—whenever Amgad has felt afraid that a zombie might be eating people's brains again, he's immediately gone for help to the effeminate witch's son.

As I was saying, the night Ustaz Wahid went to see Aldo at home, Sitt Azuka came out to him, whirring like a machine, in tongues of which I think Aldo himself could only interpret the word "sultan." I have never met the Sitt, but I visualize her as a smooth, ugly woman, hunchbacked in a white shirt. I picture her as extremely small, plump without being flabby, with untidy silver hair and red eyes; her voice is loud and comes from different places at the same time, as she mutters her spells and conjurations…

But, truth be told, it doesn't matter how I envisage her.

Aldo didn't say much about his mother, or describe that night in detail. What he did confess was that the Sitt eventually decided that the evil spirit should be ravished in order to expel it and cleanse the person, which meant that Aldo—with his mother waiting in the hallway, having covered Wahid's eyes, poured the water from the container over his head, then ordered him to take off his trousers and get down on the floor—had to lower his own trousers and take the poor fiqi from behind.

Aldo would boast, and I don't think he was exaggerating, that his size was not to be believed. His genuine embarrassment at this scene was the first (almost) convincing proof of what he always claimed—that in spite of his effeminate appearance, he actually didn't fancy men. More than once he told me that it was just a question of carrying out orders, and one could sense something about him that was either embarrassment or regret. For Aldo, although he believed absolutely in her powers, was also extremely afraid of Sitt Azuka, and would do anything he could to avoid her anger.

As he told it, he had to summon up in his imagination pictures and scenes from the store of his sexual experience, and despite that could only get a proper erection after swallowing the bolus that the witch had handed him as she went out, then—God help him—he went ahead.

I can't help seeing the fiqi Wahid that night, with his eyes bound and his bottom half naked, shaking on the tiled floor, his thighs smeared with semen and blood oozing from his anus. I can't help hearing him scream and swallow his tears and spittle, banging his fists so hard that the convulsions returned more violently than any time previously: the most violent bout to overtake Ustaz Wahid since he'd begun to see the kaftan on his body.

As soon as he'd penetrated the fiqi that night, Aldo was happy to leave the room on his mother's orders—she told him to quit the house for two hours, and by obeying her he could avoid confronting his victim immediately. In fact, he didn't see Ustaz Wahid for a whole week after that, and nor did anyone else. The fiqi hid away in his house, not eating or drinking—I don't think he was sleeping either—and when he returned to view, Aldo found that he was behaving as though nothing had happened, and so kept quiet. From that day on, neither mentioned to the other the ritual purification incident even once, and Aldo didn't tell Wahid what Sitt Azuka had said.

He was, however, convinced that the evil spirit that had possessed Wahid al-Din had actually left him during that powerful seizure, because Azuka-May, as Aldo called his mother, had told him (and he believed everything Azuka-May told him) that the fiqi had lost consciousness for half an hour, and when he started to come to, he was muttering "From her there goes a wicked sultan" (it will be obvious, of course, to any idiot that what he was saying was "I take refuge with God from the wickedness of Satan," but Aldo didn't disbelieve his mother, despite the fact that, due to her weak Arabic, she couldn't pronounce her 'ayns).

What persuaded him that the purification ritual had succeeded was that when Ustaz Wahid returned to work— despite the fact that his stammer was worse, as was his compulsive anxiety, his bent back, his uneven walk, and his proclivity for stupid behavior like watching porn at his desk (he also seemed more hesitant, and afraid of everything)—all the symptoms of the disease had actually disappeared from him and he no longer complained of convulsions or of dreams. It seems that the shock of the purification ritual, even though it completely robbed Ustaz Wahid of his senses, also freed him from any consciousness of his cosmic role. In this way, by turning into a horror film, he'd finally left behind him all the indications of his role as the person responsible for assuming the sultan's spirit, even if he'd also lost the possibility of undertaking any other role in the world, with the exception of the comedy he performed in the office.

Thanks to the beliefs of the Makua tribes in Dog Alley, when the sultan appeared in bodily form to Amgad—or, a full eight years later, to me—he had no news for anyone. At that moment, in a new way, I understood why our Master had called Wahid "poor," and I went home more convinced than at any time previously of the truth of the words of the Muslims' Imam.

Note: I photographed myself a short while ago, and again confirmed the remarkable nature of the camera, for instead of my face, there appeared on the small screen an obscure talismanic drawing which disappeared as soon as I downloaded the picture onto the computer, at which point my face as I'd photographed it reappeared. But I could see in my features on the screen a slight difference that reflected the lines of the talismanic sketch.

Return to the conversation with Aldo:
Saturday evening

After Mustafa heard Aldo's story of Ustaz Wahid—the coffee-colored giant had spent an hour hovering over Mustafa, suffocating him, and Mustafa couldn't wait for the opportunity—he would get up to go to the restroom, and on his way ask the waiter for a real lemon, a kitchen knife, and a can of soda. He stood in front of the mirror and looked at himself for a long time, contemplating the new scars on his face—as if to check what he'd noticed that morning in the car mirror, when he'd felt he was the Chosen Çorbacı—and he saw clearly that his features really had changed. There were lines, circles, and textures that had either not been there or else he hadn't noticed, but which he thought had started to take on a definite shape as the pieces of the puzzle came together in his head. Some gaps would remain in the puzzle, of course, as an integral part of its construction. Despite that, however,

Mustafa noticed the first signs of new features on his face, linked to the map of Cairo that he was trying to sketch. Merely a feeling, but it was there. A strange feeling, almost comic, but no stranger than all the developments that had occurred since the day he dreamed of Mehmet the Conqueror.

After his latest discoveries, as these feelings settled inside him in front of the mirror, Mustafa decided to photograph himself with the new camera as soon as he got home: the effect of the story on the face of its hero.

As he made his way back to the secluded table where Aldo Mazika was sitting, he realized that the real reason for the call was the desire of this family-size creature to "beat and knead the dough," as they say, to stir up suspense, nothing more, and perhaps also his unacknowledged need to unburden himself. What was certain was that Aldo, in his heart, was no different from Amgad Salah.

"Saf–suf–ti." That was how the mass of flesh would try to make sure that his confessions didn't become public, with his left eyebrow raised: perhaps his camp smile had never been anything but an expression of suspicion. "I told you these things because I TRUST you and because my heart is absolutely broken over Amgad. If I hadn't said that, you wouldn't have come. Don't let Azuka-May send me straight to hell!"

"A good thing, anyway," Mustafa replied as he steadied the lemon with one hand and pulled the knife with the other—he'd now recovered the steeliness with which he was accustomed to confronting Aldo's theatrical actions—"that you had a pretext to bring me here in such a rush."

"This was no pretext, Safsaf, okay?" But the fat African couldn't pretend to be offended for long. A moment later he was leaning over his friend Çorbacı ("Look!"), before continuing his usual beating and kneading. Within three minutes, Mustafa had convinced himself that his supposition was correct.

Aldo had been quarreling with Fustuq for some time (that's why he hadn't attended the party) and was perhaps the only one in the office who'd already known everything. He knew that Mustafa's wife had had a relationship with the puppet, and that when the puppet had sensed that Mustafa could no longer stand him he had begun to broadcast the news. Now that Aldo suspected the news had reached Mustafa himself in Sand Port a few hours before their meeting, he didn't want to deprive himself of the pleasure of gloating over another man's weakness.

Aldo did his usual thing to lead Mustafa on, with a couple of words about Fustuq like "This boy didn't turn out to be good at all, by the way!" or else, blatantly playing the fool, "Did he tell you anything about your wife?" He'd told him about the rape of Wahid al-Din to purge his conscience of the past, something he did periodically when he felt comfortable with someone whose life he'd been watching for some time. But apart from that, nothing at all. No Amgad, no "disaster," nothing. When Aldo told him Amgad was having a crisis and that they shouldn't leave him alone, he only meant that their Sunni friend had suffered a new nervous breakdown and his brothers would be putting him back in the asylum. All his life, Aldo had rejected asylums and psychiatric treatment, saying these things were cursed by the devil. So much so that, as far as Aldo was concerned, it was now clear that saving Amgad meant nothing but preventing his fellow officers from treating him—something he knew was unlikely, but he thought that Mustafa might have some influence with Amgad's family.

He wouldn't say so openly, but Mustafa concluded that he wanted to take Amgad to Azuka-May as well, so that she could see if the sultan had moved into the body of the retired policeman, who was going mad again eight years after the sultan had first driven him mad. And he wanted to make Mustafa feel responsible for Amgad's breakdown, the better to persuade him this might be a good idea.

But even this mattered little to Aldo.

All there was to it was that if he made Mustafa concerned for Amgad, he would have an opportunity to lead him on to speak about Fustuq, to find out what had gone on at the engagement party, and to see if the information that his friend "who didn't know how to draw" was lacking had caught up with him during the event. All this drama without any news reaching him of the story of the sultan's appearance, and no report reaching either him or Fustuq (with whom he was quarreling) that Mustafa had divorced his wife.

You son of a madwoman, Aldo!

The effeminate African would just stare, then distance himself, when he saw Mustafa take a napkin, squeeze half the lemon over it with his fingers, then after dowsing it with the can of soda, take off his ring from his finger and sit rubbing it hard with the napkin. For a quarter of an hour or more, whenever Aldo tried to lean over him and bring up the story of Fustuq's engagement party, Mustafa would leave whatever was in his hand and take a gulp from the can, as he held the knife up to his face, bringing it closer and closer to the ice cubes that bobbed up and down in the undulating sea of coffee. "Eh? What do you say, you barbarian?" Aldo would ask him, and lift his left eyebrow with the same camp smile on his face. But Mustafa went back to polishing the ring in silence.

Until he gave him the other half of the lemon, smiling at him enigmatically and burping in his face, then left without paying and without giving the effeminate African one word of comfort, Mustafa continued to brandish the knife at him and polish. As he passed the Khan on his way to Sayyidna al-Hussein, he would laugh from the bottom of his heart because Aldo had no idea, no idea whatsoever, what the ring might be that he'd decided to polish with lemon and soda, or what had made him finish it all off by belching in his face without a word in reply.

PART SEVEN

The Epistle of the Ring of the Dove

From Sand Port to the Beginning of the Road

Mustafa's Extensive Documentation of Fatimid Cairo and His Meeting with His Beloved

Sunday, April 15
and Monday, April 16

The Chosen Çorbacı said:

Dear Rashid,

Today a month has passed since I left Cairo. I am writing to you from beside the sea in Beirut, knowing more than ever that an email or a phone call would be of no use. Even if every detail of the story were included over a number of telephone conversations—from the start of my separation on account of the breakdown of my marriage and an overwhelming feeling that the world was against me and was punishing me, through the dream of Islam's entry into Europe and my discovery of the tughra in my daily itinerary before I noticed it on the ring, then the appearance of the sultan and the research into the history of Islam that followed it, and the implementation of the decision to get a divorce... all the way up to my shock at my ex-wife and Fustuq, and my discovery of Amgad Salah's real role in the story—the information and events would be unconnected and, worse, particular degrees of feeling wouldn't reach you—especially in the final developments.

Today, I tell myself that if I hadn't written *The Book of the Sultan's Seal*, the tale could only have taken root in your head as fleeting glimpses. And that is a failure I could not abide.

You have to remember, may God give you a good evening, that the text around the quotations is like a sponge; its dimensions are nothing less than the entire amazing tale whose features I am still reviewing in order to relate them to you. Sometimes, as I focus on a detail like my falling in love with a married woman within forty-eight hours of my divorce, I feel I really am mad. Praise God, I have learned not to always take everything that happens to me too seriously. What bothers me, Rashid, is that today you yourself are in Cairo, and I have failed to keep my appointment with you there after all these years. Now that your sudden return, which I anticipated year after year, has at last happened, it happens in my absence. But that's what the world is like, Abu al-Siyout. As that horrid popular proverb says (and there's more than one English proverb with the same meaning): "Find the faggot, and there'll be no waste ground to screw him on; find the waste ground, and there'll be no faggot to screw."

On love and writing

Now, it disturbs me to think that you may misunderstand this section of my account. I wouldn't blame you, now that you know I was so quick to fall in love, if your first reaction was to curse religion. I have to compose a respectful letter to you in the hope that you'll believe that what happened between me and the woman in question really was love—love of a sort that had never happened to me before—and that you will, incidentally, gain an idea of my views on writing.

Know, may you be exalted, that people began to write letters when they were separated from their loved ones because this was easier than facing long journeys and dangerous roads. Later, things came (train, car, airplane, telephone, telegraph, email) that brought people closer together, though they also brought complications and a rhythm of life that increased the distance between them and their loved ones. The difficulty of travel remained, as a question of time and peace of mind.

When this happened, some people thought to make their letters longer and direct them not to one friend in particular but to the world as a whole. Then, as a new development, something called "literature" came into being. Among the exponentially expanding populations there emerged a small group of people who read and wrote letters. There was a revival of writing, as an alternative to the difficulty of travel.

Some so-called philosophers claimed that God (may He be exalted) created each spirit rounded in shape in the fashion of a ball, then cut it in two, and put half a spirit in each body; and whenever a body met the body with the corresponding half, there was a yearning between them for the old affinity. —Ibn Da'ud, *Kitab al-Zahra* [Book of the Flower]

Love, may you stay cool, begins in confusion and ends in writing.

You, of course, know the theory of the orange halves. Every couple is like a complete orange that has been split in two, male and female—sometimes two males or two females—and after the sifting of souls that takes place among the planets, each of these halves has wandered somewhere, to live in the conscious or unconscious hope of finding its other half. The theory states that our souls are incomplete, that each one of us lives with half a spirit.

Or that each person has an old affinity with someone he has never met. (In ancient times the word "old" [*qadīma*] was used in the sense of "eternal"—did you know that?—as in the dispute between the Ash'arites and the Mu'tazilites over whether the Qur'an was eternal or created. Did I read about that too? To God alone belong all might and power!) This "old affinity," according to the theory, governs everything. If half of the orange meets its other half, it will be like Adam returning to Paradise; it will be at home, where the souls have not been sifted and the world is complete, with no desire to leave or depart for a single moment.

To put it more clearly, it will feel that its organs are complete, Abu al-Arshad. It will have become healthy and magnificent. But most important, it will feel that its knowledge of the beloved is deeper than anything else.

Leave aside the dates and details: without having met even once, or even heard of its existence, the half of the orange will feel that it knows its other half better than it knows itself. Without any effort, or even consciousness, each of the two halves will find that love has peeled from it layers of rind that have built up over the years, so that only the fruit now remains, naked and moist, and when one half is placed on the other, the fruit will ripen at once...

In love—be patient and you'll see why I'm speaking to you of these things—death is very close, because life loses its value. This happens equally in the presence or the absence of the beloved. Either Adam will feel on his return to Paradise that he's been expelled a second time (death is easier) or he will look at a bare roof and feel he's reached the end of everything (if he died, nothing would grieve, or else he's already dead and gone to Paradise, and is now sitting there). Even if the motive is different in each of the two cases, death is as near as Paradise is near (and perhaps Hell also—the Hell of waiting, in absence, separation, parting, and all these things). And if I were to tell you that this love of mine confirmed my belief that I am the Chosen Çorbacı, a *mustafa* and a *mukhtar*, perhaps you would be even more surprised.

When this happened, I felt that the timing was logical: the last chapter of the story before my departure. Because love in the manner of the half orange really was what brought me closest to God, as I went to praise His name, and because what begins with separation must end in union. Within just three days of my divorce, I for the first time understood what people mean when they say that love is devotion. All devotions, may you be cool, all the stillness or revelation that devotions can produce, all the death and resurrection that they bring to your mind, are as nothing compared to love.

Imagine me now, may God give you a good evening, sitting beside the sea in Beirut. You can see the towering cypresses behind me, and the waves breaking calmly on the rocks. In front of them, the lights of the nearby town of Jounieh have started to glitter over the mountains in the distance. And the sunset is orange juice as I write to you:

"In days too long gone for us to remember their features— though they must have been passed in a country like this one— we had something whose shape, whose essence, and the reason for its presence, we have forgotten. Something like those same days, whose features we do not remember, nor when or how we lost it. We know only that we preserved it with our blood, even though it was neither pleasant nor hateful, even though we'd become so used to it that we no longer even noticed it was with us. We know that its presence allowed us to stay in one place, and that, since it has been gone, we have worn ourselves out moving backward and forward. Sometimes we think we might recover it. And though its return has become more distant than a dream, we exchange smiles of hope as we pretend to remember, and say to one another that a time will come when what we once had will return to us and we can stop coming and going."

On the thoughts of Saturday night

Coming back from meeting Aldo on the third Saturday night, I stretched out my journey to Dream Bridge, to reflect on the strange things that had become clear to me, beginning with the ease of the Organization's work with the Christian communities of the Sublime State to the blood trickling from the fiqi Wahid's anus. After emerging from the Cairo of al-Mu'izz I passed the Citadel, the Muqattam Hills, and the Cemeteries, drove in the direction of Dog Alley for a bit, then turned around and went back through World's Gate. The night was fine. All the time I was driving, I was listening to Radio Nugum FM, various things coming into my mind: how strange it was that people in Cairo, for example, despite the enormous differences between them, all had the same mentality, even the supposedly persecuted minorities.

The values and suppositions on which their lives are built don't differ essentially, from the rebab seller to the owner of the orange Hummer. A man can't have a relationship with a woman, even if she is cool and bicultural, without being a family man; religion, from beginning to end, if it isn't a beard, a mark on the forehead, and an endless number of prohibitions, is just a system of right and wrong devoid of any intelligence and knowledge; patriotism, even if within us we hate the nation, is self-evident and a settled matter, and anyone who doubts it is a traitor or a foreign agent (just as anyone who questions the foregoing definition of religion is an unbeliever and an atheist, and anyone who tries to form a different sort of relationship with a woman is shameless and immoral, a son of a bitch). I thought it remarkable how differences didn't change these things.

But the most important thing on my mind was that I had to speak to Yildiz and I didn't want to. I tried to recollect things that might attract me to her in some way. When I found my dislike of her increasing for no apparent reason, I tried to use the sexual desire that had come back to me to unlock some realm of intimacy. It was no use! Yildiz continued to appear in my head in the form of the witch my father's mother had told me about when I was a child—my grandmother died at Dream Bridge when I was seven years old, but I still remember the ring of the words as she spoke, and that broken, jumpy, provincial accent whose remnants clung to my father's tongue to the last day of his life—though my reaction now was different from the laughter the idea provoked in me then, when I would look at Yildiz naked and see an actual copy of the seductive witch whose ability to transform herself terrified me when I was a child.

Now when Yildiz appeared in my head in this strange form, I felt real terror.

For some reason, despite all these revelations, I believe that the moment in which I reclaimed the city occurred during this trip, as I returned home from meeting Aldo Mazika with all these things rushing into my head. I believe that for the first time since feeling shattered and overwhelmed, following the rapid transformations Cairo had gone through between the time I went to Shubra with a woman on my conscience and the time I returned with my conscience clear, I began to see my city in a steady state—or else it had begun to settle down again in my consciousness. I don't know how to prove this to you—the fact is that, in the middle of all the ideas and goings-on, the matter didn't enter my mind directly—but it happened that I felt the city achieve a state of completion, its various parts coming together before my eyes.

You know the static that used to appear on the television screen after the transmission ended? As if the blurry, grainy image on the screen had slowly pulled itself in until a new scene appeared, made up of all its sounds and colors...

At this moment, I started to form a plan to walk through Islamic Cairo on foot, before and after work the following day, Sunday. For some reason that I didn't immediately fathom, it seemed that this walk had something to do with calling Yildiz, something I'd postponed since the subject first entered my head. I also realized the walk I'd be undertaking wouldn't represent a repossession of my city or a rebuilding operation; it was clear to me that Islamic Cairo wasn't a part of the city I sought to repossess; the walk was motivated rather by my desire to see the old city complete, so that I could make a connection between its perfection and the perfection of the Cairo that concerned me, whether through direct observation or imitation of some kind...

It didn't occur to me until I was drawing up the plan that it might actually solve the problem of Yildiz.

The best way to resolve the crisis, I thought, was to pluck up the courage to speak to Yildiz at the Sultan Hasan mosque. I feel a strange peace whenever I'm there, though I haven't been there in a long time. At this point, when I recalled the golden verses embossed in calligraphic *thuluth* script around the lofty mihrab, an image of Claudine, Yildiz's elder sister, lit up before my eyes.

•　　　•　　　•　　　•　　　•

I'd only ever sat at leisure with Claudine once, at dinner with Yildiz, about seven years ago. She'd been settled in Paris for over a year at the time. She had an extremely smart young Frenchman with her by the name of Adrian Pasqua, who kept playing the harmonica and spoke to me in English with an outrageous accent. I remember this meeting because it was a really pleasant evening and because Claudine did something for me. It's hard to explain to you now how or why, but there was something about her face that made her stick in my mind. In her face, Abu al-Siyout, or more precisely, in her manner.

Claudine was thin and almost flat, like Yildiz, so you would be both surprised and delighted to find soft flesh and the contours of a woman under her clothes if you undressed her. She also had the same dough-colored complexion as Yildiz, and short hair that was neither rough nor smooth. But despite these strong similarities, it was perhaps her difference from her sister that overwhelmed me on the night of our dinner. Far from showing off the languages she knew and pronounced as well as Yildiz—witness the ostentatious way Yildiz switches from English to French to German and vice versa—Claudine hadn't developed a faux American accent like most of the graduates of the American University. When she spoke English she retained all the mistakes of French pronunciation, like substituting a "z" or an "s" for "th," would you believe it? This was quite apart from the fact that she didn't need to use tricks, as Yildiz did, to achieve a slim, childlike body—which made her youthful appearance infinitely more attractive.

I remember that I particularly liked how she smiled shyly, as if she weren't sure whether she'd done you wrong but knew you'd forgive her anyway…

Seven years ago, then, at dinner with Yildiz, I'd observed in her elder sister an attractiveness of a sort I seemed to have been looking for all my life. There was a sparkle in her eyes that I'd never seen in anyone else. Even when she was still, her eyes would sparkle, and her manner and the feelings she radiated were always changing, so that you felt you could never catch hold of her, or anything about her. At the time, of course, there was no opportunity to think about anything between us, not just because she was so much older than me—in her eyes, I was just a baby the same age as her little sister—but also because I'd discovered that the young Frenchman with her had actually been her husband for over two years, and that she was now expecting her first child with him...

From that single meeting—you see my point—I'd retained in my mind an image that wasn't exactly pale, but was certainly on a small scale, of a woman with an uncommon ability to mix with other people so effortlessly (quite the opposite of Yildiz) that you felt that every look, every glance or movement she made, every word she spoke, she actually meant, even if in reality she didn't.

After the night of that dinner and specifically while things were going on with Yildiz, I believe I was in a narrow, far-off place searching for Claudine, her sister. This is proved by the fact that when Yildiz started to make her coarse, "short-sleeved" gestures, as we say in Arabic, I constantly reflected that Claudine would never behave like that. I retained both her image, which flashed through my mind in miniature from time to time, and an unwavering, unspoken desire to grasp her youthfulness in my hands, set it down in one place, undress her, and run my fingers and tongue over her whole body.

But for seven whole years, good God, not a whisper of this desire.

Claudine disappeared and was almost finished with before my relationship with Yildiz began. I no longer thought about Dr. Murad, although he was so exceptional, the last representative of a dying breed of Egyptian intellectual. But now, going home after seeing Aldo, I tell you, Claudine flashed before my eyes as if she were a sheet of dough ready to be folded. She moved with the same sparkle in her eyes, and her face bore the most captivating expressions: when in her presence Yildiz said, for example, "I only read the books Oprah recommends," something between disgust and distress appeared there completely spontaneously.

On preparations for the tour of Islamic Cairo

The night I polished the ring with lemon and soda, as I was telling you, I resolved to make a tour of Islamic Cairo. So I took out my history and tourist books and sketched out a route in my notebook while sitting on the bed, a B-movie on the TV screen just like the night of the first dream. With great enthusiasm, I sketched Faisal Street as it had revealed itself to me when I went to Fustuq's farm, and my route from Dream Bridge to Sand Port, then sketched the whole of Islamic Cairo and circled the area that I wanted to have a thorough walk around…

I'd gone back to Dream Bridge, laughing about the Serb girl I'd thrown into the canal, at the African whose face I had belched in, and the Sunni who cried if his plug was unplugged. I changed my clothes, repeating the hip-hop song that had played while I drove the Serb girl to the canal ("Because the sound I make will break down walls, because they make me feel hate and that hate is thirsty"), and for the first time since visiting the registrar in Shubra I felt that divorce had not only been the right decision, but had also been, particularly in light of what I'd discovered in Sand Port, necessary.

I said this to Mama as for the second night in a row I enjoyed the meal she'd prepared, reassuring her again about me and my future as I sat talking to her and teasing her—"How come you're looking so pretty today, nonna? A real beauty, honestly, just like the moon!"—hoping she might understand what I was saying as I told her in a roundabout way that my ex-wife wasn't perfect.

The odd thing, brother, is that she didn't react, either in the way I was expecting—calling on God to reassure herself that the divorce had been the right decision—or in any other way. She just looked me in the eye for a long time as a depressed expression spread over her face like a crack in a windshield and said: "I've not been pleased with you these last few days, Mustafa!"

Perhaps when you're in Cairo you can contact her and try to understand what was going through her head before and after the divorce. I really don't know. In the last week when I was staying with her—after I found out I was to leave my job and travel, but even before that—something about her manner surprised me. From roughly that moment on she gradually began to speak to me less. Gradually, too, it happened several times that I noticed her looking at me from a distance—by now she'd stopped watching over my food and sleep and things like that—and saw in her face fear and grief, like a woman who'd woken up and not recognized her son. Either a woman who didn't recognize her son, or one who had found in his place a zombie that resembled him.

But the evening I came back from seeing Aldo, I couldn't settle down with my mother. After supper, I listened to a piece of Andalusian music from the city of Tétouan in the north of Morocco, and kept repeating the words as I took a shower: "Ask the pretty girl in the black veil, what have you done to the pious hermit? Ee—ah—ee—ah." And although thus far I hadn't seen a pretty girl to fall in love with, whether in a black veil or not, tears welled up in my eyes, and for a full half hour, as the water from the shower bounced off my back, I squatted in the bathtub in tears.

When I came out of the bathroom, Mother had shut herself in her room. I went to my room intending to prepare for tomorrow's trip and go to sleep. I didn't at first begin to flip through the books I'd put on the bedside table for the second night in a row, but when I switched on the TV to fill the empty time, as was my habit by now, I took the brown notebook out of my bag and put it on my lap as I sat up in bed to watch. As if to reassure myself that it was there. The film *The Headmaster* had started some time ago, and because I love this film I thought I'd postpone my preparations to watch it. But I don't know what happened after that.

Perhaps because I knew all those things, or because the new image of the city had lodged itself in my brain, I felt inspired. As soon as I'd picked up the thick black pen from beside the books on the table—with 'Ala' Wali al-Din (God have mercy on him), the fat film hero, bellowing in the face of Ahmad Hilmi, the slim actor who stood in front of him and grabbed him by the collar: "I want to be a nobody. Ruin me, ruin me, 'Atif!"—as soon as I'd picked up the pen, I tell you, I began sketching furiously.

First of all, I composed myself and shut my eyes to draw my route, all at once, to Sand Port (you will find it on the opening page of the sixth part of this part of the book). When I'd finished, I got up and made coffee—'Ala' Wali al-Din was under a Bombay mosquito net, talking to a Russian prostitute via a formally dressed interpreter who was leaning over the side of the bed—and opened a new packet of cigarettes before spreading the books around me, open to the pages I needed.

As I understood it, you could sketch Islamic Cairo using seven focal points: beginning from the southwest, if you walk counter-clockwise (like the magic circles that I make for my drawings): al-Rawda, al-Fustat, al-Qarafa, al-Muqattam, Bab al-Futuh, Bulaq. I made an auspicious beginning with number seven. I searched on maps, to copy the Nile and with it Bulaq and al-Rawda, then al-Mu'izz's Cairo, and Old Cairo, including Fustat and the Seven Churches, and with them the area where they intersect, which contain the monuments of the Tulunid empire, then the Cemeteries with their northern and southern parts, and the Muqattam Hills between them. Finally, I drew a circle around the lines to contain them, as I had done twice before, in the first week after leaving Dog Alley: once with my daily route, and once with the five important places. Then I had the idea to add four small drawings at the four points of the compass, to make the sketch into a map as well as an amulet.

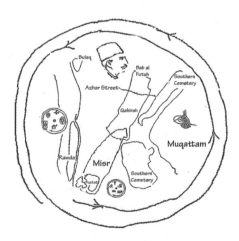

I put the sultan's head on Azhar Street in the north—the sultan's head was the largest thing in the picture—with his seal above the mountain in the east, followed by a circle of my five places, half of them within the Nile itself in the west, and my daily route, on a smaller scale, between the Cemeteries and al-Rawda in the south.

This sketch took time, my friend—I was struck by how much time I took—and once I'd finished, I turned off the TV, and in my notebook I made a detailed plan of my walking tour in Islamic Cairo, so that the following day, the third Sunday, I'd know my route easily.

I decided where I'd go and when, knowing that I'd have to be at work for at least three hours starting from eleven in the morning (on Sundays there's no need to be there longer than that—there's no work to be done, and in any case, in such a large corporation it's rare for anyone's absence to be noticed after the first couple of hours of the morning).

I decided to be realistic, and said to myself that I would just stick to Fatimid Cairo and forget al-Rawda, Old Cairo, and Bulaq. In any event, Fatimid Cairo was the largest place that was complete in itself. I would park, as usual, on El Galaa Street, arriving there before 6:30 in the morning, then take a taxi and tell the driver to take me to Bab al-Sha'riyya, get off at Bab al-Futuh, and start my walk along al-Mu'izz Street, as if to greet the Fatimid City by moving along the main artery in its body.

The final thing I thought about before sleeping was that I had to find an excuse to contact Yildiz when I arrived at Sultan Hasan, even if it wasn't a particularly convincing one. I racked my brains until I recalled that ten days before I separated from my ex-wife, Yildiz had asked me to return two sci-fi books I'd borrowed some time before. Nearly a month had gone by since this request, I told myself, but responding to it now would be a plausible excuse.

Today I can't remember, Abu al-Rushd, whether I'd got up out of bed to fetch the two books or just fixed their position in my head, but after I saw—either in reality or in my imagination—the black covers engraved with thick red lines I immediately went to sleep.

Record of the second dream

That night, without any comic influences like the Hosta Costa song, I had a second dream. I woke up remembering it all, despite its length and complexity—which would make the last sketch of my face I made during the weeks of the tale a portrait of myself sleeping. You know that sleep is like a little death, and while sketching my face for the third time that week, I'd feel I was recording the last moments in the life of a dying man: the last revelation of the person I'd been, and wouldn't be again after I woke; the person who'd worked at the economics paper; who'd married then divorced; and who was the friend of Amgad Salah.

After I woke, this person would really be dead, and the sketch of his sleeping face would be the last thing left of him. As for me, I would be resurrected as a different person, one who had new meaning to his life and a light-hearted woman who promised him harmony.

This second dream seemed to sum up everything. It had come to me on the third Sunday after I'd felt I had recovered the city I'd lost when I left the marital home, after I'd prepared for a tour of Islamic Cairo to complete my reclamation of the city, and before I'd decided to complete this task in the shortest time possible. Perhaps, in this sense, it created for me a state of psychological stability and calm reflected in my sleeping face, perhaps it even foretold my meeting with Claudine, with whom I fell in love during the actual Islamic tour as soon as I heard her voice on the telephone:

I dreamed, may God make it turn out well:

I was in a hall, its high ceiling painted with small golden stars on a dark blue background (it didn't occur to me in the dream that this could be a dark corridor in the sultan's private quarters in the Yildiz Palace). The gilded furniture was heavy and imposing in the Napoleonic style (they call it "style," pronounced the French way like "steel," as opposed to "modern" in Egypt) but there was some extremely Oriental Oyma work as well. There were thick carpets on the floor as far as the eye could see, decorated with the tughra of Abdülmecid. My foot sunk deep into them and their wine-red color reminded me of the felt used for fezzes. They were so thick that my feet actually disappeared, only to reappear when I took another step. The scene was like the preparation for a farewell or a departure, as if I were here at the last moment to say goodbye to someone leaving—though at first there was no one with me amid the thick walls inlaid with ivory. Only this dome with its heavenly workmanship above me, while I turned this way and that like an idiot, without knowing where.

Suddenly, the hall was not so dark and I was no longer alone. I was sitting as I had been, but around me were people waiting just like me, some on their feet and some sitting. In the silence that descended on us, there was a feeling of anticipation. I couldn't see clearly the faces of those who were with me, but they were wearing black suits, Istanbul-style, or else colored kaftans with cloaks over them, and turbans or fezzes on their heads. I noticed that some of those wearing suits had turbans, and some of those wearing cloaks had fezzes. I also noticed, almost shamefully, that I was the only one in the gathering who was bare-headed. I was wearing my normal clothes that I wore to travel between Dream Bridge and World's Gate, so I must have looked strange and vapid. When I felt my head and found that it was completely shaven, I felt even more ashamed and stood up to walk toward an empty corner near a tall buffet with a glass pane on top of it. Under the glass were medals and antiques and a single old, rusty sword.

For one fleeting moment, in the mirrors above the glass pane, I saw the reflection of the most famous oil painting of Sultan Mehmet the Conqueror, though I could find no trace of it in the whole hall, however much I looked. I understood this detail as an allusion to the moment I kissed his hand in my first dream while he, the young sultan, was inside Ayasofya on the back of his horse… The person we were waiting for had come, but at first I only saw him from behind. I was surprised that those waiting with me paid no attention to him at all, and only greeted him with a simple nod of the head or wave of the hand. I was thunderstruck when I recognized him, not because his appearance was odd but because I didn't believe I would succeed in meeting him: Ghazi 'Abd al-Hamid Khan II in person, the engineer of the three decades that preceded the First World War and led to the collapse of the Sublime State. I looked at him, dazzled, like a man looking at a film star whose image he has often seen on screen but whom he's now seeing for the first time in real life.

He was much smaller in size than the image in my head, though he had broad shoulders—or perhaps what made them seem broad was that, despite all his ostentation, he was much thinner than I'd expected, so thin and fragile indeed that everything on his body quivered. Despite the fact that his Istanbuli suit was starched and covered with badges and medals, and his shining fez a little shorter than it appears in pictures (making, together with his square chin, a cardboard-like cube that enclosed his face just as his suit enclosed his frame), he looked to me very, very old, and in a way decrepit, as though, if not for these reinforced containers, he would collapse before my eyes, like a skeleton that crumbles and disintegrates into dust. His beard, Abu al-Rushd, is what struck my eye as I spoke to him. Despite being very thick, it was nonetheless wispy, reflecting his own skinniness, and it was all of it gray-green, the color of my father's robe, with not the slightest variation from one place to another. He kept his eyes on the floor, or so I thought, as he moved slowly between the buffet with the sword in it and the part of the wine-red carpet decorated with his seal, which the guests had begun to circumambulate like planets around the sun, in circles that expanded and narrowed around the same point. He was muttering expressions in colloquial Turkish without directing his words to anyone in particular.

I felt he was behaving like someone shutting the windows of a house, turning off the taps and lights, and checking that everything was closed up and in its place in the last few moments before traveling. Then he put something beside the chair and sat down. People were coming up to him in turns with papers or petitions, then returning to where they had come from, walking in a circle again. I was the only one sitting by his side. When I plucked up my courage and addressed him in classical Arabic, he seemed not to understand. I'm certain we'd switched to English or some other language that people speak in dreams, when he said to me something that meant "I read classical Arabic but I don't speak it," then added literally, "But I speak the Egyptian dialect very well!" As soon as he said that, Abu al-Siyout, my face broke into a smile, and suddenly I felt a strong sense of love toward him. After a moment, he leaned over the thing he'd put beside him when he sat down, and I discovered that it was a bright orange Kipling backpack, the sort that's tied with a handle and a little cloth monkey for a fastener. The bag seemed odd and tasteless, out of keeping with a Padishah's suit and fez, and with the air of gravitas in the hall. But he simply put it on his shoulder and headed toward the door, shaking.

Had I woken up for a moment with the exit scene, as it were? I don't know. My next memory is of walking toward the buffet. It was still in its place but there was no glass on it now. The sword had moved to the surface and was new and shining. When I looked in the mirrors where I'd seen the image of Mehmet the Conqueror, the wall was empty, but I was astonished to see that I myself was now in historical dress: a short white gown with a blue kaftan over it, and a conical fez, a white head-cloth hanging from a metal mold on its rear face. In the middle of the mold was a gold star with eight sides, fashioned from the intersection of two squares. Under the gown were baggy Turkish pants reaching just below the knee, with a sheath in the belt that I sensed was the same size as the sword in front of me. I slid it in, and it fit into the waistband astonishingly smoothly, confirming to me that this actually was the sword's sheath. As I stretched my back in disbelief, I heard a voice behind me say: "Çorbacı, sir! Çorbacı, sir!"

Then I was with three others who wore the same outfit, standing in a formation with our assistants, like chess pieces moved by an unknown hand, until we created a shape like the eight-pointed star on my head, facing a velvet throne embroidered with gold. I knew that I was Çorbacı, while those with me were the Grand Vizier; the "Kizlar Agha," or Agha of the Black Eunuchs, who was in charge of the harem; and the Sheikh al-Islam, or Grand Mufti of the Hanafi Rite. Gradually, a light like a revolving spotlight started to descend on each of our heads so that it changed momentarily from a jellylike phantom to the body and face of a recognizable human being. You understand that directions become confused in dreams. The four of us were all facing the throne, standing to attention, our heads not moving at all, but I could clearly see the others' faces as the light came down and the spotlight illuminating them revolved from one to the other, just as my unknown companions had turned in the first part of the dream.

Looking at their complex garb and their different kinds of headwear, I recognized Michel Fustuq, Aldo Mazika, and Amgad Salah. I wasn't all that surprised, until mirrors appeared over the throne, the spotlight was turned off, and the only light in the place was directed at the mirrors or thrown back by them. This made the mirrors ripple gradually as though they were turning into a flimsy curtain the color of silver and ice. Then the curtain opened and a harem girl emerged, in an embroidered dress with a long train, like a sixteenth-century European princess's. I fancied her from the very first moment. She was calm and serene, although her eyes had a look of rebellion and challenge in them. She appeared in the folds of the flesh of the Kizlar Agha, where she stood still like a white spot in an oil field that might swallow her up at any moment. Her shape looked very familiar. She was thin, almost flat, with dough-colored skin and hair that was neither smooth nor rough, but I woke without recognizing her.

Recapitulation

Why must I now break the flow and anticipate events, to let you see how I too contradict myself about the essence of love? Perhaps because I am being punished in Beirut. I think that if I hadn't changed into a zombie I couldn't have put up with my punishment. It is now about a month since my meeting with

Claudine, from April 16th to the middle of May. Do I have to hate her first then see her again to know the secret of my torment?

The soul is the translator of interpretation, and the mind is the translator of change. —al-Niffari

This torment, so far, has had no fixed features. But, as in our relationship, there is something closely linked to the transformation that I will call my resurrection: a sense that destinies do not end with the end of their subjects' bodies; my repeated feeling of loss (of my ex-wife, and my life with her in Dog Alley, of my father who died, of my sister who departed this life before she could bury him, of my homeland—my estrangement from which has been confirmed to me in a million ways over ten years, of the Muslims' Imam who visited me and the Islamic umma that I discovered; the loss of you yourself, of course, since you emigrated to London, and now of the person I was before I turned into a zombie enlisted in the army of the Imam). Plus my feeling as I slept with her that I was falling into a bottomless pit, a pit that actually transcended history, Rashid...

I've never been much bothered, either now or previously, with the intellectuals' idea that there's some hidden link between love and death. I've never bothered with these abstractions. I didn't believe I really died when the sultan appeared to me. It's just that from here I can draw a connection between things: to have your love of an émigrée defined as a feeling like loss, while you yourself are abroad; and to be where you are—to be a zombie, with all that the term implies, and to have first met this girl at the time you turned into a zombie—while everything is happening to you in an attempt to understand the meaning of being Arab and a Muslim in this age.

Today, when I think of the impossibility of my relationship with Claudine, it's no exaggeration to say I want to die. Then I remember that I am actually dead, and I say to myself in an affectionate tone: she is yours, so long as you undertake the task of resurrection and revival. Only my consciousness of my death enables me to overcome the impossible. For love is the only thing that can overcome politics and economics. My longing for Claudine is like days too remote for us to recall their features, Rashid, days passed in a land like this land, when we had something else whose features we cannot recall, nor how or why we lost it. My longing for Claudine is like a memory of that thing, and nothing but our meeting can give me rest from the movement that has destroyed me since it left.

I want to die, I tell you. I remember the moment when she said to me, with her face beneath my arm, that something strange happens when two bodies are joined, something, as she described it, akin to grief. Pleasure is like Paradise, my friend, but Claudine burst into tears. In the end, I would spend only three days with her—Monday, Tuesday, and Wednesday of the third week after leaving Dog Alley—three days broken up by work, staying with my mother, and from the Tuesday morning (after she'd unwittingly put my feet on the start of the road), running around, arranging to travel to Beirut.

The moment we parted, I recall, she came down after me from the apartment where we hid away on Tree Hill. She met me in the road behind, where I parked the car well out of sight of her mother. There, as we walked up and down from one end of the street to the other, she clung to my arm. Like a white bird, hanging by its beak on the tail of an obstinate camel— her frame was that small next to mine, you know?—she kept clinging until I turned and opened my arms to take all of her in my embrace, so that nothing of her body was visible to an onlooker, as my arms wrapped themselves around her, and she stood between my legs.

I pull her to me and press her ribs to feel I have been made whole, that a hole gaping in my stomach has been filled. Who could say that someone you've been with for only three days can't make you feel right and wonderful?

On the nature of love

I'm writing to you from beside the sea, knowing more than ever that nothing except writing will be of any use. I'm writing to you—this is what I've wanted to say from the beginning— to recount some things that were said or happened while I was with Claudine, and through which I can glimpse some definitions of love. It will be like a break from looking for the parchment of the sura, sitting all day in the Rawda Café beside the military baths on the Beirut Corniche, with the sea beside me, recording very slowly in the final pages of the same brown notebook three of these definitions.

Of course, there are more, but I will write only as the mood takes me, perhaps because everything that has stuck in my head from those three days is associated not just with sexual desire and sadness, but also with being out of breath: running from one place to another to finish as quickly as possible and reach Claudine, then fucking and smoking a lot, a lot of smoking and fucking, Rashid.

I now feel that the three definitions that I will have set down before the sun disappears are the most important in this sequence of events. As if they—the definitions—were the key to our vigorous lovemaking, twelve times in total.

If the cause of Love were physical beauty, the consequence would be that no body defective in any shape or form would attract admiration; yet we know of many a man actually preferring the inferior article, though well aware that another is superior, and quite unable to turn his heart away from it. Again, if Love were due to a harmony of characters, no man would love a person who was not of like purpose and in concord with him. We therefore conclude that Love is something within the soul itself. —Ibn Hazm, *Risālat Tawq al-Hamāma*

The Chinese artist whose book I read makes a connection between ignorance of the self and the failure of relationships. For a man ignorant of himself, so he claims, relationships are only a distraction from his inner emptiness, which exposes him to collapse. It was my opinion that it was knowledge, on the contrary, that precipitated the collapse of my marriage: my knowledge of my propensity for misery—that here was the last thing I could bear, or the last thing I wanted.

But the Chinese artist's words would perhaps have some application if I were to turn them on their head. When you fall in love, your self-knowledge returns to you, and you are filled from the inside, feeling compassion with no thought of compensation, able to go beyond the rules of logic.

When we parted, when I finally pulled my teeth away from her lips to get in behind the steering wheel, Claudine would tell me she didn't like oranges. Just like that, for no apparent reason. I found this expression of the pain of parting strange—for a moment, I might doubt whether she really was pained to leave me—but since then, whenever I see oranges or a picture of oranges, I remember the trembling of her voice, the prominent arc of kohl under her eyes, like a bag to catch her tears, and the sorrow that afflicted us amid our joy in one another.

The first definition of love, may you be the coolest: Never to distinguish between sorrow and joy when you see oranges.

That night, as I drove off and down the mountain, I had in my head a verse of poetry by Sidi 'Umar, which I'd later look for to set down here: "*Nothing pleased the eye after they had moved away; when the heart was reminded of them, it was not happy*" ('Umar ibn al-Farid).

I remember I looked at the dark rocks on the barren mountain slope, suddenly convinced that she was the one. There was no one else in the world. All the way to Dream Bridge, as I looked at the sleeping city for the last time, I seemed to be floating on my beloved's perfume while I recalled her movements and her needs. I record them, because I know how much I will need them later.

I was perhaps at the Majra al-'Uyun Wall—thus far, God be praised, I had still kept at the bottom of my mind the historical information that it had been built by Qansuh al-Ghawri so that water could be brought to the Citadel inside it from the mouth of the canal in Old Cairo, opposite Rawda Island, though the wall now appears like a series of gates made for aliens of varying sizes—I was perhaps there when I recalled how Claudine received me on the Tuesday evening…

I'd gone to her that evening after a heavy day. I crept up the stairs for fear of being noticed by Kariman Hanim, who stayed up all night eavesdropping, so Claudine had warned me. But when I reached the door, rather than tapping lightly as we'd agreed, I hesitated. I stood in front of the door for a long time, knowing that she was also standing there, on the other side—don't ask me how, I just knew—and at the same time as I was standing there, she knew that I was outside, just as I knew that she was inside, but I wouldn't knock and she wouldn't open. Two people waiting, with a door between them: could this in itself be a definition of love?

After a time—I was scratching on the wood with my nails, like a cat—she opened up. I couldn't see all of her in the darkness, but behind the door, her face was caught in the light of the one lit corridor, and I could see she was blushing. The blush in Claudine's face, this was something I'd learned since Monday, the sign of embarrassment that accompanied her joy and confirmed it was the joy of love—her eyes would sparkle, and tension would paint a sort of a picture on her face, something that made you long to put her, all of her, in your mouth and swallow her to protect her from fear and torment…

Suddenly her body went limp, as if the tightness in her face had created a softness in the rest of her. Despite the feeling of being lost that came over us both at the start of each meeting, I didn't touch her immediately. After asking "How are you?" I didn't know what to do with myself, except to follow her flowing footsteps along the dark corridor. Suddenly, she stopped and squatted on the ground with her back to the wall, then put her head between her knees and sat there, muttering that she was scared and confused. When I bent over her and sucked the bridge of her nose, before asking in a whisper in her paper-thin ear what was frightening her this evening, she said that a moment ago she'd realized the only thing she wanted in the world was to make me coffee. Would you believe it? Without my saying anything to her of my thoughts of the past two weeks, she wished she were from Upper Egypt and had never been to school and that her sole aim in life was to please me. A Sa'idi girl to make me coffee and leave me in peace! The fact that she recognized this shook me more than anything.

Second definition of love, then: to be, for your sake, a Sa'idi girl who'd never been to school.

That evening, as I was noticing that she pronounced almost all English and Arabic letters a little oddly, Claudine talked to me about the danger of discoveries. We were in bed, naked and exhausted, and when I put the ashtray on my belly and we sat up to smoke, she sighed and said: "Discoveghy, ah, discoveghy!", pronouncing the English word with a French "r," unaware how strange it sounded. When I gave her an inquiring look, without moving any part of my body, she said: "Like the TV station, you know, the Discoveghy Shanellle?" (she pronounced the word "channel" without the English "ch"), and went on to say that her life after forty was just like that channel: a screen on which things appeared that the viewer couldn't be expected to recognize until he fixed the remote on this channel rather than any other. She was no longer sure she knew anything.

Little by little, she began to tell me about her on-off relationship with Dr. Murad. "You know that he's extremely ill at the moment?" she said. "I think there's a lot of things, you know." Then she explained to me how he represented everything she liked in the "male sex"—she laughed shyly when she saw I was smiling—"I mean, the male of the human species, you animal!"—how Dr. Murad represented everything she might like in the male sex and at the same time contradicted it. And that despite what she'd gone through in her life since being his "one and only young missy," whom he wooed with hot chocolate and hair bows, she'd continued to see in him a Sa'idi whose strongest feelings would still be for Upper Egypt, even if he did apply the enlightened doctrines he believed in— women's rights, liberal values, and all kinds of other things that were not in the character of that region.

After forty, so she said, she'd discovered this was what she really wanted from a man—for him to be a Sa'idi in his love for her—and that the life she'd been striving toward for all these years, even though it had in fact led her in completely the opposite direction, had been merely her way of making this discovery. Ever since she'd graduated in French literature (unlike Yildiz, who'd studied at the AUC, Claudine had insisted on going to Cairo University) right up to this moment, it was as if everything she'd done in her life had been done solely so she'd know she didn't actually want this sort of life at all.

She'd left the family home for five years with no financial support from her parents. This was a second period of formation, in which her deep sense of loneliness became apparent, together with a continuing need to be among people, and to distribute her time between them. She had been quiet and withdrawn, but she perfected the social arts, learning the pleasure of spending hours with other people, how to stay occupied, and how important it was to do so, and she became addicted to making acquaintances, then quarreling with them... She forged relationships with the scum of the earth and kept some of them after she'd emigrated (now, when she says "my friends" to me, I am annoyed and laugh to myself, saying: "That easy, huh?"). She then moved into an apartment in the neighborhood of al-Munira with a French historian called Adrian Pasqua who'd come to write a doctorate about the final years of the life of the great Mehmet Ali and met her at a hashish session at a mutual friend's. She married this Adrian and started another life with him in Paris, where even she, entirely voluntarily, started on the academic ladder, even though she'd refused all her life to imitate her father, saying that his life disgusted her. And after forty came a new self-knowledge. (She kept on saying she'd met me at the wrong time, though time was of no consequence so far as we were concerned, indeed it was impossible for time to be of any consequence.)

God filled the place where she had left Adam with yearning for her; he had compassion for her as he had for himself because she was part of him, and she had compassion for him because he was the place where she had come from. —Ibn 'Arabi

Tormented in Beirut, I tell you. But happy that, for Claudine, I was the flesh and blood of this new knowledge. Claudine's self-knowledge means a lot to me. Even though I suspected that it was merely a fancy frame for the picture of family misery that Claudine lived, like all miserable wives, even though by means of it... She knew that I wouldn't be a bomb she could throw at her routine, to explode a marital crisis that both preceded and followed my appearance—a crisis that she and Adrian seemed to me to have been cooking for themselves over a gentle flame for a whole lifetime. (The woman who wants you depressed so she can snatch you from the claws of despair—I've seen all sorts of sweethearts in my life: the woman who deceives you; the woman who uses you to make someone else mad; the woman who feels marvelous just

because you exist; the woman who wants you as a lavatory…
and the woman who makes you into a traffic sign to indicate
the direction she won't have the courage to go in.) Even if I
suspected, Rashid, I'd keep waiting. And just as I am waiting
to find a certain man—I intend to go to Damascus to look for
him there if I don't find him here this month—I have no idea
what return my waiting will bring.

On Wednesday night, I proposed to her that we should test
our feelings somewhere far from Cairo, Paris, and everything.
At every moment we imagine life together like this forever (or
for an "ever" as small as we are), each of us breathing in the
soul of the other as on Tree Hill, but now without caution or
hesitation, so that we don't even notice when "forever" expands
again. She will finish her research about the link between
the body and revolution in twentieth-century France, and I
will finish the book of drawings and photographs I've been
dreaming of putting together, even though the appearance of
the sultan has changed my conception of its content.

The third definition of love, may you be cool, is that the
size of "ever" should change more than three times a day.

An account of the tour of Islamic Cairo (a return to the Epistle of Maps and Antiquities)

The tour of Islamic Cairo took place exactly as I'd planned the
morning of the third Sunday, Abu al-Arshad. Here is a very
condensed record of the most important things that happened
to me during that tour, after I'd gotten out of bed and driven to
World's Gate, where I parked in El Galaa Street before taking a
taxi to Bab al-Futuh.

7 AM to 9 AM. In the soft morning light—the whole place
was quiet—from when I entered al-Mu'izz Street and went past
Bab al-Futuh, until I reached Khan al-Khalili, heading for the
café I love, I saw many, many things, most of them in ruins and
hard to recognize among the little shops, cafés, and houses. I
passed the palace of the Amir Bashtak: son-in-law of al-Nasir
Muhammad ibn Qalawun, the father of Sultan Hasan, who
built the mosque I'd intended to call Yildiz from, and perhaps
the most important of al-Mansur Qalawun's family, which
continued for a full century during the First Mamluk State,

despite the power struggles and bloodiness of the Mamluks. Between this palace and the Kuttab of 'Abd al-Rahman Katkhoda, built during the French expedition, lay the Bayn al-Qasrayn area that used to divide the Palace of al-Mu'izz li-Din Allah on the east side from the Palace of al-'Aziz billah al-Asghar on the west side. That was in the days when only rulers and soldiers were permitted to enter the earliest city. The sultan's baths, built by a nobody called Inal during the Second State and inaugurated two years before Mehmet the Conqueror entered Istanbul. The Khanqah, or Khankah (or Sufi dwelling-house, the one I saw being large enough for sixty dervishes) of al-Zahir Barquq, the first person to introduce plums into Egypt (where they are called *barquq* as a result, though in Greater Syria they are still known as *khukh*). The Gothic Gate, which is set in the face of the Madrasa of al-Nasir Muhammad (I already knew that this gate had been ripped from the face of St. George's Church in Acre by Sultan al-Nasir's brother during one of his battles with the Crusaders). And the Maristan of al-Mansur Qalawun himself (a Maristan being a hospital, not necessarily a mental asylum), that enormous building that one can only enter today through a window…

When I reached Bab al-Futuh, I was thinking about the awe-inspiring walls where Bonaparte's soldiers hid, widening the holes designed for arrows so that they could insert the muzzles of their guns. The walls were built to be wide enough for two men on horseback to ride side by side on top of them. I looked at the lambs' heads that you can make out carved atop the gate to celebrate the Conquering Planet (Mars, the planet of Aries) or ward off its evil. I recalled that the Bab al-Nasr and Bab al-Futuh which exist today (their correct names are actually Bab al-'Izz and Bab al-Iqbal) were built by Badr al-Din al-Jamali, the Caliph al-Mustansir's vizier, about a hundred years after the time of Jawhar al-Siqilli and al-Mu'izz, in order to expand the city so that the ruler's mosque could be inside it and to protect it from the attacks of the Seljuks…

But the most impressive thing during the first part of the tour was the appearance of an albino beggar who seemed to emerge from the remains of a small mosque in the middle of the gate to the Copper Polishers' Quarter—the only Ottoman remains I'd had noticed so far—holding his chest wide as if to block my way. He was wearing a torn black gallabiya, and snot was dripping onto his thin white beard. His eyes were slightly closed against the light, like all albinos', and his mouth was crooked and wide open. He stood there until I approached him, when he gave me a smile that made his mouth even more crooked, then, before I could put my hand into my pocket, gave me a military salute. As soon as I held my hand out, though, he gestured to me to stop:

"No, no, don't give me money. Look, the sultan's my friend! I've come to bless you because the sultan's my friend!"

To be frank, I was scared, especially as the quarter was completely deserted, as was al-Gamaliyya Street in front of me. I hurried past the beggar and walked on toward al-Mu'izz Street to get away from him and continue my tour. All the time I was walking, I could hear him repeating in a voice distorted by snot: "The sultan's my friend, my friend's the sultan!"

•   •   •   •   •

9 AM to 2 PM. At the café I like, they were sweeping up the sawdust in the narrow room and the corridor leading off it where I used to sit, set off a little from the wider square with the gold and souvenir shops and the tourist police in the evening. Nothing special happened, but I thoroughly enjoyed my tea, and when I stood up I felt remarkably rejuvenated; here was a pleasant sense of intimacy with Islamic Cairo. I walked through the Mouski and Zuqaq al-Midaqq then returned via al-Mu'izz Street, recited the fatiha for Sayyidna al-Hussein, and crossed through the tunnel to the Ghawriyya, where I wandered for a bit before leaving again to take a taxi downtown.

The Fiat 128 was ancient but in working condition. The driver was a short, very dark young man with a nervous tic in his left shoulder, which he shook without warning every couple of minutes. He didn't say a single word to me but he had a friendly smile the whole way. I was preoccupied with the Islamic monuments I was seeing, and if it hadn't been for this nervous tic of his, perhaps I wouldn't have taken any notice of what he looked like at all, even though he was noticeably cheerful. It was only when I was giving him the fare that I saw a small tattoo in the shape of a star over his right eye. It reminded me of the stars in the blue dome in the dream.

At work, two things happened that in context I think were important:

The first was that the fiqi Wahid appeared in the office at an unusually early hour for him (you know he only ever came very late in the evening). Aldo wasn't there, and the fiqi seemed lost and frightened in his absence, wandering all over the place. I was in my cubicle with the door shut, putting together a trivial article about the emo phenomenon in rock music, the black clothes, hair dye, and makeup that have spread among teenagers in Plane Yard.

Despite an unsettling, and constantly growing, feeling that with the fiqi there Sultan Wahid al-Din must also in some way be present, I tried not to pay any attention to him. At one moment, however, I raised my head to think about the drafting of a certain sentence, then thought of lighting a cigarette and turned slightly to look for the packet on the right of the computer—a single, completely unplanned moment—and I saw him standing outside the door of the big room that contains the cubicles, looking straight at me. The transformation had happened, as if by chance, at that very moment. Through two doors, I saw, in a fleeting and unexpected way, not the fiqi Wahid but our Master the Sultan. He was looking at me sympathetically, nodding his head in encouragement as if to say: "Be brave!" But as soon as I'd looked at him, the transformation was reversed, and the eccentric fiqi seemed to find it odd that he was standing there. I believe that he left the office as I was finishing the article. That was the last time I saw either the fiqi or the sultan.

The second thing was that I went out to the visitors' reception room, where the prayer room was situated; it too was a cubicle, though only marked off by a curtain. Someone from the corporation advertising department was waiting for me there to ask about something even more trivial than the article I was writing. But as I was leaving the room, I bumped into the girl engaged to the boy and the dark-skinned girl, heading together to the prayer room, one behind the other.

I smiled to disguise my sudden agitation when the dark girl turned her head and winked at me. I quickly moved in front of her, and she interrupted her friend, who was taking nonstop in a squeaky voice, to whisper to me: "Why did you look so lost at Michel's engagement party?" But the engaged girl didn't stop talking, didn't even let up the pace of her speech. She seemed to me to be not so much talking as making a succession of spluttering noises like a defective exhaust pipe on the freeway. One splutter was only separated from the next by the expression "I mean, why?", uttered in a disgusted tone that reminded me of when she'd talked to me about her family: "I can't do anything that would annoy them. I mean, why?"

God forgive me, Rashid, but I think the dark girl must have gestured to her as she handed her the veil to wrap around her head to pray, at the same moment she was putting on her own veil. Because the engaged girl only stopped spluttering when she took the veil. She seemed to have stopped completely; the expression on her face changed, and a mixture of embarrassment and rapture appeared on it, as if—God forgive me—some youthful lust had pinned her from top to toe. The dark girl was smiling wickedly with her eyes as she led her to the prayer area, and took off her shoes like a husband undoing his belt to make love to his wife. They were both silent, which made the blood boil in my body. Although I was tied up with the advertising executive awaiting me, as I shook hands with him I sneaked a glance in the direction of the little cubicle. Was it just my imagination that when the dark girl put her chin on the engaged girl's shoulder before they disappeared together behind the curtain, she bit her on the neck and smoothed her hair?

I left work with nothing in my head except for the gate on which Tuman Bey had been hanged, and how this would lead me, one way or another, to a place where I would be calm enough to speak to Yildiz. I knew that the conversation with which my tour of Islamic Cairo would end as a symbol of the city's reclamation would lead me to the start of the path toward fulfilling my mission. Did the return of my desire mean that I would fall in love in the meantime? Although the image of Claudine had returned to me often since I'd recalled her yesterday on the way back from meeting Aldo, and although I'd recognized her (and been very surprised) after awakening from the dream, I hadn't thought of her as a possible lover. A joyful danger…

On another level, though, I was delighted—or at least I was optimistic about the future. When I didn't find a taxi in El Galaa Street I didn't get angry or frustrated or take it as an evil omen. I just said to myself that it was easier to go from Ramses Street anyway, and I walked under the flyover and crossed the side road to get there.

Perhaps I need to tell you again that I'm not mad. The things I'm telling you all happened just as I'm telling them. I hadn't had a nervous breakdown for any reason, any previous or subsequent breakdowns notwithstanding. As soon as I started waiting for a taxi, a Fiat 128 stopped for me of its own accord. I looked inside in astonishment, because taxis in Egypt, as you know, don't stop for anyone until they know where he's heading. It was the same short, dark driver, smiling amiably at me and gesturing at me to get in. I was stunned but got in beside him and shut the door, and he moved off without saying a word. This time, I paid more attention to the star tattoo over his eye. I was certain that the first time it had been over his right eye and was small as a pin head. But now, I swear it was over his left eye, the same side as the shoulder with the nervous tic, and it had grown as big as a finger joint. I kept looking at it in disbelief until we turned off, when I pulled myself together.

"Bab al-Khalq, please!" I said.

"I'll drop you at the Mitwalli Gate," he replied.

"What? Who told you…?"

"I know where you're going, don't worry, I know where you're going!"

In response to his smile, which seemed to me positively angelic, I stayed silent; and neither of us said anything else for the rest of the journey. The albino beggar had suddenly come back to me with the first twitch of the driver's shoulder, and fear alone would have been enough to shut me up (the driver was silent and smiling anyway). Still, I don't think it was fear that kept me silent; there was also a feeling like the one that comes over you as you fasten your seat belt in an airplane in preparation for take-off: a feeling that you're committing your soul to an action over which you have no control. You can only trust the pilot's ability to do his duty. This doesn't mean that you're not afraid, but both fear and lack of it are pointless. It must have seemed to me that if I tried to understand this driver's nature or the hidden role he was playing in my life, I'd be like a traveler trying for the first time to learn (in full, during just one take-off) how a plane worked and how the pilot flew it.

•　　　•　　　•　　　•　　　•

2 to 6 PM. After he'd taken me to Bab Zuweila, totally smoothly despite the difficulty of penetrating the area by taxi, he took the fare in silence, like last time—his smiling face and sweet smile were incredible, Rashid!—and I got out to find myself among the crowd in the lap of the gate named after a Berber tribe who supported the Fatimids and came with them from Tunisia. Their troops had settled there as soon as the city was founded (I knew that the mosque had acquired the two minarets that flanked it from a mosque built by the Sultan al-Mu'ayyad, who had started out as one of Barquq's Mamluks, four hundred or so years later; it was built in place of the Shimali prison, which he destroyed when he came to power because he'd been imprisoned there as a young man). But by this time the 128 taxi, through divine providence, had disappeared.

I walked through the Tent-makers' Quarter more relaxed than ever, because I really was on the right track. From then on, before reaching the Sultan Hasan mosque (I was completely calm), I saw the Sugar Exchange built by Sitt Nafisa al-Bayda', known as the mother of the Mamluks (a woman so powerful that she invited Bonaparte personally to visit her). I was saddened by the state of the place, which had later become so famous for its sweetmeats that they named it (and the area around it) al-Sukkariyya. Garbage was piled against the gate a meter high—just bean porridge and salad and torn clothes. I saw the madrasa of the mother of Sultan Sha'ban, the Ayyubid minaret, the fountain of Ibrahim Agha Mustahfazan, and many other things whose names I didn't know.

But again, what detained me had no direct connection with the antiquities. I was tired from walking through al-Darb al-Ahmar. The distance between me and the wall built by the eunuch Qaraqosh for Saladin got narrower as far as the Tabbanah Quarter, then became wider again as the Bab al-Wazir area spanned out. Here I passed the tomb of the traitor Khayr Bey, whose nationalism so resembled my own, and whom Yavuz Selim, as I knew, had made the first Ottoman pasha over Egypt.

As I turned with the road toward the mosque I was aiming for—the al-Rifa'i mosque, where the last king of Egypt and the last shah of Iran lie buried side by side, stands in front of it—I had a feeling I'd eaten a rich meal that I was now digesting. Of course, there was a sense of wariness as I approached the place from which I would make the call. But my overwhelming sensation was of the process of digestion—and that I was actually, in some sense or other, dead. The sense of being a dead person was what stuck in my head, because it was this that had made me stop, and because, when I took my shoes off and went into the mosque, instead of sitting in the corner and reading the Qur'an or praying, I found myself walking around the large domed ablutions fountain as though hypnotized, muttering over and over verses such as "*And death's agony comes in truth;*" "*Oh soul at peace;*" "*Every soul shall taste of death.*"

I was like a man in a stupor, Abu al-Arshad. Once again, I saw those unknown companions, turning around each other in an out-of-the-way part of the corridor in the sultan's private quarters, in the second episode of the dream. I didn't stop walking until I noticed more than one person watching me curiously. At this point, I hurried over to the mihrab, stood in front of it, then squatted down in the first empty corner I came to.

What made me stop was something extremely simple, really: before going in, as I looked toward the ticket window where tourists paid money to look at the mosque as if it were there to provide entertainment (the more knowledgable among them, perhaps, lamenting a bygone civilization, without it occurring to them that the heirs to that civilization might be alive), I saw in the distance a young man who seemed to be a foreigner. He was thin and fair, with thick, soft hair and a very trendy outfit. Clinging orange trousers, and a white shirt with a round navy blue collar, decorated with twinkling, luminous stars, which I noticed were again the same as the stars on the dome in the palace, and the same as the star that had moved and grown larger on the driver's forehead. He was standing on the edge of the sidewalk as if he was waiting, but he didn't respond to the taxis, the unlicensed tourist touts, or the guides who stopped in front of him. What happened was that when I got closer he turned toward me. I'd noticed something hanging in his right hand that in that moment I realized was a rosary. He lifted it up in front of his chest as if to show it to me, while with his left hand he brushed away the hair from his forehead, where (would you believe it, Rashid?) a prayer mark appeared. A large, round, prominent prayer mark, exactly in the center of his forehead, a little lighter in color than Amgad Salah's.

I tried to walk past him but my legs failed me. I heard him interrupt his devotions to smile at me with a mixture of sympathy and pleasure in revenge. To put it in absolutely plain and correct language, he looked into my eyes and cleared his throat before saying: "The dead meet on the threshold of the mosque." Then he looked annoyed and immediately returned to his devotions.

I continued standing there for a while. I wanted to pounce hard on him and ask him who he was and what he wanted from me, but the shock had almost paralyzed me. By the time I'd recovered and started to move, he'd hurried over to the Rifa'i mosque and disappeared in the direction of the Imam al-Shafi'i's tomb. "There is no God but God!" I shouted. And, not knowing if I'd attracted attention, I went in through the main gate and from there, carrying my shoes, to the open courtyard with the ablutions fountain in it.

•   •   •   •   •

I hadn't reached the end of the formal prayers when I got up from beside the mihrab, feeling quite calm, and a voice whispered to me that if I prayed, I'd be successful in the first steps of the commission. Just two prostrations, feeling extremely pious as I performed them, for it was as if I were continuing the prayers I'd begun after prostrating myself behind the young sultan in the first dream. As I recited the supplementary prayers and committed myself to God, my heart actually stopped. And as soon as I'd finished, I carried my shoes outside.

I took my mobile out of my pocket in front of the wall. As I searched for Yildiz's number then pressed the key to call it, I recalled the sight of the two sci-fi books with their black covers decorated with thick red lines in the Arabic tableau. I didn't waste much effort in ridding my mind of the frightening image of the sprite, but I needed these two books to be there. My heart was racing as the number connected. Immediately, a voice like Yildiz's replied. It didn't have the same boom or hollow self-confidence as Yildiz's voice, but it had a different power, the features of which were not clear at first. For a moment, I was confused, then I asked: "Is this Yildiz?"

"No, Claudine, her sister. Sorry, she left her mobile with me. Who's this?"

"Claudine! Oh!"

"Wait, wait a moment, I know that voice!"

Something in her tone made her sound tired and totally preoccupied. How could she convey a sense of genuine concern to the person she was talking to in the middle of all this?

We continued to play "Guess Who" until she sighed and said: "Mustafa Shurba, the journalist!"

We laughed innocently, then we both sighed. I could feel a kind of euphoria run through the length and breadth of my body. Only then, as we exchanged news without going into detail, and an unexpected mutual understanding emerged between us that turned all my fears into passion, only then did I tell her the story of the two books, and discovered that Yildiz, contrary to what I had thought, really was traveling. Claudine gave me to understand that Yildiz was in the middle of a new love affair and had left her mobile with her because she didn't want to be disturbed. She also told me that she—Claudine—had been in Cairo for some time because she was fed up with her life in Paris. "I left him the children and everything," she said, laughing. And without even intending to, we agreed to meet at the Sea of Japan on the pretext of me giving her the two books at six the following evening.

The most striking thing was that when we made the agreement, her voice gave the impression that she was as happy as I.

•   •   •   •   •

With the sea spray reviving me, let me tell you about the last stage in my tour of Islamic Cairo, after that fateful phone call from in front of the mosque as it grew dark. I was in a small alley branching off Muhammad 'Ali Street. Already madly in love without knowing it, I thought I'd take a walk to the al-'Ataba al-Khadra' area without thinking about any antiquities, and when I arrived there I'd either carry on walking or take a taxi to El Galaa Street... until I found myself alone in this long alley in the dark, a row of pickups behind me, one after another, their lights out and nothing to indicate if they were approaching, or when. How could they move forward like that without making any noise? It was as if they were moving on velvet, with not a living soul in any direction.

I'd suddenly be aware of one at my back, before being assailed by its horn, which the driver sounded as if he were claiming his dues from the world. I was nonplussed and, to let the pickup past, hunched my body crosswise between the asphalt and the cars parked in a single direction all along the alley. I was unexpectedly frightened. For no obvious reason, I sensed a Satanic presence, as if the sequence of events that had begun with the angelic taxi driver, and continued with the albino carrying a rosary (whose mystical power you could feel, without knowing whether it was more good than evil)—as if this sequence of events must inevitably end with fiends.

I started to turn around, disturbed by the lack of space and the hurry. I couldn't see either end of the alley. The lights were so few and far between that it was pitch black. I felt shut up in a disquieting place and I wanted to escape. I kept walking but the alley wouldn't end. Suddenly, the angle or the surface seemed to change and I became aware of houses on the left, but in the general emptiness even this didn't reassure me. I heard firm footsteps coming from the opposite direction and I slowed down again, heart thumping. The pickups were still coming behind me, scaring me with their horns. Then, as the dimmest of lights appeared from the house windows as though specifically for this purpose, I started to see them:

An apparently never-ending stream of bearded Sunnis in short or long white gallabiyas, or else in shirts and trousers, their heads either shaved or covered by colored skullcaps. They crossed my path quickly, one at a time, two together, or occasionally in small groups. Their faces glowered and their eyes shone as they suddenly appeared out of the darkness, then, having passed me with their shoulders rubbing mine, disappeared again.

The strangest thing was that I could only hear their footsteps as they came toward me. After they'd crossed my path, just like the pickups, their feet made no sound, as if they were treading on velvet. For hours I could hear them muttering among themselves in a low voice, but they always flashed past me silently without any greeting. I panicked when our shoulders started to come into contact more violently, Abu al-Arshad. Once or twice a brawny shoulder bumped against me on purpose but I said nothing. I was breathing with difficulty, struggling to control my movements until the lights of the main street appeared.

I saw the last of them at the street corner. He was square-built and stocky, with a large, cubical head. His face looked like a copy of Fustuq's, except that he had a beard that reached down to his navel, and his head was bald. The gallabiya he was wearing barely reached his knees, with nothing to hide his lower legs. He was on his own—I'm sure he was on his own—but he was muttering more loudly than the others, and his voice was loud enough for me to hear it over the din of the main road.

I hurried on, thinking I'd shaken him off, but suddenly he reappeared beside me, pretended to knock against my shoulder, then said in an ironical tone: "Mustafa Kemal sends you his greetings. Don't think he will leave you alone!" When I turned round after recovering from the blow, he had disappeared into the darkness of the alley.

Today, with the sea in front of me, I recall how, as the plane took off, I put down the notebook and gazed at the clouds. Was it possible that the view could change so quickly? As soon as we took off, I made out the Nile, like a narrow, navy-blue carpet amidst the thin black lines of asphalt, above which the flyovers were smaller and lighter, then shades of yellow and red—all the colors of Mars—in the buildings crammed in everywhere, and vehicles moving like ants, singly and in groups.

But the navy-blue carpet was the most prominent because it cut through everything, while on either side of it stretched a hollow, low-lying area, the home of the Pharaohs and dwellings of the giants. When I first noticed the Sea of Japan, I thought that it was a large hole or burn mark on the edge of this carpet, until I recognized the Gezira Sheraton Hotel building (I think they've changed the name now) like a cylindrical shape at the very edge, and realized that it was Gezira.

For a moment, as I looked at the city turning into a map, I recalled Muhyi al-Din Piri Reis. As I studied the maps of the Bosphorus on Wikipedia in the course of my research, I had chanced on the biography of this Ottoman sea captain, the first person to produce detailed maps of the world in the Islamic period. I found a large-scale photograph of his first map, dated 1513. Its corner had been scratched off, but you could appreciate its beauty, with its drawings of animals, plants, and ships representing the different regions and constellations, the writing in different directions, and the warm colors—totally different from European cartography. I felt that the form of the earth I was flying over was much nearer to Piri Reis's map than the unadorned images we are used to.

As I was saying, all this was before we flew up and away and the city took on the form of a talisman—the city had by now assumed a clear shape in my head that was completely new to me. Now the talisman itself had disappeared and the window was all clouds. White on blue, making me think that even if I was a long way from my beloved, I was close to God, God in whose hand are men's hearts, Rashid. And although I knew that it was just a delusion, I went with the shapes and forms, as if instead of squeezing Claudine's ribs and feeling myself fall into the pit, I should be satisfied with sleeping on those light, fluffy things, falling, falling, falling. And as I fell, it would become clear to me how difficult and ugly the city was when compared to clouds.

At all events, I was near to our Lord because I was going to play a part in reviving His nation. But amid the white clouds (or above them: we'd be above them for hours, with the glint of light on their edges like a fairy tale), I would feel that being close to God was the same as being distant from the city, even if love had been born among the city's quarters. You are only in the clouds when you sit beside an Airbus window like this on your way to another city, and are complete and well because a woman exists who can sew up the tear that cries out in your stomach, even if she eventually decides not to do so.

Being close to God, then—and love is part of this—means traveling. Now I understood: all my wanderings inside Cairo, all the journeys and itineraries that led nowhere, were simply unconscious attempts at this same journey, at the revival of the nation preceded by falling in love. The plane seat where I sat with your brown notebook on my thigh was so much better than polished wood and chinois carpets. My marriage, my closeness to Fustuq, my relationship with Aldo, and my friendship with Amgad Salah, weren't all these just distractions along the way?

After seeing my city as a talisman, and with Claudine's smell on my body, everything became clear: Mustafa Efendi's marriage of East and West, the place of Cairo and its possibilities; Turks and Arabs, white faces and Muslims... Now this life has a clear meaning, Abu al-Siyout... I just have to find a man about whom I know nothing, except for his name and profession.

Recapitulation, on the nature of love

Today, at the seaside, I won't hide from you that my encounter with Claudine has left me thinking about disturbing things. I think about Adrian Pasqua, her husband, for example. I sympathize with him, then despise him again, and think it impossible for me to be like him. Then I reach a sort of accommodation with the collapse of his life, which coincided with, or ran parallel to, my new love.

What would remain of Claudine's family, I wonder, if he had to look after the children on his own? As if a woman marries a man who is content to assume the woman's old (eternal?) burdens, simply to prove to herself that she's like a man.

The fact is that Claudine never talks about civilization, freedom, or independence. Perhaps she believes in these things in an honest and coherent way, a way that doesn't require talking. But women's rights are like a kick in the crotch to the man who loves her, whether she acknowledges it or not. And sometimes (so much do I want her, and want her to give herself to me, so that I could kill her if I wanted to), these women's rights seem to me—contrary to what I have believed all my life, Abu al-Arshad—to be an injustice, a stupidity, and a crime that only a coward could accept.

East is East and West is West. We are One. These are our Two Worlds. —Sargon Boulos

Today I must stop putting myself in the position of her husband and posing questions so light and empty that they jump around like a ping-pong ball.

In brief, I cannot bear family at all, so why should I put up with a family in which I'm beaten around the head? Does this mean that I am, or Claudine is, an example of backwardness that is the reverse of Adrian's civilized attitude? Does it mean she will exploit the idea of civilization to deal with her backwardness with a person who doesn't properly understand it? On the assumption that I had some manly dignity and would rise to the occasion if required to, would I divorce or kill her if I were in Adrian's shoes? A Sa'idi girl to make my coffee and leave me alone: how many years of independence and provocation for my beloved to feel for a single moment that she was this person? How many years of deprivation for me to tell her, or myself, just tell her that I want her to be like that?

By what divine power can we live in this state for even a single day of this life?

• • • • •

You should know, yes indeed, that since coming to Beirut, I've been buying little things for Claudine, to stuff in a cardboard box with her Paris address on it. Today, having written the three definitions of love, and having quit the Rawda Café with the definitions in my brown notebook, I'll pass by the lingerie shop in the Hamra to buy the negligee I've imagined her in ever since I saw it, and as soon as I've gone back to the Bay View Hotel, I'll put it into the envelope, carefully folded. Then, after the camisole has settled on top of the other presents, I'll spend some time fastening it with tape and glue, to drop off at the post office in the morning. And then I'll go back to the Rawda Café to write something like a poem:

Without much effort, I think, your fingers, slender as cigarettes, will realize how many tears my hands shed to secure this fastening. This aimless wanderer to test you, smuggler of secrets through airports. I imagine your fingers exerting an equivalent effort to undo the wrappings that I perpetrated as I hurried to get some shining fabric that I would have a chance to see over your knees. A few days ago, this precious thing was nothing but a shell, the color of a dilapidated wall dividing our street from a long-lost village. But as soon as I let it go, it became a rock, so well packed are the things in it, my weight on your ribs. The cardboard container, minted in two folds. For days, the books and jewelry will push at its edges, and the leather will be filled with a compact weft. But I will never feel it is full until I put into it a piece of silk underwear, befitting the magnificence of your small body. One of its two sides has a human softness, a softness that I sensed powerfully before we parted. So much so that I almost ask the postman to recite the name of God over it as I give it to him. A rock that will become a sack if you empty it, large enough for you to squat naked inside. And you will scream with pain from the wounds left by its collapse in your hands. Now I will drink of your blood then carry you on my back in this sack. Before the family tank catches us, you will be the happiest woman in the world, the sweat of my back like pearls on your temple, like pearls on your temple in the morning light.

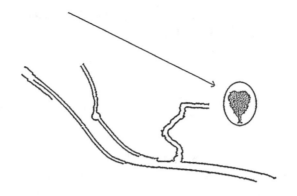

PART EIGHT
The Book of ʿUmar

Tree Hill

How the Narrator Concluded *The Book of the Sultan's Seal*: Scenes Subtitled with Verses by the Sultan of Lovers

Monday, April 16
to Thursday, April 19

We choose the beginning but the end chooses us, and there is no road but the road. —Sargon Boulus

Praise be to God

And so on Tree Hill, after dawn on the third Thursday, a few hours before his departure from Egypt, Mustafa Çorbacı would discover that he'd never be rid of Dr. Claudine Yusuf or leave her, ever, however much he was tormented by her love, however much the world collapsed around him, or his days went up and down with his separation from her, and her thoughtlessness intensified the pressure of separation. He would only leave her if his neck or back were broken.

No question about the merits of a certainty based on three days' acquaintance. The madwoman's daughter! As he contemplated all these torments with a sort of divine insight, he concluded that he wouldn't leave her even if he ended up killing her, even if he was forced to throw her down on these rough stones, to break her head, rip her skin from her flesh, then suck her blood with his lips and tongue.

Till thou has passed away
Wholly in me, thou hast not loved me true
And till my form is manifest in thee
Thou hast not passed away

Now, although the tour of Islamic Cairo had ended with the threat by the Sunni who was a copy of Michel Fustuq, and who spoke for Mustafa Kemal—the tyrannical atheist, the caliph's enemy—it didn't stop Mustafa Çorbacı thinking about three things that we now suspect lay at the heart of the story: first, that unintentionally, and without even admitting it to himself, he had fallen badly in love as soon as he'd left his wife; secondly, that this had happened hard on the heels of a piece of historical research that had made him take a fresh look at life; and thirdly, that the search had led to something like death, and it was this that allowed love, no matter how impossible, to continue.

Had some of the characteristics of the living become dead to him? The zombie, of course, is a person buried in the tomb of history. And his consciousness of being buried is what allows him to undertake the one thing in the world that exists outside that tomb: a zombie is the principle character in a serial written by a voodoo *bokor*, a magician with extraordinary hidden powers like those of the sultan. Among the plotlines of this serial is the meeting of the other half of his orange and their union, not from personal weakness or emotional dependency, not from wisdom or patience in suffering, or even out of hope for the future, but simply because he—being dead, or carrying his tomb instead of his cross—can no longer control what paths his movements now take.

As we were saying: the tour of Islamic Cairo ended with the Sunni's threat. Mustafa became convinced that both angels and devils, as well as the dead, had appeared in this city. But what really took him out of it was the shock of his eagerness to meet Claudine, and the conviction that she would actually put his foot on the start of the road. A psychological shock that began to manifest itself that same night in the form of a physical flicker in his left eye: in a narrow, undefined place between the edge of his upper eyelid and the bone of his brow, as he walked back from Islamic Cairo to World's Gate, and began to feel a gentle but extremely rapid throbbing that was neither pleasant nor painful but seemed like a hint or a warning... When it recurred as he drove from World's Gate to Dream Bridge, he recalled the whistle that sounds in some new cars when the speedometer exceeds the speed limit on the highway.

An illogical sensation: when he felt that flicker, he seemed to be seeing how his experience of the relationship would develop before it had started, consuming its impossibility. He knew that his disappointment in the person he was would be matched by the sorrow he would feel, for example, when he imagined Claudine disappearing under her blanket like a teenager, clutching her phone like a prize, for her to talk to her lover or vice versa, then discovering that at the time she was simply having dinner with her friends and her phone was off, wholly unaware that he needed to hear her voice (of course, his loss had a more profound equivalent in love itself, in murder and dismemberment, in the beauty of their meeting, and in the deadly pleasure that he felt as he spoke to her for the first time and compared it with the moment of ecstasy). And so on...

Purity (yet 'tis not watered), subtility (yet not as with air),
light (and no fire there burning), spirit (not clothed in body)

Until he learns that they are like two lovers lost on their way home, he drunk and she mad—and like Jalal al-Din Rumi addressing Shams al-Tabrizi in the *Mathnavi*, he asks her (without expecting an answer) "Who will take us home?"— until he is convinced that the thing that binds them, like the thing that has driven him since the sultan's appearance, is more powerful than reality and entirely outside it… he will continue trying to make sense of things.

●   ●   ●   ●   ●

The three expressions that he would write for Claudine (at least ten times on average for each expression) during the month following his departure from Cairo: "Everything can be forgiven except misery"; "How can I sit quietly with a corpse in the room?"; and "I should be more important to you than André Breton."

●   ●   ●   ●   ●

On Sunday night, before going to bed, Mustafa found himself droning from memory after Sheikh Yasin al-Tihami. He took out the works of 'Umar ibn al-Farid and flicked through them until he read:

My death in passion's ecstasy for her
Is sweetest life, and if I do not die
In love, I live for ever in death's throes
Then O my heart, in amorous transport melt,
And O my ardent pains, dissolve me so;
O my fair fortitude, unfaltering
Accord thee with her pleasure whom I love,
Nor succour Fate to triumph over me

I offered up myself
To win her favour, counting it for her
Alone, and hoping for no recompense
From her; but she did draw me nigh to her

On the third Monday, April 16, Ibn al-Farid's verses were ringing in Mustafa's head as he went to work. He had walked from al-'Ataba to El Galaa Street. He'd gone to bed, gotten up, and was now, in a state of half-demented ecstasy, contemplating the complex relationship between love and death for the first time since the caliph had appeared to him. One cannot love seriously before one has in some way died. At the Dry Nile Dock, he frowned a little and suddenly seemed to become two people—one saying to the other that even though he'd been frightened and tired by his meeting with the caliph and everything that followed (the historical research, the social discoveries, and the interaction with creatures that seemed to have come from another world or from dreams), it might also lead him to the love he'd spent a lifetime searching for without even knowing it, and this love would not benefit him.

Actually, it would happen more than once in the following days, that the Chosen Çorbacı would suddenly feel he'd become two people, one speaking to the other. Mustafa was late for work because the road was hideously congested and everything was at a standstill, but he felt nothing, so preoccupied was he with Claudine. He conjured up her features and felt relieved that it was she who had come to him instead of Yildiz, whom he'd planned to meet. Something inside him was sketching a wider, deeper circle than the sexual desire that was returning to him, even though she was stirring it deeply. By the time he reached the office, he had made a connection between this and his mad desire for Claudine, even before seeing her.

As we were saying, Mustafa was preoccupied with Claudine, in a detached state of readiness that he reckoned would be followed by a departure—to where, he didn't know, and it didn't matter. The whole city had become his again, and so he could leave it. He would make the craziest of U-turns from the Red Crescent Hospital, in the direction of the twitch in his left eye that had begun to remind him not just that he was a zombie but also of Claudine. For the first time he felt that, even if he was moving within it after reclaiming it, he was carrying the whole of Cairo inside himself. Did that mean that you had to die before you could have a city?

Surprisingly in the light of all these developments, nothing worth mentioning happened at the office that day. Maybe this was because he left early, or because people there noticed that he didn't want to engage. He finished his work in silence during the first three hours, then took out his notebook and sat scribbling while he waited for his date with Claudine. Aldo Mazika came in for just five minutes, dancing around with that silly laugh of his that made him sound like a fifteen-year-old girl. Later, Mustafa would recall that these five minutes were the last time he saw Aldo, but at the time, with the funnel-shaped man filling the cubicle to the last centimeter, he paid no attention to what was being said, thinking he was looking at the ghost of the Kizlar Agha from his dream. He wouldn't even remember that he'd seen him that day.

On the following day, the third Tuesday, Mustafa would bump into Michel Fustuq as he was leaving the chief editor's office, and listen as Fustuq criticized him for his behavior with the Serb girl on the day of the engagement party in Sand Port, but Mustafa would do no more than nod his head at Fustuq as though he were a rich homeowner welcoming some poor guests. Michel Fustuq... this was the last time he'd see him, too.

Death she accordeth me, when she granteth me her desire; and
that indeed is cheap—my yearning in exchange for my doom

Now, as his eagerness for his meeting with his prospective lover gradually increased (tonight, he knew in advance, a lustful vigor would commence that would end in either murder or forgetting—forgetting being in reality much more distasteful than murder), Mustafa found himself thinking of the "five stages of grief," a naive theory that some American woman had come up with from her research into patients with incurable diseases who died in the late sixties. (The theory was subsequently also applied to the grieving, on the basis that they went through the same stages the deceased had gone through, when they had to cope with the death of someone near to them.)

Mustafa had read about this theory somewhere and forgotten it. But now, as he scribbled against the background of the flicker in his left eye, forming words like "misery" and "passion" with the thick pen to produce patterns like children's drawings, he suddenly recalled the five stages with an unexpected clarity, and wrote them out in order as he considered the possibility that they might apply to him. Denial (no, this hasn't happened, it couldn't happen); anger (how could this happen? And how could it happen to me, of all people? Impossible, that isn't fair); negotiation (okay, I've accepted that this must happen, but can we postpone it for a bit?); dejection (it happened and that's it; no use); and acceptance (it happened because it had to happen; it happened with the smile that is the most precious gift, as they say...)

Denial when he refused to believe that the fiqi Wahid was the sultan, and dejection (perhaps) when he became overwhelmed and fell to pieces. The acceptance came when he started to fulfill his mission by calling Yildiz, and Claudine answered him. But there was no anger and no negotiation. At least, not in that order... he thought the theory of the five stages was really dumb, but could there perhaps be something to rationalizing grief like this?

Fascinated by his own inner death, he found himself—without planning anything—drawing an eight-pointed star like the one he had seen on his head while he wore the chief janissary's clothes in the dream.

Then, as soon as he'd finished the star, he proceeded to tell the story of his own grief, which he'd started to become conscious of, by putting a single word over each point—moving as usual counter-clockwise, from right to left, as the sun moves around the earth: separation, punishment, the dream, the ring, the appearance, search, discovery, requital.

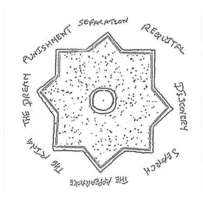

Afterward, as he cast his eye around the words, each of these eight things started to assume the form of one of the stages of grief, which in his head was mingled with happiness. The flicker in his left eye reminded him of this. It was like a new theory about a dying man's reaction to his death invented by the Chosen Çorbacı as he sat there: the eight stages of grief.

You know you're dying, and the first thing that happens to you is that you separate from your wife. After the separation—something that also happens before and during it, though you only see it clearly afterward—amid the confusion, the pain, and the terror, your harsh, merciless punishment begins: you are, as Muhammad al-Maghut says in one of his poems, "alone and hard: I'm a stranger, mother!" You feel you're responsible for the failure and the futility, that you're the only person in this world put to shame by the marriage of civilizations. But within this punishment—the third stage of grief—you have a mystical dream that changes your outlook on things. The dream both frightens you and makes you happy—a mixture that reminds you of the sense of danger with which your dying originally began, and is the first sign that one of the characteristics of the dead is to dream. When the dream is fulfilled (your punishment is ongoing), you gain something that can remain with you wherever you go, something engraved with the mark of the end or of resurrection. Let's say that this thing is a ring, and that you wear it on your ring finger. The difference between the grieving man who has reached the fourth stage, and the ungrieving, or the grieving who has not reached this stage, is that the first has on his finger a silver ring that he never takes off. In the fifth stage a ghost or phantom appears who confirms to you that you're now about to die, and proves what he is saying by interpreting the words of your dream, and by the fact that it turns out your ring actually bears his name. A messenger from the angel of death, or a historical zombie, or even a demon called Sultan, that is, a mystic being whose mission this is. You'll have covered roughly half the distance and will cope with your bewilderment by research and reading: a continuous rummaging through paper and digital sources to arrive at ideas. As you delve into a short-lived period of prosperity in the life of the Ottoman Empire between 1719 and 1730 (a period that ended in a revolt led by an Albanian janissary with a bad reputation called Patruna Khalil), during which the Ottomans knocked themselves out growing tulips, for example, you learn that the name of this flower in Arabic was *khuzama* and in Turkish *laleh*, and observe that your own flower that you drew over the Orman Gardens as a symbol in your first sketch of your daily journey from Dream Bridge to World's Gate has by chance the same shape (so you draw it again):

After the search comes joy. Contentment. Little by little you accept that you are dying, and see in death a resurrection that you have wanted all your life. In front of you lies just one final step after the days you've spent coping: to use your joy in this resurrection—your joy in escaping from a life you were ready to toss into the garbage can, and the lust that has returned to you with this joy—to use all this to confront the people coming into your life. You divorce your wife without hesitation and continue to move about the city. You contact your friends. You contemplate. You mingle and meet people. And with the discovery that the woman you have divorced was hiding her relationships from you, with the discovery that your Sunni friend is a coward, that the Christian is really despicable, and that your African colleague's mother is a witch—all the possible anger and negotiation come during this stage of discovery, incidentally—you will become ready to receive your retribution. Retribution is the best way of expressing it, by the way. The eighth stage of your self-grieving parallels the stage of final acceptance according to the American researcher:

an undiluted feeling that you deserve everything good despite what you've suffered, and that you suffered it all precisely because you deserve everything good. By the time you reach this point, you will have embraced your death, believed in its necessity, and loved it. When the time comes for you to die, a woman will appear before you with whom you've fallen in love in a dream. You're now making your tour of Islamic Cairo as a different person, but you will make the acquaintance of this woman, and it will be easier for you to mix with the angels and devils in the city itself.

The important thing, thought Mustafa when he'd finished recording the stages, is that this woman actually appeared to you, and that in the course of the night when you died to awaken as a new person, you became ready to meet her. The woman captured by the sultan's army. In this connection, he imagined that the little circle he'd drawn at the center of the bereavement star without thinking must be a sign of the love to come. This was the first time he'd felt that unexpected connection between his death and his readiness for passion.

For a second time, he became two people, one saying to the other: "You forgot that the star itself is a historical symbol, and so is your loss of yourself. Your death was simply an acknowledgment that you and your whole world are in the grave of the relevant historical narrative; and that this resurrection of yours that you are so happy with has but one aim: that you should play your part in bringing the world out of the grave. The circle of love is the hole your pain digs in the seamless wall of history. And today, only today, my dear, does the journey of ascent begin."

●   ●   ●   ●   ●

The time was drawing near, but Mustafa, without being aware of it, was thinking these words. He was still both eager and wary, but preoccupied with the snapshots that had flashed through his mind since sensing the exhilaration of danger after Michel Fustuq's prophecy at the 'Uruba Café (he was now, for the second time since his divorce, returning to the Sea of Japan). For some unknown reason, he began to picture his journey to Tree Hill (as yet, he still didn't have any clear reason to go there) and his erratic passage by car from the middle of the cemeteries, via Salah Salem Street, through the two halves of the city, to the road that climbed up to it.

For the first time, he sketched a route before taking it. In front of him was a decree of 'Abd al-Hamid which he'd printed from the net and glued into his notebook. Now he took just a small section of it, and imagined that that section was also a book or a box closed over words. As on the first and second occasions, the words of the decree, which naturally sloped upwards, formed the weft of the space in which the car was moving. As he marveled at the way the decrees were written, he imagined that on these lines he would be ascending not to Tree Hill but to heaven.

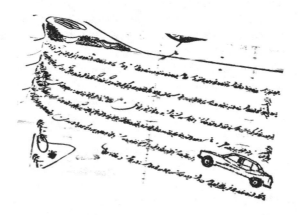

Mustafa contemplated the picture carefully. There were twenty minutes left before his appointment with Claudine. The weather outside was cloudy, and he was shaking slightly—quite apart from the flicker in his eye, which was getting worse. He didn't know if it was cold or anticipation. He was supposed to speak to her on Yildiz's mobile to set a precise place to meet. He shut the notebook and put it in his bag, took the phone out of his pocket and contemplated the lines of Abu al-'Ila that the sultan had looked at when he said: "The images of decline are revealed to the eye of your intelligence in the place of this diwan." He was supposed to be happy when he heard her voice.

So why? Why, with the bag over his shoulder—he hadn't summoned the elevator yet, and her voice was just like it had been yesterday, a tone of distracted concern in the midst of tiredness and indifference—why did Mustafa Çorbacı feel, as he went to meet Claudine Yusuf, as if he were climbing the heights of sadness?

Since that primeval time
Of the High Covenant, before the age
Of my created elements, before
The warning was delivered men should be
Ready for resurrection

When she'd asked, he'd replied without thinking: "The 'Uruba Café." She felt a spontaneous joy because she liked cafés (those places traditionally reserved for men, like all Claudine's places and exploits). Why, he asked himself, did he love boyish women? He was captivated by that sharp look, warning against any harassment. An improvised performance with a touch of the ribald… He drove slowly. He would hand over the car and its keys to the first parking attendant he met at the Diwan bookshop. Why did he drool over small, tired feet?

He was now approaching the Sea of Japan, the cold continuing. Crowds. Women like ducks in gallabiyas. He could almost see the whole of the Island of Bulaq on the page of an atlas. That hollowed-out bend between two circles—World's Gate and Dream Bridge—as if he were stepping over a raised threshold to enter. He passed over the 15 May Bridge, leaving himself behind. Only a few moments before, he'd poisoned his mother and father, and leaked his country's military secrets to the enemy. And, following such total destruction, he went back to the place of the prophecy, the place where his marriage had begun and the place where he'd broken with Amgad Salah. A single step. Everything he'd known in this world was the aftermath of a crime. The life of an informer and murderer, in which he comprehended nothing. Ruins or ashes. Caution is unbearable when mixed with overwhelming sadness. But why this overwhelming sadness?

Unexpectedly, he found a parking place as soon as he came off the bridge. He stumbled around. From the Ahram alcohol store where he'd parked to the 'Uruba Café, the route was surrounded with questions. The moon that had just appeared had grown smaller then crept away without either splitting or remaining a crescent. With two sci-fi books in his bag and an Andalusian poem in his ear ("Tell the beauty in the black veil...") he made his way along the sidewalk.

I say my prayers, chatting right well as I make mention of her
in my recitation, and I rejoice in the prayer-niche, she
being there to lead me

In the moment Mustafa's life ends (as a young man, an old man, or God knows), on his second and final death bed— or possibly wallowing in his blood on the asphalt, consumed by fire or hit by a bullet (maybe), exploding or breaking into fragments, crushed under metal or choking underwater—at the moment of his body's final death, he would remember nothing of the two halves of his life (before and after the appearance of the sultan, that is) except for the moment he noticed Claudine coming toward him as he sat outside the café, her miniature body throwing a diagonal line across 26 July Street, for the third time inexplicably quiet.

This belief had no explanation at that moment: not the shape of Claudine as she came toward him; not the Sea of Japan in the background, nor his sudden feeling that something in the scene summed up the whole of his story; not the disturbing greed in her face—which sometimes, for no particular reason, would change into consternation or anger; not the confused climax of his ardor as he got up to greet her... nor the smell of her perfume, her short hair, combed straight with a kind of bohemian elegance; nor even the powerful sense of déjà-vu that came over him without warning, as if he had lived this scene in all its detail before.

The belief sprang from the piety and godliness that struck him as soon as he recognized her, and which reminded him of what he felt when he'd prostrated himself in the first dream, and again when he sat beside the sultan in the second. It brought back his sense of mission, and the piety of the two *rak'a*s he had prayed in the Sultan Hasan mosque toward the end of his tour the previous day.

Perhaps it was because, although she wasn't the most beautiful woman in the world, he had from the first moment wanted her and no one else for himself alone; or because the tiredness and sadness that made you need to protect and calm her (also from the first moment) were apparent on her face even then. Or perhaps because you sometimes look into the eyes of a particular human being, and know that this human being holds your salvation and destruction, and that you are present in the world to take them into your arms. Simply...

The piety wouldn't continue so strongly, of course. Mustafa was only conscious of it for a few seconds before they started talking, with tea, coffee, and cigarettes, but no shisha (while she approached Claudine was a bullet drawing a triangle from two points on the flyover and the ashtray in front of him), but something of this stroke of piety would color all their interactions, despite her shamelessness and openness to forbidden things. Godliness. From his viewpoint, if not from hers. As though by loving her he was performing devotions. As though, despite everything about her, she was his direct means of ascending to heaven. Her body was the rosary he clasped in remembrance of God.

As she approached, her body was so steady that it was almost wooden (was she always such a grumpy hedgehog in public space?), under a black dress whose material at first glance seemed hard and grainy, like emery paper. Mustafa saw this rosary of his, small and tenuous to the point of invisibility. Was it just its size that suggested it was invisible? And what was that absent look that came into her eyes when she walked, as if her head had no connection with what was happening around her?

The following night, she would complain to him that "People don't see her." She meant that they didn't appreciate or value her suffering or what she was going through. The complaint would repeat itself in various forms, for it was Claudine who didn't want people to see her. But as he watched her approaching him for the first time, Mustafa would continue to understand her as a reminder of what had happened to him: she was a transparent being, and like the ghosts of the dead who appear before a buried city to give notice of its re-emergence, none but the Chosen could enjoy her sight.

The secret was in the triangle.

An overwhelming sadness... scorched bullets scorched his desire. From where, indeed? Despite the appointments she'd had before, afterward, and during (even here, she had innumerable friends of all ages and motivations, most of them of course male and café addicts, people of the streets of her kind); despite the family, academic, and even consumer obligations that seemed to him valueless, though she dealt with them as if they were sacred duties owed to the male sex; then again, the lost look in her eyes... this was, if truth be told, the most beautiful woman in the world.

Her quick steps had the speed of people from a cold climate, moving over the earth with a seeming confidence that in time he'd recognize as no more than a heroic challenge to the loss of an almost absolute poise.

My joining is my separating, my
Approximation is my distancing,
My love is my aversion, and my end
Is my beginning

In Mustafa's hands Claudine's shoulders felt like two thin quails as he kissed her on both cheeks in a sort of fraternal greeting. Something of her own fragrance seeped through to him from beneath her perfume, and he realized how hyped up she was about their meeting, how her eyes widened when she saw him, and how eager she was to sit beside him. Then his old fear came back to him, together with a sudden worsening of his tic—because he realized he was near the start of the road he was seeking; or rather, to be more precise, he realized that passion was the condition, or the price, for reaching the starting point. As if, in order to reach the point at which he would leave her, he had to fall in love with her first, making leaving her a trial.

From our own planet, we do not know what they talked about for two hours on the 26 July sidewalk. The night was rapidly drawing in. From the distance, they seemed preoccupied, but if you drew closer, you'd have realized that they were busy gazing at each other. They might have been engrossed in discussion of books and films, drugs and psychological problems, sleep and dreams. Perhaps they recalled their only meeting and gossiped about Yildiz a bit, or exchanged news of work at his paper and her university, the difficulties of everyday life in Cairo and Paris. It doesn't matter.

He savored the words from her mouth, her lisp always a surprise. He hid from her the smile that formed despite himself as soon as he discerned a word coming out like a chick being hatched. She had a way of forming words as if the organs responsible for joining the letters hadn't developed since childhood. As if her tongue held within it a child learning to speak.

When he took the two sci-fi books out of the bag and handed them to her, he found himself ready to say two words to her that he hadn't said with such simplicity to his ex-wife for fifteen months, since before the beginning of history.

Ready to embark on marriage to a married woman older than you whom you've only seen once in seven years?

The only thing he could think of was to enquire about her relationship with her husband. How, why, and were they (where?) in harmony? The easiest way, he thought. Claudine would later tell him that if he'd asked, she would have changed the subject. But he didn't let himself ask. Afraid, embarrassed, he decided to be realistic. It doesn't matter.

The oddest thing was that until she stood up in front of him and again became a bullet making a triangle with no base (again, the twitch in his left eye), it didn't consciously occur to him that anything could happen between them. Even when he discovered she had an appointment in the Sea of Japan and she'd be pleased if he could drive her home afterward, he didn't acknowledge to himself that this might be an invitation for him to embrace her, to breathe in her flesh and chew her veins, disturb the arrangement of her hair, and sink his teeth into her living skin.

The oddest thing was that it didn't occur to Claudine either. She'd tell him so herself, as dawn broke in the bedroom she'd slept in alone for years during her visits to Cairo, even when Adrian was with her. The change only occurred as the car passed the Semiramis Hotel. That was when she became conscious of her desire, with an embarrassment that both frightened and angered her. She felt an impossible closeness and intimacy.

> *Still I travelled on and on*
> *Through certainty's degrees—its knowledge first,*
> *Second its essence, third the truth thereof*

To be honest, when she got in beside him a little over two hours later—Mustafa had spent the time dozing in Café Beano's, by the British School behind the ceramics museum—he remembered the moment she'd pulled his right hand to look at the ring: "A ring too—wow!" There was warmth or electricity in her fingers. A force promising something he had to pretend to ignore. "That's nice..." Mustafa had again become two people, one talking to the other: "She wants you, just like you want her. But when you really want someone you don't move as easily as usual, you're not ready to take the risk. You turn into a coward. She wants you and you're completely indifferent. Until you feel comfortable. But you've never in your life wanted anyone so much and she wants you..."

Here he is, making an epic journey across the city. The stumbling blocks seem like mountains as the car speeds off. A new journey within the usual bounds. But Ahmad 'Adawiyya is singing and is impossible to ignore. "Tell him if you're cool or without equal...!" We don't think they exchanged a single word until Salah Salem Street. She was silent, a look of puzzlement on her face, and he was smiling into space. "My heart is no theater for the hobby of acting." From the Sea of Japan to Kasr al-'Ayni—over the Kasr al-Nil Bridge, with its Khedival lions—the way was smooth and clear. Why did he remember the route as being all ups and downs, all bumps and potholes?

If you'd seen them then, if you'd been with them... It was as if they were having a conversation without speaking. Feverish negotiations without either knowing the subject of the session. Global warming and the future of life on the planet? On the way to Tree Hill, a bilateral summit about nuclear weapons. Laws and declarations. But Mustafa was concerned only with her shyness, that ethereal thing that appeared one drop at a time after they passed the Semiramis, creeping up on her from a place that only she knew. He'd follow her as she hid her face behind the usual masks, one after the other. Until her mind wandered and something like hesitation made the masks vanish, then her embarrassment showed and she was angry. The seriousness of the professor had only just been replaced by an uncouth delinquency before that too, despite her efforts, collapsed. She turned a somersault. Exchanged delinquency for the arrogance of an aristocratic girl, then that too dissolved.

Her left tit held within it a coquette the size of a finger joint, so Mustafa found himself thinking. A tit too small to be seen behind her frock. Where had this tomboy been for ten years? The coquette was struggling to get out. But she was the size of a finger joint, shut up in her tit. Opposite the Kasr al-'Ayni Hospital, did he imagine it, or did it really happen, that her body relaxed for a second, while he—giving in to the enchantment of the tune—repeated "My heart is no theater"? When he looked to her at the traffic signal before Majra al-'Uyun, after he'd turned left, her body was wooden again—and she was silently crying with anger.

'Adawiyya wouldn't lower his voice at the light. "What's become of us… don't we satisfy anymore?" The jasmine seller came and went. Both knew well that the natural thing, the right thing, the thing set out in the instruction manual, so to speak, was that he should buy her a garland of jasmine and put it round her neck. With a look, too late, he asked her if she'd like some jasmine. Why had he let the moment go? She wiped away tears she hadn't acknowledged were there, the words "I suppose so" in a critical tone etched on her lips. Too late! Should he call to the seller after the light had turned green? "Okay, go and ask them what's become of us…" Mustafa actually braked, sat up straight, and put his head out the window. Laughing with the car horns, frightened by the crowds, Claudine gestured to him not to hold up the traffic.

"You want to get us killed, don't you?"

The first thing that had been said in the car since he picked her up from in front of her friends' house in Hassan Sabri Street.

"Look, we're passing the City of the Dead." He roared with laughter at the tourist name for the graveyards. As if he were mocking her foreign culture. He turned down the cassette so he could hear her and she him, then turned it up again. "Or should that be 'La Ville des Morts'? I thought, since we didn't actually die back there, we might as well say hello to the dead."

"By the way..." She sighed before the pleasure could be heard in her voice. "I said that you could drive me home, not bury me..."

"By the way, you're capable of burying the country..."

"You know, if we wanted to show off by talking French, which we don't understand"—for the first time, he heard a mocking tone in her voice, and instead of being annoyed or upset, he wanted to kiss her—"maybe we could try and correct our pronunciation, could we not?"

But in the "City of the Dead"—perhaps because it was really the roughest stage of the trip—he felt the need to turn off 'Adawiyya. There was a certain reverence amid the gravestones. Your help, O Saints! Something different from piety and godliness although very close to them. A kind of need... A large moon in a dark sky. With bright stars surrounding it. Isn't that so... At last, the mountain appeared.

He recalled his favorite line: "Cling to the coat tails of love, and cast off shame, forget the way of the ascetics, even if they are sublime!" Then he recited the opening of the Qur'an for the Sultan of Lovers (who is buried in the vicinity). "You're really reciting the fatiha?" The same sarcasm in her voice, but in a whisper. He imagined that more than one Yildiz was shining like a giant over her head. Where had all these stars come from?

When he stretched out his hand to turn off the cassette, he found that she too was looking at the sky. One piece of asphalt after another as the car sped off. Silence again. The opposite of his feelings when he drove Amgad Salah to the Khan of Secrets (the person sitting beside him then was his link with the world), knowing that the car with everyone and everything in it ("Everything in Everything," like the title of 'Adawiyya's song) had finally, irrevocably fallen to pieces. There was nothing but the lines of writing sloping upward, and the car balanced upon them.

A punctuation mark in an imperial decree.

●　　　　●　　　　●　　　　●　　　　●

At the middle hill, the ascent maneuvers began. To reach the house, cross the staircase landing, go into an apartment that is usually empty. As if they were about to carry out a secret operation or a spy raid.

"Would you like to come up and have a drink, or do you need to go home and get some rest?"

He no longer hid his desire.

"Of course, I'd like to come up... Claudine," he stammered. "I'd like every motherfucking thing possible, please."

His mystical terror mingled with caution and with the feeling she gave him that they were about to commit a crime. At this very moment. A dry anxiety. And following the logic that her fear would calm him—it would happen, it would happen—he seemed to be on the point of buying a ticket to depart on the start of his mission. The price would be paid with his flesh. The flicker at its fastest since yesterday.

"Look, your Tante Kariman will be awake and on the lookout with the doors. Be careful as we go up, I don't want her to know I've got someone with me. If she comes down, God help us, okay?"

The first signs of anxiety in her voice. As they left the car, her voice was breathless. "Say something!" Something like a plea for help between embarrassment and anger. Then she noticed how surprised he was at her fear.

"We'll climb the staircase like ghosts, Mustafa, okay?" she whispered, covering up her nervousness with a laugh. "I mean, does it make sense to be forty-one years old and still afraid of my mother?" The street actually leaned upward: the same angle as the lines of the decree he'd transcribed part of five hours ago in the office while waiting for his date with her. "Shameful!" It had been a long time since he was here. He slowed down to look at the scene. "Come on!" She pulled him impatiently as she rushed ahead: "Hurry up, man!"

Then, in a milder tone: "Be careful"—was Claudine really such a coward?—"for my sake!"

He followed her confident steps to the gate. The green metal surrounded by trees. One step, then another. A metallic ticking, then the house's spiral staircase, in the darkness... pitch-black darkness, as they held their breath. Claudine draping herself over the ornamental banisters, climbing up. In the faint light from the street, Mustafa could only catch a glimpse of her at one curve, where the fretwork glowed dimly. She seemed to be twisting around, though without losing the woodenness in her body. She almost tripped as she turned. Shhhhh! Disaster at any moment! A secret operation or a spy raid. Another deep breath, the banister shaking. His heart was beating a little more slowly, but danger was just as imminent. Shhhhh! Could someone be creeping around on the floor above them? As they went up, he was certain he could hear her heartbeats like a muffled drum (he didn't know where this heart could be in a body the width of a sheet of glass). Mustafa kept his eye on what he thought was her waist. Haste and confusion. Until she stopped and he heard the clink of keys in her hand, life remained a spiraling darkness surrounded by collapse.

Finally he stretched out on the sofa while she closed the door in silence. He could only hear the key shyly turning in the lock from within. He turned to see her hurrying across the balcony, drawing the curtains. He could see she was panting, but still he laughed out loud. Without thinking, he stood up and embraced her from behind. "Why are you trembling like that, doctor?" he asked. She sighed and smiled at him, holding her breath. The same pleading in her eyes as she gently detached herself.

If they are threatened with abandonment they die of fear, and if they are threatened with murder they turn to murder

"Too hot!" she moaned when he placed his hand on her shoulder, as if in the course of conversation. A laugh appeared on his face. Beside each other on two chairs. The tea on the table, no music playing. What to talk about? "I know, it's really hot!"

Now completely calm and confident, he withdrew his hand and moved to the sofa opposite. "I mean, I know we're not teenagers..."—she's angry, for real—"but if we wanted to act like teenagers, we could." Because the room wasn't hot, and she was still coping with her embarrassment. "Be really naughty!" She finally responded to his laugh with a laugh of her own.

How, within minutes, did she join him on the sofa? What made him aware of her rough black dress against his skin, distinct from any other sensation? Perhaps her body was more wooden now than ever, but when he kissed her breathless hand as if to restore it to her after a long absence (so she would cryptically inform him a very long time later), he would feel her gradually coming loose. His rosary was coming apart in his hand, and he wouldn't let a single bead escape.

Until the softness of her neck came to his lips, he wouldn't realize how soft and pliable this childlike body was. Its transparent dimensions. As if it had depths that could only be felt when it was naked. Now she was sitting relaxed in his lap, the fabric of her dress between them. (In the last part of the night, as they lay silent in her bed, Mustafa would see this first meeting of theirs—like his research into the history of Cairo and the Sublime State—as a melody condensed from an infinite number of tunes. A mad synopsis of stages of perception and development. As if they were living three centuries in three hours. How else could a man love a woman?)

As soon as she was in his lap, the last remnants of perfume disappeared. With an ordered savagery he'd never shown to anyone in his life, and didn't know he was capable of, he gathered her hair in his hand and bent her head toward him with a one powerful squeeze, while with his other hand—thumb on her throat—he pulled open the neck of her dress. Not a breath could be heard from her.

Her neck now lay under his jawbone, like a piece of sown ground. If he'd taken a knife to it, he could have drawn from its depths the blood he could sense boiling as it gushed through her veins.

With a practiced enjoyment, a torture to crack the beauty spots, he runs his tongue along delicate hills, then suddenly squeezes them. He follows valleys like threads to a place where the delicate fur meets the bone. "You know that you're wasting away?" He bites so hard that he makes the skin contract, then licks again, widening the rectangle with the tip of his chin to push his nose into the open space. As if she'd said: "Eat me!"

He sniffs before sucking. Claudine lies unmoving in his lap. By what inner force does she respond to him, and he sense her impulses? By what power does she put her will (more powerful than anything in the world) under the power of *his* will? And what on earth is sad in this harmony?

The moment his life ends, as an old man or as a youth, floundering in his blood or in the grip of fire, Mustafa may well invoke the smell of her neck as it was soaked by his saliva at that moment. Nothing in the world can express the intimacy of that smell, its sensitivity, the warmth of the mutual need for it to flow into his blood through his lungs, his recognition of himself in it as he inhaled deliberately, or the perfection of the absolute power of his nose. Mustafa wouldn't call Claudine's smell a "scent," wouldn't give it a name at all. In time he'd realize she was also smelling him. Was it pleasure that was on her face? Nothing in the world could he call her smell.

"By the way, I already told you I love your touch." Every word was a chick hatching, but it emerged from the egg crying, or about to cry. "Do you want me to tell you I love your smell too?"

"If it was up to me…" It was as if his soul was speaking while he—without letting go of her hand, without testing the suppleness of her limbs or sitting up straight under her—lifted her feet toward his face and said: "I'd have you say I was God!"

No fear, no flicker. Nothing but the feeling that he was dead in her vastness.

Crushed under metal or choking underwater, Mustafa might recall the sharp bones of the pelvis stretching across her buttocks to his thigh, feet raised, while her fingers turned from pencils into threads of mastic. Threads of Turkish mastic in his mouth, and the kisses all twists and turns. He encircled her whole face with his hands to bite her lips. "Give me your tongue!" How could giving orders turn into power over him? Her wavering cries of pleasure were like electric shocks. There was shyness in her eyes but no anger now. He drank from her mouth as he sat. All this energy without him wavering? Claudine was calm and still, she had stopped resisting. Each foot was like a fish, quivering a little until its tail disappeared, then relaxing. She stretched out and went to sleep. He massaged her feet with his hand, her big toes out of line with the others. But where did this overwhelming sadness come from? And how could it be so at one with this pleasure?

· · · · ·

Now she sighed. With a scarcely audible sound, as she lay in the shape of a triangle on his lap, her toes slipped into his lips one by one, for his teeth to mark the root of each, then clamp it until his lips could separate and enfold it. And every time Claudine Yusuf would sigh, telling him, wordlessly, to take her home. The pleasure was an overwhelming sadness on her face.

· · · · ·

He would kiss her again in the dark corridor, standing, on the way to bed. A longer kiss, a new daring in her mouth. She swallowed his saliva and pulled his tongue, chewing it gently, then hard. He turned her neck and pressed it. She had to stand almost on tiptoe, waves of the sea breaking on her lips. He imagines his hands covered in blood as he runs them from her underarms down to her buttocks then lifts up, raising her dress. As if the crinkly material in his hand really were emery paper. The dough-colored flesh slowly softened before his eyes. She would make way for him in the apartment's narrow entryways. A fierce war in the dark corridor, as the saliva of anxiety turned into a battle. "I'll kill you, Claudine!" he gasped in her face between two bites. Patience was more distant than the stars. With a pleading look like the one he'd seen on the way here, she challenged him: "Show me!" He pushed her, with her dress lifted. Blood and dreams. He wrestled with the material—he'd give a lesson with his teeth to every inch that was showing. Her sighs were louder now. She was almost crawling on her back as he pulled off her bra. A retreat? Her breast fell out of his hand as she gasped for breath. Her tiny breast, as if grown giant with pain. The nipple, swollen with desire, which he had grasped like a wild infant, was full and radiant. A fickle woman in his throat, the nipple. He tried to pull her up by the torso but she clung to his shoulders and he fell on her, passing his hand over her hip. His member felt secure.

•   •   •   •   •

On the bed—no light except for that coming from a balcony in the distance—her legs were raised and his head was between her feet. Balanced on his knees at an angle, to make room for the light. Like an inspired garbage man, he removed clothes and jewelry with startling efficiency. With a mechanical energy, he pulled everything from her body and cleared it out of the way, then did the same for himself, until his shirt was on the floor, his belt on the bedpost, and his underwear under the sheet. He put his ring on the bedside table, to her side. Then he leaned sternly over her face again.

And so his breathing in became her breathing out, her whole neck between his jaws. On his knees, he explored her from above. The same ordered wildness to his actions as he rubbed her belly. She twisted on her narrow bottom. Her impatience did not invite haste. She folded herself across the bed as if to escape from him, but at the same moment called him by name.

There was something in her voice distinct from moans of pleasure and supplication. "Lovers are either fish or birds. They either kill me by drowning or make my lungs burst. So how is it I can breathe so easily now underwater, dangling from the edge of a pool?" He stretched his hand out to lift the silk from the gateway to her womb he had so long awaited.

Because he knew she'd had two children, or because he had the idea that she was experienced and independent— whether for an objective reason or otherwise—he anticipated an organ open wide to the world, a shameless circle that cared for no one. Why, then, did she have this line, hidden like a tulip bud, which if it opened would match the flower he'd drawn a few hours ago? And the trembling line itself, where did its softness and refined appearance come from, this delicacy…

As soon as he saw it he pulled at the silk eagerly. Did he tear her tiny silk underwear, narrow as her bottom? She was paralyzed with embarrassment but softened again as he kissed her there. Until she moved to pull him by his head, but couldn't reach, and her voice broke on his shoulder as she snarled "enough!" he really hadn't believed that her cunt could be such a shy, small thing.

And when she
Appeared, 'twas given to me to contemplate
My occultation, and I found myself
There to be she in the unveiling of
My privacy

When Mustafa penetrated Claudine for the first time, it seemed to him that the fractured world had healed itself and become perfect. The same world, every inch broken, full of anxiety, confusion, and need, dyed in a thousand colors, and no color free of another in its light… the world that his heart had been sick of had filled its cracks, had composed its extension into space, and no longer did a rainbow stretch over its surface. There was no longer any place for the thought of right and wrong, light and darkness. In the whole world, there was no longer up and down, I and you, East and West. Only this one thing that made him and her a paragon of perfection, he and she, she and he, shhee.

The world's conscience.

When he lay down beside her, hanging her arm around his neck—he was still inside her, either by some miracle, or through the heroic efforts of the tulip bulb around his still hard member (his heart's vessel in her belly)—then started to whisper to her drily about life and suffering; when he spread out her arm, thin as a matchstick, with her earlobe in his mouth like a postage stamp he was wetting to stick on an envelope that he'd burn with a lit match; or her face lost itself beneath his arm as she waited expectantly and grumbled, he would feel that it was *his* heart that pumped the blood that flowed in her and that if he tightened his grip on her neck until she choked, the life would go out of *his* body.

At first, he moved back and forth rhythmically, his whole body on top of her, but with the smell of her skin, damp now with his sweat, he felt again the urge for battle. As he kneaded her chest with his whole weight on his hands, he began to lift his trunk and vary the rhythm. "Wrap your legs around my back!"

Her short legs were like a pair of pincers ready for his backbone. Before he could gobble up her thigh to check, everything was in the right place. Sometimes he stopped completely. But she shifted from side to side in a way that moved him perforce. She cried for help. She crooked her face away, unable to open her eyes, even when he was saying "look at me!" (She'd open them tomorrow, tomorrow she'd open them!) Despite this, she could still stop him with a look. She came closer to him and forced him to turn in a certain direction. She got up, sat down, then lay down again. Suddenly, she said to him: "Talk to me!" After a few moments' confusion—on this first night, he didn't know what to say—he whispered to her again, into her nipple. The world that was no longer divided was like a taut sinew, the thread of a rosary of burning beads. A rope running through furrowed pottery.

Her round face in his hands, and her eyes closed. There really was life after death.

Before he was aware of it, she had to resist her climax. Then, with a cry for help whose meaning he at first didn't understand, with a sob like the song of a Berber woman in the Atlas Mountains, the beating began. Her arms were a fan from whose edges not even his face was secure. With a slightly excessive indulgence, he could answer her only with his penis. Claudine struggled to wait for him, for them to come together. He held back his climax, the struggle began; as soon as she lost, she whimpered "Animal!", but as she came the world was created anew.

By the time she moved her feet to his shoulders or buried them under her knees behind her back, a second struggle would have begun which he tried not to lose again. The most beautiful thing in the world was to see her struggle.

Save that my body's curtain being drawn
Disclosed that secret of my inmost soul
It had till then most strictly screened from him

On Monday night, Mustafa made love to Claudine three times without the subject of their love coming up. The second time was gentler than the first, and the third slower and more polished. He discovered a capacity for violence in sex he'd never known he'd had. Before the start of the third session, Claudine noticed the ring lying on the table beside her. The table lamp was on, and the light shone on the Padishah's seal.

"Wait, wait!" she said. "I think I recognize this!" She turned the ring over in her fingers to examine it more closely as she sighed: "By the way, this is a *turra*! Isn't it called a *turra*? You know, I love calligraphy. I read a book about it once. But tell me, honestly, what's made you wear a ring with this *turra* on it, or whatever it's called?"

"It's actually called a *tughra*!" His flicker came back. No fear, but the flicker in his left eye was back. He turned into two people, one speaking to the other. "You were about to come, when your lover noticed the *tughra*. Your lover? Yes, really! While you're lying here, with her cigarette butt in the ashtray on your belly, your body bathed in her sweat, and surrounded by the smell from her skin just soaked in your saliva, not yet sated with her, she accepting your blows, and you sunk into her, you'd kill her and she'd say 'eat me!,' and the world is healed and recreated—how could she not be your lover? You've really fallen for her, even if you haven't told her yet. But don't worry! Since you've fallen for her, and she's noticed the ring, she'll definitely show you the start of the road!"

He turned his head to look at her as if waiting for something. "No, I just liked its shape. You know I've drawn for a long time, but recently I've been taking a bit of an interest in calligraphy!" Then he kissed her, to show that this was what he'd expected.

"Because, you know…" She started to speak but didn't finish the sentence.

"What?" He took her nipple between two fingers and pressed it sadistically. "Speak up!"

"No, it's nothing, but you know that daddy had a friend who was a calligrapher, a real artist, I mean, and I think he used to draw the same *turra* on a larger scale." She kissed him in turn. "You know, the things I took from daddy I left here, so if you like, I could show them to you."

He was seized by fear. "I'd like to see them now!" She looked at him dubiously, then enquiringly, then, as if she couldn't believe she'd found an opportunity to escape from bed (at home, excited, and with no excuse for moving), as soon as he added "I'm serious, Claudine!", she jumped up. "You know, you're really strange!" She was shy about walking naked in the apartment ("I'm honestly not used to it!"), and without his seeing where she'd suddenly got it from, she wrapped a silk kimono around herself.

Yet this morn thou art possessed
Of knowledge what befell men long since gone
And mysteries of others yet to come,
And boasteth of thy ken

So, after dawn of the third Tuesday, the Chosen Çorbacı found himself on Tree Hill, between their second and third bouts of lovemaking, sitting half naked at the dining-room table in a strong light. Claudine was beside him, like a flat loaf of sugared bread just out of the oven, wrapped in red cellophane, stretched out in a zigzag shape across an armchair. In front of him was a gray cardboard dossier, containing around nine pieces of extremely fine Arabic calligraphy. He could have spent a whole day contemplating their beauty.

The pieces were of varying size, the biggest being A4. They were all originals, written in old-style Chinese inks on different materials. But no tughra of the Sultan Vahdettin, or anyone else, among them, Mustafa muttered to himself.

Only after he'd spent some time rummaging through them did he notice one the size of a medium-sized book cover written on fine leather. Even before he made out the words, "and likewise to cherish my mother; he has not made me arrogant, unprosperous (32). Peace be upon me, the day I was born, and the day I die, and the day I am raised up alive!", and before he realized that the script was what he'd encountered in the book of Islamic art as *qalam muhaqqaq*—he knew that it had some connection with the sura he was looking for. He held it up to his eyes and continued reading. "That is Jesus, son of Mary, in word of truth, concerning which they are doubting (34). It is not for God to take a son..."

Can you believe it?

The parchment was cut off at the top but he went on looking at it, Claudine paying no attention, then turned it over onto its back and brought it up to his eyes, an inch at a time, to see if there was any writing he could decipher. He began, with difficulty, to read an extremely fine *naskh* hand: "The pen of God's servant known as al-Shalchi, Beirut, in the month of Rajab 1425." Then, in a finer *ruq'a* script, under the first phrase, and at an angle: "a transcription of the third of the seven parchments of the sura of Mary written by Sultan Abdülmecid ibn Mahmud, may God have mercy on him."

Çorbacı could hardly contain himself. With a speed that would later astonish him, he grasped that 1425 was 2004 in the Christian calendar. And Claudine had told him that "Uncle Rufa" had been living in Beirut since precisely that year.

All at once, Salah Salem Street appeared before him, the part leading to Plane Yard, and without thinking about it, he knew he would travel to Beirut. All his life, he'd wanted to go to Beirut, he recalled.

Desire was returning to him with renewed force. A volcanic desire that would take Claudine to the edge of unconsciousness as it merged with her own. Before he could lift the paper in front of her and strike his hand on the table, he heard a voice like the Padishah's reciting another verse of 'Umar ibn al-Farid, for whom he'd recited the fatiha on the way:

"There I found the creatures had joined in alliance, that they, with my help, should assist me."

"Claudine," he whispered, so as not to shout. "Could I take this with me and not return it?" He breathed with difficulty. "I'll give you absolutely anything you want for it…"

He who is over under, over all
Under him being, to his guiding face
Is all direction turned submissively

We forgot to record, in speaking of their lovemaking on Monday night, that they did not keep to one position in any of their three sessions. The second time, Claudine was on top of him most of the time, even when he was thrusting. On the third occasion, his body shook not just with renewed desire but with the panic, intoxication, and madness of the start of his mission, his soul calm after he'd put the parchment signed by the Iraqi calligrapher Ma'ruf al-Shalchi into his case and locked it. This time he was squatting opposite her, her feet squeezed first against his belly, then his chest, then over his shoulders like two signboards on the sides of the entrance to a deserted street.

An old dream started to come back to him, that he was falling into a ditch with soft leather or pieces of leavened bread at its bottom. Everything was the color of Claudine's neck, and though he hadn't moved at all, the world was far away. By the light of a fragrant candle she'd lit while he was rummaging in the dossier, to cover up the smell of cigarettes in the bedroom, it seemed as though, by ravishing her, he was reaching the bottom of this ditch for the first time, cutting through the surface to discover what was in its depths. Soon he forgot the mission and the Iraqi calligrapher, and even the woman he was penetrating. Nothing was left but the genius of the harmony of the world at the moment he sunk into her belly. And the beauty of the two fishes, as he sucked their tails, and his ardor increased… and he sunk further.

This final time, when she turned and spread herself out for him to take her from behind, Mustafa pulled her hair and sat tweaking her buttocks, scratching her back with his elbow and leaving his thumb sunk in her anus, and she stammered and shouted while she waited (meanwhile, he probed her depths relentlessly), until she came again and again, crying from pleasure, pain, and the suicide of the will.

After he'd tickled her and licked her armpit, he made her lie on top of him on her belly, just lie without moving. So that the extent of their touching could be as wide as the furthest possible limits.

She spread in the sea of your body a land, to which loyal fingers pointed

That night, as they were in this position—and without her saying anything to him—he understood everything by intuition, and felt a redoubled affection, through which he didn't know how to convey his tenderness (in time, he would know that his intuition was correct). He understood the feeling of failure for which she couldn't forgive herself, in the face of things no human being could succeed in. He understood that this feeling was rooted in some old anger at the world, a rejection of everything she could take from the world without fighting for it. In her head there were shameless powers that controlled her behavior and detached her from herself—powers she accepted as a substitute for her father and mother, as though she were escaping from a kind guardian to attract to herself a hundred jailers—and so she only knew herself in pockets of time stolen from her life. He understood her most stupid shortcomings, too: her quarrels with time and duty, her quarrels with her direct instincts when she went from here to there, her constant fear that she might have let go of some piece of information, profit, or confession to be divulged to enemies more present in her head than anywhere; and then, her frightening capacity for recklessness.

Suicide attempts and mental asylums—he understood this too—and then her continuous efforts to avoid pressing questions at difficult times, which made solutions come from outside despite herself. All those indefinitely postponed destinies of hers...

As we said, he understood, and the elastic hope came back to him. What was hope for now? And hope for what? Apart from the fact that she was married with children and lived on another continent, apart from the fact that he had only met her because he was a zombie who had received instructions to travel, Mustafa immediately knew that Claudine was more intelligent and more selfish than any other woman he'd known; that she was obsessed with herself, and that imbalances in her temperament made her behave in an annoying way. No one who started a relationship with her could be happy.

As soon as he embraced her—not shrinking from his feelings, but allowing them to develop—he questioned the idea that his ex-wife was most at fault in their history. He regretted his marriage to his ex-wife—regretted it in the sense that he knew that if this marriage hadn't happened, nothing in the world would've been different—and this in itself was enough for him to realize that the mistake hadn't been an existential one, hadn't been the end of the world, or rather, perhaps, that his fulfillment didn't depend on leaving it behind him. "It's written on the brow, my dear," Claudine would tell him on the phone when he asked her from Beirut why they'd embraced disaster on the pretext of love.

He knew he would embark on this new mistake, despite all the possible reasons for regret.

•   •   •   •   •

That night, he said nothing to her about his fear of the things he understood: of his counter-revolution against the liberation of women, for example, or that he saw in her a model of a person whose fear of loneliness traps them in a vicious cycle: as they distribute their time and emotions among a larger and larger number of people they become more and more lonely, which in turn drives them to distribute their time and emotions among more and more people still. Claudine also reminded him of other types, types he'd had ten years to chew and spit out. In her "impossible" column she'd entered nice, faultless things that were still quite possible, and it would really distress him if she didn't correct the error.

He just told her she was beautiful, and that all he wanted was to see her always as she was now. That he should keep feeling what he felt when she was spread over him like a winding sheet, not covering him completely, her belly on his chest and her nipples at his Adam's apple, her belly on his chest and her face in his mouth. That this feeling should stay with him despite everything. He didn't say this, exactly, he whispered. He sucked her chin and raised her head to bite her cheek and make her moan. He spat his words out intermittently as his fingers burrowed into her armpits. He kneaded her back with his palms, pressing her ribs into his flesh. When she gasped, the woodenness returned again for a moment but he ended it with a lick. Once again, her tears were in his nostrils.

Lights like stars glinted through the window.

> Let him be with me, and I know not at all to be abroad in a
> strange land; and wherever we are together, my mind is
> wholly untroubled

So on Tree Hill, after dawn on the third Tuesday, before Mustafa, through a series of small miracles, was able to actually leave his city in the space of two days, he crept out of Dr. Murad Zakariyya's house feeling at one with himself for the first time in two lives (in the last dream, he'd started a second life, hadn't he?)—"at one" meaning composed, at ease, and perfectly integrated. The world, with all its fractures, had been mended and restored to health. He walked no longer half-heartedly but with a full spirit.

Outside the sky was like a Van Gogh painting. For a longish-seeming time as he was driving, he looked at the brightest galaxies of stars from a height and imagined that he was in Beşiktaş, Istanbul, where the Yıldız Palace was.

Could he distinguish the outline of the face of Aries amidst the constellations? Was there really a ram's head among them?

•   •   •   •   •

Mustafa didn't sleep that night. He noticed that his mother hadn't brought him anything to eat nor asked after him all day (he remembered this) although he hadn't spoken to her. When he went in to kiss her as she slept, she turned her face away and muttered: "God help me!" He went out broken-hearted, smelling the smell of his lover on his body, and decided to postpone a shower, to preserve it. In his room, recalling the things he'd understood, and his feelings as he passed the cemetery, he went back to the works of 'Umar ibn al-Farid and sat reading:

> And on her account I rejoice that I am exposed to shame, yea,
>   delightful is my rejection and humbling, after the proud
>   high station that once was mine;
> And for her sake is my dishonouring sweet, and that after once
>   I was godly, yea, the casting off of my shame, and the
>   commission of my sins.
> My bond and my compact—the one is loosed not, the other
>   unchanging: my passion of old is still my passion, my
>   ardour is yet true ardour.
> Love hath left naught surviving of me save a broken heart, and
>   sorrow, and sore distress, and sickness exceeding;

And I know not any, except it be passion, that knows where
I dwell, and how I have hidden my secrets, and guarded
faithfully my covenant;
To whom should I look for guidance, alas! if I sought to forget
her? Seeing that every leader in love seeks to follow my
footsteps.

After a time, he got out his travel bag, opened it, and put it in front of him while he sat studying his account book and inspecting his debit and credit cards and passport. He needed official leave, for a start. He'd go to work early, and reach an understanding with the chief editor, but what would he say when asked when he wanted to travel? He decided to say, "As soon as possible, sir!" He'd have to check he had money left in his credit card account, and that in his current account he had the equivalent of a thousand dollars that he could withdraw quickly. Realizing that his bank position was weak, he decided to call Islam al-'Azzazi, his filmmaker friend, on the dot of ten o'clock, to ask him for a loan.

If so, on his way back he'd drop by where Islam lived with his wife in Mohandiseen.

That left the ticket and the visa, he thought. If he could persuade the chief editor to treat his trip as a journalistic assignment, he wouldn't have to go to the embassy or a travel company.

Perhaps because he left very early, the route into work on the third Tuesday was actually uncongested, and the weather at World's Gate was fine. So fine, indeed, that he had a chance, having parked without needing to wait for an attendant, to stand in a juice shop on Ramses Road and drink a sugar-cane juice. He needed something sweet. As he looked into the spring daylight, he felt that existential pain that follows good sex.

Even the office was quiet today. As soon as he arrived, he went in to the chief editor.

●　　　●　　　●　　　●　　　●

"Look, sir, to be brief, because we can't sit talking all day…"

That's all he said, after a lot of give and take, courtesies and disagreements, fights, conciliations, and more fights—which

Mustafa plunged into, valiantly standing up to the enemy despite his physical exhaustion and his total detachment from the humbug of reality. He looked at the swarthy giant sitting well-dressed and measured behind his ornate desk, a swollen vein throbbing on his forehead under his bald pate, and thought that he was very tall and very fat at the same time, and that this gave his thin, carefully trimmed beard, together with his tie stuffed into his belt, a ridiculous appearance. Mustafa knew the chief editor had never forgiven him for his insulting comment in the corridor during the final days of the breakup of his marriage. But he also knew the editor would so much like to be rid of him that he'd cooperate to that end. And because Mustafa held an official appointment in the corporation and couldn't be dismissed, because he had good relations with some important people in the management as well—all this a result of editorial tasks he'd undertaken for various parties at various times—if he told the chief editor that he was going and not coming back, perhaps he'd grant him the small service he was asking for: to concoct for him an official reason for visiting Beirut in the next few days, so he could get a visa and ticket quickly with minimum effort, even if he had to pay for them out of his own pocket. Leave without pay, or even a resignation, could follow (he actually suggested this to him) after the trip.

The reason for all this give and take was simply the offer that Mustafa was in practice making: You'll get rid of me forever, sir, on condition you perform a simple service for me in exchange. But obviously, this could not be said in so many words. And Mustafa had to be circumspect in mentioning the reasons for his trip. He'd tell the chief editor he was going to get married, and give him the impression that after the wedding he'd be settling and working in Beirut. He had to speak in a plausible way that would convince him this was not just a ploy in the cold war that had existed between them for months, that the chief editor would really be rid of him without trouble… But until he received the stamped document from the old secretary in hijab whose makeup made her look like a clown, and read the words "Visit to the Lebanese *Al-Akhbar* newspaper for investigation and discussion of the possibilities of cooperation on behalf of... ," he wouldn't believe he had managed it.

After bumping into Michel Fustuq as he emerged, after hearing the Pistachio Kid say, "Are you trying to embarrass me with foreigners?", and playing fast and loose with him without a single word for half an hour in the office rooms, Mustafa would spend hours moving around the corporation offices, presenting documents and getting his papers stamped, not knowing when he'd eventually get back his passport complete with a visa for the Lebanese Republic, and hence did not have a ticket booked for him as yet. He wouldn't finish his editorial work until nine in the evening, and by the time he'd left Islam al-'Azzazi's behind Syria Street with a bundle of dollars in his pocket, it would be nearly midnight. Then he'd collect his car and go back to Claudine on Tree Hill.

●　　　●　　　●　　　●　　　●

Islam's wife was away, but the house was chock a-block with her things, and Islam was almost lost in the middle of them. Tapes, boxes, bottles, books, jewelry, medicine, clothes, not a single inch free. Mustafa stayed at Islam's for more than two hours, but the only thing he'd remember about this final visit was Islam standing at the door with a retractable leash in his hand, the end of which formed a circle around the neck of the dog he was preparing to walk.

Islam and his wife had a large flabby dog called "Mujrim," or "Naughty," who would annoy Mustafa the whole time he sat there, telling the story of his meeting with Claudine without going into detail. He was surprised by Islam's attention to the dog and his obvious affection for him. He registered the fact that another of his nomadic friends in World's Gate had married and kept a dog in his apartment, and that this really shouldn't make him sad.

When they spoke that morning, the lazy director with whom Mustafa used to swap advice in affairs of the heart had told him he was broke. But after finding a bundle of dollars at home which he realized had been left by his wife, he called back. As he'd understood from Mustafa that he was traveling on important business, he'd decided to give him the dollars off his own bat.

"I mean, you'll pay me back, of course," he said, before restraining the dog from Mustafa. (Mujrim had pushed his snout for the tenth time into the latter's pubic area.) "Be quiet, Mujrim!"

"What would I do without you, Islam?" he replied. "But please, won't you take Mujrim out?"

Of all that happened during that meeting, Mustafa would recall nothing except his friend standing in his sports clothes with the leash in his hand, while Mujrim, in his eagerness to go out, ran up and down the hall making a fearful din. He said to himself that Islam had changed since he knew him in the nineties, while Islam repeated, in an extremely sad tone, the words of an old TV ad: "Just give me a frankisami, and I'll clean the pots!"

He'd recall hearing Islam repeat this phrase, and walking with him for a bit behind Mujrim in the alleys that join Shihab Street to Syria Street, before hurrying back to Tree Hill.

And had the breaths of its perfume been wafted through the
East, and in the West were one whose nostrils were
stopped, the sense of smell would have returned to him

On their first night together, when he kissed Claudine between her thighs, Mustafa smelled nothing worth mentioning. But when he went back to her late on Tuesday night... He struggled up the staircase, and groped around repeatedly in front of the door. It was then that she squatted down in the dark corridor, her body relaxed, as though the tightening in her face had made her body softer.

That night, after she'd told him she was frightened by the feeling she was just an innocent, ignorant, Sa'idi woman, he spent some time examining her vagina, long and thin like a tulip bud (or two buds, rather, one on top of the other), which he proceeded to name Bashmuhandis or "Chief Engineer."

Because, so he'd tell Claudine, it had engineered the world for him anew, as though life was a city and this poor organ had singlehandedly replanned its streets. Later, Claudine would on one occasion say "My Chief Engineer, that you love so..."

Before completing the map of Cairo that was in his head, he would redraw the flower as a double flower, so as not to forget it:

But as we were saying from our planet: he didn't smell anything.

When he wasn't involved in a relationship, Mustafa slept with women he didn't know, but only occasionally—not because he found it disgusting, or because it gave him no pleasure, but because there was something almost taboo about the act. As if it was so special or valuable that he couldn't do it with just anyone. Sometimes, of course, the smell wasn't agreeable. He remembers that when he bent over Claudine to kiss her there, he had a fleeting notion that for the first time in his life he was doing this without the slightest suspicion that he ought not to be doing it, and that the smell he would encounter, whether pleasant or not—on that first night, in the end, he didn't smell anything—would be linked to the start of the sacred mission that he was about to perform…

But when he came back to her late at night, and they did it for the first time, gently, gently, as though he were waves on the shore and she was swimming, his nostrils began to pick up something that made him take his member out from inside her, and press his face to the source of the smell.

"Eeeeeeh?" she muttered in protest, but he paid no attention except to the beguiling fragrance that his nostrils had detected for the first time. When he returned to her face with the smell on his mouth and nose, above and below his cheeks, and the hair sprouting on his chin, even Claudine would tell him she couldn't recall smelling it in her life. "Nice?" he asked her, and she indicated her assent, without opening her eyes or saying anything, apart from another stifled sigh in response to a sudden thrust like a penetrating blow from his waist. "Nice?" he asked again, and continued thrusting until he overcame her silence and she answered him with an exasperated sigh: "Okay, yes!" The smell of her arousal, as he thought of what it might be called in Arabic: *arīj, ʻabaq, tīb, shadhā*, nothing could name that smell.

At first, he thought of a tulip soaked in red wine, but he couldn't recall a tulip having any smell. If Mustafa had found it difficult to describe the smell of Claudine's neck as he bit it—he couldn't really think of a name for it—it was even more difficult to describe the smell of the Bashmuhandis. He'd continue to ponder, though, recalling the affection he'd felt when he smelled it, and the inexplicable merging of this affection with the desire to ravish or harm her body. At one moment, Claudine said to him (he understood roughly, then checked with her later), "*Avec toi, je pense que je recherche une sorte de mort*." When he was certain of the meaning, he thought about death: how this might be the smell of the souls of the dead, alive forever. The smell of torment trembling between dismemberment and compassion: the ecstatic climax of overwhelming sadness. In time, he would recall the white musk with which his father perfumed himself in his rare good moods. He'd probably only smelled it once or twice in his whole life, but he remembered it because it was quite special (in particular, on his father's skin). In his whole life, he'd never encountered a smell like it or even near to it, despite all the varieties of white musk that had come to his nose.

The Bashmuhandis had the smell of al-Muhandis Nayif's musk, then, so it was natural to have given it that nickname without knowing, and to have imagined it—as his father had dreamed of doing in his youth—replanning an entire city. But it had another smell as well (not mixed with the musk, but accompanying or following it without blotting it out), a faint acidic smell like orange peel. Orange peel or orange-flower water. Yes, the smell of orange-flower water... accompanying al-Muhandis Nayif's musk without destroying or weakening it.

Sweet of speech, indeed it is a sweetness to shatter hearts

On Tuesday (or dawn on Wednesday, rather) there was much talking. Out of eight hours, he slept for only two before he left Claudine and went out in the early morning. They'd made love five times, and talked in between, and the time had passed in a flash.

Claudine told him about Dr. Murad, about changes and discoveries. Then, with the terseness of a woman afraid to discuss such things, about their meeting—how she really hadn't been wanting or expecting what happened to happen. How, despite that, she wanted it to go on somehow or other. "You know, this isn't something that just happened, and that's it!" Adrien appeared and disappeared again as she spoke, without his place in her life being defined. Mustafa might have been happy at the omission.

Some things he'd intuitively grasped the previous night were confirmed. He then told her he'd be traveling to Beirut in a few days. He already knew that she was returning to France on April 21 as well. "On business?" she asked. "Yes, but I don't know how long I'll stay, maybe a bit longer..." On the pretext of his admiration for the work he'd looked at yesterday, he told her he was thinking of looking for Ma'ruf al-Shalchi there in his spare time.

"It'd be wonderful if I could study calligraphy with him even just for a couple of weeks, if he's happy to do it, that is. You know I've always wanted to learn calligraphy. But Claudine, don't you have a number for him?" he asked, as though by the way.

"No," she replied, "you know he dropped out of sight a while back. I always ask after him, because I like him a lot, but daddy hasn't known how to get hold of him for ages. That's what daddy told me, anyway, when I came to Egypt this time. But he's supposed to still be in Beirut. He's not so old, by the way, and he hasn't been ill or anything. Daddy says that if anything happened to him, he'd certainly hear about it here." She didn't explain how. "You know, Uncle Rufa's got no friends apart from daddy."

She laughed again, in a despondent tone.

"But why do you love him so much?" Mustafa moved her arm from his side, put it back on top of his belly, and sat playing with it with his fingers.

"By the way, we go back a very long time with Uncle Rufa." Her laughter shattered on the same despondency.

She told him she'd known Ma'ruf Efendi al-Shalchi as a family friend in Paris in the seventies before they'd moved when she was four to Germany, and from there to Holland, and Ma'ruf Efendi had continued to visit them in Cologne and then in Rotterdam as she grew up, but he'd never come to Egypt.

He insisted on the title Efendi, she explained to Mustafa, despite being younger than Dr. Murad and having no reason to call himself Efendi, when he could have called himself Bey or Pasha, or even simply Ustaz. For some incomprehensible reason, Efendi was in his eyes the most honorable of titles, because it was the title of sultans who didn't rule, so he used to say. "I don't know what sultans, quite honestly," she added, then laughed again as she imitated his Iraqi accent: "What? Don't you believe me? I swear by God, there's nothing more honorable than that!" She also mentioned that Yildiz had never liked him. Ma'ruf Efendi had lived in Paris since the sixties—Claudine couldn't recall him having a definite job there, just that he had a large number of old manuscripts and possibly traded in them—and only went back to Iraq after the First Gulf War in 1991. "What a time to go back!"

She laughed louder. "By the way, he's a real intellectual. You know, he's got no children or relations at all. He's never married or lived with anyone in his life, he just concentrated on old books and…"

He stuck it out in Baghdad working as a calligrapher until he sensed his life was in danger, after the invasion, so he moved to Beirut.

"So his position was okay with Saddam?"

"I really don't know. Daddy stayed in touch with him until 2005. Then he disappeared completely. But Daddy says if anything had happened to him, he'd have certainly known about it. I believe him, too."

"Why?"

"I mean, I don't believe anything's happened to him."

After Mustafa had turned into two people, the second telling him that he wouldn't find out from Claudine any more than he knew already—that Ma'ruf Efendi was short and fair, had a moustache, and usually wore striped pants and black shirts—he lifted her arm from his belly and gave it back to her, so he could suddenly move on top of her with all his weight.

•   •   •   •   •

Their third lovemaking session began with talk about how he viewed her life. On the strength of his knowledge, and with the authority of the new fragrance that wafted from her as soon as she'd returned her Bashmuhandis to his body, he said something to the effect that there were too many people in her life, that it would be better if she terminated her relationship with her husband, and that love—if there was such a thing—was more important than work, more important even than children and family.

He told her these things without taking sides or starting a direct argument, but he became steadily more angry at her cold replies and ambiguous, sarcastic tone. "You know, you get all your judgments ready-made, don't you?" or, "Of course, I'll leave everything in Paris and come to you on my knees, won't I?" In this new war, both of them naked and almost one body, their lust was growing without either knowing it. With her spread over him, he naturally expressed his fear of the things he'd found out yesterday, together with the anger that he'd only feel with clarity in Beirut. For her part, as was her habit when the annoyance of someone she loved fell on her head, she withstood the attack without either defending or showing any readiness to change herself.

"By the way, I'm not like any old woman you've slept with," she told him, when he pushed her shoulder into the mattress with one hand, and without thinking smacked her lightly with the other. She returned him a light blow at once, but he merely turned her over on to her stomach. "You really still don't understand, do you?"

With the same savage calm that had brought them together the first time, he interrupted her: "But you're a bitch in heat, doctor, you're just a filthy pair of shoes!", then lifted her by her belly. She gasped as he thrust his knee between her thighs from behind and again slapped her as she knelt there, putting his hands around her throat before she tried to slap him in return. "Shoes that I wouldn't care to put on my feet!" He licked her and squashed her, knowing she'd go wild. He pulled her hair so hard that she screamed, and there were tears trapped in her voice. "Don't talk like that!" With all the anger of the months to come, he aroused her and told her to lie down again on her back. "Legs up!" He was quite calm, and if she'd resisted, he'd have turned her over roughly, lifted her legs for her, and perhaps slapped her again.

As he penetrated her now, as if he was knocking in a nail, she opened her eyes in his face and whimpered: "Gently, okay?"

All that defeat in her arousal. An insane compassion for her came back to him but his body persisted in its violence. All this violence, where had it been hiding in his body? He pulled her thighs apart with his hands, and the white musk wafted from her more strongly than ever. "What were we saying you were, doctor?" He moved back and forth so hard she was unable to speak, but he felt the Bashmuhandis throbbing around his member with the same insistence, feeling it contract more with every pinch or blow, as he switched from one position to another and leaned over her face again. "I am Claudine Yusuf," she challenged him again, on the verge of tears.

His thrusts had even greater effect than his blows. "Who?" He overpowered her completely and pulled her hair again. "Claudine Yusuf!" Her tears were flowing, so he licked her round face and gave her some little kisses before gently biting her nipple and pulling her shoulder. "Who are you, I'm asking?" without letting up. And in a moment, with his finger in her ear, she broke. Claudine Yusuf broke completely, and fell to pieces, with the Bashmuhandis like a piece of iron around his member.

Until, looking her in the eye, he returned for a moment to the gentleness of the earlier session, and she said: "I want you to take me on the floor," the words seeming to come from her womb...

The floor was hard against his knees, but he felt she really was his dog now, and her body belonged to him, thoughtless. "Speak!" A moment, perhaps, but how long would it take to recreate the world? He'd return to his mercilessness as he pressed her spine, one vertebra at a time, his soul clinging to her belly. "Now I feel that I really am yours!" she gasped. He leaned over her neck to bite it. "At last, doctor!" There was something in her crying that was not defeat. "But still not your shoes, you beast!"

Once again, the dream came back to him, the dream of falling into a ditch with flesh at the bottom and no light. He passed through the pitch-dark flesh and emerged in a space that was blacker but so sweet he would have liked to die there. He was swimming in white musk as he expired.

The whole world was her cunt.

•   •   •   •   •

On the third Wednesday morning, Claudine was sleeping when he left. He remembered his mother. He hadn't seen her since the previous day. He suspected that she was also sleeping. It was a nice morning on the middle hill, but he headed for the bank on Dream Bridge to withdraw whatever was left in his account and settle his credit card so that it would last him as long as possible.

The waiting room was crowded as he sat dreaming of coffee. An albino in a full suit smiled at him in the distance. Was it the beggar who'd blocked his path in al-Mu'izz Street? A brawny Sunni who looked like Amgad Salah hurried by in front of him. A few seconds before his turn came, his mobile rang with a call from a corporation number. An extremely loud voice with the tone of an archivist: "Yes, Mr. Mustafa, this is Khalid Gamal from Employees' Affairs. At the moment, sir, there are no tickets for two weeks. I know that the form has urgent written on it, but can you travel tomorrow?"

He didn't have time to think, but he knew he couldn't wait two weeks.

"I mean, there's no chance of a ticket in a day or two?"

"Sir, these tickets have been reserved for the corporation for months, at reduced prices. There's one left that we can't dispose of, Ustaz Mustafa. You know, sir, if I could, but, if you went to any travel agent now, you couldn't find anything in less than two weeks. I'm telling you…"

"Okay, if I can go tomorrow, will the visa have come, Khalid?"

"Leave it to me, Mr. Mustafa."

Khalid Gamal disappeared, disappeared so long that Mustafa lost his place in the line at the window. His stomach churned with the fear that had taken complete hold of him in such a strange way: the same anxiety, though he hadn't felt it with such force until now.

"Hello, yes, Mr. Mustafa, your passport's in front of me with the visa in it. You're traveling to Lebanon, aren't you? Ah, yes, in front of me. I don't know how they managed to get it in one day, to be honest. Your trip tomorrow seems to be sorted for you. OK? Should I confirm the ticket in front of me for tomorrow or will you wait two weeks?"

Before he could grasp exactly what this conversation meant, he was sitting down again waiting his turn at the window.

> *My folk feigned incomprehension, seeing me thus distraught,*
> *and cried, "On account of whom hath madness touched*
> *this youth?"*

He called Claudine from home. There was a sadness in her voice as she asked: "So today's the last day?"

When his mother asked why he was leaving so suddenly, without any beating about the bush he replied, "Work, mama!" She was sitting sifting rice in her bedroom wearing her reading glasses. Her manner was calm but sad, as if she'd been expecting this for a long time and had left it in the hands of God. How had she known he'd leave her to travel? "And where did you spend the night yesterday?" For the first time since Saturday, he sensed genuine concern in her voice, though she didn't lift her eyes from the rice for a moment. "Work again?" He started. "Calm down, mama. What do you know, Amgad Salah had a heart attack!" He was astonished by his capacity for improvisation, knowing she would uncover his lie. "We had to take him to hospital and sat with him until morning. God help him!"

Without looking at him or asking about Amgad Salah, she asked, "You didn't sleep? Aren't you going to work today?"

"No, I'm going!" The flicker in his eye was distracting him. "I'm going, but I'll rest for half an hour before I go out."

"Yes, you must, or you'll find yourself spending tonight in hospital with your colleague as well..." He looked into her eyes with a smile of genuine affection before spluttering: "My God, I'll miss you in Beirut, nonna!"

●   ●   ●   ●   ●

In the three hours between one and four he collected his passport, paid the fees due, completed several forms, then said goodbye to the chief editor and his clown of a secretary. The last day in this office? Mustafa sat in the cubicle for ten minutes. The lunch break, and no one. The weather was really nice. The roofs of Abu al-'Ila glinted in the sunlight. Should he play Lost Ark? He found that he was happy he wouldn't see anyone before he left. Not just because he didn't want to get into a discussion about why he was going, but because he felt that they—all of them—would be distant and inauthentic, like characters in B-movies that couldn't hold his attention. The same feeling he'd had the first day he'd come to work after moving from Dog Alley to Dream Bridge, when he discovered he wouldn't be meeting Yildiz. He laughed at the paradox that the woman he'd become so attached to for two days was the sister of a colleague and friend, someone willowy as fire. What a strange person you are, Çorbacı! He also had another feeling, a feeling like the one he'd had when he stayed late at the office, with no colleagues there and no possibility of anyone coming in after Aldo except for the fiqi Wahid. Today he left his bag at home. No notebook and no pens. Now that his mission had begun, he no longer wanted to draw.

The drawing: the trace. And it is said: the remains of the trace.
The strange thing was that he wasn't thinking about Ma'ruf
Efendi al-Shalchi, or trying to visualize how he looked in
striped pants and a black shirt. In his head there was only
the image of the Bashmuhandis and Claudine's look when he
was thrusting inside her and she was saying, "I want you to
take me on the floor!" Tonight, he would use the camera to
take a picture of her naked by the light of the bedside lamp,
to keep with him her memory, her trace, Claudine—the most
important thing in his story, and perhaps his story's real goal.

Suddenly, the security man blocked the door. "Good
evening, Darsh!" he said. The same security man who'd been
with him the night the caliph appeared. This time, he came in
before Mustafa could stand up to greet him, the same amiable
smile on his face: "I hear you're traveling. It's good that I found
you because someone left this letter with me for you." He put a
yellow envelope with Mustafa's name on it on the desk.

"A very odd man, to tell you the truth. He looked like a
foreigner but very religious, somehow. He had a rosary in his
hand and a prayer mark on his forehead." Once again, the
anxiety. "He spoke proper, formal Arabic, but wore strange
clothes. He passed by reception this morning and left it for you
without giving his name. Do you know him, Darsh?"

"God only knows, your guess is as good as mine!" he
muttered. "But is there anyone who isn't a bit strange these
days?"

Waving the envelope in the air like a signal, then clutching
it close to his chest, Mustafa hurried out before anyone could
notice him, leaving the security man in the office. "See you
soon!" he said. He headed toward the elevator to call it. And,
another definition of a drawing: *the trace of that which is not a
person.*

•　　　•　　　•　　　•　　　•

Mustafa left work early, but Claudine was busy with her friends.
Was it reasonable for her to deliberately make appointments
on their last day? He went back home at about five o'clock.
Before shaving and showering he locked the door of his room

and opened the envelope. There was nothing in it except for a piece of leather, the size of a cigarette packet, on the lighter side of which he recognized the Padishah's handwriting—the same handwriting in which he'd explained to him the composition of the tughra and written for him the word *yeniçeri*.

Just one sentence confirmed, as it had no doubt been intended to, that he'd really put his foot on the beginning of the road. "Roads open up in the arms of lovers." And underneath: "And another whom you love, and near victory, and give good news to the Believers. God's word is true." Mustafa was overwhelmed with joy. He kissed the letter and put it on his head, then slipped it into his brown notebook with the sultan's photograph. Then he had lunch with his mother, insisting that she should sit with him. The entire time he ate, he tried to drag her into conversation, but without success. Only when he asked why she was sad did she give him a look between rebuke and contempt.

He spent two hours packing his bag. He took all his clean clothes, put some notebooks and two or three books in with them, then said goodbye to his mother on his way out. He told her he was putting the bag in the car, and would bring the car back from the hospital, park it in the garage, then take a taxi. "You're still talking about the hospital, Mustafa." Suddenly, she wailed in pure panic: "Why are you determined to make a laughingstock of me and make me feel I no longer know who you are?" But he couldn't think of anything to say in response.

He understood that in order to conciliate her in any meaningful way, he would have to spend his remaining time with her. But he couldn't miss his final meeting with Claudine. He was surprised how cold he was being with his mother when he was leaving her for an unknown period, especially when he recalled the day of his divorce: when he'd woken her that morning, he'd felt such warmth and compassion.

Now, he told himself, she was like a character in a film. There was nothing to link him to her, nothing to link him to this world.

Take-off at nine in the morning: that was what was on his mind as he tried without success to kiss his mother. Whenever he brought his mouth close to her face she turned her head and shouted. He had to be at the airport at seven, which meant leaving Claudine's at five. Could she really be wasting all this time with her friends?

He'd put his passport, ticket, money, and new camera into his hand luggage, together with his brown notebook, the only notebook not yet full. Between two pages, wrapped in cellophane, he put the parchment that Uncle Rufa had transcribed from the handwritten work of Sultan Abdülmecid, may God have mercy on him.

> I beamed with joy (for I had reached myself)
> Full of a certainty protecting me
> From the necessity to bind my pack
> And saddle to a journey

Dawn on the final Thursday, the Thursday of setting out. The thick mist on the middle hill presaged a hot day all day. The Chosen Çorbacı had taken his time on his way to Tree Hill. He parked more than once and got out of the car to look around. Although he wanted to spend as much time as possible with Claudine, he had the feeling he wouldn't be seeing this city again for a very long time, and perhaps wouldn't see it again ever. Finally, she opened up for him apprehensively, wearing her red kimono. The most beautiful woman in the world. Apprehensively also, he slept with her four times, during which he took several pictures of her with his camera. She was shy about being photographed, but the camera aroused her. There was a state of denial on both sides that their parting was really near. Eternal sorrow in union, joy undiminished, but apprehension, like a Turkish flute in the background, tempering the violence a little. For about an hour before he left, before the last time, she would stay clinging to his body as he licked and smelled her. He didn't shower (and for days after he arrived in Beirut would preserve her smell on his body). After he'd led her to the back road, extracted his teeth from her lips, and she'd told him she didn't like oranges, he saw nothing except the slope of the mountain: the mountain of the Citadel and the Cemeteries, the mountain of Sidi 'Umar and al-Hakim bi-Amr Allah… Then he recalled another line, as though he could see in it his situation throughout the coming month: *Nothing delighted the eye after they had left; when the heart keeps company with memory, it is not at ease.*

He looked at the damp stones on the mountainside, the same stones on which he'd imagined himself killing Claudine. All the way to Dream Bridge, as he was looking at the sleeping city for the last time, as if floating on the musk of the Bashmuhandis, he recalled her looks and the expressions on her face... He would reach Dream Bridge at a quarter to six. In the morning air, he felt his brain was empty, completely empty, empty of everything. Carrying his suitcase, with his hand luggage over his shoulder, he stopped the first taxi he met and immediately agreed to the fare the driver demanded. Along the Dry Nile, as he smelled Claudine's smell on his body, joy would return to him, becoming more and more intense until the taxi entered Plane Yard. And although there was nothing in the whole world but the sound of the breeze breaking against the windshield, he would hear, as if coming from an instrument hidden in his ear: "Tell him if you're dull or matchless; my heart is no theater for the hobby of acting."

•   •   •   •   •

And you who desired the nakedness of the adventure, then burned the map, sleep now in the doorway of the dragon. —Sargon Boulus

"Where are you traveling to?" the taxi driver asked.

"I'm going to heaven," replied Mustafa Nayif Çorbacı. "Haven't you heard? They now have a direct flight to heaven!"

PART NINE

Scrapbook

Plane Yard

Short Facts and Fancies,
Assembled by the Narrator in the
Order of the Book's Parts,
Followed by the Conclusion,
Containing His Confession

Fancy

"If it so just happened that they should bomb the High Dam" (so wrote Mustafa Çorbacı in a small black notebook in the final week before his final separation from his wife), "if they hit the High Dam with a single large bomb and it collapsed and dissolved and Lake Nasser was released into the Nile Valley (all the water accumulated behind the dam, that is), how long before the flood reached Cairo, how long before the corporation's building, the Mugamma in Tahrir Square, and the Radio and TV building became like sinking ships? How long before people started to splash around, quarreling with fierce-looking fish until they died? Would any signs of life be left above the water or would we all go at once? Now I see torrents like mountains destroying the Corniche towers and the Ring Road, or calmer floods carrying cars on their arcs from Giza to al-Qanatir in a single movement, freeing them from the traffic jams as the gas settles inside them. Until they drown, the Cairo Tower, the Pyramids, and the Citadel sway on silken surfaces even vaster than the area that surrounds them, and the length and breadth of the October Bridge is just a tongue, bobbing up and down in the water that surges from desert to desert. By now, the asphalt is just another layer of floating filth. How can I be calm as I juxtapose in my head the images of this watery end and them all swimming naked: Amgad Salah, balanced on his chin, with Aldo Mazika like a round submarine beneath him; or Yildiz Zakariyya spinning like a top, her arms looking like sails or wings, holding the dark girl and the girl engaged to the boy; the chief editor on his own like a lost whale, and Michel Fustuq, holding Ustaz Wahid al-Din on a plank of wood in the shape of a cross, with water passing though his mouth to emerge from his anus in bubbles and blisters? How is it that I see the world without light, taking on the color of green and blue oil—bread, trees, and air-conditioning—as the mosques spew out their guts below the surface, with grocers, minibuses, and police stations? *Matrimony*

Fancy

"A City Founded with Mars in the Ascendant" (from the observations of the Chosen Çorbacı in one of the notebooks he took with him to Beirut; he hadn't looked at this paragraph when the eighth part ended): "Like those born in the signs of Aries and Scorpio, it is natural that her temperament should be impetuous, and that she should have a tendency to anger. She makes quick judgments without thinking things through and confronts things head on without regard to others' differences. Perhaps her anger will quickly vanish. But it produces a dryness like parched earth. Everything becomes dry inside her. If you stay there long enough, and without necessarily changing your ways, you will disappear into the asphalt paste spread any which way over her surface. I have read horoscopes about 'Mars people'—people born while Mars is in the ascendant—and discovered that although they learn quickly and have a copious imagination, they forget more quickly than they learn, and just as suddenly lose their liking for things that they have let their imaginations loose on, so that their love turns to hatred. Cairo is like these people. There is nothing shorter than her memory, and her mind has an insatiable appetite for all sorts and races of men, whom she consumes as her memory consumes events. Her imagination is deficient, not through any fault of its own but because it is always ablaze: the fire of Mars eats the land and makes the waters boil. Like the people of Mars, this city accepts situations as they are, because its memory isn't long enough nor its imagination strong enough to change them. Horoscopes say that the people of Mars are suitable for work as smithies, because they're associated with the surface of the conquering planet, where the proportions of iron are very high, and they like to forge metal. They can also blow air from their lungs with great force, which qualifies them to play wind instruments. Nothing can fill the space they possess, and they are associated with masculinity rather than femininity. Cairo is a woman, sure, but it is also a blacksmith or a piper with fire in his heart, tearing him apart with drought and anger. *Subject and Predicate*

Fact

In a conversation between some eminent writers and the political sociologist Burhan Ghalyun some words occurred that Mustafa noticed and which seem almost like the political lining of *The Book of the Sultan's Seal*. "As well as the crisis provoking an explosion, the preservation of the society in crisis can only be achieved by an increasing reliance on force… by imposing laws and regulations directly on the people through military orders and martial law, or through bogus 'parliaments'" (so the Syrian scholar says; he goes on): "This force [material, political, legal, judicial, symbolic] can have only one aim: to drive people to plumb the depths of fear, anxiety and self-contempt… in order to suppress them and paralyze their will, and encourage them to distance themselves by themselves, and hence guarantee their absolute submission to external authority, and to the regime. Unbridled force is not the only characteristic of the 'crisis regime.' There is a second characteristic, which I should like to call 'the dead taking the place of the living in all spheres.'" (This last sentence is the important one and might have given Mustafa pause: "the dead taking the place of the living in all spheres.") "In the Arab world, this dynamic is embodied in, and given expression by, a stultifying bureaucratic authority. All decisions are made by an executive authority totally remote from any genuine societal life or connection, a self-motivated bureaucratic authority which makes laws and decisions, and executes them, without being subject to any scrutiny or accountable to anyone. It is also self-renewing without recourse to anyone's opinion, and indeed is not concerned with anyone's opinion. It creates its heads, just as it creates its chamberlains, and dismisses and guides them without consulting anyone and without anyone's knowledge. This is the basis of the total silence and complete paralysis to which the bureaucratic class gives the names 'stability' and 'continuity'." *The Demons*

Fancy

The first thing the Chosen Çorbacı would do when he arrived at Beirut was to put his three routes together side by side and look at them. He'd keep looking at them until he was struck by the possibility of joining them at certain places and angles. He'd then transfer the three drawings onto three pieces of tracing paper and move them around in front of him until this possibility was realized.

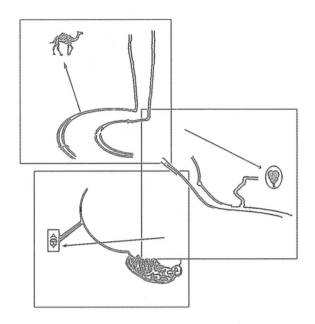

But before he completed a large-scale version of the drawing that resulted from superimposing them—before his successive journeys over three weeks were connected, and the transformation of his Cairo into a tughra complete—he would write a new account in the same brown notebook: "The map is complete. My story is more or less finished. I have no idea how much time I've spent staring at the Cairo tughra. I realized immediately that there were mistakes in it but I am still amazed that the map of the city forming in my head since I left Dog Alley really looks like this. Perhaps I saw its shape while the plane that brought me here was taking off, when I saw my city in the shape of a talisman. Now I shall redraw it and write on it the names of the districts I made up. Until I learn Arabic calligraphy (as I really intend to do) I will content myself with showing how its shape is linked to the tughra: to the seal, the ring, and the sultan's name. For the first time, it occurs to me that even if I don't find the lost sura of Mary, I may perhaps become a skilled enough calligrapher to write it in my own hand." *The Sultan*

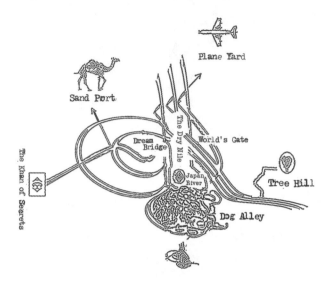

The map shows labels: Plane Yard, Sand Port, Dream Bridge, World's Gate, The Dry Nile, The Khan of Secrets, Japan River, Tree Hill, Dog Alley

Fancy

"Organization, conspiracy, a zombie's bite: the thing standing behind the disaster… may actually be just an infectious disease." That's what Mustafa wrote to Rashid at the start of one of his notebooks. "Maybe the story isn't the story of a group of people deliberately devising existential conspiracies, as we thought at first. If there hadn't been a CIA, there wouldn't have been Taliban, but it may be that the conspiracy lies not in any dirty deed that the developed nations have committed or caused to be committed. Not in humiliating and punishing the blacks in South Africa, for example, or in forcibly preventing the whirling dervishes from whirling. Not in screwing the refugees in Sabra and Shatila in 1982, or in making innocent people wear orange coveralls and squat in chains in Guantanamo Bay after 2001. The conspiracy might be just a vision of the world or a mode of thought that first appeared in Northwest Europe, stamped with the color of the people living there. The Enlightenment, the Industrial Revolution, colonialism: all the modernistic things that denied Islamic history and in a complex, circular way, left me, as I sit now on Dream Bridge, sick in my heart of this world… All this results from this mode of thought, this vision. The vision may be no more than a virus that attacked those pale faces first, before it spread it to other peoples. That the world is all against me, that Muslims are beggars and jerboas, that their civilization is just myths and terrorism—there may be nothing more to it than a deadly virus, a virus that has become so powerful and virulent that it controls the whole world. (A virus can't live in isolation from the living creature that nourishes it, isn't that right?) You of course understand bacteria and viruses better than I, but in so far as I understand it, one of the properties of viruses is that they are half alive (exactly like ideas and attitudes), and among their other properties is that they do not kill with their own hands but rather neutralize the systems necessary for the continuation of life. It occurred to me that the conspiracy may be a virus like that, and that we have to treat it, whether we hate the whites or not. *Plans and Antiquities*

Fact

When Rashid Jalal Siyouti returned to Egypt after an uninterrupted absence of three years, eager to meet his lifelong friend Mustafa Nayif Çorbacı, he was very disappointed not to find Mustafa in Cairo. His mobile was permanently switched off, and when he emailed him—until he returned to England, where he received a PDF of a manuscript entitled *The Book of the Sultan's Seal*—he received no reply. The night he arrived, when he found Mustafa's mobile switched off, he called him at home and his mother replied, with a strong hint of impatience in her voice, as if she'd be overjoyed to hear anything connected with her son. Poor woman, she thought he'd know something about Mustafa or have a letter from him. When she understood that Rashid had only called that evening to ask about his friend, her voice again acquired a strange apathy and coldness, and she turned into someone a good deal more obnoxious than Tante 'Aziza, with whom he used to enjoy a chat. She told him she didn't know anything about Mustafa except that he'd stayed with her for three weeks after he left his wife and made up his mind to divorce her quickly, then all of a sudden, just like that, had told her he was traveling to Beirut on business. Mustafa had only rung her once, three days later, and hadn't given her an address or a telephone number or said when he was coming back. Rashid was depressed when he heard what she said, quite apart from the tone of her voice. He decided not to call again, and apologized for disturbing her, hoping that the warmth would return to her voice. It was no use. Mustafa would turn up when he turned up, he thought. He was most likely okay. But after that an odd thing happened to Rashid that made him call Tante 'Aziza again before leaving, and in this second call he went on and on so much that she fell apart and screamed and told him that Mustafa had changed so much lately that they must have swapped him for someone else. She hadn't been that alarmed by his departure because it hadn't really been him who had left, and now, having lost her husband to death and her daughter to emigration, she was losing her son in a third way that she couldn't exactly name. "Do you understand now, my dear," she asked Rashid, "why I'm sad and silent and my voice is choking?" *Friends' Secrets*

Fancy

"Madwoman! How many potholes on the road to her embrace! You too smelled her armpit in the darkness." So Mustafa Çorbacı wrote to Adrien Pasqua, Claudine's husband. "You inclined your head to chew on flesh whose very existence, let alone its tenderness on the lips, the eye could not suspect under her clothes. You saw melodies in lines that curved for your eyes alone, just as I saw poems. You too shook hands with God when half your soul was in the pit of grief, and were healed. You believed the promise of possible happiness and found rest in a legalized eternity. You too were restored by the smell. Cracks in the hard surface of the meadows by your house, from a fairy tale the pair of you could not invent… the vivid color of blood spattering on ice, gusts from the exhaust pipe with the same hiss along each route. Drowsy cracks where there are also trees, perhaps closer to the miniature deserts of dust on the asphalt than we thought. You who hurry to the doctor to heal discord, hold back from the oxygen of an entire life in her madness, say goodbye to wretchedness. Play your music well, just as I bear her separation with no help from your defeat. In her harsh departures from your presence, when she seems small and lost and in need of affection, remember that between her and me there is a distance as great as that between the two of you on this earth. And in your calm, which gives me pain, the fatal journey of release, thank geography and children. Now I am certain you are there, looking at her, knowing that I, here, know she is with you and am awaiting the end, and that this is really a calamity… the madwoman. When I rip this page from my notebook, I will call to mind all the curiosity or love I harbor for you, any personal coloring to make you believe I am completely serious, before I fold it in an imaginary envelope with your address on it, crowned with your name preceded by the word 'Dear.' How many potholes for me to acknowledge the essential lie in the letter: that I am writing to you in order to be near my love?" *Ring of the Dove*

Fact

Before a single year had passed since their meeting, the Chosen Çorbacı would feel not that it was impossible for him to possess Claudine, but that this Claudine was basically a mirage. There was nothing there to be possessed for more than a moment. Even knowledge, which can actually melt geography and history, wouldn't succeed, in any way that would satisfy him, in making her submissive or available. Until then, possibly always, when Mustafa had been with Claudine, and no one and nothing else, there really was no one else in the universe, and he'd feel she was his rib and his home. But as soon as a third party appeared, or the topic of living arrangements came up, he would be struck by the certainty that the oranges and their halves meant simply a union that would heal him when he lapped the white musk from her Bashmuhandis, or his nose picked up the scent of orange-blossom water while she was on all fours, howling like a dog, as he took her from behind. That life would last for several hours at most. Nothing else had any relevance: not his desire to make her happy, not her stupid wars, one giving birth to another… not her stories that (were it not for his devotion, which it would pain him to see disappear) left him with every reason (in terms of loneliness, despair, and freedom of movement) to be with other women. In short, the human "case" that was Claudine was not the person he loved, which confirmed to him that souls really do not live in their owners. Extremely painful, this, really painful. But Mustafa would learn to accept it, on the basis that it proved she was, as he'd seen her the first time, a flimsy being. Even al-Mukhtar could only see her at set times, stolen from the midst of a life they didn't live together. Like the dream with which the Sublime State had begun, or that had sparked off his tale, Claudine was an epic and a story, a legend impossible to weave into the threads of reality. But reality, despite everything, was more wonderful through her. Çorbacı's life, which he was prepared to throw into the garbage can, his life that he would've been happy to lose after discovering in the minutest of its details a universal conspiracy the size of an elephant, if not a mystical device to restore the umma, was merely an excuse for a tulip able to make the world heal itself. *'Umar*

A Reference

Near the end of his research into the Sublime State, as we recorded, Mustafa withdrew at random a volume of al-Jabarti, printed by Dar al-Sha'b, from the books piled up in the hall balcony and, after shaking the dust from it, placed it between two notebooks on his desk, with the intention of reading it at a later date. But he didn't read a single word of it until he reached Beirut, where the volume had by chance been transported with the two notebooks, Mustafa having forgotten it completely during the events of the sixth part. When he found it in his bag as he rummaged through the notebooks in his hotel room in Ain el Mreisseh, he felt a familiarity and affection, and suspected the coincidence might have some significance that would help him to fulfill his mission. He sat on the balcony that day with a large coffee pot, reading. There were no clues or information in the volume to help him find Ma'ruf al-Shalchi. Mustafa simply loved the final paragraphs, which were a succinct summary of the two years preceding the French invasion (1796–98), and which confirmed to Mustafa that some things he'd written (as some of those who'd read them had told him) had really been poetry. Because al-Jabarti too, without intending to, had written poetry in these paragraphs: "No events happened in those two years of the sort that people were expecting... except for those that have been referred to previously... they were all ordinary causes and signs, and no effects could be attributed to their influence. By looking at the kingdom of heaven and the earth, they sought guidance, and they were guided by the stars. Among the most significant of those things was the total eclipse of the moon that occurred halfway through the month of Dhu'l-Hijjah at the end of the year 1212 with Gemini, with which the province of Egypt is associated, in the ascendant. The band of Frenchmen arrived immediately afterwards in the first days of the following year..." Mustafa got up from the hotel balcony, his heart full of emotion, and went out, saying to himself that poetry, like miracles, is always to be found where no one expects it. *Scrapbook*

•   •   •   •   •

What the narrator said in explanation, by way of an ending

Thank God I don't know the people Mustafa has been talking about, as he involved me in treating them badly and exposing what they'd resolved to keep hidden, not just through his own words but also (in parts such as this one) through mine. As we agreed, I made his style and opinions my own. He agreed that I should intervene if I felt that the account was illogical or contained mistakes, on condition that I was sympathetic to his ideas as far as I could be: I am not at all sympathetic to the Ottoman State, for example, and I prefer Atatürk to Abdülhamid a thousand times. But I carried on translating, subtracting and adding to such an extent that I started writing like him, exactly like him, in this fluctuating language that belongs nowhere culturally. It's true that I like the state of harmony that has grown between us, but why should I put myself in the wrong with these people? Perhaps, as Mustafa says, what is meant by "talking transparently about people" is loving them. But it is a hard love, this, more like the love of God for man. I mean, is this the meaning of love? To shame people and expose their wounds? To screw them, torment them and slap them on the head (and consequently be transparent in looking at them)? Possibly. But Mustafa, although he justifies the situation in this way, is still determined that what we are writing is only a "book" to a friend, a "book" in the sense of a letter. I have comforted myself and set my mind at rest with one simple fact: no one reading this book will know my name, whether it be Rashid al-Siyouti or the blue jinn. To be honest—although I can see madness in his story, and I am disturbed by something resembling reactionism in some of Mustafa's ideas—I've had considerable sympathy with Mustafa since meeting him ten days ago, perhaps because I went through a similar experiment in marriage (even though it lasted three years longer and didn't involve pregnancy or children), during which I suffered the same confusion between heritage and (God help us all!) modernity. This is the reason for my coming to take up residence here, to be honest—plus the fact that living in Beirut is a little easier for someone who likes to drink every day, likes to live on his own, likes to see women in the street, and hates the sights and practices of Islamization that are spreading in Cairo like the plague. The Lebanese have taught me to love life. I savor my food, enjoy sex and wine, and I dance. I get up in the morning like a real human being, and I deal with other people and things the whole day. I hadn't forgotten, exactly. But meeting Mustafa reminded me of the years that I lived, like him, without really living. In that meeting, I confessed to myself that—quite apart from the other details—I'd come to Beirut because I'd failed in my private life, something I'd never acknowledged in six years. Of course, during this period I encountered other serious problems in Beirut. The fact that I didn't go back, I mean, was not so much the result of my liking the life here as a rejection of Egypt and everything that happened to me there. Mustafa opened up old wounds, for I immediately recognized his social allusions and revelations of general despair that he described with the phrase "at the end of one's rope." I sensed it precisely whenever he said: "When a girl who's been brought up abroad behaves like that, what can you do?" I sensed it—without saying anything to him—so much that I wanted to cry. How can people live in a single house after losing their respect for one another? How can you wake up and go to bed with someone you've started to think of as garbage? By lying and resorting to clichés which you continuously repeat to yourself? (Mustafa prefers the word "platitude": that is, an expression that is repeated, trivial, and most likely wrong, and that's said as if it were the deepest and most honest truth, now being revealed for the first time.) Through boasting, swaggering, and flattery? Through scenes and settings? Silence and tears? *How* is perhaps easy, for those who can bear it. Most people can bear it. Mustafa, like me, decided not to bear it. And this is what quickly attracted me to him and made me eager to help him document his tale. Although I don't know whether inserting his marriage and love for Claudine Yusuf in the tale is justified from a literary point of view, I do know that, if it weren't for the connection between the tale and the values linked to his life and work, I wouldn't have been at all enthusiastic about it. He himself tells Rashid al-Siyouti that the tale and the observations in the notebooks are everything. He says: "The words around them are like a sponge," but to be frank, if it weren't for the surrounding text—his problem with his wife, his Muslim friend's conversion, and his Christian friend's prophesy—if it weren't for the sponge, in short, I couldn't have digested either the tale or the observations. Disregarding an infinite number of individual causes and motives that reflect the confusion and restlessness of those concerned—as I was saying—people live with each other after losing respect for one another because they are afraid. This was my feeling at the time I left my wife, more than seven years ago. I woke up one day convinced that the only reason that could possibly be keeping me with her was fear. Fear of loneliness, of the consequences of divorce, of leaving a known "here" for an unknown "there." Fear that I might be the villain of the film, of being tormented by feelings of guilt or others' accusations, that my decision might be mere revenge or a violent reaction to an unintended blow or a stray fleck of spit (like a bullet that kills the shooter), and that I might live to regret it. Fear that I might not be like other people, in short. I believe that people live after losing their respect in fear that they may become outsiders. We all like the inside, we're all inside until further notice. No one is ready to confess that "inside"—because of the religion they spout all the time, among other things, of course—has become hell on earth and unbearable. In this sense too, I shall understand Mustafa's words about resistance—not resistance to some supposed universal conspiracy, but rather, and before any theories contrary to the laws of reality, resistance to the "fed up to the back teeth" mood that you encounter in Cairo on a daily basis. Mustafa is my double in more than one context, and although my own story differs considerably from his, and I still speak to my father (may God grant him health) every ten days, I merged myself with Mustafa so much that I digressed to tell my own story, like him, and say much more than was necessary. As each part of the book was completed, I felt myself becoming more and more entangled. Despite that, I'm extremely happy for this story to be present in my life, so long as we continue to respect the pledge we gave each other: that you won't know my name, whether you're Rashid or anyone else. My condition for working with Mustafa on *The Book of the Sultan's Seal* was that I should remain nameless. I am no one, and the same condition applies to anyone claiming to be an author. I even almost forgot my voice while writing. My aim was to start and end the task without appearing even for a moment, and for nothing to be known about me. My aim and my condition. Mustafa accepted. And although he repeatedly insisted, and there was a lot of give and take in the first three days, after that he stopped asking me if I believed him. Perhaps he thought me odd. That's his business, even though people who live in glass houses shouldn't throw stones. Anyway, I explained everything to him at our second meeting, as we drank bitter coffee in the Rawda Café, and we both observed how similar the Rawda Café was to those places by the sea at Chatby Beach in Alexandria at the end of the eighties. He told me this was his first time in Beirut and he was finding it hard to understand the Lebanese dialect, so I pretended to be annoyed and asked him in a Lebanese accent: "What's the matter, man? Do you need an interpreter to converse with the world?" We laughed. That night, the night of April 22, 2007, the weather was fine, so we walked along the Corniche from the Military Baths to Ain el Mreisseh. I left him in front of the hotel there and took a shared taxi to Zarub al-Tamlis, where I live. What I told him then during our walk was closer to the truth than anything I told him, or even told myself, later: that it was really important to write down the story he'd spent the previous evening telling me, after we'd met by chance with Pierre Abi Saab in the office of the new newspaper *Al-Akhbar*, which Joseph Samaha (may God have mercy on him) founded before they moved to the Monoprix building in Verdun. Even if it was all fantasy, even if he'd made it up, there were things in it that needed to be documented, not because they'd lead to great events, nor because I particularly agreed with their contents. But because the story of Mustafa Çorbacı and his sudden transformation during twenty-one days from a Europeanized intellectual to a semi-madman who believed he could perform magic deeds to resurrect the Islamic caliphate—and this is what I'd really become convinced of—the story of Mustafa Çorbacı was not just a set of fairy tales.

GLOSSARY

Notes
1 All dates are given in AD (CE) form.
*2 Persons are generally listed under the first element of their names: thus,
"Ahmad Hilmi" rather than "Hilmi, Ahmad."*
3 "T" denotes a Turkish term; Arabic terms are unmarked.

15 May Bridge: bridge linking Bulaq to Sphinx Square, crossing the
two branches of the River Nile at Zamalek and Abu al-'Ila.

26 July Corridor: one of Greater Cairo's main freeways, which runs
south of Sheikh Zayed City, and leads to the Cairo–Alexandria Desert
Road.

26 July Street: one of the busiest commercial streets in downtown
Cairo. Planned by Ibrahim Pasha, it was previously called Fouad
I Street. Its present name commemorates the abdication of King
Farouk in 1952.

6 October Bridge: twelve-mile bridge and elevated highway south of
the Kasr al-Nil Bridge. The bridge, whose name commemorates the
start of the 1973 October War, crosses the Nile, runs through Gezira
Island to Downtown Cairo, and connects to Cairo International
Airport in the east.

6 October City: satellite town in Giza Governorate, established in
1979 in the desert, twenty miles outside the city of Cairo.

'Abbasids: a major Islamic dynasty, founded by descendants of the
Prophet's uncle, 'Abbas; based in Baghdad from 750 until its sacking
by the Mongols in 1258.

'Abbasiyya: neighborhood in northeast central Cairo, where the Coptic Patriarchate and cathedral are located.

'Abd al-Qadir al-Jilani (1078–1166): Islamic scholar and preacher, founder of the Qadiriyya Sufi order.

'Abd al-Rahman al-Jabarti (1753–1825): Egyptian-born biographer and historian, best known for his account of the French invasion of Egypt in 1798.

Abdülmecid I (1823–1861, r. 1839–1861): Ottoman sultan and caliph.

Abdülmecid II (1868–1944): served as Ottoman caliph 1922–1924, following the abolition of the sultanate; exiled in 1924 on abolition of caliphate.

al-Abshihi (sometimes al-Ibshihi) (1388–c. 1446): Egyptian writer, author of the encyclopedic *Mustaṭraf fī kull fann mustaẓraf* ("A Quest for Attainment in Each Fine Art").

Abu Ayyub al-Ansari (576–672/674): close companion of the Prophet Muhammad, and one of the Ansar ("Helpers") who supported Muhammad after his hijra to Medina in 622; died during the first Arab siege of Constantinople.

Agouza: suburb of Giza, on the west bank of the Nile between 6 October Bridge and 15 May Bridge, between the more prosperous Dokki and Mohandiseen suburbs.

Ahmad Hilmi (b. 1969): well-known Egyptian comedy actor and TV host, born in Benha.

Ahmad ibn Tulun (835–884): founder of the dynasty that ruled Egypt briefly between 868 and 905; he had originally been sent by the 'Abbasid caliph as governor to Egypt, but established himself as an independent ruler.

Ahmad 'Urabi, Colonel (1841–1911): Egyptian nationalist leader whose uprising of 1879–1882 prompted the British to occupy Egypt.

Ain el Mreisseh: neighborhood on the Mediterranean in central Beirut, fronted by the Corniche.

'Ain Shams: suburb of Cairo; location of 'Ain Shams University, the third-oldest public Egyptian university, founded in 1950.

Aisha Fahmi Palace: palace overlooking the Nile in the Cairo district of Zamalek; currently being restored to be reopened to the public as an arts center.

Akhnatun arts complex: arts complex in Zamalek, Cairo.

'Aja'ib al-athar fi 'l-tarajim wa'l-akhbar ("The Marvelous Compositions of Biographies and Chronicles"): title of chronicle by the Egyptian-born historian al-Jabarti (1753–1825).

'Ala' Wali al-Din (b. 1963): Egyptian actor and comedian, graduate of 'Ain Shams University, who became a household name with films such as *Al-Nazer* ("The Headmaster," 2000).

'Ali al-Maqri: modern Yemeni poet and novelist.

'Ali Pasha Fahmi (1834–1897): leading Egyptian official under the khedives Isma'il and Tawfik.

'Amr ibn al-'As (c. 585–664): Arab military commander who led the Muslim conquest of Egypt in 640.

'Amr Khalid (b. 1967), aka 'Amr Mohamed Helmi Khaled: well-known and influential Muslim satellite TV preacher, born in Alexandria, who rejects extremism.

Ard al-Liwa': a poor and uncontrolled informal housing area on the outskirts of Cairo.

al-'Ataba al-Khadra': square in Cairo, located between the old and modern cities, and site of Cairo's largest fresh food market.

Ash'arites: an early theological Sunni school of Islam founded by Imam Abu al-Hasan al-Ash'ari (d. 936).

awlad al-nas: "children of the people"; the foreign military elite during the Mamluk sultanate of Egypt and Syria; also, the descendants (to about the fourth generation) of politically significant people who were foreign by descent but born Muslims.

Ayasofya: Turkish adaptation of Greek *Aghia Sophia* (Saint Sophia); a patriarchal basilica in Constantinople / Istanbul, built in 537; subsequently converted into an imperial mosque 1453–1931, and a museum from 1935.

'ayn: spring of water, eye; also, the eighteenth letter of the Arabic alphabet.

al-Azhar: mosque and associated university founded in Cairo in 970 or 972 by the fourth Fatimid caliph, al-Mu'izz li-Din Allah, as a center of Islamic learning; it is the oldest university in Egypt to grant degrees.

al-'Aziz billah al-Asghar (955–996; r. 975–996): the fifth caliph of the Fatimid caliphate. His palace is currently unlocated.

Bab al-Futuh: north-facing gate in the walls of Old Cairo at the northern end of al-Mu'izz Street, completed in 1087.

Bab al-Nasr ("Victory Gate"): massive fortified gate with rectangular stone towers, originally built south of the present one as part of the Fatimid city.

Bab al-Sha'riyya: one of the main commercial central areas in Cairo, northwest of Muski, with a very high population density.

Bab Zuweila (also Zuwayla): famous medieval gate, originally built in 1092 by Badr al-Jamali as the southern gate on a second wall around Cairo; also the area of Old Cairo around the gate.

Bada'i' al-zuhur fi waqa'i' al-duhur ("Beautiful Flowers on the Events of the Times"): six-volume history of Egypt by Muhammad [ibn Ahmad] ibn Iyas (1448–1522), an important Mamluk historian who witnessed the Ottoman invasion of Egypt.

Bayn al-Qasrayn ("Between the Two Palaces"): an area in al-Mu'izz li-Din Allah Street, named for the site of two great palaces in medieval Cairo.

Bayn al-Sarayat: low-income district of Giza.

Beşiktaş district of Istanbul: municipality (*belediye*) of Istanbul, Turkey, located on the European side of the Bosphorus, with many important municipal buildings, including the Dolmabahçe Palace.

Birkat al-Fil ("Elephant's pond"): ancient pleasure quarters, just outside the Cairo city walls; developed mainly by public figures from the fourteenth century onwards.

Birqash: small village, 22 miles northwest of Cairo, on the edge of the cultivated land of the Nile Delta. Egypt's largest camel market relocated to Birqash in 1995 from Cairo's western suburb of Imbaba.

al-Buhayra (also al-Beheira) province: coastal governorate in northern Egypt in the Nile Delta; its capital is Damanhur.

Bulaq Abu al-'Ila: working-class area of Cairo, to the north of as-Sabtiyyah.

Bulaq al-Dakrur Bridge: bridge linking the Giza district of Bulaq al-Dakrur with Gezira Island.

caliph (from Arabic khalīfa, pl. khulafā'): successor; specifically, holder of office as successor to the Prophet Muhammad, and thereby leader of the Muslim community.

Champollion Street: a main artery in Downtown Cairo, close to Tahrir Square. Named for the French scholar Jean-François Champollion, who deciphered Egyptian hieroglyphics in 1824.

Cow, sura of: the second, and longest, sura (chapter) of the Qur'an.

al-Darb al-Ahmar ("'Red Road"): medieval Cairene neighborhood of narrow, twisting alleyways, lined with mosques and medieval facades, which accommodates a variety of different trades and crafts.

Dayir al-Nahiya: village on the outskirts of Cairo, in the Dokki area.

dhikr: lit. remembrance [of God]; Sufi prayer ritual.

Dokki: district in Giza, on west bank of the Nile directly across from Downtown Cairo, with many embassies and schools.

Dolmabahçe Palace: palace on the Bosphorus shore in the Beşiktaş district of Istanbul; built between 1843 and 1856, it was the principal administrative center of the Ottoman Empire from 1856 to 1922.

El Galaa Street: important main Cairo thoroughfare and location of the *Al-Ahram* newspaper offices.

Ezbek ibn Tatakh al-Atabeg: Mamluk emir who is believed to have created the Ezbekiyya Gardens in 1475.

Ezbekiyya (also Azbakiyya) Gardens: area of lakes and gardens in the former Frankish quarter of Cairo, fashionable in the nineteenth century. The lakes are now drained.

Faisal ibn 'Abd al-'Aziz Al Sa'ud (1906–1975): King of Saudi Arabia 1964–1975, assassinated by his nephew, Faisal bin Musaid.

Faisal Street *see* al-Malik Faisal Street.

faqih or "fiqi": one skilled or qualified in Islamic jurisprudence ("fiqi" being a colloquial corruption of the more formal term faqih).

fatiha: the "Opening"; the first sura of the Qur'an, whose seven verses are used in daily prayer.

fatwa, plural *fatawa:* a legal interpretation given by a specialist of Islamic law or mufti (i.e., an issuer of a fatwa).

fellahin (*fallahin*), plural of fellah (*fallah*): peasants.

Forty Days' Road (Darb al-Arba'in): one of the five great caravan routes of North Africa, running from Assiut via Kharga, Selima, and Bir Natrun to Darfur.

fuqaha': plural of faqih.

al-Fustat: the earliest Islamic capital of Egypt; built by general 'Amr ibn al-'As just after the Muslim conquest of Egypt in 641.

gallabiya: long, simple traditional robe worn by Egyptian men.

al-Gamaliyya: area of Cairo; the heart of a trading district in the medieval city.

al-Ghawriyya (also al-Ghūriyyah): district in Cairo; a complex of *awqaf* (sing. *waqf*, "religious endowment") around the mosque of Sultan Qansuh al-Ghawri in medieval Cairo, including the Silk Market.

Gezira Club: fashionable sporting club in the heart of the island of Gezira, Cairo.

Ghazi Yavuz Selim *see* Selim I.

Grand Vizier (from Arabic wazir, "minister"): the prime minister of the Ottoman sultan, with absolute power of attorney.

hadith: a saying of, or story about, the Prophet Muhammad; collectively, the second source of authority in Islam after the Qur'an itself.

halal: that which is allowed under religious law.

Hanafi: one of the four main law schools of Sunni Islam.

haram: that which is forbidden under religious law.

Hawsh Qadam: area within the al-Ghawriyya district of Cairo.

Heliopolis: in Arabic *Misr al-Gadida*, or "New Cairo": suburb of Cairo to the northeast of the city, built around 1907; previously the Greek name for the ancient city of On.

Hijaz: region in west of present-day Saudi Arabia, which includes the holy cities of Mecca and Medina.

hijra: [e]migration; specifically, Muhammad's migration from Mecca to Medina in AD 622, which provides the starting-point for the Islamic calendar.

howdah: riding seat, often with a canopy, carried on the back of a camel or elephant.

Hussein al-Imam (1951–2014): well-known Egyptian actor and film musician, who composed many film scores and film tracks.

Ibn Da'ud al-Isbahani (c. 868–910): Islamic jurisprudent, compiler of an anthology of poetry called *Kitab al-Zahra* ("Book of the Flower").

Ibn Iyas, aka Muhammad [ibn Ahmad] ibn Iyas (1448–1522): an important Mamluk historian who witnessed the Ottoman invasion of Egypt; author of a six-volume history of Egypt, *Bada'i' al-zuhur fi waqa'i' al-duhur* ("Beautiful Flowers on the Events of the Times").

Ibn Khaldun, 'Abd al-Rahman (1332–1406): traveler, historian, judge, and philosopher, born in Tunis of Andalusian descent; one of the founding fathers of modern historiography, best known for his book *Al-Muqaddimah* ("The Introduction").

Ikhshidids: dynasty who ruled Egypt from 934 until they were defeated by the Fatimids in 969.

imam: Muslim prayer leader in a mosque; also, a community leader, and a title for respected Islamic scholars.

al-Imam al-Shafi'i *see* al-Shafi'i.

Imbaba, district of northern Giza, near Gezira Island and Downtown Cairo: historically, the terminus for camels brought from Sudan and beyond, to be sold in its Friday market.

Isaaf Square: square in Downtown Cairo.

al-Jabarti *see* 'Abd al-Rahman al-Jabarti.

al-Jahiz (c. 776–c. 868): Arab prose writer, usually reckoned the most accomplished exponent of *adab* (imaginative prose) of the 'Abbasid period.

Jamal al-Din al-Afghani (1838/1839–1897): one of the founders of Islamic modernism, and a political activist who promoted Pan-Islamic unity.

janissaries: elite infantry who provided the household troops and bodyguards for the Ottoman sultans. Created by Sultan Murad I in 1383, they were abolished by Sultan Mahmud II in 1826.

jifa: corpse.

jubba: traditional ankle-length garment, usually with long sleeves.

Kaaba (Ka'ba): a large cuboid-shaped building in the courtyard of al-Masjid al-Haram in Mecca, the most sacred location for Muslims. When performing daily prayers (*salat*), Muslims face the Kaaba, wherever they may be.

kaftan: loose-fitting shirt with long sleeves.

kapıkulu (T): lit. "palace guard." Military corps founded during the reign of Sultan Murad I (r. 1362–1389).

Kasr al-'Ayni (also Qasr El-Einy): one of the oldest streets in Downtown Cairo; named for the palace of El-Einy Pasha, now one of the oldest and most prestigious medical schools in the Middle East.

Kasr al-Nil (also Qasr al-Nil) Bridge: bridge across the Nile in central Cairo, opened in 1933; formerly known as Khedive Isma'il Bridge.

Kirdasa (also Kerdasa): touristic village in Giza Governorate, famous for its hand-crafted textiles.

kitab: book; also used more widely in pre-modern Arabic to refer to other pieces of writing.

Kizlar Agha (Turkish: Kızlar ağası = "Agha of the [slave] girls"): head of the eunuchs who guarded the imperial harem of the Ottoman sultans in Istanbul.

koshari: Egyptian dish made of lentils, rice, and macaroni, to which may be added a variety of sauces.

Kuttab of 'Abd al-Rahman Katkhoda: an important Cairo monument, combining a school with a public fountain and blending Ottoman and Mamluk styles; built in 1744 for the Mamluk emir 'Abd al-Rahman Katkhoda (d. 1776).

Lisan al-'Arab: authoritative Arabic dictionary, compiled by Ibn Manzur (1233–1311).

Maadi Corniche: riverside highway along the Nile, to the west of the affluent Maadi district of southern Cairo.

madrasa: school; in medieval times, more specifically, a college of Islamic law.

Majra al-'Uyun Wall: part of an ancient aqueduct in Old Cairo, used to transport Nile water to the Citadel.

al-Malik Faisal Street: an often congested main thoroughfare in Giza, which leads to the Pyramids area.

Mamluks: lit. "owned"; trained slave soldiers, who formed the sultanate that ruled Egypt and Syria from 1250 until 1517, when their dynasty was extinguished by the Ottomans.

Mansur Muhammad Street: street in Zamalek, Cairo, with expensive restaurants, publishers' and lawyers' offices.

Mar'i ibn Yusuf al-Maqdisi (al-Qudsi) (d. 1623): writer; author of *Qala'id al-'uqyan fi fada'il Al 'Uthman* ("Necklaces of Pure Gold on the Virtues of the Ottomans").

Mary, sura of: the nineteenth sura (chapter) of the Qur'an.

al-Maryutiyya: area in Giza along the al-Maryutiyya Canal, just north of the Pyramids, famous for its open-air family restaurants.

mastaba: seat made of mud or stone built against a wall of a house.

al-Mas'udi (c. 896–956): Arab polymath, historian, and geographer, noted for his accounts of non-Islamic civilizations.

Mawlana Jalal al-Din (1207–1273): Jalal ad-Dīn Muhammad Balkhi, also *Mevlana* or *Mawlana* ("Our Master"), known in the West as Rumi; Persian poet, jurist, theologian, and Sufi mystic, whose works include the *Mathnaviye Ma'nawi* ("Spiritual couplets"), widely considered to be one of the greatest works of mystical poetry.

Mehmet VI (also Mehmed Vahdettin Khan; Hazreti Sultan Mehmet Vahdettin; Mehmed Vahideddin; or Mehmet Vahdettin) (1861–1926): 36th padishah and last sultan of the Ottoman Empire (r. 1918–1922), after which the Ottoman sultanate was abolished.

mihrab: prayer niche in mosque, oriented toward Mecca.

Mitwalli Gate: local name for Bab Zuweila, after the Muslim saint al-Kutb al-Mitwalli, who worked miracles near there; the gate defines the southern limits of Fatimid Cairo.

Mohamed Naguib (1901–1984): first president of Egypt following the Free Officers' Revolution of 1952; succeeded in 1954 by Gamal Abdel Nasser.

Mohandiseen (also Muhandisin): middle-class suburb built in the 1950s in Giza, where engineers (*muhandisin*) were offered cheaper housing than elsewhere.

Muhammad ibn Ahmad al-Hanafi *see* Ibn Iyas.

Muhammad Heneidi (b. 1962), aka Mohamed Henedy: Egyptian comedy actor, well-known throughout the Arabic world.

Muhammad al-Mutawakkil 'ala Allah III (d. 1543): the last 'Abbasid caliph, based in Cairo, r. 1508–1516, and again in 1517. He was defeated by the Ottoman sultan Selim I, and sent from Egypt to Istanbul in 1517.

Muhyi al-Din Piri Reis (also Muhyiddin Pîrî Bey and Hacı Ahmed Muhiddin Piri) (c.1465/1470–1553): Ottoman admiral, navigator, and cartographer known for his maps and charts in his *Kitab-ı Bahriye* (*Book of Navigation*); probably executed in 1553.

al-Mu'izz (properly al-Mu'izz li-Dīn Allah) Street: one of the oldest streets in Islamic Cairo, running from Bab al-Futuh to Bab Zuweila in the south. Named for al-Mu'izz li-Din Allah, the fourth caliph of the Fatimid dynasty.

al-Mu'izz li-Din Allah (932–975; r. 953–975): fourth caliph of the Fatimid dynasty, during whose reign the Fatimid dynasty moved its center of power from North Africa to Egypt. Al-Mu'izz overthrew the Ikhshidids and directed the construction of the new capital, al-Qahira; his palace is currently unlocated.

mukhtar: lit. "chosen."

Muqattam Hills: range of hills, with an associated suburb, situated to the southeast of Cairo.

mustafa: chosen, selected; in particular, an epithet of the Prophet Muhammad.

al-Musta'sim: al-Musta'sim Billah (1213–1258), the last 'Abbasid caliph in Baghdad, who ruled from 1242 until his death.

al-Mutanabbi, Abu Tayyib (c. 915–965): Arabic poet, reckoned as one of the greatest exponents of the medieval Arabic poetic tradition, and known particularly for his panegyrics.

mutawalli: trustee of a *waqf* (religious endowment); an official appointed to care for a shrine.

Mu'tazilites: Islamic sect active in Basra and Baghdad in 8th to 10th centuries AD, which stressed the rational aspects of Islam.

al-Nasir Muhammad Ibn Qalawun (1285–1341): ninth Mamluk sultan of Egypt (r. 1293–1294, 1299–1309, 1309–1341).

naskh (script): a style of Arabic calligraphy.

Nasr City: a "satellite city" to the east of the Cairo Governorate; established in the 1960s as an extension of Heliopolis.

nasta'liq (script): an Arabic calligraphic style.

Nur al-Din Zangi (1118–1174): member of the Turkic Zengid dynasty, who ruled the Syrian province of the Seljuk Empire from 1146 to 1174.

Padishah (also Padişah; Padeshah; Padshah): royal title of Persian origin (roughly = "Great King") adopted by various monarchs, including the Ottoman sultans, the Shahanshahs of Iran, and the Mughal Emperors of India.

al-Qahir: lit. "conquering"; epithet associated with the planet Mars, which was in the ascendant on the day the city of Cairo was founded by the Fatimids in 969.

al-Qahira: Arabic name for Cairo.

Qaitbay (c. 1416/1418–1496; r. 1468–1496): eighteenth Burji Mamluk sultan of Egypt.

Qalyubiyya: Egyptian province, to the north of Cairo.

Qansuh al-Ghawri (also al-Ghuri) (r. 1501–1516): Circassian Mamluk, second-to-last sultan of the Burji dynasty.

Qala'id al-'uqyan fi fada'il Al 'Uthman ("Necklaces of Pure Gold on the Virtues of the Ottomans"): literary work by Mar'i ibn Yusuf al-Maqdisi (al-Qudsi) (d. 1623).

qalam muhaqqaq (script): a style of Arabic calligraphy.

al-Qarafa: graveyard; specifically, an Islamic necropolis and cemetery below the Muqattam Hills in southeastern Cairo, usually known in English as the "City of the Dead."

Qasr al-Nil Bridge *see* Kasr al-Nil Bridge.

Qattamiya (also Katameya): neighborhood on the southeastern outskirts of Cairo, near the road linking Cairo with the Red Sea coastal towns at Ain Sukhna.

qibla: direction of prayer, oriented toward Mecca.

qisma: fate, destiny (ordained by God).

Qolali tunnel: tunnel leading into Shubra from the Ramses area of central Cairo.

Qurayshi: of the tribe of Quraysh, to which the Prophet Muhammad belonged.

Rafic Hariri International Airport: Lebanon's only international airport, formerly known as Beirut International Airport; named for Rafic Hariri, Lebanese Prime Minister assassinated in 2005.

rak'a: a single prostration in the Muslim prayer ritual.

Raouché: coastal suburb of Beirut, famous for its rock formations.

al-Rawda (also Roda): garden, paradise: island in center of Cairo, famous for its Nilometer; also, a common name for cafés, parks, etc.

rebab: stringed musical instrument.

al-Rifa'i mosque: mosque near the Cairo Citadel, commissioned by Khushyar Hanim, mother of Khedive Isma'il, and constructed between 1869 and 1912 to replace the *zawiya* (shrine) of the medieval saint Ahmad al-Rifa'i.

ruq'a: Arabic noun meaning "a patch or piece of cloth," from which the calligraphic style "Ruq'a" is derived, as it was originally written on small scraps of paper.

Sa'idi: of or from the Sa'id, i.e., Upper Egypt.

al-salam 'alaykum: lit. "peace be upon you," the standard Muslim greeting.

Salafi movement: a strict and literalist approach to Islam, often identified with Wahhabism, that developed in reaction to the spread of European ideas in the late nineteenth century. Its name refers to the early Muslims (Arabic *salaf*, "ancestors"), who are held to epitomize best Islamic practice.

Salah Salem Street: ring road round eastern Cairo, completed in the 1960s; named for Salah Salem (1920—1962), an Egyptian military officer and a member of the Free Officers' Movement that coordinated the Egyptian Revolution of 1952.

Sargon Boulos (1944–2007): Iraqi poet of Assyrian descent, and a close friend of many leading Lebanese writers including Adonis and Yusuf al-Khal, the founder of the magazine *Shi'r*.

Sayyid Qutb (1906–1966): Egyptian thinker, author of over 24 books, and a leading member of the Egyptian Muslim Brotherhood in the 1950s and 1960s. He was hanged in 1966 after being convicted of plotting the assassination of Egyptian president Gamal Abdel Nasser. His works on the social and political role of Islam continue to influence Islamists in Egypt and elsewhere.

Sayyidna al-Hussein: mosque built in 1154 near the Khan al-Khalili bazaar in Old Cairo ("Sayyidna," "Our Master," being an honorific title).

Selim I (1465/1466/1470–1520; r. 1512–1520): Ottoman sultan, sometimes known as "Selim the Grim," who conquered the Mamluk sultanate of Egypt in 1516–1517, thus consolidating Ottoman control over much of the Middle East.

Selim II (1524–1574; r. 1566–1574): Ottoman sultan, sometimes known as "Selim the Sot" in the west and as "Sarı Selim" (Selim the Blond) in the east.

Sha'ban II (also al-Ashraf Sha'ban) (r. 1363–1377): Mamluk ruler of the Bahri dynasty.

al-Shafi'i, Imam Muhammad ibn Idris (767–820): early Muslim jurist, founder of one of the four main schools of Sunni law.

Shajarat al-Durr Street: street named for Sultana Shajar al-Durr (d. 1259), a Turcoman slave who became politically powerful after the death of her husband, Salih Ayyub, the sultan of Egypt, in 1250.

Sharm El Sheikh: popular tourist resort on the Red Sea at the southern tip of the Sinai peninsula, in the Egyptian South Sinai Governorate.

Sheikh (Shaykh) al-Islam: title conferred on distinguished scholars of Islam; more specifically, in the Ottoman Empire, the foremost legal authority on Islamic matters.

Sheikh Shaarawi, i.e. Muhammad Metwally al-Shaarawy (1911–1998): Egyptian Muslim jurist and teacher, best known as a popular preacher able to explain Qur'anic teachings in readily accessible terms.

shisha: water pipe for smoking.

Shubra Khit (also Chobra Kit): medium-sized town in al-Buhayra Province; site of a defeat of the Mamluks by Napoleon's French forces on July, 13 1798.

sipahi (also sepahi) (T): member of an Ottoman cavalry corps made up of freeborn mounted troops, other than *akıncıs* (irregular light cavalry) and tribal horsemen.

Su'ad Husni, aka Soad Mohamed Hosny (1943–2001): Egyptian singer and actress, born in Cairo of Syrian Kurdish descent, who performed in over 83 films between 1959 and 1991 and was widely known throughout the Middle East.

al-Sukkariyya: district in Old Cairo, made famous as the title of the third part of the Nobel prizewinner Naguib Mahfouz's novelistic trilogy.

sultan: originally Arabic for "strength, authority"; title of Ottoman (and some other) rulers.

Sultan Qaitbay *see* Qaitbay.

Sultan Selim *see* Selim I.

Sultan Sha'ban *see* Sha'ban II.

Sunni: related, or adhering to, the majority or mainstream branch of Islam, which comprises some 87–89 percent of Muslims worldwide. The term derives from *sunna*, "established practice," i.e., the sayings and actions of the Prophet Muhammad.

sura: chapter of the Qur'an.

Taba: town in Egypt on the Gulf of Aqaba, near the border crossing between Egypt and the Israeli town of Eilat.

Tabbanah Quarter: an area of Cairo, situated between Bab Zuweila and the Citadel.

ta'liq (script): cursive style of Islamic calligraphic script with rounded forms and exaggerated horizontal strokes; developed in Persia in the tenth century.

Tanzimat: a series of reforms, heavily influenced by contemporary European practice, implemented between 1839 and 1876 during the reigns of the sultans Abdülmecid I and Abdülaziz and intended to transform the Ottoman Empire into a modern state.

Tawfiqiyya Market: small village and railway station in al-Buhayra Province near the Cairo–Alexandria Agricultural Road.

thuluth (script): a large, elegant, cursive Islamic calligraphic script, developed from the eleventh century and often used for mosque decoration.

Topkapı Palace: palace in Istanbul, built following the Ottoman conquest of Constantinople in 1453 and the primary residence of the Ottoman sultans for nearly 400 years (1465–1856); now a museum and a major tourist attraction.

tughra (modern Turkish spelling: *tuğra*): the seal of the Ottoman sultans.

Tughrul (also Toghrul I, Toghril Beg, etc.) (990–1063; r. 1037–1063): Turkmen founder of the Seljuk Empire.

Tuman Bey I (al-'Adil Sayf al-Din Tuman Bey): the twenty-fifth Mamluk sultan of Egypt, who ruled for c. 100 days in 1501.

Tuman Bey II (al-Ashraf Tuman Bey): Mamluk sultan of Egypt after the defeat of Sultan al-Ashraf Qansuh al-Ghawri by the Ottoman Sultan Selim I at the Battle of Marj Dabiq in 1516.

Turguman: square and bus station near Tahrir Square in central Cairo.

'Umar [ibn 'Ali] ibn al-Farid (1181–1235): Sufi poet, born and died in Cairo; lived for a time in Mecca; often considered the greatest mystical poet to write in Arabic.

umma: the community of Islam.

ustadh / ustaz: teacher, professor; the term is also widely used colloquially (in the form *ustaz*) as an honorific title for musicians, artists, and other professional persons.

Wadi Natrun: valley in the Egyptian desert, about 25 miles south of Alexandria, famous for its many Coptic monasteries.

Wahhabism: radical and ultraconservative Islamic revivalist movement of Sunni Islam founded by Muhammad ibn 'Abd al-Wahhab (1703–1792) in Najd (in present-day Saudi Arabia). The movement, which seeks to return to the earliest Islamic authorities, has been linked to a number of modern terrorist organizations, including al-Qaeda.

waqf (pl. *awqaf*): a religious endowment, often in the form of a building used for religious, educational, or charitable purposes.

al-Wastaniyya: small village in al-Buhayra Province, on the Cairo–Alexandria Agricultural Road, just south of Kafr El-Dawar.

yıldız (T): star; also used as girl's name.

Yusuf ibn Najm al-Din Ayyub Salah al-Din (1138–1193): famous Muslim Kurdish leader, better known in the west as Saladin.

al-Zahir Khoshqadam (r. 1461–1467): the first Mamluk sultan of Anatolian origin. His reign saw the beginning of the struggle between the Egyptian and Ottoman sultanates, which led to the incorporation of Egypt into the Ottoman empire in 1517.

Zamalek: affluent district of western Cairo, including the northern part of Gezira Island in the Nile River.

TRANSLATOR'S AFTERWORD

Youssef Rakha's *Kitab al-Ṭughra* [*The Book of the Sultan's Seal*], his first novel, set in the spring of 2007 and completed at the start of 2010, was published less than a fortnight after mass protests centered on Cairo's Tahrir Square forced the resignation of the then Egyptian President Hosni Mubarak on February 11, 2011— a move that prompted the transfer of power to the Supreme Council of the Armed Forces (SCAF), and everything that has followed since. The work attracted enthusiastic (at times, hyperbolic) reviews, though more than one commentator noted that the timing may not have been entirely fortunate, since (to quote Mona Anis) "a historical event of such wide import as the Egyptian uprising will naturally overshadow the appearance of any new novel, no matter how accomplished." Be that as it may, the timing of the work's publication makes attempts to relate it to current developments in Egypt and the wider Middle East almost inevitable; and indeed, the recent emergence of ISIS (Islamic State of Iraq and al-Sham) has arguably given a new urgency to Rakha's tale of a man's "transformation during twenty-one days from a Europeanized intellectual to a semi-madman who believed he could perform magic deeds to resurrect the Islamic caliphate" (p. 349). To say that this is a complex work, however, is to understate the obvious, for the novel may be read on several levels: as an exploration of the Ottoman contribution to the make-up of the contemporary Middle East; as a study of the contemporary Arab Muslim's desperation for a sense of identity (heavily dependent, like all identities, on history); or simply as a rollicking good tale—by turns, suspenseful, riotous, and erotic.

Themes apart, Rakha's novel is a complex work in other ways also, being written in what the author sees as a new version of "middle Arabic," which makes extensive use of contemporary colloquial idioms, as well as reflecting the range of foreign (mostly English) vocabulary that has recently entered the language. On a literary level, the work is full of intertextual references—explicit and implicit—both to the medieval Arabic canon and to more modern writers: some chapters, indeed, almost mimic their classical counterparts. These features pose particular problems for the translator, and indeed can arguably be regarded as rendering the work essentially "untranslatable," since the range of linguistic subtleties embedded in Rakha's text can never be reproduced in English, or indeed, in any other language. That said, I have attempted to capture as far as possible the spirit of Rakha's text, in general resisting the temptation to "spell things out" in the text for the English-speaking reader; on rereading the translation, I am conscious that one or two passages in which I have attempted to preserve the narrative structure of the original Arabic (most notably, the account of Egyptian history on pp. 53-55) may perhaps prove a little too allusive for some readers; but if anyone finds these passages too difficult or obscure, I suggest they may safely be skipped.

In its original published Arabic version, the text of Rakha's novel was followed by three appendices, comprising (1) notes on the history of the Ottomans; (2) details of well-known historical figures mentioned in the text; and (3) a glossary (in Arabic) of potentially unfamiliar terms and expressions. The third of these appendices is in any event irrelevant to any non-Arabic version of the novel, and for the purposes of the translation the remaining two appendices have been replaced by a glossary, which, together with the additional explanatory notes on transliteration and other matters that form part of this afterword, was felt would be more useful for the English-speaking reader.

Acknowledgments

As already noted, Rakha's work is rich in quotations from other Arab authors, both classical and modern. Quotations in the translation are generally printed in italics, followed by the name of the author concerned, but in Part Eight, where the author makes extensive use of quotations from the mystical poet Ibn al-Farid, it has not been felt necessary to repeat the name of the author on each occasion.

Most translations from other authors are my own, but in a few cases—most notably the quotations from Ibn Farid in Part Eight—I have made use of existing published English versions, for which acknowledgment is duly made as follows:

1. The quotation from al-Jahiz on p. 3 is adapted from the translation by R.B. Serjeant, *The Book of Misers*, Reading: Garnet Publishing, 1997.

2. The quotations from Ibn Hazm on p. 10 and p. 261 are taken from the translation by A.J. Arberry, *The Ring of the Dove*, London: Luzac, 1953.

3. The translations of the short verses from the Qur'an on p. 273 and p. 311 are taken from A.J. Arberry, *The Koran Interpreted*, London: Allen & Unwin, 1955.

4. The majority of the translations from Ibn Farid have been taken from A.J. Arberry, *Nazm al-suluk*, London: Walker, 1952, and A.J. Arberry, *The Mystical Poems of Ibn al-Farid*, Dublin: Walker, 1956. Translations of verses not found in those volumes are my own.

In bringing this translation to publication, I have been fortunate in enjoying the help of several people. First and foremost, thanks are due to the author, Youssef Rakha, who read the entire draft, saved me from many errors, and made numerous suggestions for changes and improvements, as well as redrawing a number of his sketches for the English version. I am also grateful to all staff at Interlink Publishing for their constant support, particularly Hilary Plum, who copy-edited the translation, and whose concern for clarity and precision is, in my experience, unparalleled. Thanks are also due to my wife, Janet, who helped to compile the glossary, and to my colleague Aziza Zaher for help with some particularly obtuse Egyptian colloquial expressions.

A Note on Arabic Transliteration and Pronunciation
Transliteration—or how to write in one alphabet words normally spelled in another—is a perennial problem for scholars and translators working with texts in Arabic, whose phonetic structure is markedly different from that of English. At one of end of the spectrum, academics use a number of different systems to render into English the various Arabic sounds without precise equivalents in English—to make vital distinctions like those between *haram* ("pyramid"), *ḥaram* ("sacred space, particularly those in Mecca and Medina"), and *ḥarām* ("forbidden"), for example. At the other end of the spectrum, T.E. Lawrence once famously returned a set of proofs to his publisher, who had queried some inconsistencies in his transliteration, with the words: "I spell my names anyhow, to show what rot the systems are." In the present context, I have tried to be reasonably consistent in the spelling of individual names and other terms, but have not used strictly transliterated forms where another form is more commonly used in English. Thus, the reader will find "Beirut" rather than "Bayrūt," and "Sharm El Sheikh" rather than "Sharm al-Shaykh." I have also taken the view that diacritics (dots under letters and lines above vowels, as in the examples above) are likely to constitute a distraction rather than an aid for the average reader, so with a very few exceptions I have omitted them.

That said, as various references are made in the novel to how different characters pronounce Arabic, readers unacquainted with the language may wish to note a few of its more salient phonetic features, which frequently pose problems for foreign learners:

—certain consonants (t, d, s, z) occur in two sets, the first set being pronounced roughly as in English, the second (known as "emphatics") pronounced with the tongue halfway back along the roof of the mouth;

—in addition to the ordinary "h", roughly equivalent to the English sound, Arabic has a breathier form of the same letter, usually transliterated as "ḥ", which occurs, for example, in the name Muḥammad;

—the letter *jīm*, pronounced in most parts of the Arab world as "j", is in most parts of Egypt (including Cairo) pronounced "g" as in "go";

—the letter "q" (called *qāf* in Arabic) is not the initial "qu" of "queen," but a "k" sound made further back in the throat. This sound is frequently replaced by a glottal stop (called *hamza* in Arabic) in urban colloquial Arabic varieties, such as that spoken in Cairo;

—particularly problematic for foreigners is the letter *'ayn*, a guttural sound made from the back of the throat. This letter has been rendered in the translation as ', but for practical purposes the reader may safely ignore it—though it is worth noting that it occurs in a large number of common words, including, for example, *'arab* ("Arabs") and *'Abd* ("slave" or "servant," the first element in compound names such as 'Abd Allāh).

Those wanting to pursue these distinctions further can find the sounds on a number of easily accessible websites (just search for "Arabic alphabet pronunciation" or something similar); alternatively, you may console yourself with the thought that neither the Persians nor the Turks (both of whose languages absorbed large quantities of Arabic vocabulary as they came under the influence of Islam) ever really got the hang of them either.

Turkish Spelling and Pronunciation

A particular problem for the translator of Rakha's novel arises from the interplay of the Arab[ic] and Turkish elements in the work. During the Ottoman period, Turkish was written in the Arabic script (with a few extra letters), but as part of the process of modernization led by Mustafa Kemal (Atatürk), the Arabic script was replaced by the Roman script in 1928. Again, most of the letters are pronounced more or less as they are in English, but the reader unfamiliar with Turkish may wish to note the following:

—"ç" and "ş" are pronounced "ch" (as in "church") and "sh" (as in "ship") respectively;

—"c" is pronounced "j" as in "jam" (and *not* as in English "come" or "nice"!);

—"ı" (undotted "i") is a short neutral vowel, a bit like the "u" in "radium"; try pronouncing "dr" quickly, and you will have a rough equivalent of the Turkish word "dır" ("is");

—"ö" and "ü" are pronounced as in German, or like the French vowels in "deux" and "tu" respectively.

Arabic vs. Turkish

Ottoman Turkish names (and other words) sometimes look a bit different from their Arabic equivalents when transliterated: Muḥammad 'Alī, who ruled Egypt for most of the first half of the nineteenth century, appears in Turkish as Mehmet Ali, for example, while the Ottoman sultan Selim would be Salīm in Arabic. Generally speaking, I have used Turkish forms for Ottoman personalities and Arabic forms for Arabs in the novel, but total consistency is impossible—a measure of the extent to which the history of the two peoples and languages has been intertwined for several centuries, as well as of the cosmopolitan nature of certain aspects of the Ottoman Empire: Muḥammad 'Alī, for example, was actually an ethnic Albanian, born in Kavala, which is now in Greece.

Exceptionally, also, the name of the novel's protagonist, Çorbacı, has been spelled Turkish-style rather than in the form it would take if transliterated from the Arabic (Eshorbagy / Shorbagy / al-Shurbaji or some such). The reason for this has nothing to do with any scholarly or academic argument, but simply that following the publication of Rakha's novel the character began to acquire a life of his own as Çorbacı in discussion on English-language websites, and it was thought too confusing to change it.

Names and Titles

Pre-modern Arab names present something of a challenge for the uninitiated. In traditional Arab society, a man would be known by his given name, followed by the name of his father, and then that of his grandfather (a chain which could, in theory, be extended almost indefinitely)—the names being generally linked by *ibn* ("son [of]"), with a feminine equivalent *bint* ("daughter [of]"). Thus Muḥammad, the Prophet of Islam, for example, was Muḥammad ibn 'Abd Allāh ibn 'Abd al-Muṭṭalib. This admirably logical system was complicated, however, by the fact that many people acquired names of other kinds, either as nicknames, or as descriptors of various sorts—to specify their place of origin, celebrate the name of their eldest son, or whatever. The tricky bit is that there is absolutely no way of telling by which element(s) of their name the person concerned was (or is) generally known. Thus al-Jahiz (who provides Rakha's quote on p. 3 of the translation) was actually named 'Amr ibn Bahr, but in practice he is always called al-Jahiz, which means "goggle-eyed"—a reference to his notorious ugliness. A particularly interesting case (from the Persian rather than the Arab world) is presented by the mystical poet generally known to English readers as Rumi ("from Anatolia") and referred to on p. 54: his given name was Jalal al-Din, but he is commonly referred to in the Middle East simply as Mawlana ("Our Master") or, in its Turkish form, Mevlana (hence the "Mevlevi" Whirling Dervishes); added to which, he was not actually born in Anatolia at all, but in the province of Balkh, which straddled parts of present-day Afghanistan and Tajikistan—the sobriquet Rumi being acquired as a result of his subsequent residence in Konya, where he wrote most of his poetry.

Modern Arab names are a good deal less complicated than medieval ones, and many (probably most) people use what are effectively Western-style "family names," though practice varies in the different countries of the Arab world. Turkish names in general also present fewer problems, since from 1935, as part of the process of modernization, every Turkish family has been obliged by law to choose a surname. The Ottoman sultans' propensity for acquiring nicknames and titles, however, means that one sultan may be referred to in several different ways: Selim I, for example, is in Turkish commonly referred to as Yavuz ("Steadfast") Selim or Yavuz Sultan Selim, but in English as "Selim the Grim"; while the ruler commonly known in English as Suleiman the Magnificent is in Turkish usually called Kanunî ("The Lawgiver") Sultan Süleyman. Readers should note that I have made no attempt to simplify any of this for the purposes of the translation and that names almost always appear in the English version in the same form as in Rakha's original text.

Paul Starkey
July 31, 2014